To Terea

Enjoy the book!

David [illegible]

STALKING HORSE

Inspired by true events

DAVID KNIGHT

Horizon Publishing Group™

Published in 2016
Horizon Publishing Group
PO Box 275
Cherrybrook NSW 2126
Australia
www.horizonpg.net
Email: orders@horizonpg.net
info@horizonpg.net

First published by Horizon Publishing Group in 2016.

National Library of Australia Cataloguing-in-Publication data:

Author: Knight, David, 1949- author.
Title: The stalking horse / David Knight.
Edition: 1st ed.
ISBN: 9781922238535 (pbk.)
ISBN: 9781922238696 (ebook)
Subjects: Drug traffic--Fiction.
Suspense fiction.
Dewey Number: A823.4

Cover by L Harris.
Typesetting & Page Design by Inception Press.

Disclaimer

This book is a work of fiction. All characters, names, dialogues, situations, events and incidents, and places are either the products of the author's imagination or are used fictitiously. Any resemblance to actual events, places or persons, living or dead, is entirely coincidental.

*****

Dedication & Acknowledgment

The cover of The Stalking Horse shows a surfboat crashing through a wave. This image was taken in the early 1970s and the crew includes four great friends of the author, as well as the author himself. They know who they are, and I pay tribute to them because this was one of many experiences in surf lifesaving that helped shape this book.

As well as acknowledging the role played by all Australians involved in the Vietnam War, I would also like to pay tribute to Tony Hammett, who appears in the second part of 'The Stalking Horse'. As a major, he was commander of D Company 1 RAR during the period in which the fictitious Jack Martin served in that company I had the privilege of serving with Brigadier General Tony Hammett in the mid-1980s in a military posting in Canberra. As a man and as a leader, there weren't too many better. Tragically Tony lost his life in a plane crash later in life. Vale, Tony Hammett.

As this novel came together a number of friends provided expert advice and read early drafts. My thanks go to Professor John Ramsland, a prolific author in his own right, for reading the first draft and suggesting that it was good enough to seek to have it published. Also to Peter Tilley, sculptor extraordinaire, for his encouragement, suggestions and proof reading, to Dr Peter for his medical expertise and enthusiastic willingness to act as a sounding board for my ideas, to Reg Ware for his scrutiny of the manuscript, and for my eldest son Andrew for taking the time to read an early draft and not act too shocked at the sex scenes penned by his father. I owe Andrew's partner Cassandra a vote of thanks for delving into the archives of the computing section of the University of NSW in the early 1970s and providing me with background material to enable Jack Martin to study there.

Of course, none of this would have happened without the

support of my wife, Diane, who encouraged me to keep going when my enthusiasm waned.

Finally a special thanks to the excellent editorial direction provided by Dale Jacobsen. I am indebted to you for your excellent suggestions to further refine the novel. And thanks to Horizon Publishing Group for giving me a chance when others had rejected my manuscript.

David Knight
December 2015

*****

PROLOGUE

Early 1992

Jack Curtiss picks up a car from the hire car counter at the Newcastle Airport and takes the half-hour drive into the city. He notes that the place has changed a hell of a lot since the late 1960s—just like his surname. Jack drives up the long main street, formerly a bustling and busy place. It is almost deserted. He recalls that the earthquake in the late 1980s has done a lot of damage, but it obviously has precipitated an exodus of businesses from the city centre to somewhere else—possibly the surrounding suburbs.

Booking into the beachside hotel, using one of several false credit cards he has with him, Jack enters his room and throws himself onto the bed, not before setting the alarm. He is tired and a bit jet-lagged after the long flight into Australia and then up to Newcastle, but he knows that after a few hours' sleep he will be up for the reunion. Jack knows he is taking a risk in returning to his old stamping ground, but he reasons that after almost twenty-five years any surveillance will have long since ceased. His passport is expertly forged, and besides, no-one knows of his visit. Well, almost no-one.

Several hours later, refreshed after a nap and a long shower, Jack steps into the surf clubhouse and pauses, letting his eyes adjust to the darker interior after the glare of the late afternoon sun outside. The hall is already crowded with current and former members. Laughter reverberates around the room as old stories are retold. *There will be a lot of bullshit spread around here this evening*, he thinks wryly.

He glances around. The club isn't in too bad a shape for an old building exposed to the elements of surf, sand and salt as it has. Jack pauses, surprised. He hadn't, at first, noticed the changes to the layout. Gone are the stairs down to the changing rooms, and to the beach proper. The hall has been reshaped, and as he peers towards the sea he can see that the balcony area has been changed as well. And the bar is in a different place. The changes seem to have worked. The place is looking pretty bloody good.

He heads for the bar to get a beer but is intercepted by several of his old mates. One remarks about the difference in his appearance. 'I almost didn't recognise you, Jack,' the friend observes, 'even with that beard hiding most of it, your face is somehow changed.'

Jack smiles. 'In twenty-five years a person can change a lot.' He does not let on that some subtle plastic surgery has contributed to these changes.

His old friend's puzzled look quickly disappears as warm exchanges are made amongst the group and questions asked about what those from outside of Newcastle are doing now.

'I'm doing okay,' Jack responds when it is his turn, 'I've got a nice business in Sydney that's making money, so I can't complain'. That part is true, up to a point. What he doesn't say is that it is run by a proxy manager and there is no trace of his previous identity there.

There are several comments made, some obviously in envy, but not all. This is a working-class town, he reminds himself, and most of these guys don't like the boss man—or being too far away from their birthplace.

Another old friend asks him how he feels about the Vietnam War. Jack pauses: 'That was a while ago,' he replies neutrally, 'and I don't dwell on it, what's the point? No bastard could give a stuff now, anyway'.

Sensing something deeper underneath this statement, his former mate sees fit to agree, and the conversation turns to more familiar topics—football, surfboats, how much the surf lifesaving game has changed, and old flames. Someone shoves a beer into his hand, and the reunion kicks into full gear. The beer flows, speeches are made, stories told, and the noise level rises appreciably. No one notices one of the club members briefly leave the clubhouse to make a phone call from the public phone on the street outside.

Several hours later, his belly full of beer and steak, Jack sways towards the toilet, trying not to appear too pissed. After a deeply satisfying pee, he washes his hands and, now steadier on his feet, walks back into the clubhouse.

He notices a lot of newish photos on the walls and walks over to study them. Someone has placed them in decade order, and his eyes instinctively seek the pictures of the 1960s. There he is in one photo, looking so young and innocent. His glance falls on another photo of a boat crew. His younger self peers out at him and, as his eyes move along the other crew members, his face tightens when he registers the face of Terry Bannister.

Biting down on the emotion that threatens to overwhelm him, Jack turns away from the images of long ago and makes his way back to the bar for another beer. Hopefully, this visit to his old stamping ground will help expunge the demons that occasionally get the better of him. If not, no harm done. No-one here knows about his life over the past thirty or so years, and that's all the better.

Rising early the next morning with a dry throat and a slight hangover, Jack crosses the road in front of the hotel and trudges down the sand to the surf. He dives into the water and, refreshed, returns to his hotel room, showers and dresses, eats breakfast, and then drives back to the airport for a flight to Sydney. There he will quietly and discreetly meet someone from his past. Then he will be off on the long trip back to where he has been living since the early 1980s.

Jack, lost in reminiscences of the past, fails to notice a car shadowing him as he drives to the airport. A tip-off from someone attending the reunion has sparked urgent action. The driver stays well back, and then surreptitiously follows the man into the airport and notes which flight he catches. He then goes to a payphone and calls a number. When someone answers, he gives the flight details and then hangs up—his job completed.

*****

BOOK ONE

THE YEAR OF THE HORSE: 1967

'May you live in interesting times.'

Ancient Chinese proverb or curse.

'So the deaths of local Novocastrians, fallen soldiers and surfing heroes, are remembered in different aspects of their lives in a monument aux morts—a monument to the dead, a true "bearer of collective memory".'

John Ramsland, *Cook's Hill Life Saving and Surf Club: The First Hundred Years*. Brolga Publishing, Melbourne, 2011.

Chapter 1

Billy Wilson glances approvingly out at the warm and sunny mid-February morning on display outside the bathroom window. The radio in the bathroom is playing *Last Train to Clarkesville* by the Monkees, and Billy hums along tunelessly. It is a beautiful summer's day at the beginning of what the Chinese call the Year of the Horse. Billy peers ruefully at his reflection in the steamy mirror. He's put on a few kilos in the past couple of years, and it shows. His gut sticks out prominently and he attempts unsuccessfully to suck it back in. *Perhaps I should go on a diet or maybe do some exercise*, he thinks unconvincingly. Part of him acknowledges that this may be a bit tough to do, given the hours he's working down the mine. Still, he knows he's over forty, and he shouldn't let it go too much longer. *Maybe tomorrow*, he thinks. As he finishes his ablutions his mind drifts to the coast. He hopes that the family will love the beach today, even though it's a bit of a drive from Cessnock, but he knows it'll be a damn sight cooler than here. Billy dresses into his swimming togs, shorts, T-shirt and a pair of thongs.

'Brenda,' he calls to his wife of twenty years, 'make sure the kids have got plenty of suntan lotion on, it's going to be a bloody warm day'.

Brenda cheerily acknowledges his shouted instructions and busies herself in the kitchen, setting out the breakfast things for the family of four. Their son, Don, rushes out of his room, as excited and nervous as only a thirteen-year-old can be, eagerly awaiting the family's departure to the beach. In contrast, Emily, his sixteen-year-old sister, saunters into the kitchen, seemingly indifferent to the family outing. Brenda, however, knows otherwise.

That knowledge has been recently gained from a friend whose daughter goes to school with Emily. Emily's friend's daughter has let it slip to her mother that Emily has a boyfriend—an item too juicy not to pass on. The friend and Brenda made a bet that the boyfriend will make an appearance at the beach today. Brenda hasn't passed this on to Billy for fear that he will do the father thing and erupt and spoil the day. Brenda does not want Billy getting upset. *He may not be in the best shape he's ever been in*, she muses, *but he's still as adorable as ever*. Brenda resolves to keep a discreet eye on Emily—just in case. She turns her thoughts to the food in front of her, putting any notion of trouble out of her mind.

Breakfast complete and the dishes washed and packed away, the family climbs into the car amongst bags, towels, the beach umbrella and other stuff.

'I hope that swimsuit isn't too racy, young lady,' exclaims Billy, as he catches a glimpse of what appears to be a bikini under Emily's shirt in the rear-view mirror.

'Don't be an old fuddy-duddy, Dad,' she responds, 'I'm wearing what every other girl will be wearing, and anyway, my one-piece is so old the elastic is wearing out!'

Don sniggers; his thirteen-year-old brain actively imagining the sights he will see in the near future. *Why can't we live nearer the beach, then I could get to see girls in bikinis every day in the summer*, he thinks enviously.

'Honey, you're only sixteen, and your mother and I won't stand for anything outrageous from you today. You make sure you behave yourself, okay?' Billy is well aware that Emily is growing up fast, and her recent behaviour reflects her desire to be seen to be older than she is. *Daughters, what a pain in the bum they can be at times*, he thinks.

Pulling a face behind his back, Emily demurely agrees to behave, eliciting a giggle from Brenda.

'Don't you remember that day we had together at the beach when we started to go steady?' Brenda smiles at Billy. 'You weren't so prim and proper then.'

Billy's neck reddens in embarrassment and Emily immediately pesters Brenda for more details. Smiling, Brenda refuses to answer, but puts her hand on Billy's knee—an action not unnoticed by Emily.

'Yuck, Mum, you're both too old for that,' she cries, secretly excited as her thoughts go to the new boyfriend, Stevie, who will be at the beach. She hopes that he will find a way to kiss her like he did the other evening—and as for those wandering hands …

Her reverie is interrupted by the car lurching forward out of the driveway.

*****

Jack Martin eats the last of his toast, finishes his orange juice and goes into the bathroom to brush his teeth. A strapping twenty-year-old, Jack focuses on today's surf patrol. He is a patrol captain for a local surf club at Bar Beach in Newcastle, and he is on duty this morning. Competent and strong in the surf, Jack will be the surf-belt swimmer during any rescues. Concentrating on his patrol members as he rinses his mouth, he considers them. Not too many weak spots there, most of the guys are experienced and confident. Jack knows from the weather forecast there will be a reasonably rough surf pounding onto the beach today, but even without the lifeguard on duty this Sunday—his day off—he is confident his team can handle the conditions.

Kissing his mother, Gladys, goodbye and nodding to his father,

Henry, Jack grabs his beach hat, sunglasses and towel, and walks up the backyard to get his pushbike out of the garage. It is only a ten-minute cycle ride to the beach, but he wants to arrive well before nine in order to ensure all the lifesaving gear is working and set out on the beach. He glances at the sky, noting the deep blue colour and the lack of clouds, and feels the first stirrings of a north-east sea breeze on his body. A perfect day! There will surely be a big crowd on the beach. His pulse quickens as he straddles the pushbike and peddles quickly towards the beach.

*****

Rolling out of bed, dressed only in his jockey shorts, Terry Bannister curses his aching head—too many beers the night before, and a few hits of weed haven't helped either. He grabs a large glass of water from the bedside table and gulps it down in one swallow. Terry staggers into the bathroom and finds some Panadol. *Oh shit*, he thinks, *I'm on patrol this morning. I can't miss it, I've done that too often, and I don't want to be suspended by the surf club. That won't help with my parole officer if he hears about it.*

He makes his way slowly into the kitchen, passing his parents' bedroom. He can hear the usual muffled cries and snores from inside, signifying they had been on the drink and drugs again. He curses them. *What hope have any of their kids got* he thinks bitterly, *with a couple of losers for parents*? There is no sound from the other bedroom; his younger sisters are obviously still asleep.

Terry checks the fridge. Empty apart from a small bottle of out-of-date milk. *Typical, the useless bastards would rather spend their dole money on grog and dope than food for the family. Fuck 'em*, he thinks savagely.

He goes back to his room and finds his pants and wallet. Dressing in a pair of shorts and a dirty shirt, he quietly unlocks the front door and walks a short distance to the local convenience store where he purchases some basics—enough for the younger kids to make some breakfast when they get up.

Lighting a smoke and swigging from a bottle of Coke, Terry grabs his swimmers and a towel and quietly shuts the front door. He will get some food later from the kiosk at the beach.

*****

Her night shift in casualty at the Royal Newcastle Hospital over, Susie Adams begins to relax as she makes her way to her small flat in Newcastle East. The suburb is becoming trendy these days, with an influx of uni students flocking to the cheaper rentals available in the area. Most of the houses are weatherboard, and many need a good paint job, but they are handy to the beautiful yellow-sanded beaches of inner Newcastle, and to the numerous pubs and night clubs at the eastern end of Hunter Street. Shopping is okay too, with a Woolworths nearby and plenty of cheap clothing stores along the almost two-kilometre-long Hunter Street.

Most of Susie's nurse friends live in the nurses' accommodation at the hospital. Susie raises the ire of the matron when she defiantly announces that she is going to live elsewhere. Matron is old school, and looks down her nose at Susie as they discuss this. Matron tells her imperiously that it is not the done thing, but, adamant, Susie gets her way.

Her parents are dead, killed in a car accident in the Hunter Valley several years ago. She is an only child. She was devastated for a long time afterwards, but is now over the loss as much as she ever will be.

Susie's dad was a butcher, and her mother ran the home. Her father was friendly and outgoing, with an eye for the ladies. Her mother was the quiet one, content to be a housewife. They doted on Susie, and she misses them something fierce.

After the sale of the family home and the butcher's shop—and parking the money in the bank—Susie has moved from the historical town of Maitland to the big smoke of Newcastle to complete her nursing training. She has purchased a second-hand baby-blue Mini Minor to get around. This still leaves a sizeable nest egg earning interest in the savings account.

Although tired and a bit frustrated at what she sees as an overly bureaucratic medical system at the hospital, Susie is reasonably content with her life to date, now that her nursing training is over. She is learning fast on the job, and although her love-life is currently a bit sparse, no doubt that will pick up now she has more time in the evenings and at weekends, despite the unsocial shift rosters. A slim and attractive girl, Susie has an easygoing air that draws more than a few admiring glances from the boys. She thinks one of her best features is her eyes—they are a very unusual and striking sea-green colour.

Deciding, on a whim, to forego sleep for a while, Susie changes quickly into a bikini and eats a quick breakfast of cereal, toast with jam and coffee to sustain her for a few hours at the beach. *Where will I go?* she muses, *Newcastle Beach, or farther afield? Perhaps Bar Beach, only an easy short drive away. Yes*, she decides, *Bar Beach it is. But for no more than four hours*, she reasons, *sleep will be necessary before my next shift at ten.*

Throwing on a shift over her bikini, Susie locks her flat and climbs into her Mini, parked outside.

*****

Jack Martin wheels his pushbike into the surf club and walks out onto the balcony to check out the surf and the beach. The tide is falling, and the large sandbank in front of the surf club is beginning to reveal itself. The surf is starting to pound on the sandbank, and Jack frowns as he watches the wave action. Voices call out from inside the clubhouse. His patrol members are arriving. Friendly banter diverts his attention from the water. He turns and walks inside.

Four patrol members are there. One missing, observes Jack; Terry Bannister is not amongst those present. *Shit*, he thinks, *I hope Terry turns up, I don't want to be the one who has to dob him in to club committee. We need him for the boat crew. And we could be one short on patrol on a day when we might all be needed.* Jack is a little sad that the two former friends seem to be drifting further apart after their strong boyhood connection. There is something going on in Terry's life, but Jack doesn't know what, and Terry has become more withdrawn of late.

Jack greets his fellow patrol members and, trading jokes and friendly insults, the group descends the stairs into the area where the patrol equipment is stored. Jack gives some orders and he and the rest of the patrol gather the gear and carry it out onto the beach. They set up the patrol area, then move the surf-reel into position in front of the patrol area down closer to the water's edge. Jack instructs two guys to erect the flags that signify where the public should swim safely, as well as the flags to keep the boardriders away from the swimmers. *Bloody boardies*, thinks Jack irritably, *they are always trying to encroach on the swimmers' area. Why can't they just stay out of the flags?*

Through habit, and because it is his responsibility as patrol captain, Jack checks the surf-reel. He is well used to its operation, as well as its strengths and weaknesses. He knows there are a number of critical elements that, if they malfunction, can turn a rescue into a nightmare. Turning his attention to the surf-belt, Jack checks the quick-release mechanism. He doesn't want anyone who uses the belt—least of all himself—drowning on his watch. Having the line pulled in too quickly during a rescue by an overzealous patrol could mean being pulled underwater, with potentially fatal consequences.

Satisfied that the mechanism is working, Jack lays out the belt on the sand, ready to jump into it if a rescue is necessary. He then examines the surf-reel, satisfying himself that the brake is operating and that the line is properly wound around the drum. He finishes his inspection, now confident that everything is working as it should.

Just then he hears his name being called. He turns and sees Terry looking sheepish and obviously pretty hung over. Jack stifles an impulse to get stuck into him.

'Glad you could make it Terry,' he says, sarcastically.

'Sorry mate,' replies Terry insincerely, 'I slept in a bit'.

Scrutinising him, Jack can see that it will be pointless in taking it further.

'You'll be third linesman today.' Terry smiles in relief. He knows he is off the hook and that Jack has assigned him an easier position in the team. Terry decides to take advantage of Jack's leniency.

'I'll just grab a bite to eat and be back in a jiffy.' Jack's eyes narrow, but Terry has already gone. *Maybe he'll be all right with a bit of food in his belly*, Jack hopes.

The beach is beginning to fill up with people as they flock to the water to avoid the heat of the morning. Colourful beach umbrellas dot the warm sand, and young kids run to the water's edge to cavort in the waves; their parents watching over them.

*****

In Canberra, a bureaucrat from the Federal Department of Labour and National Service draws numbers out of a barrel in a ballot, as if for a lottery. But this is a very different sort of lottery; winners aren't grinners here. Each number corresponds to a birth date, and those twenty-year-old men in Australia whose birth dates come up are eligible to be called up into National Service. Registration is compulsory. Do it, or most likely go to jail.

Many of these Nashos are going overseas to serve in Vietnam in an increasingly unpopular war that seems to be endless. This ballot will change the lives of many young Australians in ways no-one can foresee. Jack and Terry will be among them.

*****

Chapter 2

Billy Wilson slings the bag over his shoulder and picks up the beach umbrella. He herds the family out of the car park and down onto the beach. The trip has taken longer than expected due to delays caused by a traffic accident. It is late morning as he and Brenda search for a good spot amongst the crowd to stow their gear, urging the kids to keep up. Emily gazes around, hoping to catch a glimpse of Stevie. Don's eyes are everywhere, the bikinis on display almost too many to count.

The family settles on a spot on the northern end of the beach, where a series of rocks in the sea offer protection from the large waves that are breaking elsewhere. After checking that the kids have enough suntan lotion applied, Billy and Brenda erect the umbrella and lay out the towels, whilst the younger pair head down to the water.

'Don't forget you two—either swim here or go down and swim between the flags, that way your mother and I know you're safe,' calls Billy as Emily and Don run off. The pair wave in acquiescence.

Billy asks Brenda, 'You okay, darl?' She gives him a smile in return. Billy relaxes onto his beach towel and adjusts his hat and sunglasses, careful not to stare too much at the attractive young mums who surround their spot. After a while, Billy closes his eyes and dozes in the warm sunshine.

Don splashes in the shallows, enjoying the coolness of the water and trying to catch little waves as they make their way towards the shore. Seeing her brother sufficiently distracted, Emily strolls along the beach, her eyes peeled. She sees Stevie and moves in his direction, glancing around to check that her parents aren't watching.

Stevie lounges on the sand at the water's edge, trying not to seem too eager as Emily approaches. She drops down beside him and he casually puts his arm around her shoulder, pulling her closer.

'Hey, gorgeous,' he whispers into her ear. That gets the desired response as she turns her face towards him, smiling. He gives her a quick kiss, instantly aroused, and crosses his legs in an attempt to disguise his erection. To his pleasant surprise her hand fleetingly brushes the front of his swimmers as she squirms on the sand next to him. His heart races.

Emily is pleased with Stevie's reaction, but this is right out in public, and she isn't about to let things go any further—at least, not here.

'Let's go for a swim,' she suggests, 'out there on that sandbank'.

'Okay,' he replies, at that moment willing to do anything she asks.

*****

Jack watches the surf with growing alarm. As the tide drops, conditions on the sandbank in front of the surf club worsen, to the extent that he is considering erecting the 'Dangerous Surf' sign. He is torn: there are a lot of people on the beach and they will be very unhappy not being allowed to venture out into the surf—but on the other hand, his patrol is responsible for their safety. He decides to give it another thirty minutes.

Jack has already placed several members of the surf patrol on the southern end of the sandbank, where the gutter between the bank and the shore meets a deeper channel taking water out to sea. The lads have already effected about twenty minor rescues, as kids and weaker swimmers are swept south by the rip of water rushing through the gutter into the channel. Terry is prominent amongst the rescues and, given his shaky start, Jack is happy with Terry's performance.

Terry, however, getting a bit pissed off with plucking idiots out of the rip, wants a break. His hangover has diminished, helped by some greasy food and a can of Coke. He resents having to play second fiddle to Jack, who is playing generals on the beach.

Oblivious to Terry's thoughts, Jack turns back towards the surf club, noticing Wally Quinn, the club president, lounging against the railing of the balcony. Jack jogs up to the club and shouts out to Wally: 'I'm probably gunna have to put up the "Dangerous Surf" sign soon, Wally, it's getting too treacherous. The rip's really working now. What do you think?'.

Wally again examines the water. 'Yep, I agree,' he replies. 'When you're ready, I'll make an announcement over the loudspeaker and ring Newcastle branch headquarters to advise them. Give us a shout.'

Jack walks back down the beach, not noticing the attractive girl lounging on a towel near the patrol area who glances his way as he passes.

Susie had positioned herself quite well, she thinks. With those lifesavers nearby, there are plenty of attractive men around. She covertly notes the tanned bodies, the muscles, and the flat bellies. *That one who just passed me isn't bad at all, a bit serious but nice blondish hair, good looking, broad shoulders and a great bum. And there's another one just out there in the water in front of me—tall, dark and almost handsome. I reckon he likes to party. I'm enjoying this very much.*

*****

Emily and Stevie wade out through the shallow water on the sandbank, jumping waves that threaten to push them back. Emily holds Stevie's hand tightly—it is a bit scary and she isn't used to the surf. Neither is Stevie for that matter.

Billy opens his eyes and stands up, automatically scanning the beach for the kids. Brenda dozes beside him, oblivious. *Where are they*, he asks himself. Suddenly he spots Don cavorting in the shallows in front of him. *He's okay*, thinks Billy, relieved. He casts his eyes around, but can't see Emily.

He walks down to the water's edge, searching anxiously. Looking south, he spots what he thinks is her, but she's with some boy, and they are holding hands! *Bloody hell, what's that girl doing? I'll teach her a lesson when I get my hands on her!*

Billy runs along the beach, waving seaward in a vain attempt to catch Emily's eye. But she is facing the other way, moving further out into the waves, edging to the south slightly away from the other surfers.

Billy plunges into the water and wades as fast as he can through the gutter and onto the sandbank. *God, I wish I'd done more exercise*, he thinks, as he quickly begins to tire, his breath coming in gasps. *What are those two doing? Shit, he's kissing her, and she's kissing him back! I've got to stop this.*

Further into the waves Billy rushes, adrenalin kicking in and giving him extra momentum, then he feels like someone is choking him. He feels a tightening in his chest.

*****

Chapter 3

It is the third wave of the largest set to hit the beach that morning that collapses the southern edge of the sandbank. Immediately the depth of water changes from waist-high to over two metres deep as sand cascades off the bank into the deeper water. Some sand caught up in the aftermath of the sandbank collapsing sweeps seawards and in an instant the surf becomes confused and very dangerous.

Emily and Stevie are knocked over and dumped heavily. Stevie swallows water. Panicked, he lets go of Emily's hand, his thoughts only for himself. He is buffeted by the strong current but, by some miracle, manages to find bottom with his feet and push upward. His head breaches the water, allowing him to take a quick gulp of air before he is pummelled again. Instinct takes over and he thrashes around, trying to keep his head above the water.

Suddenly, he feels a hand grab him and he hears a calming voice: 'Easy, mate, I've got you. Don't struggle against me, or I'll have to belt you one, and you won't like that!'

Terry had seen the sets coming and instinctively moved further out onto the sandbank—his dark thoughts banished from his mind at the impending danger.

'Emily,' Stevie gasps, 'where's Emily?'.

'That your girlfriend, mate? Don't worry, we'll get her.'

But Emily has disappeared.

From the shore, Jack watches with mounting horror. Although most people seem to be okay, there are three that are in danger: a youth, a girl and an older man who, only metres away from the youngsters, is slightly less impacted by the last wave of the set. Suddenly, the man dives into the deeper water and begins to swim awkwardly towards the girl.

'Al, man the reel,' Jack shouts, 'I'm taking the belt. Get other club members to let the line out, will you? Most of the patrol is on the sandbank, and can't get back in time to help here'.

Without waiting for an answer, Jack dons the belt and races into the water as three off-duty surf club members act as linesmen, helping Al the reelman to play out the line after Jack. Quickly pushing through the gutter and onto what remains of the sandbank, he high-steps through the water. Ahead he can see several patrol members assisting people and, further out, he sees Terry pulling the young guy back onto the bank.

As Jack reaches the sandbank, Terry nods towards the girl and the man. 'What should I do? I can't get them both.'

'Mate, you go after the girl and I'll take the older bloke.'

Jack keeps on jumping through the waves and shouts back at Terry: 'Just keep her afloat. Someone will come to get you'.

With that Jack dives into the rip. Although the weight of the line starts to slow him down and he is unable to properly kick his legs because of the line trailing behind, he makes good progress, assisted by the seaward sweep of the rip.

Terry reaches the girl who is screaming in panic, her head repeatedly sinking under the water as she thrashes around. She lunges at him but, experienced in this situation, Terry quickly gets behind her and dunks her. Swallowing more water, the fight goes out of her and she submits meekly.

'Okay, girlie, listen to me: I'm going to pull you along backwards and you're going to help me by holding your arms close to your body.' Sensing that she is still panicking, he adds in a serious tone, 'And if you play up, I've leave you out here'.

By this time the pair is about a hundred and fifty metres off the beach, but moving seaward more slowly as the rip weakens. *I've gone further than this plenty of times*, Terry optimistically tells himself. *Help will be along soon, anyway. I hope.*

Adopting a sideways stroke and doing his best to conserve energy, Terry moves parallel to the beach, gradually pulling the girl out of the worst of the rip.

*****

Breathing hard from the effort required to drag the line through the water, Jack lifts his head and spots the man in front of him, about twenty metres away. Ominously, the man has stopped swimming and is flopping about, trying—but not succeeding—to keep his head above water, flagging as each wave hits him. Jack becomes increasingly concerned as he powers towards him.

Jack grabs the man—now too far gone even to lift his head out of the water—and begins mouth-to-mouth resuscitation as best he can while treading water. Lifting his right arm high in the signal for the linesmen and reel man to commence to pull them in, Jack kicks his legs rhythmically in a scissor kick, holding the man's face out of the water, waiting for the tug on the line that signifies that the patrol members have commenced to retrieve the hundreds of metres of wet line.

*****

Seeing the rescue unfolding from his vantage point of the surf club balcony, Wally sprints into the clubhouse and grabs the phone and dials 000.

'Police and ambulance,' he demands to the operator. 'There's a major recue going on at Bar Beach and there's a fair chance that some people may be in some strife. Get here as quick as you can.'

Slamming down the phone, Wally dashes to the loudspeaker system.

'Attention, attention, on the beach. All club members please report immediately to the bottom of the club. This is an emergency.'

He runs back outside to organise his club members.

People start to stand up on the beach to see what is going on. Fingers point out to sea at the developing rescue operation. The crowd surges to the water's edge.

*****

Now very tired, Terry's heart lifts when a patrol member on a rescue board suddenly appears in front of him, surging through a wave. With some difficulty, the two lifesavers get the girl onto the board.

'Hang on tight to the straps on the front of the board,' the patrol member shouts at Emily, 'we're about to hit the surf zone, and I don't want to lose you'.

Emily obeys, exhausted, and the pair catch a wave. The crowd onshore cheers loudly. Relieved of his burden, Terry begins a leisurely swim to shore, conserving his energy.

*****

Jack locks his hands around the chest of the man and anxiously endures the long tow into the beach. Their progress pauses momentarily each time a wave hits them. *That first linesman is on the job*, Jack thinks tiredly. *No drowning risk here.*

But the man doesn't seem to be breathing, and Jack can only provide spasmodic mouth-to-mouth as they are towed back to the beach.

Chapter 3

Willing hands grab Jack and the man as they reach the shoreline. A crowd presses around, watching with excited voyeuristic eyes. A women hysterically screams 'Billy, Billy, is that you?'

The lifesavers push them back, giving Jack space as he commences resuscitation in earnest. He tilts the man's head back to clear the airway; provides several breaths to the mouth followed by firm chest compressions to stimulate the heart. Jack repeats the cycle again and again. In the meantime someone grabs the woman and pulls her away from the prostrate form of the man. She collapses to the sand, sobbing pitifully.

Exhausted, but with adrenalin pumping though his body, Jack determinedly continues CPR. The man shows no sign of life. Jack sits back on his haunches, resting briefly, searching for any sign of breathing. The man's chest remains motionless. A soft female voice speaks next to his ear.

'Hi, I'm a trained nurse. Do you mind if I have a go for a while? You seem a bit tired. My name is Susie, by the way.'

Startled, Jack looks up and is momentarily lost in the vision above him—dark hair frames high cheek bones, a delicate nose and red lips. He notices the beautiful sea-green eyes and a smattering of freckles across her cheeks.

'Uh, okay,' he stammers, rising to his feet to give her room. She kneels on the sand and commences CPR. All he can see is a tanned back, slim waist, pert bottom and shapely legs. *Jeez,* he thinks, *she's gorgeous.* Embarrassed at his thoughts, Jack glances around, but everyone is focussed on the drama.

Jack hears loud voices cut through the low noise of the surrounding crowd and the high-pitched, plaintive cries of the women who seems to be with this man. He sees several ambulance personnel, assisted by a couple of policemen, push their way through the throng of people.

Jack talks them through the situation as the ambos drop to the sand next to the man. Without interrupting the girl's efforts, one of them puts a stethoscope to the man's chest; the other searches for a pulse on the man's neck. After a short period, the ambo with the stethoscope shakes his head at Jack. Gently, he speaks to Susie, asking her to stop the resuscitation while he puts an oxygen mask onto the man's face—just in case. The older woman lets out a fresh wail of despair.

Jack, helped by several surf club members, assists the ambos to move the man onto a stretcher and cover him with a blanket. The group then trudges with the man up to the waiting ambulance. The man appears to be dead. The distraught woman follows, supported by her two children, all crying softly.

Although he is dispirited by the outcome of the rescue, Jack makes a point of thanking his patrol members for their sterling efforts in getting them in through the heavy surf. Terry appears at his side.

'Well done, mate,' Jack says quietly.

'You didn't do too badly yourself, Jack.'

The cops speak to Jack.

'Can you come up to the club, out of this crowd, and tell us what happened, mate?'

Jack obeys, momentarily forgetting about Susie. As he stumbles up the sand he turns, searching for her, but she has disappeared, swallowed up by the crowd.

Jack belatedly remembers Terry and tells the police of his involvement. Terry scowls—he doesn't want a bar of any coppers—but he follows.

Supported by Wally, Jack and Terry give separate statements to the police. When the cops are satisfied they have the facts, they inform Jack and Terry that they might be called upon to give evidence if there is to be a coronial hearing.

Jack is shattered. The bloke is almost certainly dead. His mind fills with dark thoughts—if only he had taken the decision to close the beach and get the bathers out of the water, the bloke would be alive and his family unaffected by tragedy.

Wally speaks quietly to Jack.

'Easy, mate, it's not your fault. You did a bloody good job, you and Terry. Sometimes shit happens, and there isn't too much you can do about it. It's gunna take some time to get over this, so you'd better start now.'

Terry is indifferent to Jack's anguish. He has saved the girl. Jack is too distracted to notice his lack of empathy.

Later in the afternoon, a phone call confirms what Jack fears: Billy Wilson has been pronounced dead on arrival at the Royal Newcastle Hospital. When he asks after the family, Jack is told that they are being taken care of.

Jack cycles home, feeling numb and, in a wooden voice, informs his parents about the death and his feelings of guilt about not acting more decisively. His father pulls him in tight and hugs him as tears well up in Jack's eyes. They stay in an embrace for a long time before Henry releases him and says quietly: 'You did your best, Son, and that is all anyone can do. We're proud of what you did today. Let's have something to eat, and a beer to wash it down'.

Jack is unable to sleep much that night.

*****

Chapter 4

The engine of the 250cc Honda motorbike purring sweetly beneath him, Jack rides to his place of work several weeks after the incident at the beach. The bike is his pride and joy, and he keeps it well maintained. Smiling, he remembers his license test several years before. The cop had ordered the small group of riders to go around the block on their bikes, and if they came back in one piece, they had their license. *There was a bit more to it than that*, Jack recalls, *but after the theory, the practical was a breeze*.

He pulls up at the main gate of the Newcastle Steelworks, owned and operated by the large Australian corporation known as Broken Hill Proprietary Limited, and shows his pass to the bored guard. Parking in the allocated area of the BHP carpark, Jack strides to the dressing rooms to don his overalls and stow his lunch box.

Jack is eager with anticipation; it is only a few weeks until uni resumes. No more of this boring crap for a few months until the next academic break. *Bring it on*, he wishes. *You can put up with this for a little while longer, think of the money*, he urges himself. *By then you will have saved enough to meet expenses for at least three months.* He silently thanks his parents for not making him pay board and lodging. That helps a lot.

Jack had taken a year off after school to work, deferring university for the period. He wanted to earn enough money to buy a motorbike and to allow him to put something away for a rainy day. He has been successful in qualifying to study for a science degree at Newcastle uni. A partial scholarship covers fees and text books. This degree stream is the only way to study the newly emerging computer science subjects. They will start this year—his second year at uni—and Jack is looking forward to it.

He doesn't know why he is so interested, but something is drawing him to this new area. Jack visited the Burroughs computer showroom in Newcastle during an excursion at the end of his high school time. He was fascinated by the photos of the huge machines and listened, enthralled, as the sales guy explained what they could do.

It is a month after the fateful rescue attempt at the beach. For Jack, life has slowly returned to normal, and he has almost overcome the feeling of guilt at not doing more to save the man.

Wally had spoken to Jack and Terry several days ago.

'There's going to be a coronial hearing, and you two will have to testify,' Wally advises. 'Just tell the court what happened, that's all you have to do.'

Jack is nervously accepting, but not Terry.

'Bugger that,' Terry said savagely. 'I'm not going to no hearing. Stuff the cops. Besides, that little bitch didn't even say thank you after I saved her life. Why should I be bothered?'

'You've got no choice, mate,' Wally replied, exasperated. 'Besides, think of the surf club's reputation.'

'Fuck you and the club.' Terry's glare at Wally was pure hatred. He wanted to smash Wally's face in but, wisely, he held back. Although Wally is in his late thirties, he has the build of a front-row forward and he is bigger and stronger than Terry. And he is more than handy with his fists.

Seeing the wildness in Terry's eyes, Wally adopted a conciliatory tone. 'Mate, you both are viewed as heroes in this town. The press is calling for a bravery award for the two of you. Whilst that may not happen, the public love you. The cops won't dare come near you, Terry.'

Backing off, Terry reluctantly agreed.

Terry is getting to be a real problem, Jack silently observes. He wishes he could help Terry more. Jack thinks back to their childhood when they were so much closer, even up until their mid teens. But since then, Jack has observed that Terry has grown more distant, and that just about every effort he has made in the past twelve months to try to understand what is bugging him has resulted in a rebuff. Jack suspects that it's got something to do with his home life—not surprising given the drop-kicks he has as parents. But away from the beach he seems to be hanging out with a dodgy crowd that are pushing drugs, which Jack views as being not very smart at all—not with the conviction for assault and robbery that earned him a short spell in goal several years ago, and his current status as a parolee. But why Terry blames Jack, or if indeed Terry blames him, is beyond Jack's understanding.

Although the inquest weighs heavily on his mind, Jack can't get the memory of Susie out of his head. He has made a half-hearted attempt to track her down, but the local hospitals won't give him any details of staff. Besides, she mightn't work in a hospital anyway. That glimpse of her face is stuck in his memory.

'Stop daydreaming, mate, and get on with it. You're here to work, not sit on your bum,' the authoritarian voice of Jack's boss scolds him. *Bullshit*, Jack thinks, *most of you bastards wouldn't work in an iron lung*.

Still, he stands and walks out of the sheds to face the monotonous job awaiting him.

Chapter 5

Terry currently works at the Newcastle State Dockyard. Leaving school at fifteen—glad to be away from the monotony of trying to learn useless facts and figures—Terry has worked spasmodically, keeping in and out of trouble with the law. The surf club helps him to keep mainly on the right side of the law, but of late he has become more bitter about his circumstances. *A dead-end job and useless bloody parents*, he thinks savagely. *Why can't they be like ordinary people, then I wouldn't be forced into a few dodgy deals to make some money to feed my sisters?* A part of him knows it is useless feeling self-pity, but this is one of the major reasons for the growing divide between him and Jack. *That bastard's got everything going for him*, Terry snarls to himself: *proper family life, university student, prospects of a good, well-paid job*. Terry conveniently forgets that Jack isn't exactly on easy street just yet.

Terry is also worried about his oldest sister, Mary, who, at fourteen, is showing signs of getting into trouble. She's been hanging around with that weasel Freddy King. *That prick needs a good warning to keep away from her.*

His thoughts turn to a planned meeting later that day with a guy called Macca—a shady character who seems to peddle drugs, usually through intermediaries. Maybe things will turn around. Macca has connections, and he seems to always have plenty of cash.

*****

Of medium height and heavily tattooed, Macca has a shit-eating grin on his face as Terry approaches him at the bar of the Star Hotel in Hunter Street that evening.

'My man, it's good to see you,' Macca says insincerely. 'Let's walk. There are too many flapping ears around here.'

Terry has done work for Macca before, on a casual basis, usually as a drug courier. Macca is impressed with Terry, for one reason—he doesn't rat. A year ago Terry had been picked up by the cops whilst in possession of a small quantity of grass that he was taking to one of Macca's customers. Terry got a beating at the time—or, as the cops described it, he resisted arrest—but he didn't give up Macca or the customer. Despite his parole status, he got a suspended sentence from a lenient magistrate, to the disgust of the police.

'I may have some work for you,' says Macca as they stroll along. 'Are you up for a bit of excitement?'

'What exactly did you have in mind,' asks Terry, guardedly.

'I need someone that I can trust to deliver some stuff for me to a guy up the Hunter Valley. Can I trust you, Terry?'

'Of course you can. But what sort of stuff?' Terry lights a cigarette and glances around to ensure no-one is near.

'Oh, just a bit of grass, nothing to worry about. And you can have a bit for yourself, if you like.' Macca replies nonchalantly.

'I'd rather be paid in cash,' Terry flatly states.

'No problems, mate. How does a couple of hundred bucks sound?'

Terry nods, pleased. Macca proceeds to tell him where and when.

'You know, Terry,' Macca grins, 'this could be the start of a beautiful friendship'.

Under instructions from higher up the chain, Macca continues the slow process of grooming Terry for bigger things.

*****

Chapter 6

Although it is getting towards the end of summer, the weather is still warm for March. Jack swims strongly out into the surf to catch a few waves, glad it is the weekend.

A broken wave sweeps towards him, and at the last moment Jack sees the riderless surf board that is being propelled in front of the white water. Ducking instinctively, he feels a sharp pain as the fin of the board strikes him on the back of the head. Stunned, he treads water, running his hand over his head. He feels a lump, but it is impossible to tell if there is anything else wrong. Swearing, he turns around and heads for shore.

Baz Lawson, the council-employed lifeguard, meets him at the shoreline. Baz carries the errant board under his arm.

'The bastard who owns this won't be riding it for a while, Jack,' exclaims Baz in an angry tone. 'Did it hit you?'

'Yep, right on the back of the noggin.'

'Turn around and let me have a look,' commands Baz. He swears. 'Mate, there's blood pissing down your back. You're going to need some stitches in that. Come on up to the tower and I'll ring for an ambulance.'

Jack protests, to no avail, that he will be okay. 'Bullshit, Jack, there's enough blood coming out of that gash to fill a nine-gallon keg.'

Before long the sound of a siren can be heard coming down Memorial Drive. Holding a blood-soaked towel to Jack's head, Baz helps him up the steps to the ambulance waiting at the curb. He is quickly assessed by the ambos and, without delay, he is off to the hospital.

Sitting on a stretcher, Jack is hurried into the Emergency Department. The ambos sit him on a bed and pull the curtains across.

'Well, who have we here?' a female voice speaks from his side. 'It's the hero from the beach.'

Turning, Jack spies Susie. Even dressed as she is in a dowdy blue uniform, she is still a stunner.

'Remember me?' Susie asks.

'Yep,' replies Jack, 'it's ... Sue ... no, Susie!'

Thank goodness I've got a good memory, he thinks.

'Err ... my name's Jack ... Jack Martin.'

'Jack Martin, have you been up to some more heroics?' she asks in a bantering tone.

'No, some bast ... I mean bloke ... his surfboard hit me in the head in the surf.' Jack grimaces at the pain.

Instantly Susie is solicitous. 'Here, show me your head.'

Wiping the blood away, Susie examines the wound and frowns. She grabs a clean pad and puts it in his hand. 'Hold this over the wound, and press firmly. I'm going to get a doctor to examine you.' She hurries out.

Jack sits quietly holding his head, excited to see her again, hoping she will return. Within a few minutes she is back, ushering into the cubicle a man wearing a white coat.

'Hi,' the man says, 'I'm Doctor Charlesworth. I'm going to

examine the wound on your head'. The doctor examines the back of Jack's skull, gently probing.

'I'd say you are going to need a reasonable number of stitches in that to close it up,' he observes, 'and an X-ray of your skull, just to make sure there isn't a fracture. Nurse, will you fetch me a suture tray, please?'.

Susie is back before he knows it, carrying the tray.

'Now, I'm going to put in some local anaesthetic to deaden the area. It will sting a bit going in, but then you'll feel nothing when I stitch you up. Then we'll get you an X-ray. Okay?'

Jack nods agreement, his eyes never leaving Susie's face. Trying to avoid his gaze, she watches as the doctor completes the procedure. Jack winces at the sting of the needle, but it is quickly over.

Finished with the stitching of his head, the doctor tells Jack he will arrange for the X-ray. He leaves Jack and Susie alone in the cubicle.

'Uh, I've got to get on with my work. It was good to see you again,' Susie tells him, turning away a trifle reluctantly, it seems to Jack.

Jack summons up his courage. 'Hey, do you want to go to the movies, or something, one night?'

Susie turns back to him and examines his face, undecided. *I like his smile*, she thinks, *open and honest*. She makes a decision.

'Well, I don't usually date patients, but seeing as we've both kissed the same guy, I suppose that would be okay.' Jack is a bit taken aback by this macabre joke, but then smiles. She tears off a piece of paper from a notebook and scribbles something on it.

'Here's my number. Call me when you're feeling better.'

With that, she sweeps out of the cubicle and is gone.

Later, the X-rays completed and with a clean bill of health, Jack finally unclasps his hand and memorises the number on the piece of paper.

Chapter 7

Terry silently watches through the half-closed door as his sister and that asshole Freddy recline on her bed. Arriving home early, Terry heard soft voices upstairs. They are entwined on the bed, with Freddy's hand up Mary's skirt. Mary is whispering for him to stop, but Freddy is having none of it.

Terry strikes, grabbing Freddy by the leg and pulling him onto the floor. Without hesitation Terry manhandles the boy to the open window and, before Freddy can make a sound, he is dangling upside down out of the window, suspended in midair by his left foot. Freddy lets out a scream of terror as he stares, horrified, at the concrete below.

'You little turd. Give me a good reason why I shouldn't drop you on your head,' yells Terry. Freddie wets his pants in terror, convinced he is going to die.

'Terry, please, please, just let him go,' pleads Mary, 'I promise I won't see him again. Terry, please'.

Sighing, Terry reluctantly pulls him back up into the bedroom. Freddie, overcome with relief, crouches on the floor, eyes fixed on Terry.

'Get up, you piece of shit,' Terry orders.

As Freddie rises, Terry hits him hard in the face. Blood immediately starts flowing from Freddie's nose—probably broken. He moans with pain and terror.

'Get the fuck out of here, now. And if I see you anywhere near this place, or her, I swear you will be dead next time.'

Edging past Terry, Freddy scampers down the stairs and out the door, holding his face.

'Mary, Mary, what am I going to do with you?' Terry is suddenly exhausted. Mary, eyes downcast, doesn't reply.

*****

The extra cash that Terry is earning from running Macca's errands is great. He is able to put regular, healthier food on the table for the kids, and he carefully stashes away the remainder of the money. *Another few jobs and I'll have enough to get myself a decent used car and some nice clothes*, he thinks. Things are looking up. He has free access to good quality weed for personal use—he had taken a decision early on to leave the hard stuff well alone. Distribute it, yes, but use it, no way.

Macca is offering Terry more and more jobs, and although there is an element of danger associated with being caught in possession, Terry is confident that, by taking simple precautions, he can minimise the risk. *Besides*, Terry thinks, *Macca has connections within the cops, so any run-in with them would most likely go no further than a thumping for my trouble*. Terry can handle that if it comes to it. And Macca is dropping hints that bigger things are in the wind—something about dope coming out of South-East Asia, wherever that is. If he plays his cards right, Terry can become a player, not just a courier.

Any misgivings he has are being quashed. *Let the mugs do the honest jobs*, he thinks, *it's much easier to make big money this way*.

*****

Chapter 8

Sipping on a white wine, Susie—in multi-tasking mode—is also painting her nails when the phone rings. She answers it.

'Uh, hi, it's Jack,' the voice on the other end announces nervously.

'Oh, hello, Jack,' Susie answers coolly. Better to have him eager.

'I was wondering ... are ... are you doing anything this Saturday night? If you're working, that's okay,' Jack babbles, out of his comfort zone.

'Well Jack, as a matter of fact, I'm free. What did you have in mind?'

His imagination running riot, Jack almost blurts out what he really wants, but somehow stops his mouth from running away. He squirms uncomfortably. His lack of experience with the opposite sex is showing.

'Perhaps a movie, or a drink and some dinner?' he mutters lamely.

Susie knows she has him on the hook, but decides to give him a little more wriggle room.

'Why don't we combine them, and do all three?'

'Okay,' Jack sags with relief, 'where would you like to go?'.

Susie has had enough of his indecisiveness.

'You choose, and pick me up at my place at six-thirty.'

Susie gives him her address. Jack regains some composure.

'Make sure you don't wear a short dress,' he advises cryptically, and rings off before she can ask him what he means.

Maybe he isn't such a wuss, she thinks, suddenly more interested. Her attention turns to what she will wear. *What's wrong with a short dress?* she thinks, *I've got the legs for it*.

*****

At the club's training shed inside Newcastle Harbour, Jack eyes the surf club's new surfboat with approval. He loves the sleek shape. Bill Clymer, a legend when it comes to these boats, has moulded layers of ply—glued and heavily varnished with a keel, horizontal ribs and stringers made of silver ash—into a boat, eight metres long, that is as beautiful as any woman could be. At least in the eyes of Mick Roser, the boat sweep. Named after a club stalwart and champion sweep, the *Dave Wylie* showcases the latest in surfboat design.

Jack looks around at the assembled rowers from both the junior and senior crews. The junior crew consists of lads who are still about seventeen-years-old and have a fair bit to learn, whist in the senior crew, he and Terry are the youngest at twenty. Mick has been training the members of the current senior crew for over five years now, and they have evolved from learners as kids of fifteen or sixteen to a very experienced and skilled group of men. Jack knows he was chosen as the stroke hand because of his steadiness under pressure, even as a youngster. The experience in rowing together as a team seems to be paying off, as the senior crew has a few wins in local surf carnivals under their belt already this season. Jack thinks it will be a challenge to beat the formidable Caves Beach senior crew at the fast-approaching Newcastle branch championships, but Mick says he is confident of an upset, and Jack thinks this new boat may well make the difference.

Jack and the others take the oars down to the edge of the water and place them on top of each other, conscious to keep any sand away from the grease on the collars where the oars will rest in the rowlocks. Then they manhandle the boat, all four hundred kilograms of it, down to the shore where Mick ties on the sweep oar and instructs the senior crew to place the oars in the boat. Mick tells them he has decided to subject the crews to several sprints of about eight hundred metres out and back—to get their heads in the right space for the championships. Jack will be pleased to do it, and pleased when it's over.

The senior crew goes first. Jack, Terry and the other two rowers jump into the boat on Mick's command and pull strongly on the oars, racing four hundred metres before turning and coming back. By the time they return, Jack and the others are breathing heavily and glad of a break, sweat glistening on their bodies as they watch the junior crew in action. Then Jack leads the charge into the cooling waters, savouring the feel of the sticky salt water on his body, washing away the fatigue. Within five minutes they are off again.

After taking the crews twice, Mick decides to give a trainee sweep a turn with the junior crew. Whilst the five senior crew members rest up on the beach, Jack lets slip that he has asked a girl out and doesn't know where to take her for dinner before the movies. Much gratuitous advice follows, most of it explicit and completely unrelated to his question. Even Terry, who has been avoiding him of late, chips in with a few ribald suggestions. Mick, who is older than the crew, and married, provides the only serious idea.

'Take her to that new cafe on the corner of Hunter and Darby Streets. I took my missus there last weekend. It's called *Le Petit Vache*. Something about a cow, the waitress told me. The food's quite good, if you like French.'

Jack, who has never experienced French cuisine, worries that he won't know what to order. Mick tells him to relax, the menu is in English.

After several more sprints, Mick calls a halt to training, much to the relief of the rowers. All they want to do is pack the boat up and get home to have a shower and a cold drink, followed by a decent feed.

At home, after dinner, Jack studies the movie guide in the newspaper. A new James Bond film called *Casino Royale* is showing at a cinema close to the cafe. Perfect. Jack sits back in satisfaction. French food, and what sounds like a movie with a French setting. How romantic is that?

*****

Chapter 9

Gladys calls out to Jack. 'You can't stay in the bathroom all afternoon. Others need to use it. Get a move on, Son.'

Jack studies his image in the mirror for the umpteenth time. In keeping with the fashion, he is wearing a pink shirt, blue flared trousers, and his favourite pair of winklepickers on his feet. *Bugger it*, he thinks in resignation, *I'm either good enough or I'm not. I'd better get a move on.*

He walks out the front door, straddles his motorbike and heads uptown.

Susie has finally decided on a figure-hugging pants-suit, although she is annoyed at herself for taking any notice of what Jack said. *I should have shown off my legs in a miniskirt*, she thinks. But she has to admit she looks good. Her dark hair is down past her shoulders, her false eyelashes and dark eyeliner make her eyes seem huge, and her lips are adorned in pale lipstick.

She answers the knock at the door. Seeing her, Jack's mouth falls open. *God, she is drop-dead gorgeous. That figure. Those lips.*

'Hello, Jack,' Susie greets him demurely.

Jack is tongue-tied, but manages to mumble a reply. Susie sashays past him out the door, allowing Jack to get an eyeful of her posterior outlined in the tight pants-suit.

Susie comes to an abrupt halt when they reach the curb. *He has a motorbike!* She bursts out laughing. Jack, fearing that he has offended her in some way, is worried and his face shows it.

'It's okay, you dear, sweet boy,' Susie consoles him. 'I see now what you meant about not wearing a dress. You were only trying to save me from embarrassment.'

Jack grins, his spirits soaring.

'Hop on behind me,' he calls, and the couple speed off into the evening. Susie clings tightly to him, squealing in pleasure as the wind blows her hair out behind her. Jack revels in the feel of her body pressing against his back and her hands locked tightly around his waist.

The cafe is perfect and the food is great. Importantly, it comes out quickly. Jack has a beer and Susie a glass of white wine. As they eat, her foot seemingly accidentally brushes against his under the table, causing his heart to beat faster. She quizzes him expertly, extracting a brief life history and what he is studying at uni. Susie is less forthcoming with her own story but Jack, lost in her eyes, doesn't care for the moment.

Susie is delighted to discover that Jack is able to carry a conversation as they eat their main course and then dessert. At her instigation, they cover a wide range of current topics. Jack is a bit taken aback with her vehement denunciation of the Vietnam War, and she feigns anger when his fervour doesn't match hers, but she accepts his explanation that he has a soft spot for the Aussie soldiers fighting there. Susie realises she is enjoying herself in his company.

Jack is not only smitten with her looks, but also finds himself attracted to her intellect. *She is a bit of a firebrand and she isn't afraid to say what she thinks*, Jack reflects admiringly.

Suddenly curious to find out more about her, Jack asks, 'Susie, what's your last name?'.

She regards him appraisingly and responds, 'My full name is Susan Domenica Adams'.

Jack laughs disbelievingly. 'Domenica—that's an unusual name. Where does it come from? It sounds sort of foreign.'

'My father named me after his first girlfriend. He was all of five years old when he met her,' she replies seriously. 'My father was born in Italy. His surname then was Adamo. He changed it when he immigrated to Australia after World War II.' Susie leans forward, a challenging expression on her face, her eyes blazing. 'Have you got a problem with Italians?'

'Now I can see why you're a bit fiery,' Jack laughs, then immediately regrets this.

To his surprise, Susie doesn't take offence. 'You'd better believe it, it's in my blood,' she responds firmly, and then smiles.

When they finish their meal, Susie insists on going halves in the bill. 'You're a poor uni student, and I'm working,' she explains—those green eyes flashing.

The movie theatre is close by and, after purchasing their tickets, they find some seats in the middle of the theatre. The movie starts, and Jack is momentarily at a loss when the cast speaks English. He whispers his misunderstanding in Susie's ear, causing her to giggle in amusement. She holds his hand all the way through the picture. They enjoy the James Bond spoof, even though it is a bit silly in places.

Susie is quiet on the bike ride home. Jack, now awkward again, hesitates as she gets off the bike at her flat. She takes the initiative.

'Jack, I had a lovely evening, thank you. I won't invite you in, not this time anyway. I enjoyed going out with you, and I'd be happy to do it again if you want to.'

She kisses him on the lips and, before he can react, she hurries inside her flat.

Jack rides off, smiling. He likes this girl. A lot. He will certainly be asking her out again, and soon.

Chapter 10

Macca and Terry meet in a quiet back bar down near the wharf.

'Terry, I want you to go to Sydney, to King's Cross, to meet a guy and bring a parcel back for me. It's worth five hundred bucks to you, but you've got to do this right. If you stuff up, you could lose more than the money,' Macca states ominously. 'I'm bloody serious here, you pass this hurdle, you are a step up the ladder in the business.'

Terry is keen, but caution stings him.

'Mate, haven't I done the right bloody things so far?' he challenges.

'True, but this is special. The blokes you will be dealing with take no prisoners. I'm just giving you fair warning.'

Terry snorts. 'I get it, Macca. I fucking get it. Stop worrying.'

'Okay,' Macca backs off. 'The bloke you will meet, this name's Bernie ... Bernie Houghton. He runs a bar in the Cross called the Bourbon and Beefsteak Bar. And you'll need to be dressed decent like.'

Macca gives Terry detailed instructions on the meet, to be held on the following Saturday evening.

ooooo

Chapter 10

Alighting from the train at Kings Cross Station, dressed in a new sports coat and tailored trousers, Terry rides the escalator up to the entrance of the subway. He gazes out onto Darlinghurst Road. It is packed with people. Following Macca's instructions, Terry turns left and strolls along, his eyes wide, drinking in the sights and sounds.

Shit, this is a far cry from Newcastle, he thinks. Strip clubs abound, and bouncers in tuxedos spruik outside their establishments. Glossy photos of half-naked girls stare out from the walls surrounding the clubs. The street is packed with people gawking. Huge neon signs advertising everything from Cocoa Cola to Phillips electrical appliances shine out above him. American servicemen on R and R gather noisily outside the strip clubs and the numerous bars.

Terry crosses Darlinghurst Road and spots the Bourbon and Beefsteak Bar. Several girls, obviously prostitutes, faces painted garishly, loiter outside the entrance. A very large man speaks to them, apparently ordering them to move along. He is massive across the shoulders and his face looks like it has been rearranged by a sledge hammer.

Terry approaches him and nervously asks if he can speak to Mr Houghton. The bouncer gives Terry the once over, his face impassive.

'What ya want him for?' demands the big guy, in a deep voice.

'Uh, a guy named Macca sent me,' Terry responds apprehensively.

'Well, okay, why didn't ya say so straight away? I'm Dozer,' the big guy replies in a friendlier tone.

'I'm Terry.'

'Follow me.'

Dozer escorts Terry inside, taking him through the crowded noisy bar, and parts a curtain, motioning for Terry to follow him down a narrow corridor.

Terry asks, somewhat naively, 'Uh, why do they call you Dozer?'.

'Well man, its short for Bulldozer. You can figure the rest out for yourself.'

Terry realises that Macca has spoken the truth. *Bloody hell, I'd better be very careful here*, he thinks.

His fears are realised when Dozer, quick as a cat, spins and grabs Terry, who instinctively shies away from the big man.

'No offense mate, but I need to see what you've got under that coat.'

Terry is helpless as Dozer quickly and expertly frisks him.

'I've got nothin' against you personally, mate,' says Dozer, 'but the boss would kill me if you're carrying anything unfriendly'.

Terry believes him. Dozer knocks softly on a door.

'Come,' says an American voice from inside. The pair enters.

'Mr Houghton, this here is Terry. Macca sent him. He's clean,' explains Dozer.

'Ah, Terry, come in. Thanks Dozer, I'll take it from here.'

Bernie speaks in an American drawl that Terry later learns is Texan.

Terry glances around. The office is opulent: expensive furniture; plush carpets and fancy paintings on the walls. The bar area can be seen through a large window on one wall, seemingly one-way glass. Terry is in awe of his surroundings.

Bernie reclines in a comfortable chair behind a large desk, which is completely clear. He has a drink in one hand and a cigar in the other. A heavy-set man in his late thirties with a full head of greying hair, he is impeccably dressed in a well-cut suit. Terry's gaze is attracted to the heavy gold rings he wears on several fingers.

'Sit down, Terry. Wanna drink?'

'No thanks, Mr Houghton,' Terry declines politely. He decides he needs all his wits about him. Bernie smiles appreciatively and blows a perfect smoke ring.

'Our mutual acquaintance, Mr Macdonald, speaks highly of you, Terry.' Bernie smiles, but it fails to reach his eyes. Terry assumes he is referring to Macca. He continues: 'Yes, he says that you're someone to be trusted ... to do a job properly ... and to keep your mouth shut. Those attributes are very important to my organisation'.

Bernie sits forward and fixes Terry in a direct gaze. 'I know a lot about you and your background, Terry, from lots of sources. Although you've only been in my business for a little while, I'm thinking of taking a punt on you. What do you say to that?'

Terry stammers that he is happy to be involved and that he won't let Bernie down. He wills himself to be calm, sensing that Bernie is shrewdly assessing him as they speak.

'Good boy,' Bernie says approvingly. 'Go and find Dozer. He'll introduce you to a few guys who also work for me. They'll give you the package that you'll take to Mr Macdonald. He'll give you further instructions.'

'Oh by the way,' Bernie adds as Terry rises and heads for the door, 'you won't need to be working at that Newcastle Dockyard anymore. And keep your nose clean. No more brushes with the law. We have plans for you. But Terry, once you're in, you're all the way in. I do not tolerate anyone that rats on me or tries to cheat me. The consequences could be ... fatal'. Bernie fixes him with a cold glare.

Terry wonders how Bernie knows about the dockyard, and his criminal record, then realises that Macca has probably told him. Or perhaps he hasn't. Perhaps he has connections into the cops as well?

Before Terry can respond, Bernie turns to face the window dismissively, gazing out towards the punters who are silently carousing in the bar. Terry leaves, gently shutting the door behind him.

Once Terry is gone, Bernie lifts the phone on his desk and places a call to Newcastle.

'You know who this is. Your new man will do just fine, but keep an eye on him just the same. One can never be too careful. And get him to meet up with our connection in Singleton. He can be useful in keeping tabs on things up there.'

Bernie hangs up and resumes his scrutiny of the bar, contemptuously regarding the customers. *That's right, you suckers, keep on drinking that watered-down booze and trying to chat up my girls. Spend all the money you want.*

Escorted by Dozer, Terry meets two of Bernie's underlings and quickly completes the pickup. There are several small parcels, which he slips into his pockets. As he leaves with Dozer, Terry asks: 'Mr Houghton, he's a Yank, right? What's he doing here in Sydney?'.

Dozer regards Terry for a moment.

'Terry, you seem like a smart guy. Sometimes it's best to keep your mouth shut. Too many questions can be dangerous. Understand?'

Terry nods.

'Now piss off, mate. Perhaps I'll see you again.'

Dozer's attention is drawn by two drunks that are causing a disturbance at the entrance to the bar. He quickly moves to them, and before they know it, they are flat on their backs on the street, their faces bloodied.

Terry spots two uniformed coppers on the other side of the street watching the commotion. The younger one speaks animatedly to the older, who shakes his head and whispers something in the other's ear, gesturing towards the Bourbon and Beefsteak. The pair turns and walks on.

Shaking his head in admiration, Terry takes Dozer's advice and heads for the train station. It would seem that Mr Houghton has got the local cops on the payroll. What a player.

As he walks away, Terry reflects on the Yank he has just met. *What's he doing here?* he ponders, and then smiles as the answer comes into his head. I bet it's something to do with all those Yankee soldiers in the Cross.

*****

Jack is having a drink with Susie in a bar in Cooks Hill when Terry walks in. Terry sees Jack and is about to go the other way when he spots Susie. He seems to change his mind and comes over. Jack isn't too pleased, given their recent differences of opinion.

'Jack,' Terry greets him coolly, 'who is this beautiful woman? You've got more taste than I realised'.

Jack reluctantly introduces Susie.

Terry takes Susie's hand in greeting, gazing into her eyes boldly. She realises she's seen him before, at the beach on the day of the rescue. She smiles at him. *He is easy on the eye, but in a different way to Jack. Somehow more dangerous.* She notes the dark glint in his eye.

'Pleased to meet you,' he says smoothly, running his eyes over her figure, his face breaking into a smile.

Before Jack can say anything more, Terry speaks again.

'Well, I'm just passing through. I hope to see you again, Susie,' he smiles again at her and, ignoring Jack, walks away.

Jack has an unhappy expression on his face.

'Sorry Susie, but that bloke and I don't get on too well these days. It wasn't always like that, but for some reason he has taken a dislike to me.'

Sipping her wine, Susie glances after Terry briefly, and then turns the topic of conversation to other things.

*****

Chapter 11

Six surfboats line up for the final of the senior boat race at the New South Wales State Surf Lifesaving Championships. The weather at Sydney's Newport Beach on this early April Sunday afternoon is atrocious. Heavy rain falls, drenching participants and the few remaining spectators alike. The wind is strong and gusting out of the south. The surf is huge. Apart from a large shore break, there are two further lines of breaking waves, the last and biggest about four hundred metres out to sea. The cans, around which the surfboats will turn, are bobbing wildly a hundred metres beyond the last break.

A number of events have been cancelled. All junior surf races are off after several competitors had to be rescued in the semifinals, and at least a half-dozen surf skis have been smashed to pieces in the ski final. If it wasn't for the fact that the senior boat race is the premier event of the carnival, it would have been cancelled as well.

Jack, Terry, Mick and two other rowers, Simon and Dan, form one of the crews in the final. Simon and Dan are a year older than Jack and Terry, with more experience. The crew is in the race courtesy of wins in their heat and quarterfinal yesterday, and their semifinal first up this morning. The first two races were close, but they won the morning race in convincing style, drawing the favoured number six alley—the southernmost—and hitting the beach before half the other crews could reach the cans.

But the surf is now more chaotic than this morning, and their crew has drawn number one alley, at the northern end of the area. This means they will have to push up into the strong southerly conditions to reach their can, and then head back to the beach in a diagonal path in order to finish inside the designated area. This is a tough ask.

There is only one thing working in their favour: a strong rip sweeps seaward just to the north of their alley, and Mick plans to use it as a springboard on the way out to the cans.

They have form behind them. Although by no means the biggest crew, their timing is excellent regardless of the surf conditions, and Mick is a first-class sweep—aggressive and confident. They claimed victory at the Newcastle branch championships several weeks before in big surf, beating the more fancied Caves Beach crew, a most satisfying triumph. In that final, Mick put them down the wave of the day, holding the boat straight through the white water. They swept past their one remaining rival as the opposing sweep panicked and swung his boat, overturning it, dumping the crew unceremoniously into the water.

Still, Jack is nervous. He glances at the Dee Why crew in the next alley. *They are huge guys*, he thinks. One smiles back at him insolently and flexes his shoulder muscles. *You cheeky bugger*, Jack thinks angrily, *we'll soon see who's smiling*.

The crews get the order to move their boats into the shallows in preparation for the start.

'Now, listen,' Mick calls to them, his voice deep and calm. 'I want the same start as this morning. We have to get past this shore break or we're cactus. So, when I say go, pull the boat past you for a step and then jump in and row like buggery—but in time with the stroke hand. Make sure you get your feet in the foot straps, I don't want an oar to crab. Jack, I want the same cadence as this morning. Terry, as bowhand you're crucial here too. You make sure you get your oar in the water and get a good wack of water with that blade in the first stroke. Don't any one of you take any notice of the starter, that's my job. Block everything else out. You just pay attention to what I'm saying, okay?'

The crews tense as the boat official prepares to fire the starting pistol. Suddenly there is a bang and the race is on.

'Run the boat … in the boat,' Mick screams, his face contorted in concentration. The crew obeys, and the momentum of their actions sees them rise up and, barely, over a large shore dumper.

'You fucking idiot,' Mick screams in the direction of the starter, 'you've almost put the whole race in the shitter'.

But Jack, rowing furiously, his side of the boat facing the other five competitors, sees that several—Dee Why included—have been hit hard by the wave. In fact, Dee Why's boat is swamped, and a boat in alley four has shipped a lot of water.

Mick, looking around, sees it too. 'Row, you bastards, row, it's a four-boat race. You're in front.'

Using the rip skilfully, Mick engages the sweep oar to steer the surfboat out towards the second break. They hold a narrow lead over the boat in the favoured alley six.

Mick stands tall and scans the water ahead, searching for a gap in the confused surf. The rip helps, and he spies a spot where the waves are not breaking as heavily. *It must be deeper water*, he thinks, and instinctively heads for it.

The crew settles into a steady rhythm, oars dipping in unison, and the surfboat powers ahead. Again Mick glances right to check on the opposition. He sees Jack sneaking a peek and screams at him to watch his oar. One mistake and they're history in these conditions.

Chapter 11

The four boats approach the second break, the crew coming last only about twenty metres behind. Mick glances right again. He notices that the other sweeps are ordering their crews to dig their oars, waiting for a lull before tackling the ten-foot waves in front of them.

'Drop a gear,' Mick yells at the top of his voice, 'the opposition's stopped. This is our chance. Go. Go!'.

Led by Jack, the crew up the tempo, rowing feverishly, their oars biting the water powerfully. They surge forward, gaining speed swiftly as the other crews come to a temporary halt.

'The rip's given us a bit of a lull, all we have to do is get over the next wave, and we're almost out,' cries Mick, conveniently omitting to mention the last and largest break that they have to scale.

The lip of the big wave in front of them starts to break as their boat rises up its slope, steeper and steeper, until it seems that the boat will crash down backwards to disaster. But the faster rowing tempo has given them just enough extra momentum, and the boat scrapes over the crest before crashing down into the lee of the swell.

His heart thumping, Jack glances down at the bottom of the boat and sees that they have picked up some water in the narrow escape.

Mick quickly orders Simon to put his foot on the venturi valves under his feet, pushing them open, allowing the water to gradually escape. He peers over but can't see any other surfboats as yet.

'Long slow strokes, lads,' Mick calls. 'Conserve a bit of energy, but we still need to go fast enough to get this water out.'

The crew obeys, their breathing easing slightly after the last big effort.

The last break looms.

Mick glances around and sees two other boats emerge through the raging water, about fifty metres behind but well to the south. *Shit*, he thinks, *they're still within striking distance.*

Frustratingly, there are no more gaps evident, so Mick has to pick his wave and bash through the wall of broken white water, hoping that there isn't a larger wave behind that may swamp them and surely end their chances. It will mean taking in water, but he must retain the advantage over the other crews. He knows his crew is tiring; they have put in a big effort, but the hardest is yet to come.

He coaxes the tired rowers to greater efforts as a huge broken wave approaches and, accelerating, the boat smashes into the wall of white water. Momentum slows and they are almost stopped by the impact, but Mick screams at the two stroke hands to lock the handles of their oars into their stomachs so that the boat does not slip too far back. He cajoles the bow hands to row as hard as they can.

Suddenly, they are through the break and Mick can see the cans. The boat has taken a lot of water, and it will be heavy to row—but row they must, so that the venturis can do their job of sucking the water out.

Mick steers at an angle to the beach to reach their can. The crew is struggling, exhaustion written on their faces, grimacing as they pull the oars through the grey-green water. The water level in the boat slowly drops.

They reach the can and Mick steers the surfboat around it. They head back towards the beach. Mick can see that they have about an eighty-metre advantage over the three surviving boats. *Bastards*, he thinks savagely, *they've all made it out.*

As Mick angles the heavy boat to the south, the crew picks up runners as the swells move powerfully underneath them. It is easier rowing, both physically and psychologically, and the boat's momentum builds. Mick finds it difficult to steer as the bow dips on the runners and the remaining water in the boat rushes towards the bow.

Mick wants to go at least another fifty metres south before he turns the boat for home, but the surf has other ideas. Alerted by

Jack's moan, he glances behind and sees a huge swell looming, about to break. They must catch it or it will break on top of them.

'Row, lads, we have to get out in front of it,' Mick shouts. Adrenalin pumping, the crew complies.

The large swell, cresting, picks them up and carries them forward.

'Trail your oars … back you come,' Mick commands and the crew throw their oars over their heads and push them to the sides of the boat before climbing carefully back to the stern, looking upwards at the rapidly tilting rear of the boat as it accelerates down the big wave.

Jack is furthest back, under Mick's feet, and the others pile on top of him, clinging to whatever they can. They gaze in awe at the size of the wave as they head down its face, steeper and steeper. The remaining water in the boat surges forward to the bow, making it increasingly more difficult for Mick to hold the boat straight.

'Steady boys, keep the boat level,' Mick calmly calls as he lines the boat up, preparing for the massive jolt when the wave breaks and the white water surges around the boat.

It hits, and Mick struggles to hold the sweep oar as the raging wave, combined with the volume of water inside the boat, makes steering almost impossible. Gradually at first, then more quickly, the boat swings to the right on the wave, white water slopping over the side into the boat.

'Lean to the left,' Mick calls urgently to the crew. 'Try to keep the right side high. If more water comes in, we're fucked.'

Mick fumes silently. *Why didn't the boat swing south? We'd still be in the finish zone.*

About a hundred and fifty metres from the shore, the wave peters out as the next break looms. Mick gets the crew back into their seats and they retrieve their oars. The boat is now half-full of water and very sluggish to handle. The other boats aren't in sight, so Mick senses his crew still has a chance of reaching the finish line first.

Again, the crew rows diagonally to the south, Mick searching for the northernmost finishing marker. He spots it, but they are still not in position for the final run to the beach. Knowing time is running out, he takes a calculated risk.

'We gunna have to head into the wave area and hope we get a lull,' he calls, 'we can still win this sucker'.

Slowly they make their way parallel to the beach, fearfully searching for any waves that might hit them. They almost make it when another big breaker looms across the stern. Mick decides instantly to take it, or it will turn them over.

Again the crew respond to his command. Rowing furiously, they catch it, only to once again swing to the right away from the finish area, the weight of water in the boat making it impossible to control.

They hit the beach about thirty metres north of the finish zone. Members of their surf club swarm towards the boat, wanting to help them.

'Stay the fuck away,' screams Mick, 'we have to finish under our own steam, or we'll be disqualified'.

The exhausted crew jump out and push and drag the boat to the finish line, half in and half out of the water, dodging, as best as they can, the heavy shore break. But in the two minutes or so it takes to get the boat across the finish line, the two crews from alleys one and two cross ahead of them, cheering wildly. Jack and the crew slump to the sand, dog-tired, as Mick finally allows the helpers to carry the boat up the beach out of the water.

Mick is a dejected figure as he sits on the stern after the race. Still breathing heavily from the efforts of the past fifteen minutes, Jack picks himself up off the sand and tries to console him.

'If I hadn't swung north twice we'd have won that,' Mick says bitterly.

'Mate, you did an amazing job to get us out there and back in those conditions. I'm just pleased we got a place,' Jack gasps, 'and

I'm sure the rest of the guys agree'. The rest of the crew, apart from Terry, nod their heads. Terry has an angry expression on his face.

'Come on guys, let's head up to the presentation dais and wait for the medal ceremony,' suggests Jack.

The five trudge through the sand towards the official platform, Simon, Dan and Jack talking animatedly about the race. Terry says nothing, staying slightly behind the others.

Jack notices, and drops back to talk to Terry, who stares at him sullenly.

'What's the matter, Terry?' Jack asks, pretty sure he knows why Terry is angry.

Terry has an irate glint in his eye.

'You and I know that Mick blew it. We could have won, if it wasn't for him.'

Jack replies angrily: 'What a load of bullshit, mate. He did a great job under the circumstances. We all did'.

'Fuck off, pretty boy,' replies Terry coldly, and walks on, leaving Jack standing there, stunned.

Mick, pausing to wait for the two stragglers, overhears the exchange. He shakes his head silently.

After the medal ceremony, and with the boat secure on its trailer, the crew and other club members repair to a local pub for a beer to celebrate and to more closely examine their bronze medals. Jack can't keep his eyes off the medal, really excited despite the harsh words exchanged with Terry.

Mick gets in the first shout of beers for the crew.

'Well lads, I don't say this often, but I'm proud of you all. That was a terrific race, and one for which you can claim a moral victory. Something to tell your grandkids about. Here's to you.'

Mick raises his glass in salute. They all join him, even Terry.

'Lads, you'd better think about whether you want to nominate for the Aussie titles in a few weeks' time. They're on the Gold Coast, from memory. I reckon we're in with a good chance, on the form you blokes have been displaying.'

A robust conversation follows as pros and cons of going to Queensland are discussed loudly. Simon, Dan and Jack are keen, but Terry is quiet.

Mick turns to him. 'What's your view, Terry? You in or what?'

Terry puts down his beer and stares defiantly at the rest of the crew.

'You'll have to get another bow hand for that, I'm quitting the crew. I've got other—better—plans.'

With this bombshell, Terry downs his beer and walks out of the bar, leaving his fellow crew members to look at each other in astonishment.

'Leave this to me,' Mick commands. 'And Jack, I don't know what is going on between you two, but you stay away from him.'

Jack says nothing, dumbfounded. The problem is that he doesn't know what's going on either. He is angry, frustrated and upset. In a short period of time, Terry has changed so much, and not for the better.

*****

Chapter 12

Jack parks his motorbike in one of the car parks at the university and locks it. He looks around appreciatively, admiring the leafy surroundings. The uni buildings are located in a bushland setting and the native gums tower over the complex, which is spread out over a couple of hectares. Kookaburras, rosellas, and other native birds call in the trees, interrupting the otherwise silent atmosphere. It is a very relaxing locale.

Jack walks briskly up the path through the trees to the science faculty buildings and climbs the steps into the concrete structure that houses the Mathematics Department. Standing in a small crowd of students, he checks the noticeboard on the ground floor for any changes to lectures and tutorials. Jack likes to be organised, and hates not to know where his classes are.

Hearing familiar voices behind him, Jack turns and warmly greets his mates, Merv and Tim, who are studying similar second-year subjects to him. Merv has long brown hair and is a bit of a radical. Tim, short and with fair curly locks, is more academic. He is in contention for honours studies down the track and possibly a University Medal, such is his brilliance. Neither of them is a surf club member—Tim hates the beach and Merv is mad on soccer. Somehow, despite their disparate lives, the three are firm friends, drawn together by the subject choice plus a liking for cold beer and pretty girls.

Jack has elected to study two mathematics subjects, plus psychology, needing a third field of study, also non-science, to complete his second-year quota. The bonus of the last subject is that there are certain to be a lot more girls in class than in maths. He is a good, but not gifted, student and has no wish to study pure maths, a subject at which Tim excels. Both Tim and Merv are taking three maths streams in year two.

The three exchange friendly banter, ribbing each other about hot girls and topics they are studying. Tim and Merv are well aware of Jack's love for the beach, and give him a hard time about surf clubs and boat rowers with their swimmers tucked up the cheeks of their bums to avoid getting blisters.

'Come on down to the union building,' Merv enthusiastically entreats them, 'there's a protest on about the Vietnam War. There are some good speakers up from Sydney. Later, there will be a march in town to the Army Recruiting Centre. Hopefully that should stir the bastards up'. Merv is rabidly anti-war and has refused to register for National Service, claiming conscientious objector status.

Tim and Jack aren't so stirred. Tim excuses himself; he has to meet one of the lecturers to discuss something or other. Jack also begs off attending the protest, keen to check out whether there are any games of snooker on at the union building.

*****

Dressed in her nightgown, Susie brushes her hair and thinks about Jack. They have gone out several times since their first date, and she knows their relationship is blossoming, even though they have to fit in outings around Susie's work shifts. Jack has told her he likes meeting her during week nights, as the places they go aren't as crowded. Susie knows it gives them more opportunity to talk without having to shout over the noise generated by the weekend crowds.

Susie has elected to play hard to get, refusing to go any further than kissing, although she acknowledges that this has become pretty passionate. She is aware this leaves Jack frustrated but, to his credit, he doesn't push things. Susie is almost sure about Jack, but at times he seems a bit straitlaced and a bit of a goody-two-shoes. He won't smoke pot and is more content with a quiet night out than a rage. Part of her thinks that she wants someone more dangerous and adventurous, but another part likes the safety and security he offers. And he is good looking and has a great body. She is torn.

She thinks back to her childhood, to her father. Handsome and wild, he adored her, but he wasn't a good husband to her mother, who repeatedly caught him with other women. Finally, in despair, she had left him when Susie was fourteen. They had got back together a year or so later, and seemed happy. Then came the car crash.

Maybe I'm too much like him, she thinks, *too much of him is inside me. Never content to settle for the quiet life.*

This had influenced her teenage years. A bit of a wild child, she constantly defied her mother's wishes and ran fast and free. Her part-time father did little to discipline her.

Staying out late and sexually active at fifteen, she had been lucky to avoid a pregnancy at sixteen, suffering a miscarriage at ten weeks. This had slowed her down a bit, and she decided to study nursing. *The best thing I ever did*, she acknowledges.

She wants to sleep with Jack and to build on the relationship, but she senses neither of them is ready just yet. She decides to wait for a sign.

*****

Gladys hands Jack a letter when he gets home from uni.

'It's for you. It's from the government.'

Gladys wears a worried expression. She is joined by Henry, and they stand in front of their son as he eyes the envelope.

It is from the Department of Labour and National Service. Jack's heart skips a beat. *Oh please, God—if there is a God—don't let it be my call-up.*

Jack opens the envelope and reads the letter closely. After what feels like an eternity to his parents, his face transforms into an ear-to-ear grin.

'I haven't been called up,' he cries. His mother weeps tears of relief and Henry, to Jack's surprise, grabs him in a bear hug, a tear in his eye too.

What Jack doesn't tell them is that the letter advises his birth date has come up in the ballot, but because of his university enrolment he is deferred until the completion of his studies. *That's two years away*, he thinks. *The bloody war will probably be over by then.* He decides to tell them later, not wanting to spoil their joy right now.

'I'm off to the pub to celebrate, I'll get a hamburger later, Mum, don't worry about my dinner.'

He bursts into the public bar of the pub, anxious to broadcast the news to anyone who will listen. By chance, Mick is there, talking quietly to Terry. Jack interrupts their conversation with his news, unable to wait until they have finished talking. Mick gives him an exasperated glare that Jack, on a high, misses completely.

'That's terrific news, Jack,' acknowledges Mick in a quiet tone. 'But you won't have heard, of course—Terry has been called up.'

Jack gapes at Terry in astonishment, his mouth falling open. He has forgotten completely that they are of a similar age. Terry glares back, rage and anger in his eyes. *The prick*, Terry seethes, *why do I always draw the short straw? Why not him?*

This is the final insult for Terry. His resentment of Jack boils over and he throws a wild punch at Jack's face. Jack instinctively ducks, and before any blows can reach their mark, Mick is between them, pinning Terry's arms to his sides.

'I think it's best if you go, Jack,' Mick advises. 'I'll sort out Terry. I'm sure he doesn't mean it.'

Not so sure about this, but cursing himself for his stupidity, Jack obeys.

Outside on the pavement, Jack hesitates. Upset and angry with himself, he doesn't want to go home. On a whim, he enters the public phone box nearby and dials Susie's number. She answers, thank goodness, and he blurts out his news.

Susie is excited and pleased for Jack. *Perhaps this is the signal I've been waiting for*, she thinks.

Making up her mind quickly, Susie invites Jack to her flat for dinner. He accepts eagerly.

When Jack arrives, Susie greets him with a long kiss. She sits him down in the tiny lounge room and fetches him a beer.

'I'll be back in a minute,' she tells him.

In her bedroom, Susie quickly disrobes. Dressed only in a brief pair of panties, she dons a short robe but doesn't tie the belt. She takes a quick peek in the mirror. *You'll do*, she thinks.

Jack is studying his beer bottle when she returns. He looks up and almost spills his beer in astonishment. Susie is standing there, mostly undressed, the robe open at the front. He can see her full, creamy white breasts and erect pink nipples. Her belly is flat, and her brief knickers accentuate her long slim brown legs.

Jack is instantly aroused.

Susie crosses to him and stands above him, gazing down at him, eyes heavily lidded. 'I thought I'd give you a little present to go with your good news,' she purrs.

Bending slightly, she thrusts her breasts against his face, allowing him to nuzzle them. He kisses her nipples and delights in their feel, further exciting him.

'Take my panties off, Jack,' Susie whispers throatily. Jack needs no further urging.

As he pulls them down, Susie steps out of them and arches her pelvis into his face, allowing him to taste her sex. She moans as he does so and rhythmically rotates her pubic bone against his lips. Before long she orgasms, crying out and arching her back in pleasure.

After she has recovered, Susie kneels in front of Jack. She helps him out of his shorts and jocks, and grasps his erect penis in her hand before moving it to her mouth. She takes him in her mouth and expertly works on him. Jack groans and thrusts as she increases her tempo. Jack ejaculates, noisily, and she sits back on her haunches, well pleased with the outcome.

Wiping her mouth on her knickers, she smiles at Jack, who stares back at her, for the moment spent. She places her hand on his cock, which has become flaccid.

'Don't think you're finished, Jack my boy,' Susie grins at him, 'we're just getting started. We're going to have a lot of fun this evening'.

With that she gently puts her hand on him and massages slowly.

'We'll have Jack Junior here up and about in no time.'

*****

Chapter 13

Terry is desperate, and makes contact with Macca, arranging a meet at a local hotel.

'Mate, I'm stuffed,' says Terry, anxiety all over his face. 'I've been called up by the bloody government. I'm gunna be a Nasho. That's gunna fuck things up completely,' he says dejectedly.

To Terry's surprise, Macca seems more thoughtful than angry.

'Can't you pull some strings, or get Mr Houghton to talk to somebody?' Terry pleads, his future plans and hopes seemingly in tatters.

'Quiet, man, I'm thinking,' responds Macca. He ponders for a minute whilst Terry waits anxiously.

Suddenly, Macca smiles wolfishly.

'Terry, mate, this could actually work out pretty well.'

Terry cannot see how this can be so.

'What … what are you talking about?' he stammers.

Macca places an arm around Terry's shoulder and explains his blossoming idea. Terry listens, his panic slowly subsiding.

'So, you're in the army for a couple of years. No big deal. I hear you don't have to go to Vietnam unless you volunteer, so don't put your hand up. Sure, you'll probably have to do some shit jobs, but there is opportunity here.'

Macca goes to the bar and brings back a couple of schooners. Sipping from his beer, Macca continues with his idea.

'I was gunna get you to go up to Singleton to meet a guy, anyway. This guy is in the army and works at the base there. We've been a bit worried about him lately, and we were gunna get you to keep tabs on him. This way, if we can swing it—and I'm sure Bernie can with his contacts—you can do your training in Singleton. Kill two birds with one stone. It'd be worth a fair bit of dosh to you.'

Terry sips his beer, considering the idea. *Why not?* he thinks. *I'd be out of that shithole at home. And hopefully it would earn plenty of brownie points with Mr Houghton.*

Macca goes on, warming to the theme.

'Shit, this idea is getting better and better. We would have a trusted contact inside the army for the next couple of years. Those guys are an important client base for our operations.'

Macca pauses, realising he might be imparting more information than he intends.

'I'll let you in on something you wouldn't have known about until much further down the track,' Macca confides. 'A lot of the drugs we bring into the country come from a place in South-East Asia called the Golden Triangle. It's where they grow opium, and it's a bloody big area smack in the middle of three shitty little countries. But the product is top grade, and it fetches top dollar here and in the States. And that's where Bernie comes in, him and another guy—never mind his name. Both him and Bernie are Yanks, and they have a lot of clout.'

Macca finishes his beer.

'Leave things with me, Terry. Just relax and do all the things you need to with the government and the army. I'll talk over the idea with Bernie, but I'm sure he'll go for it. Mate, your star could just be looking very bright indeed.'

With that, Macca gets another shout in.

Chapter 14

The relationship between Susie and Jack reaches a new level now that they are sleeping together. They see each other at least twice a week when Susie's shifts and Jack's uni studies permit. Mostly, it is at Susie's flat, where the sex is frequent and intense.

It is mid-autumn, and the days are sunny and milder. They go for picnics in Susie's Mini up into the Hunter Valley, and Susie introduces Jack to the pleasures of wine tasting in the growing number of vineyards being opened in the area to the west of Cessnock where the rich alluvial soil is ideal for growing good-quality grapes.

Although his preferred tipple is beer, Jack develops a taste for Tulloch's 'Private Bin' burgundy. Susie, on the other hand, fancies a Rhinegold semillon. They argue good-naturedly about the merits of each as they laze under shady trees and eat sandwiches they have brought with them.

On the weekends, they go to pubs for drinks and food, and Susie manages to drag Jack along to the Conquistador nightclub in the West End one Saturday night, and to the nearby Star Hotel on another. They see Terry in the back bar at the Star, and Terry raises his glass to them in a mock salute, but stays away.

Susie says the Conquistador is her favourite. Both places are notorious for drugs, underage drinking and brawls. The Star is a dump, full of sailors, transvestites and petty crims. The Conquistador is a bit classier, but still full of low-life and young people searching for adventure.

Jack is out of his comfort zone in these places. He can handle himself, but he doesn't want to get involved in any fights whilst in Susie's company. And she seems to like smoking grass. He doesn't mind this too much—plenty of his uni mates do it—but she keeps persuading him to try some. She sometimes gets angry when he refuses.

Jack's studies are suffering a little, due to his infatuation with Susie. His mind can't seem to focus on anything else for too long. His parents have noticed that something is up, and suspect female involvement, but Jack won't talk about it. Gladys is worried, but Henry is secretly pleased. *That's my boy*, he thinks with pride.

Obsessed though Jack is, a tiny seed of doubt clouds his happiness. Susie is everything he wants: smart, funny, full of life, and very, very sexy, but she's a bit of a wild child. Not that there's anything wrong with that, but if she's not careful, she may bite off more than she can chew. Those places she wants to frequent are a worry.

Jack has a mate, nicknamed Beaver, who works as a bouncer at the Conquistador. Beaver has regaled Jack and his mates with stories about the place. Grass, LSD, cocaine, and even heroin are available if you know the right people.

Susie has admitted to Jack that she has tried LSD. Dropping acid she calls it. She says she has only done it once. She describes feeling euphoric and so, so aware of her surroundings. She knows friends who have had bad trips and weird reactions, but she is not deterred.

Jack is a little concerned, but is reluctant to challenge her. He thinks he is in love, knows he is in lust, and he is blinded. Perhaps if he tells her about his feelings, she will stop this silly behaviour. Jack is not aware that Susie thinks of him in a way that falls far short of love.

She has been reflecting on Jack. He is a great guy and she likes him a lot. *We have fun. The sex is nice, but it could be spiced up if he would loosen up a bit. A toke or two would help, but he won't touch anything but alcohol. Maybe I want more than he can offer*, she reflects, not meaning anything like love and marriage. *He is too down-to-earth and too square. I want a bit more danger in my life. He doesn't like partying, and hates the places where I want to go.*

But Susie is not yet prepared to move on. She enjoys the security, even though she thirsts for more exciting and risky escapades. She is content, for the moment, to continue to see him, make love, and enjoy life—although she is becoming increasingly convinced that each of them has a differing agenda.

*****

Chapter 15

Terry meets up with Macca at a local pub for a beer and to discuss the army thing. Macca casually mentions that he has had a word to Bernie about Terry's situation.

'Terry, my man, this is like a godsend. Bernie reckons you will provide an entree into an emerging market created by the National Service scheme. He wants you to go to a place called Holsworthy after your initial training. It's out past Liverpool in Sydney, so you'd be not too far from home. He thinks you should stay there for the duration of your Nasho service. There are a shitload of army people there, and Bernie reckons it will be a snack to get drugs onto the base. You'd be the man, Terry, and the money you'd make would be sensational.'

Terry sits silently, digesting this. *The money sounds good, but what about the risk? Surely that would be where Bernie comes in with his connections.* Terry decides to take the opportunity to do a bit more probing on Bernie's background.

'That sounds promising Macca, but, given I would be the kingpin at the base, I would like to know a bit more about Bernie.'

Macca looks dubious at this, but Terry is adamant.

'Mate, you've got to give a bit to get what seems to me like a lot. I just need some background. What harm can it do? I've proved my worth.'

Glancing around to check there is no undue interest in the conversation, Macca lowers his voice and grudgingly answers.

'Now, I don't know a real lot, but what I do know is that he served in the US Army in World War II as a youngster, and used his connections to work in Vietnam during the early part of the war, including being linked to some of the Aussie troops there at the time. I think that's where he made his pile of money, because he arrived in Australia a few years ago and opened up several nightclubs in the Cross. This would have taken some doing, knowing the crims who control that area, not to mention the politicians and the coppers.'

Macca hesitates, then decides to continue. 'Maybe I'm speaking out of turn, but I know he has a buddy called Michael Hand, another Yank who fought in Vietnam and who now lives in Sydney. Mike seems to have his fingers in a lot of pies.' Macca stops, takes a drink and says: 'That's all I know, Terry. Now, are you in, or not?'.

Terry doesn't hesitate. 'Yep, mate, I'm in.'

As they part, Macca opens the bag he is carrying and surreptitiously hands Terry several thick envelopes. Each is stuffed full of twenty-dollar bills.

*****

It is early afternoon when Terry drives the new Holden out of the dealer's yard. It is a two-door HB model Torana S, hot off the press, bright red with a black racing stripe painted along the bonnet. Although it only has a four-cylinder engine, Terry loves it.

He tests the four-speed gearbox gently. It has to do a thousand kilometres at a placid speed before the engine is run in, and Terry has just the place to go. The car has set him back over eighteen hundred dollars, but he reckons it is money well spent. *Sex on wheels,* he thinks. And he's got almost five hundred bucks to spare from the money Macca gave him.

He turns into Maitland Road and heads out through Mayfield—destination Singleton. He expects to be there in an hour and a half, and is due to meet Macca's army guy in the Imperial Hotel public bar at five. The return trip will give him the opportunity to drive at night, something he hasn't done before.

Driving up the New England Highway, Terry passes through the towns of Maitland and Branxton and takes in the green countryside. It is a very pleasant trip, made more so by the new car.

He tunes the radio to a local station and sings along to songs by Petula Clark, the Monkees and, of course, the Beatles. He doesn't really understand what the Beatles are getting at in their new song, *Strawberry Fields Forever*, but he likes the tune. And he quite fancies Petula Clark. Terry fantasises about what he would do to her if they were alone on a desert island. His love-life is embarrassingly lacking. He'll have to change that now he's got money, he decides.

At four-thirty he parks outside the hotel and gazes around, on alert. Macca said that there might be trouble with the guy, who apparently isn't doing what he had been told. Terry's job is not to go the heavy on him—someone else will do that if necessary—but to try to talk some sense into him. Terry hopes the guy will cooperate.

Inside the bar, he pauses to let his eyes grow accustomed to the darker interior. He sees only one person in uniform, and heads towards him. The soldier watches, his expression revealing nothing.

Warily, Terry greets the man. They don't exchange names. The man listens to what Terry has to say, but still he doesn't speak. Terry's tone is deliberately unthreatening.

Terry finishes what he has to say and waits for the guy to respond. Instead, the soldier's gaze focuses over Terry's shoulder, and he smiles. It is not a good smile.

Turning quickly, Terry is hit hard in the jaw by a fist swung by another man. Stumbling sideways, Terry manages to duck a following blow. No-one in the pub moves to help Terry. The barman turns away, suddenly busy elsewhere.

Cautiously, Terry circles, watching for another punch, the side of his face numb and beginning to swell. The stranger is bigger than Terry, but not as fast on his feet. Terry knows he won't have much of a chance unless he can beat this guy quickly. The soldier just sits there, content to let his mate do the dirty work.

The stranger lunges clumsily, trying to land a haymaker right cross. Terry skips inside the blow and hits him in the face with a straight right of his own, his arm jarring as he lands a good punch. He follows with a solid left hook, striking the man just below the heart. The guy slumps, winded, his guard down. Pivoting on his left foot, Terry kicks the man hard between the legs. The guy's eyes roll up into his head and he collapses to the floor, down for the count.

Terry doesn't hesitate. He sprints out of the front door and jumps into the car before the soldier can react. He accelerates sharply up the street, then slows as he remembers the new engine. He checks the rear-view mirror. No-one is following.

As the adrenaline in his system subsides, Terry wipes his face, examining in the mirror the angry red weal on his jaw.

That prick will pay, he thinks savagely. *It's Macca's problem now, and I bet the guy will regret it.*

Terry drives back to Newcastle.

Several days later, the *Newcastle Herald* reports the death under suspicious circumstances of a soldier based at the Lone Pine Army Barracks in Singleton. There is conjecture about the death being drug related, but nothing more comes of it with the police unable to find the perpetrator.

*****

Terry is contemplative as he throws the official-looking letter onto the table. He has received instructions to report for National Service on the following Monday. This is the bad news. The good news is that Macca advises that Bernie has been successful in arranging for him to enter the army at Singleton. Once there, he will carefully market the product—military training permitting—but this is not the real target.

After twelve weeks in Singleton he will be posted to Holsworthy, where he will be contacted by some of Bernie's associates. He is to build a market base there for the remaining time he is to serve. Macca assures him that he will be very well compensated for his efforts but, more importantly, Bernie will have a proper job in Sydney for him when he finishes. Terry is well pleased.

*****

Chapter 16

Susie's competence as a nurse is growing steadily as she experiences a wide variety of cases in the Emergency Department. She is enjoying the challenges, which involve everything from cuts and bruises to heart attacks and strokes, and whilst she doesn't enjoy the outpourings of grief from loved ones, she accepts that this is what happens. The ED team are expert and very professional, but sometimes they just can't do the impossible.

Susie enjoys flirting with the male doctors, married and unmarried, but doesn't let things get out of hand. Although she doesn't see Jack as a long-term prospect, she is fond of him and is content to keep him on the hook. Besides, although a lot of the guys are cute, the look in their eyes tells her that they are only after one thing. But she is no pushover. Well, not often anyway, and certainly not at work.

She hasn't decided what area to specialise in. She has an interest in babies—*what girl doesn't*, she thinks—but maybe intensive care might be worth a shot. She knows she will have to study to become Certificate Qualified, but she doesn't want to go there just yet. She wants to have fun before she settles down to that study. *Maybe in a few years*, she prevaricates.

She occasionally contemplates a change of scene. *Maybe Sydney would be nice. There are plenty of hospitals to choose from, although somewhere near the beach would be preferable. The Prince of Wales Hospital is in Randwick, isn't it, and that's near Bondi. Bondi beach, now that would be a great place to live.* Susie daydreams for a while about this possibility.

Several incidents of people with drug overdose have shaken her. A few weeks ago an eighteen-year-old girl was rushed by ambulance from a party where she'd had several tabs of LSD, coupled with several shots of vodka. She had been hallucinating badly, and was convinced that both the paramedics and the ED staff were trying to kill her as part of some bizarre medical experiment.

The girl sobbed, screamed, kicked and punched and tried to bite a nurse's finger off. She had to be forcibly restrained and sedated in order to calm her central nervous system down. Susie heard on the grapevine that the girl had been admitted to the mental asylum in Watts Street, close to the hospital, and will be a patient there for some time as she keeps on having flashbacks, sending her off the deep end again.

Maybe I'd better steer clear of LSD, she decides. She's heard that cocaine can produce as big a high. But she will need to be careful. She is confident that a guy she knows who goes to the Conquistador can get her some. Only for occasional use, of course. And there's always pot to help her mellow out.

*****

Jack's senior tutor, an honours student in the mathematics department, regards him with irritation.

'Man, surely you realise that unless you do some work you're going to fail? I can't understand it. You have shown us that you can hack the subject matter, why aren't you applying yourself more?'

Jack is on the carpet after failing several minor tests. He hangs his head, knowing he should do better, but his infatuation with Susie is doing his head in.

The tutor studies Jack's face, searching for a clue. Intuitively he asks, 'It's a woman, isn't it?' Jack nods miserably in agreement.

'Shit, dude, this is your future we're talking about.' The tutor changes tack. 'Are you in love with her?'

'Yep,' Jack replies succinctly.

'Does she know, and is it reciprocated?'

'No, she doesn't, and I know she likes me but I don't know about love.'

The tutor stands up.

'Man, I'm not a relationships counsellor, but you need to sort this out, and fast. Otherwise, you're out of here.'

The tutor picks up his notes and walks out of the meeting room. Jack thinks hard for a few minutes and makes a decision. He resolves to confess his feelings to Susie.

*****

Chapter 17

There is a big dance on at the surf club the following Saturday night, the last weekend in June. Jack has invited Susie and she is keen to go. Most of the club members and wives and girlfriends will be there.

The social committee has achieved a coup and engaged a hot local rock band called The Velvet Underground to play. They are reputedly the Hunter Valley's answer to The Rolling Stones and play cover versions of their songs.

Wally has commissioned a few of the bigger club members to act as bouncers, as there are sure to be gate crashers. The cops have been informed but, as one of the committee is a detective and he will be there, they will keep a watching brief and respond if necessary.

Jack has joined about twenty members to decorate the hall during the afternoon and, hanging bunting, he watches as the band sets up in a corner. The lead singer, Steve Phillipson, harmonica in hand, tests the sound system. One of the other band members, Malcolm Young, tunes his guitar.

That morning, Jack walked down to a jeweller store in Hunter

Street and, using some of his savings, purchased a simple friendship ring for Susie. He intends to give it to her tonight, at an appropriate time.

Wally has heard of the band's wild onstage antics, and has threatened Steve and Malcolm with grievous bodily harm if the band starts any fires in the clubhouse, as has apparently happened at other venues. They are also instructed to ignore Wally's wife if she comes too close and tries to grab hold of them. Any other women are fair game.

Tonight's going to be huge, in more ways than one, Jack thinks. He has decided on his approach to Susie. Hopefully it will have the desired result. Still, he is nervous. He is unsure of the outcome, and he doesn't like the feeling of uncertainty.

Wally is checking the Temprites in the bar, determined to avoid a repeat of the last time someone tried to spear a keg of beer. The silly bugger almost lost his head when the gas pressure rapidly forced the spear back out of the keg. He glances up at the patched-up hole in the plastered ceiling above him, remembering the incident. He calls to a mate.

'How many eighteens have we got for tonight?' He refers to eighteen-gallon kegs.

'Five, Wally, with two in reserve in the gear room—just in case.'

We will probably need the reserves, Wally thinks, knowing that the crowd will number around two hundred, with a correspondingly large thirst.

He checks the fridges to ensure that the wine is cool and there is enough meat for the barbeque. *Gotta keep the girls happy, or my missus will kill me*, he thinks.

The club members place chairs around the perimeter of the hall, leaving the centre open for people to move around in, and to dance.

Jack has volunteered to do a stint cooking on the barbeque tonight, which is sure to be busy. It is located outside on the balcony, overlooking the beach.

Wally has managed to persuade the publican who supplied the kegs of beer to loan the club several hundred plastic schooner glasses. Wally knows from bitter experience that using glass in a function like this is a recipe for disaster.

Wally checks the lock on the door to the committee room. The band will use this room for a green room. Wally will post a club member outside to keep non-authorised people out and to allow the band a breather between sets.

All preparations complete, the band and the club members leave the club and Wally locks the front door. They will be back in a few hours and the show will start.

*****

Susie is looking forward to the night with great anticipation. She has seen The Velvet Underground perform at the Star Hotel and loves their act. *This is the sort of gig that suits my style*, she thinks. *Outrageous and crazy.*

In the mood to party, she has decided to wear a micro miniskirt this evening, which will showcase her legs. *I'm sure Jack will love it*, she smiles.

She draws a bath, and as she settles into the warm bubbly water, impulsively she pours herself the first of several wines she will have during the afternoon.

*****

Terry has invited a girl he met at the Star the previous weekend. She had been dancing, half naked, on the stage whilst a band played behind her. She had seen him watching her and, uninvited, she jumped down into his arms and tongue kissed him frantically, writhing in his arms.

She is a bit skinny for his taste, with a boyish figure, but she is crazy and will do anything for a tab of LSD, as she graphically demonstrated in the laneway outside the pub after he offered her a tab.

Terry grins in anticipation as he dresses. This is his penultimate night of freedom, and he intends to make the most of it.

*****

Jack suspects that Susie has had a few drinks when she picks up him outside his house at the allotted time. She is as gorgeous as ever, but her eyes are slightly unfocused and she is a bit wobbly on her feet.

When he gets into her car he notices that her brief miniskirt has ridden high on her thighs, and Jack can see a glimpse of white panties between her legs as she turns toward him, her legs opening. She kisses him sloppily, and he tastes the alcohol on her breath. She grabs his hand and moves it up her thighs to her sex. He can feel the smooth silkiness of nylon stocking give way to the slightly courser texture of her knickers. She squirms delightedly as his fingers caress her through the fabric.

Being a normal red-blooded male, Jack enjoys this display of abandonment, but part of him queries what she is going to be like at the dance. Will he be able to keep her in check and prevent her from doing something too stupid? He naturally wants to be envied by his mates for having a hot chick on his arm, but he doesn't want it to turn into a spectacle.

'Perhaps I should drive, Susie, you seem to have had a head start on me,' Jack suggests.

Susie responds with a firm shake of her head, grinning tipsily.

'Oh, no, no, Jacky boy, it's my car, and I'm driving,' she slurs. 'You just sit there and keep on doing what you're doing. I like it. But be careful, don't ladder my pantyhose. A girl has got to look her best, hasn't she?'

Sighing, Jack does as he is told.

*****

The skinny girl accepts the LSD eagerly and swigs it down with some water she has in a bottle. She and Terry are sitting in the front seat of his Torana in the car park above the beach. It is dark, and they can see the growing level of activity near the surf club as people arrive.

She does not resist when Terry gently but firmly pulls her head down into his crotch, where she works at his fly until his cock is out. She sucks on it with enthusiasm. Terry groans in pleasure, one hand searching underneath her skirt and the other pinching a nipple through her bra.

*****

Jack presents the tickets to the guy on the door and, in exchange, Susie's and his hands are stamped. This will allow them to get drinks and food as part of the ticket price. He and Susie walk into the club to be greeted by wall-to-wall noise. The place is filling up fast and the band is in the corner giving their instruments a final tune.

The pair heads to the bar, pausing every few steps for Jack to say hello to club members and their partners. The guys are all fashionably dressed in a variety of brightly coloured shirts with big collars, and flared pants.

Jack spots one guy dressed as a hippie, complete with sandals, hair in a band, John Lennon glasses, a striped sleeveless coat and no shirt, with a large copper peace wheel medal around his neck. The outfit is impressive.

The girls are dolled up to the max. Miniskirts in widely differing colours abound. Flower power prints are popular. Most have high necks, with hemlines only reaching the upper thigh. Knee-high boots are in style, and Twiggy-style haircuts are all the rage.

A girl walks by adorned in a crocheted short dress, wearing only knickers underneath, her nipples clearly visible through the material. Judging by the ogling leers and wolf whistles she gets, the boys love this overt display of female flesh.

Some girls don't have the legs for such short skirts, but they don't care. The fashion is the fashion, and it's either be there, or be square.

They edge their way forward through the crush of people and finally reach the bar. Jack is holding Susie's arm firmly as she is a bit unsteady. Jack gets them drinks.

I'll have to watch the amount of wine she consumes, notes Jack, *at least until she shows signs of being a bit more sober. Perhaps if I get the drinks and keep her away from the bar, that will help.*

At Susie's urging, they make their way slowly towards the band, who are about to start a bracket. Taking a gulp of wine, Susie yells enthusiastically as the band begins to play. The noise level rises appreciably as they launch into a popular Stones' song, several of them jumping up and down energetically to the beat.

One band member is wearing some sort of old-style military jacket, which has gold piping on each sleeve. He has on matching pants and white sneakers. Pinned to the jacket is what appears to be a vintage German Iron Cross. Shirtless, he has a rawhide bandana around his neck. Jack estimates he is about sixteen-years-old. *That can't be right*, he thinks. Or maybe it is.

Quickly, the crowd closest to the band starts to dance. People are excitedly doing the twist, the mashed potato, the funky chicken, or just plain old rock and roll. Some are very good, others are downright terrible, but all are enjoying themselves, screaming along with the music.

Susie and Jack twist to the beat, laughing and mouthing the words of *Satisfaction*, which the band plays with great skill. *They are bloody good*, realises Jack.

The song finished, the crowd pauses for breath, applauding wildly. The band immediately launches into *Get Off My Cloud*, and the unruly gyrations resume.

Jack and Susie dance all the way through the band's first bracket.

He is not as rhythmical as her, but he manages to stay with her as she rotates her hips and, feet apart, slides her high heels from side to side, in tune with the beat. They dip to the floor and she presents her back to him, leaning over so that her delectable bottom is close to him. He grabs it and they sway together, bringing shouts of encouragement from other dancers.

Susie switches to rock and roll, and Jack follows. He is no expert, but has the sense to follow her lead. She grabs his hand and pushes him away; they both turn a circle before reuniting. Holding his hand high, she ducks under it and swings around again. Plenty of thigh is revealed as Susie rotates rapidly, her hair swinging out with the effort. She is loving it.

After several brackets the band takes a break. By now Susie has drunk several wines but wants more, her eyes full of excitement. Her skin is flushed. She is very desirable in Jack's eyes.

They head out onto the balcony for some air, and Susie kisses him passionately, then demands another wine. Jack goes back inside to get more drinks.

Terry is tired of the girl he is with. She has served her purpose, and he wants her gone. He ignores her entreaties to dance with her, instead he watches the people bopping to the music. He sees Jack and Susie doing the twist, and jealousy flares in him. *They look so good together. Why can't I dance like that? I'd like to get a piece of that ass*, he fantasises, his eyes feasting on Susie's tight buttocks shaking under her skirt.

He sees Jack and Susie walking out to the balcony and, on impulse, follows, leaving the girl to her own devices. She lurks in the shadows, watching him jealously.

When he sees Jack leave, he takes the opportunity and approaches Susie, who has lit a cigarette and is gazing out over the silvery water. The moon is up, and the surf is lit by its glow.

'Hi Susie, what's up? Has Jack gone off and left you?'

Susie turns towards him and laughs tipsily. Aroused by the dancing, she feels bold.

'Oh, he'll be back soon,' she responds airily.

Susie has heard rumours at the Star Hotel that Terry has links to drug dealing. She regards him with interest.

'God, what I'd give for some pot,' she states impulsively.

Terry smiles wolfishly.

'I might be able to get my hands on some coke,' he suggests, 'would that do?'.

Susie is suddenly very interested in Terry. She moves closer so that they are only inches apart. Her lips part, and she gives him a sultry smile.

'That would be wonderful,' she purrs. 'But I don't want Jack to know about it. Can you keep a secret, Terry?' Susie stares at him, lips parted suggestively.

'My lips are sealed. I'm very good with secrets.'

He bends to kiss her, but she averts her face so that his lips only brush her cheek.

'My, you're a forward boy,' she smiles at him.

Just then Jack reappears on the balcony carrying the drinks. Spying Terry and Susie together, he looks daggers at Terry.

Unfazed, Terry gives a little bow and walks away, a cold smile on his face.

'You stay away from that bloke, he's trouble,' Jack commands angrily.

'Relax Jack, he was only saying hello,' Susie lies, suddenly angry. *How dare he tell me what to do?* Her mood turns petulant.

Not knowing what Susie is thinking, Jack decides it is time to present her with the ring. Reaching into his pocket, Jack brings out the box. He gathers his courage and starts to speak. It all comes out in a rush.

'Susie, I have a confession to make. I love you, and I would like you to accept this friendship ring. It's not an engagement ring, but that could come a bit later, if you like …'

Jack's speech peters out as he watches Susie's eyes widen in astonishment. He thinks she is going to embrace him in joy, but instinctively she steps back a pace, and instead of elation on her face, he sees only confusion.

'Jack … Jack … this is too much,' she stammers. 'I … I'm not ready for this. I mean … I like you … a lot … and I enjoy your company. But I want to see a lot more of life before I can even think of getting too serious with one guy. You may be that guy, but it's way too early.'

Jack is stunned and embarrassed. *What an idiot you are*, he thinks to himself. *You have read this completely wrong.* He stares down at his shoes, mortified.

Susie realises, belatedly, that she has said it all wrong. Although it is true, she should have handled it better. She tries desperately to soften the blow.

'Jack, sweetie, you mean a lot to me. I want our relationship to continue, but maybe we just need to both back off a little. Just chill out a bit. It's all a bit too soon. We've only been going out for a few months. Do you understand?'

Jack mumbles his assent. Susie pulls him into an embrace and they stand there in the moonlight.

Hearing a call from further down the balcony, Jack disentangles himself from the embrace. He is wanted for his shift on the barbeque. Not trusting himself to speak, his thoughts in turmoil, he silently leaves Susie standing there. She can fend for herself for a while.

Susie hugs herself and shivers, even though the night is mild. She is conflicted. *Should I stick to my guns, or should I go to him and beg his forgiveness*, she anguishes. *No*, she decides. *I can't pretend to be someone I'm not. He'll just have to get used to it. If he can't, then so be it.*

With that she strides determinedly back into the hall, ready to dance, to drink some more, and maybe to search for Terry.

Disconsolate, Jack serves the steaks and sausages to the hungry party goers. Mick, who is on barbeque duty as well, is busy with the cooking, but eventually he notices Jack's long face. He has seen Jack with Susie earlier, dancing up a storm. Sensing that things aren't what they should be between the couple, he speaks softly to Jack.

'Mate, you okay?'

Jack's face is etched in misery. He silently shakes his head, barely able to contain the tears that threaten to spill down his cheeks.

'Want to talk about it?'

'Not really,' Jack replies in a low voice. 'There's nothing you can do, anyway. There's nothing anyone can do. It's fucked.'

Mick presses him to say more. Jack slowly pours out the story. Mick shakes his head. *Women*, he thinks. *Can't live with them, can't live without them.*

Mick offers some advice based on past experience.

'Jack, you need to take a deep breath. Go and find her and talk through whatever is wrong. Women love to talk, to discuss their emotions. We blokes aren't good at it, but you owe it to yourself, and to her, to try. Judging by the look on your face, you obviously think you've been hard done by—and that may well be true—but you need to talk to her. Go on, piss off and sort it out. Don't stand around here like a lost sheep.'

Mick's words are harsh, but they have a galvanising effect on Jack. Giving Mick a glare, he takes off his apron and pushes past Mick.

'Good lad,' Mick nods, hoping, but not confident, that the outcome will be a good one.

Walking as quickly as he can through the noisy and unruly crowd, Jack scans the room for Susie. He searches amongst the dancers, but she is nowhere to be seen. He heads to the bar, but she is not there either. He asks a girl he knows to go into the ladies' toilet to see if she is in there. The girl comes out, shaking her head.

Jack is growing agitated. *Where is she?*

The committee room door is shut. Ignoring the club member stationed outside, Jack wrenches open the door and barges inside. The light is out, but moonlight shines in the window. One of the band members is on the committee room table, his pants down around his ankles, a girl on top of him, her face in shadow, soft cries coming from her as she couples with him. Jack finds the light switch and turns it on, ignoring the shouts of outrage from the couple on the table.

It is not Susie.

Jack is both relieved and worried. He tries to think of where she can be. *The car*, he remembers. *If she's gone, the car won't be there, surely.*

He races out of the hall and pushes through the crowd of would-be gatecrashers who mill around outside, unsuccessfully trying to persuade the bouncers to let them in.

Up on the road, Jack searches for Susie's car, half expecting it not to be there. But it sits in the same spot as when they arrived, empty.

*****

Heading for the bar after leaving Jack, Susie sculls one wine and is working on another when Terry looms beside her, a shark-like smile on his face. He takes in the colour in her cheeks and the too-bright gleam in her eye. *She is like a rose ready to pluck*, he senses. *All she needs is a little push, and who knows what might happen? And I've got just the persuader.*

He beckons her to follow him, and she does his bidding, dismissing a niggling feeling that she should not do this. But she is in a mood to gamble, if only to prove that she is her own woman. She likes the impish feeling that grows in her.

They leave the hall and Terry puts his arm around her, gently guiding her towards his car. She resists briefly, but when he whispers in her ear that there is some good stuff in the car, she acquiesces.

Terry lets her into the front seat and closes the door. He walks around to the boot of the car and opens it quietly, checking that no-one is around. Satisfied, he reaches past the spare wheel and clicks open a flap, revealing a concealed space. He extracts a small plastic envelope. Again checking around, he shuts the flap and the boot, and gets into the driver's seat.

Susie asks him in anticipation, 'Have you got what I think you've got?'

'I've got the crème de la crème,' Terry responds. 'But are you sure you can handle it?'

Susie smiles and reaches for the envelope. 'Gimme,' she demands.

Terry pulls the envelope back out of her reach. 'Not so fast, my lovely Susie. What's in it for me?'

His intention is obvious and alarm bells start to ring in one part of her brain, but Susie quietens them. *I can handle him*, she thinks overconfidently.

Taking a deep breath, Susie stupidly asks, 'What do you want, Terry?'.

'Well now, you're drop-dead gorgeous, and I like pretty girls … very much. But I tell you what, why don't you try some of this lovely stuff, and then we'll see.'

Not waiting for an answer, Terry takes out a vial of white powder and, reaching under his seat, he brings out a spoon and a straw. He offers the vial to Susie.

'Rub some on your gums, and snort the rest up your nose.'

All her inhabitations fly out of the window. Susie does what he suggests and sits back to await the reaction. Terry studies her, smiling, his eyes roaming over her body.

Within seconds she begins to feel a buzz as the stimulant hits her brain. Her heart rate jumps, her pulse races, and she begins to feel sexually aroused.

Terry senses this, watching her lips part and her nipples stand out erect through her dress. This is exactly what he has hoped for.

He opens the car door and strides around to her side, pulling her to her feet. She grasps hold of him tightly and moans as he runs his hands over her body.

Terry steers her away from the clubhouse and down to the beach, as aroused as he has ever been. He is elated—she is his, to do with what he wants. His hand reaches under her skirt and she gasps in rapture as his fingers move inside her panties, tearing frantically at them.

Terry backs her up against a picnic table under a rotunda, shadows enveloping them. He hoists up her dress and in one movement has it over her head, revealing her body. She doesn't resist as he pulls down her knickers and rips the panty hose at her crotch, revealing her sex. Susie is past caring. She is in a euphoric state, barely conscious of what is happening.

Quickly he pulls his pants down and unceremoniously pushes his erection into her as far as it will go. She gasps again, and her legs wrap around him, pulling him further in. He paws at her brassiere, freeing her breasts, and sucks hungrily on her nipples.

*****

A sinking sensation in his chest, Jack decides to search the beach. He runs down the steps and scans the sand, calling out her name. Several entwined couples glance up, but Susie is not among them.

Jack runs north along the sea wall. Suddenly he sees the outline of a male and a female coupling on a table in front of him. The man turns in Jack's direction. Jack sees it is Terry, wearing a triumphant smile. The girl is crying out in passion, oblivious. Shocked to the core, Jack recognises Susie.

He stands motionless for several seconds, staring incredulously at the sight. Then, with a cry of anguish, he turns and sprints back the way he had come, sobbing as he runs. He is beside himself with grief and anger—not at Terry, but at Susie's betrayal. His heart is shattered.

Jack never hears Susie cry out his name as she climaxes.

Terry savours the moment of Jack's despair, and then turns his attention to the girl lying motionless on the table. With a savage grin, he turns her over, spreads her legs, and proceeds to sodomise her. She doesn't move, lost in some psychedelic dream.

Jack stumbles home. His life and beliefs have been changed forever. He and Susie are no more.

*****

His gear in the boot of the car, singing along to the radio, Terry drives the Torana west along the New England Highway, obeying the speed limit—destination Singleton and the army. Technically, he is supposed to catch a bus from Newcastle with all the others, but Terry is disdainful of such trivial regulations. Besides he doesn't want to leave the car at home. *The old man will probably sell the bloody thing and use the money on pot and grog*, he thinks. *I'll worry about the army when I get there.*

Satiated and grinning like an idiot, he left Susie sprawled unconscious across the table two nights ago, lost in her own world. He has won a huge victory over Jack, and has revelled in the spoils. He smiles, remembering the things he did to her as she lay comatose. *Maybe I'll have a rematch sometime in the future*, he thinks malevolently. *She is a great piece of ass. And Jack has been taught a lesson he will never forget.*

Terry settles into the seat and motors on.

*****

Chapter 18

Jack has spent a solitary Sunday in his room, refusing all attempts by his parents to lure him out. His mind is in a whirl as he clutches the box with the ring tightly in one fist. What should he do?

The image of Terry fucking Susie in the shadows is burnt into his brain. Every time he closes his eyes he sees it being played over and over in an endless, excruciating loop. What was he thinking when he offered her the ring—she would declare her love for him and everyone would live happily after?

What a crock of shit. Is this what she means by 'before I can think of getting too serious with one guy'? Look what she did within thirty minutes of rebuffing him. Went out and fucked the one guy she knew Jack didn't get on with. 'Chill out a bit' were her words. Chill fucking out? 'I like you a lot.' Total and utter bullshit.

Jack's fevered mind considers another angle. What a way to take revenge on him for his childish behaviour. It's almost as if she intended to ensure his maximum humiliation. She must have known that he would come searching for her. She didn't even have the decency to go somewhere else where he couldn't find her. She wanted him to see. Jack's face burns in shame.

What about Terry? The bastard. His rationale is obvious. In a strange way Jack doesn't blame Terry as much as he does Susie, but surely Terry has taken extreme delight in sharing the graphic details with his surf club mates by now? How can Jack ever look them in the eye again? They're probably all having a good laugh right now at his expense. He can't show his face in that club again, that is clear. Fuck Terry.

And fuck Susie. She's nothing but a whore and a conniving bitch. He hates her, doesn't he? Ninety-nine per cent of his brain believes that, but a tiny part keeps nagging at him. Is there some other explanation for what he saw? But how could that be? The time period is too short between when he walked away from her on the balcony and when he found them together outside. There must have been premeditation on both their parts. It's the only possible explanation. He considers the implications. This means the relationship in which he had placed such high hopes is now utterly destroyed. He is shattered. His self-image has taken a huge hit, and his sense of betrayal is complete.

Leaving the issue of betrayal aside for the moment, Jack contemplates his future. Can he stay in Newcastle when word will soon get around about this? It's funny, university was so important to him until recently, and now he couldn't give a flying fuck whether he continues or not. His tutor is right: if you can't lift your game, then maybe it's time to pull the plug before someone else does.

A kernel of an idea suddenly pops into his head. Jack examines it slowly, testing it in light of the demons he has been wrestling. *It just might work*, he concludes. *Mind you*, he thinks, *it's not without risk, but it does provide a chance to make a clean break*. If he defers his university studies, he can always come back at a later date, although probably not in Newcastle. Jack gnaws at this possible solution and its implications well into Sunday night.

He finally reaches a decision just before dawn on Monday

morning. When he hears his parents up and about Jack, tired but now much calmer, walks into the kitchen to tell his parents what he has resolved to do. They hear him out numbly and Gladys pleads with him to change his mind. Henry is silent. But Jack is unwavering.

Henry speaks out: 'Jack, why don't you and me have a nice cuppa tea in the garden? Gladys darling, would you be a dear and make us one please? It's time Jack and I had a man-to-man chat'.

While Gladys tearfully prepares the tea, Henry and Jack sit in some old chairs under the lemon tree. The sun shines through the leaves, making a dappled pattern on the grass underneath. Jack refuses to meet Henry's eyes. Henry sighs, and pats Jack on the knee gently: 'Come on Jack, let's hear about it. I promise I won't interrupt you. Let's have it, son'.

Jack's resolve not to say anything about his pain disappears the instant his gaze meets his father's. With a low moan, Jack launches into the story, tears flowing from his eyes as he gasps out the sordid details. Gladys appears behind Jack with the tea, but Henry silently motions for her to put the cups on the ground and then politely indicates for her to return to the kitchen. She will hear the story later, but for now it's between son and father.

When Jack has poured his heart out, Henry finally speaks in soft tones, tears blurring his eyes as well.

'Jack, my boy, you surely have been hard done by. That is the lowest act I've ever heard of. Damn the girl, and damn that Terry Bannister.' Henry pauses to clear his throat, and continues in a stronger voice. 'You say you have considered all the options and the one you presented to us is the only one possible in your view? Can you confirm that, lad?'

Jack nods, misery written all over his face. Henry goes on.

'Well, if that's what you want to do, Jack, I'll back that decision all the way. It's going to cause your mother and me a deal of personal pain, but that's for us to deal with, and deal with it we will.

Leave your mother to me Jack; I'll square it with her. And Son, in case you're wondering, I don't think you're running away—far from it. It has taken a lot of guts to make this decision, and I'm very, very proud of you. Now come here, and give me a hug, and then we'll have that cup of tea.'

*****

At opening time, Jack walks determinedly into the Army Recruiting office in the main street of Newcastle. He addresses the guy in uniform at the desk.

'Can I speak to someone about National Service please?'

After a short wait, Jack is ushered into an interview room and is soon joined by a grizzled sergeant, the left pocket area of his uniform festooned with campaign ribbons. The sergeant asks him what he wants, but the bored expression on his face says that the conversation will probably be wasting his valuable time.

'I am quitting university and, as I was deferred because I was studying, I wish to volunteer for National Service. And I want to go to Vietnam.'

The sergeant sits forward, suddenly attentive. He isn't a fan of the Nasho scheme, and neither is most of the army, but it makes a change for someone to come in out of the blue and volunteer. The sergeant asks, not unkindly: 'Are you absolutely sure you want to do this, lad? You can just get up and walk out, and no-one will be the wiser'.

The sergeant takes in the determined look on his face as Jack replies, 'I want to volunteer for Vietnam'.

With that, the sergeant is all smiles.

'Then I think I may be able to help you there. Let's get some details, eh?'

*****

Susie slumps in a chair in her flat. She is sore in some very sensitive parts of her anatomy—from what, she doesn't know, but she has her suspicions. She wonders exactly what that bastard did to her, shuddering at the images her mind conjures up. She feels completely violated, but what is worse is that she knows she has contributed to her demise.

She cries softly to herself: 'Oh, Jack, Jack, where are you? I need you. I'm so, so sorry. I'll change, I promise'.

But Jack will not come to the phone when she calls his place. His parents are coldly polite and offer her no solace. He is lost to her. As the weeks pass, she hears nothing.

One day, a month or so later at the Conquistador nightclub, Susie bumps into a surf club member that she knows slightly.

'Why hello, Susie,' the man greets her, a knowing grin on his face.

Susie ignores this and without preamble asks him, 'Have you seen Jack?'

The man's smile widens. 'Haven't you heard, Susie? He's gone and joined the army. Gone off to war.' He pauses, and then adds with distain, 'Silly bastard'. Perhaps sensing an opportunity, his smile turns predatory. 'Do you fancy a drink or … anything, Susie?'

Susie reels in shock. She manages to shout at him, 'Fuck off, you prick', before fleeing the nightclub, sobbing wildly, her guilt enveloping her like a cloak.

ooooo

Jack later hears that the coroner's inquest into the death of Billy Wilson is held in April 1968, some fourteen months after Billy's death. The delay is due to a backlog of cases. The inquest is to hear that two important witnesses are not available. Nevertheless, there is enough evidence for the coroner to make a finding of death by drowning following a heart attack. The coroner will commend the actions of those involved in his attempted rescue. Two of those involved are elsewhere, doing things that they would have scarcely contemplated at the time of Billy's death.

BOOK TWO

HORSE WARS

'You will kill ten of us, we will kill one of you, but in the end, you will tire of it first.'

Ho Chí Minh

'I'm not going to be the first American president to lose a war.'

Richard Nixon, Oct. 1969

'It became necessary to destroy the town to save it.'

A US Army major as quoted in the
New York Times May 1968

'We will abolish conscription forthwith. It must be done not just because a volunteer army means a better army, but because we profoundly believe that it is intolerable that a free nation at peace and under no threat should cull by lottery the best of its youth to provide defence on the cheap.'

Gough Whitlam, '*It's Time*' speech,
November 1972

Chapter 19

Jack starts his training in mid-1967 at an army base called Kapooka, just outside the town of Wagga Wagga in south-west New South Wales. It is the home of the First Recruit Training Battalion.

He has passed the medical examination and subsequent interview, which were held in Sydney. Jack is questioned in the interview about his education level and his employment history. His background fits the bill.

He is put on a long train journey to Wagga Wagga and then, with a large group of other soon-to-be soldiers, is driven in trucks to Kapooka. They line up and, after another medical, get issued with uniforms, most of which aren't the correct size. But, importantly for Jack, his boots fit well.

Jack has his longish hair shorn with a number two comb and stares disbelievingly at his image in the mirror. He looks about sixteen. He smiles at the similar astonished expressions on the other Nashos' faces as they undergo the same treatment. Welcome to the army. It is the army's first blow in the march towards conformity, the desired state where teamwork and discipline prevail.

Chapter 17

He joins a large group of young men who go through basic training in the middle of a cold winter. Trying hard to ignore the wet, chilly conditions, over the next twelve weeks Jack and his cohort experience a steep learning curve. Each day starts before dawn, and the pace is relentless. The trainees fall into their beds, exhausted, by mid-evening and get up and do it all over again the next day.

Jack finds that, instead of hating this experience, he revels in it. Perhaps it's his surf club experience—although that never reached this scale of attack on his comfort levels. Perhaps he needs to experience this in order to drive Susie out of his mind through sheer exhaustion. Importantly, it gives him a purpose—survival and not letting the system beat him. His focus is almost entirely on this, which allows him to sleep deeply and without dreams each night.

A few Nashos rebel, and refuse to obey orders. There is little precedent for this, even though the army has punishment for offenders down to a fine art. The Nasho scheme is political, and the top brass has given an unofficial directive to adopt a hands-off approach to those who resist—although this doesn't prevent these recalcitrant few from being given the worst jobs imaginable by the pitiless training staff.

Several try to escape the army's clutches. They are found quickly as there is nowhere to hide, then summarily despatched to the military prison at Holsworthy, where they will have plenty of time to regret their actions.

Jack, among the majority, learns new skills. How to shoot, salute, march, make their beds, iron their uniforms, spit-polish their boots and a myriad other things they have never experienced. Everything is done at a rapid pace. Everything except shooting. The drill here is painstaking and exact. The trainers take care to inculcate the correct methods in the young men. This could be a matter of life or death, and the army is very serious about killing.

Jack finds that he likes the shooting part very much. Using the combat standard self-loading rifle, he discovers a talent for accurate shooting. The SLR is a semi-automatic, with an effective range of about three hundred metres. Fully loaded, it holds twenty rounds of standard 7.62 millimetre ammunition. This calibre bullet can be relied on to kill the enemy.

Jack learns all this during his training.

Jack and his fellow recruits learn to eat, shower, shave, and shit quickly. Reveille is at five in the morning, and heaven help you if you are tardy in getting out of the sack. The food is plentiful but plain—and anyway, they have to eat it in a hurry, so it doesn't matter too much. Just shovel it in while you can.

Jack, having experienced the discipline associated with surfboat rowing, finds that the instructors are hard but fair. Even so, many recruits fall foul of the multitude of army rules and regulations that seem to have been devised by a group of sadists. The degree of punishment varies depending on the nature of the crime. The usual penalty is extra duties, but some miscreants suffer forced route marches after the others have quit for the day. The more serious will spend some time in the slammer so that they may reflect on the error of their ways. Jack learns that it is the army way. Break them and then mould them into a shape that will meet the army's requirements.

Early on he adopts a quiet, moody mindset, his anger at the recent past unabated. It helps him to focus and stay out of trouble. Jack doesn't mix too much with his fellow trainees, and this is noticed by them and the training staff. He writes letters to his parents when he has time, and welcomes their replies, full of mundane events in Newcastle. His parents don't commit their anguish at his decision to paper. It is too late for that.

Jack's attitude is the point of brief comment by the training staff, but they have their hands full with the troublemakers and the need to get these kids trained to a level that may prevent them from getting killed. Besides, he's a Nasho, and the regular army soldiers have little truck with the Nasho scheme. Many regard it contemptuously as nothing more than childminding.

But there are some eyes on Jack, following his progress. He is a Nasho, sure, but he has volunteered to put himself in harm's way, and the veterans on staff respect that.

*****

Jack, along with all the other recruits, marches proudly in step to the band. It is finally the day of the passing-out parade. They have rehearsed this for several weeks now, and things are going like clockwork. The platoon sergeant gives the 'eyes right' and, apart from the right marker, all heads turn in unison as they march past the saluting dais.

Much to his surprise, Jack's parents have made the journey down the Hume Highway to attend. He had a brief word with them before mustering for parade. He searches for them out of the corner of his eye, but they are hidden in the crowd witnessing the parade.

Some senior officer gives a long-winded speech, and then the parade is dismissed. Hats fly into the air, and guys that had nothing in common three months ago embrace each other in delight. They are officially diggers.

In the canteen, Jack and his parents enjoy tea and cake. Jack introduces them to the few mates he has made. His father beams at him in pride tinged with anxiety. His mother's smile is too bright, and fixed. But they must keep up appearances.

Jack farewells them as they drive off. Part of him is sad to see them go, but most of him wants them gone. The transformation to the new Jack is gathering pace.

That night the new diggers get their first leave and prepare to paint the town red. The town, of course, is well used to this, and fathers make up excuses to prevent their daughters from going out. The MPs are on hand, ready to deal quickly, efficiently and, if necessary, forcefully with any soldier that steps too far out of line.

Nursing a sore head the next day, Jack is told that he is to be posted to the First Royal Australian Regiment—known as 1RAR—based at Gallipoli Barracks, Holsworthy. He is to be an infantryman.

*****

Terry's recruit training in Singleton follows a similar path to Jack's, with one important difference: Terry's bad-boy attitude earns him the early attention of the training staff. This is a mistake on his part, and they ride him unmercifully. He is on their radar. Terry endures extra duties and forced marches for any slight transgression.

When he complains to his chief instructor about what he sees as unfair treatment, the sergeant shows no pity. He responds contemptuously: 'Bannister, you are getting exactly what you asked for. You give us shit, you get shit back. You have no idea of how deep that shithole is. Thus far, you're only in it up to your ankles. Just imagine when it gets over your head. And it will, if you keep on trying to buck the system. The army owns your ass, soldier, at least for the next two years'.

The sergeant dismisses him with a sneer. *Fucking Nashos*, he thinks. *Sonny, use your brains, if you've got any. Obey the rules, or suffer the consequences.*

Terry turns away, his face unsuccessfully trying to mask his hatred of the system. But he decides that he'd better keep his head down, at least until this recruit training crap is finished.

From his lowly position in the hierarchy, he is not able to make too much headway in his quest to organise a network of dealers, and he can't contact Macca or anyone outside the base until his training is over. He will have to bide his time.

In the sea of life, Terry wants to be a shark, and his association with the likes of Macca and Bernie Houghton has shown him the path to get there. But right here, right now, he is a tiddler swimming against the tide, and he has no wish to be gobbled up by a bigger, meaner predator.

Chapter 20

Near the end of 1967 Terry is posted to a headquarters unit at Holsworthy, where many of the troops in the unit are Nashos. None have volunteered for service in Vietnam. There is little real work, leaving him with the opportunity to link into the burgeoning underground network of drugs, both on and off the base. The horrors of recruit training are behind him, and the tiddler is changing shape, his teeth growing bigger and sharper.

Holsworthy Barracks, housing several thousand soldiers, form part of the Holsworthy Military Reserve, a huge and sprawling expanse of commonwealth land that has been a training area and artillery range since World War I. There is an air field, a field hospital, and a large number of accommodation barracks, mess halls, and other amenities.

Liverpool is nearby, and wherever there is a major military base, there is vice. Brothels, illegal gaming houses and SP bookies can be found in the area—if one knows where to look. The field hospital constantly has to order more supplies of condoms for horny troops with ready cash to satisfy their carnal desires.

The locals—some of them bikies—in the pubs and bars in

Liverpool don't take too kindly to the soldiers with their short hair and gung-ho attitude. A number of pubs have been declared 'off limits' by the army, but to the soldiers this is like a red rag to a bull. Fights abound, and often mass brawls erupt. The military police and local cops are kept busy.

Despite all this, the routine is reasonably relaxed and Terry is able to leave the base on short leave on a regular basis. Bernie Houghton's connections have put him in touch with a guy called The Duke—or Duke for short—a shady character who runs a brothel and illegal gaming house in central Liverpool. The scuttlebutt is that Duke has links to the brutal standover man, Lenny McPherson, the reputed overlord of organised crime in Sydney.

Duke supplies Terry's increasing demand for drugs to sell amongst the troops, and operates as a cut-out between Terry and Bernie.

Terry enjoys his visits to Duke's establishment. The bar and gambling facilities are classy, and the girls are prettier than most of the other places in the area. The girls like his growing habit of splashing his cash around. He is earning plenty now, his cut from the drug sales fattening his wallet.

But Terry is careful with the booze and the betting. He is determined not to be in debt or become a drunk like his father, and lose control of his destiny.

Things are shaping up nicely, Terry reflects. *Only another eighteen months to go, and then I can get out of uniform and back into the real world.* He has decided to seek fame and fortune in Sydney, where the prospects seem to be endless, particularly in his line of work.

*****

Jack settles into life in Finschaffen Lines, Holsworthy, the home of 1RAR. He learns these lines are named after a World War II battle in 1943 between Australian and Japanese forces in north-east Papua

New Guinea. They are a new style of barracks, which allow each soldier more personal space as opposed to the old lines where ten men share one open-floor hut. Jack is pleased about this.

On arrival at 1RAR, Jack is assigned to Delta Company, but is required to front the commander, a major named Tony Hammett, to talk about Vietnam. Major Hammett is a Duntroon graduate—class of 1958.

Jack is impressed to learn that Major Hammett represented Australia in the modern pentathlon at the Olympic Games in Rome in 1960. And he is a qualified helicopter pilot. But most importantly, the word is that he is a good egg, and is fair on his men.

At attention, Jack studies the officer. He isn't a tall man, but has an athlete's build and a pleasantly open face that will never win any prizes in a beauty contest. The major questions Jack closely.

'So, Private Martin, you want to go to war. Why?'

Jack is prepared for this and has his answer down pat.

'Well, Sir, I think we need to stop those communist bastards before they come down here and invade Australia.'

Tony Hammett, no fool, scrutinises Jack's face.

'Bullshit, soldier, don't feed me that domino-theory crap. I know you're an educated young man. I've read your record. You quit university. I would have loved to go to university, yet you just up and quit. Why was that? And you'd bloody well better give me the real answer this time.'

His defences breached, Jack decides to tell the truth.

'I gave it up because of a girl, Sir. She ... she did the dirty on me. But, that's past history. Sir, I am prepared to fight for my country. And I can always go back to uni afterwards.'

He almost convinces himself that he is over Susie. The honesty satisfies the Major.

'It must have been some breakup, fella. Still, her loss is our gain. I hear you can shoot. We're going to need that skill. Good luck,

Private Martin. Welcome to Delta Company. Dismissed.'

Jack salutes, about-turns, and marches off.

As Jack leaves, the major says quietly to the company sergeant major, 'Keep an eye on that one. I think he's got the potential to be a good'un. Make sure he is ready.'

Forewarned that the battalion will go back to Vietnam in 1968, training in radio, mortar firing, as well as more weapons training, is taking place. Jack, with his aptitude and accuracy with the SLR, undergoes sniper training. He learns the skills of camouflage, target acquisition and field craft.

Jack occasionally ventures off base on a leave pass. He stays out of trouble, content to enjoy a few quiet drinks in a friendly bar on the outskirts of Liverpool. Even though his hair is cut short, women are attracted to him, but he avoids any encounters with the fairer sex. Once bitten, twice shy, is his new motto.

Jack's and Terry's paths do not cross. This is unsurprising, as the base is huge, and Finschaffen Lines are at the opposite end of the complex to the headquarters area.

A few weeks later 1RAR is transported to the army's jungle training centre at Canungra, in the Queensland's Gold Coast hinterland. Kakoda Barracks have been around since World War II, and the facilities are deliberately basic. For the next three weeks 1RAR is put through a series of exercises designed to toughen the troops physically and mentally. Over and over everyone, officers included, undertakes a series of obstacle courses and exercises on the battle simulation ranges. The instructors drive them unmercifully until they are assessed as ready for combat. Jack enjoys the experience, despite being sleep-deprived and covered in mosquito bites.

Jack elects not to return to the family home in Newcastle for Christmas 1967, to the dismay of his parents. They know from his letters that he is to leave for Vietnam within months and cannot understand why he does not want to see them. But Jack has no wish to give them more pain. Instead, he books into a guesthouse in North Sydney and enjoys walking around the area, taking in the sights and sounds of the beautiful harbour and surrounds. He celebrates New Year's Eve alone in a bar, nursing a few beers. A friendly barmaid chats to him for a while but, sensing he is not keen on company, leaves him to drink in solitude.

As he sips his beer, Jack disinterestedly watches TV footage of the recent visit to Australia by the President of the United States of America, Lyndon Baines Johnson. The lanky Texan, nicknamed LBJ, is here to attend the funeral of Harold Holt, Australia's former Prime Minister who disappeared in mysterious circumstances in the surf off Portsea Beach in Victoria a week earlier. The TV shows file footage of the anti-Vietnam War protests when LBJ visited Sydney a year previously. Jack feels torn: he agrees with the protests, but he is the one going to war. He sighs and then deliberately switches his attention to another TV showing the preliminaries to the New Year's Eve celebrations on Sydney Harbour.

*****

On that same evening Terry drives the Torana into King Cross to attend a party hosted by Bernie Houghton. It is a lavish affair, with champagne flowing freely and huge quantities of fresh seafood eagerly consumed by the hundred or so guests.

Terry is reunited with Dozer, who greets him like a long lost brother. Dressed for the occasion in a suit, Terry is very impressed with the quality of women present. He resolves to get a piece of the action before the night is over.

Bernie introduces Terry to some of his acquaintances. Terry's head spins as he meets George Freeman, Stan 'The Man' Smith, and Perce Galea, as they enjoy the hospitality. These crime luminaries are the stuff of legend.

But Bernie has several other surprises for him. Bernie takes Terry into his office. Sitting there, deep in conversation, are two men. They turn to look at him. Terry immediately recognises 'Mr Big', Lenny McPherson, and is immediately rendered dumb. The other guy, he doesn't know.

'Terry, lad, I'd like you to meet Mr Lenny McPherson and Mr Michael Hand. Boys, this here's Terry Bannister. Terry, once you're finished playing soldier, you are going to be seeing a lot more of Mr Hand. He and I go way back.'

*****

Chapter 21

In early January 1968 Terry is caught by the military police in a sting operation on the base. A soldier he has dealt with before sidles up to Terry and whispers that he needs some pot, and Terry arranges to meet him to talk quantities near the unit latrines. The military police surround him before he can move, and quickly bundle Terry and the snitch into separate vehicles that are hidden behind the latrines.

Terry knows that to struggle is useless and will only bring retribution of the painful kind from the two large military policemen sitting next to him, so he sits passively as the vehicle drives to the guardhouse. He curses himself for his stupidity and complacency. Now he has to face the music. Or perhaps not. Has Duke put the fix in? He will find out soon.

The Royal Australian Army Provost Corps, stationed at Holsworthy, has been on the trail of drug peddlers for some time. The base commandant has instructed them to clamp down on the menace as it is spreading steadily with the ramp-up during the Vietnam War. They have had some success, but they know this is only the tip of the iceberg. The provosts know that bribes have been offered to keep people quiet, even bashings for those who are tempted to come forward. Perhaps tonight they have a chance at a breakthrough.

Terry is strip-searched, including an anal probe by a burly MP who wears a rubber glove but doesn't use Vaseline. The contents of his pockets are examined and his car keys removed. He is given an old pair of overalls to put on. They stink of piss and vomit.

The provosts search his locker and, on finding nothing incriminating, move on to his car. They are well experienced at searching, and soon discover the hidden compartment in the boot. In it they find marijuana and cocaine in small plastic bags.

Eventually Terry is hauled before a warrant officer, who regards the figure in front of him with distaste.

'Name and serial number, soldier', he snaps. The WO, who already knows Terry's identity, is determined to show this prick who is boss.

Terry responds sullenly, and is rewarded by a punch in the ribs from another military policeman standing beside him. The provost warns him after the blow, speaking menacingly in his ear, 'In future soldier, answer in a respectful tone to the warrant officer'.

The WO speaks again. 'Private Bannister, you have been caught red-handed in the course of organising to supply a substance that is prohibited under army law, and you have been found to have a marketable quantity of illicit drugs in your possession. It is no good trying to deny it. The witness will testify to this, and my lads found the drugs in your car. So, come on, do yourself a favour and talk to me about it. Tell me where you get your drugs and who supplies them'.

Terry regards him impassively, careful not to permit his face to reveal the contempt he feels. It is obvious that there has been no fix put in here to get him off. He has no wish to suffer a beating, but he is no informer. Besides, he knows what his partners in crime are capable of if he rolls over.

'I've got nothing to say, Sir,' he replies. 'I don't know what you're talking about. Someone must have planted those drugs in my car.'

'Come on, lad, we know all about you. Your disciplinary jacket is full of misdemeanours. Stop your lies. Speak up, and we'll go easy on you. What do you say?'

But Terry is silent.

The WO loses patience with him. 'Take him away.' He adds, 'and don't let him come to any harm.' He means just the opposite.

As Terry is led out, the WO has one final thing to say.

'Oh by the way, Bannister, your car suffered a bit of damage during the search my lads made. Actually it is more than a bit. They had to forcibly take it apart to ensure there were no more drugs hidden. It's in pieces. But I'm sure you'll get a few dollars in scrap money for it when you eventually get to see it again.'

Terry, enraged, lunges at him but is easily restrained by the MPs.

As Terry is dragged away, the WO turns to his subordinate. 'A week in the glasshouse might loosen his tongue. Put him in solitary so that he can reflect on his sins. And bread and water only. Then we'll see whether he is as tough after that. And no record of him being there, either,' the WO adds as an afterthought, 'we don't want any do-gooders sniffing around'.

The Military Corrective Establishment, Holsworthy, is not a nice place to be a guest. Terry endures much greater privation than he experienced at Singleton. The beating he receives after being placed in his cell is administered by experts. Using rubber hoses filled with lead, the guards leave him heavily bruised on the legs and on the torso. Only his face is unmarked.

He is filthy, stinking of sweat and unshaven when, a week later, he is visited by the warrant officer.

The WO smiles at him. 'I bet you'd love a cold beer, a hot tub and some clean clothes. They're yours—the only thing you have to do is open your mouth and sing like a bird.'

Terry is sorely tempted, but is more afraid of his certain fate if he blabs. He says nothing. Disgusted, the WO directs his staff to get him cleaned up.

'It's a visit to the base commandant for you, you low-life piece of shit. I'm sure he will agree with my recommendation of a jail term. You'll be back in here before you know it.'

Terry stares at the WO, a stricken expression on his face.

Cleaned up and quietly shitting bricks, Terry is paraded before the commandant, who follows the formal script for military tribunal hearings. The warrant officer himself reads out the charge, and the commandant asks Terry if he pleads guilty or not guilty. When Terry declares he is not guilty, the commandant directs the WO to present the evidence. It is a clear-cut case and Terry is officially pronounced guilty as charged.

The commandant calls for a recommended sentence, but before the WO can speak, the commandant's adjutant, a major with an infantry badge on his uniform who has been silently observing proceedings, whispers something in the commandant's ear. The commandant examines Terry thoughtfully.

'Private Bannister, the customary sentence befitting your crime is penal servitude, the duration of which is at my discretion. But there is another option open to you. Do you want to hear it?'

His mind in a panic, Terry stammers in the affirmative and the commandant speaks again.

'The other option is for you to volunteer for service in Vietnam. You would have to do a short period incarcerated in the lockup over there, but you would avoid an eighteen-month sentence by doing so. Your choice, soldier, what's it to be?'

Terry, caught between a big rock and a very hard place, doesn't hesitate.

Chapter 21

'I'll take Vietnam, Sir.'

The words stick in his throat, but he cannot bear the thought of the alternative. Anything has to be better than that.

The commandant smiles for the first time and directs his adjutant to have Terry posted to 1RAR, who are in the final stages of their work up for Vietnam.

*****

Several weeks later 1RAR travels to the Shoalwater Bay Military Training Area, north of Yeppoon, Queensland, to participate in exercise 'Grass Parrot', the final training before leaving for Vietnam. There, the battalion is divided into red and blue forces to conduct war games, some with live firing, in conditions designed to replicate the type of operations they will experience in South Vietnam.

Jack and his platoon do well, now well-rehearsed in war gaming. It is not Vietnam, but at least they know how to deploy, to patrol, and to dig in. The weather is balmy and not too humid, and it is exciting to do almost the real thing after all the training.

Terry is assigned to 1RAR headquarters company and is employed, under the close eye of a military policeman, in menial tasks. This suits him fine. He can use a rifle, but has no desire to get too involved in this war stuff. He just wants to do his time, keep his head down, and return home unscathed.

Although confined to base, he has been able to get a message to Bernie via Duke about his situation. Although Bernie is pissed off at Terry being caught, he acts swiftly and pulls in some favours.

Terry is reassured when he gets word from Bernie that he is not to worry, he will be taken care of once he gets to Vietnam. *Perhaps it won't be too bad after all*, he hopes.

*****

In late March 1RAR is transported by truck from Holsworthy to the Royal Australian Naval dockyard at Garden Island in Sydney

Harbour. Garden Island is a large navy shore establishment within which most of the navy fleet is based. Tied up alongside the main wharf is *HMAS Sydney*, the troop transport, getting steam up to sail, its main deck and some hanger spaces crammed with material.

Alighting from the trucks, 1RAR form up outside the navy base and march in through the main gates. Jack, on the left-hand side of the formation, notices a large contingent of anti-war protestors gathered near the gates, held back by a line of New South Wales police. There are banners and posters everywhere, with slogans calling for the abolition of conscription. Protestors scream abuse at the soldiers, some burning their draft cards, only to be hauled off by the coppers. Eggs and rotten fruit are hurled at the soldiers, staining their uniforms.

Jack is stunned. He knows the war isn't popular, but why take it out on the troops? He observes the hate and anger on the protestors' faces as he watches several girls spit on some of his platoon. *Why aren't they taking their ire out on the bloody politicians? They are the ones responsible for us being here. We're just the meat in the fucking sandwich.*

Suddenly, Jack glimpses a face that seems familiar. Is that Susie? No, it can't be. His head full of thoughts he'd rather leave buried, Jack drops his eyes and marches on. The gates close behind the troops and they file up the gangways onto the troop transport, which is to be their temporary home for the next twelve days.

The wharfies have refused to assist the ship depart from Garden Island, as part of the Vietnam War protest, and so the captain of *HMAS Sydney* orders the lines to be thrown overboard and the ship sails slowly out of Sydney Harbour.

Jack leans over the railing, taking in the view, and thinking about the future. He sings tunelessly to himself, *we're on the eve of destruction*.

The words to the popular song match his mood.

*****

Chapter 21

Susie has decided to come to Sydney to join an anti-war protest. She shares a joint with a long-haired draft dodger who wears a dreamy expression. The young people around her work themselves into a frenzy as the troops march by. She is not as stimulated, content to wave a banner that someone has given her.

She thinks about Jack less and less, time slowly healing the raw wound in her heart. She has resumed her party-girl approach, but much more carefully. She is still restless and impatient, and wants everything that life can give her.

Perhaps she'll sleep with the dreamy guy tonight after the party that is sure to follow the protest. She glances at the grim-faced young men in their uniforms as they file past. Suddenly she gives a little gasp. Is that Jack under that slouch hat? Before she can react, the figure is gone. Her attention is drawn to the joint the guy is offering her. She takes it and smiles at him.

*****

Chapter 22

HMAS *Sydney* steams north during March 1968, her four boilers driving her at a steady fifteen knots through the warming waters. She is an old warhorse and her twenty years of service have taken their toll. She has seen service in two wars now, the Korean War being the first.

Some bright spark in the navy had the vision to suggest that she be converted into a fast troop transport in the early 1960s, thus avoiding being scrapped. Her hangar has been converted into accommodation and storage, and her armament reduced to four Bofors guns. She is now the *Vung Tau Ferry*.

For the voyage north to Asia the sailors of the ship's company have been displaced from their bunks and hammocks and have to occupy the hangar accommodation. This causes a deal of unhappiness because the sailors know that it gets bloody hot in the hangar space once the ship passes Brisbane. In a concession to his crew, the captain allows the large lifts fore and aft to be lowered when the weather permits, bringing cooler air and some relief from the sauna-like conditions.

Chapter 22

The routine that Jack and his fellow soldiers experience onboard is … well … routine. Reveille—'wakey, wakey' in navy slang—occurs at first light and the ship goes to action stations in practice for entering a war zone. Early morning calisthenics led by a navy physical training instructor—PTI for short—are followed by breakfast, or 'scran'. The cooks have been working since 0400 hours to prepare meals for around twelve hundred personnel, and will do so for lunch and dinner. The sea air gives those onboard a healthy appetite.

The morning is spent checking weapons and attending lectures on the war. Jack learns about their adversary, the Vietcong. VC. Victor Charlie. Charlie. Their tactics, their dress, their habits. In the afternoon there is time for washing and catching up on penning letters home. They will receive no mail during the trip as they won't see land until Vung Tau.

The navy constantly makes announcements in navy talk, to the mirth of the troops who lay bets on what these mean. Despite himself, Jack becomes familiar with navy slang: goffa for drink; scran for food; buzz for rumour; common dog fuck for common sense; dhoby for washing; gash for rubbish; pit for bed—the list goes on and on.

When authorised, soldiers and sailors alike receive a beer issue. Two beers per day, perhaps. Those who don't drink trade their beers for smokes, or anything else of worth.

Conjecture abounds. The war is about to end. The war is ramping up. There is to be an invasion of North Vietnam, MacArthur style. Ho Chi Minh is dead. Elvis has been sighted on the quarterdeck. America is going to nuke Hanoi. US forces are operating covertly in Laos—wherever that is. And the CIA is ferrying opium out of Laos to supply US troops in Vietnam, using something called Air America.

All rumours are given due consideration, some more than others.

All are declared to be bullshit, but the last two are true. The Yanks are seeking to intercept VC supply lines in Laos and have troops covertly stationed there. The heroin supply via Air America has ramped up during the Year of the Horse, and heroin, or horse, is the by-product. The region is in the grip of Horse Wars. When Terry hears the last one, he recalls vaguely something that Macca said to him in confidence a while back. Is there a link? No way, José.

Tony Hammett leads his troops from the front. He can match the best in push-ups and scaling ropes, and leads the run around the deck—an obstacle course of trucks and equipment. He listens to their gripes and kicks their ass when needed, but mostly he is compassionate and will do what he can to address a genuine problem. The troops love him.

The temperature and humidity grow higher as they move into the tropics. Showers are limited to ninety seconds duration to conserve water. Soap up in salt water, rinse off in fresh.

A sheet is erected in the mess where they eat, and they watch movies in the evenings. John Wayne is popular, and they laugh at the antics of Peter Sellers in *The Pink Panther*. They identify with Clint Eastwood's spaghetti western character in *The Good, The Bad, and the Ugly*. They lust after Honor Blackman in *Goldfinger*, and they all want to be James Bond, if only to bed her.

Jack and other designated marksmen practice shooting at objects thrown off the rear of the ship. He matches the others in proficiency. Tony Hammett watches, pleased.

The ship crosses the equator. A sailor tells Jack that there is normally a Crossing the Line ceremony involving someone dressed as King Neptune, but as the ship is at operational status, 7RAR will enjoy this on the return journey. That 7RAR will return on the *Vung Tau Ferry* is common knowledge onboard, despite it being classified information.

It isn't until the ship passes the halfway mark on its journey north that Jack encounters Terry one afternoon during a stroll around the ship. It is inevitable in such confined quarters. Jack is surprised to see Terry and curious to find out why he is here, but he doesn't want a confrontation,—at least, not here where there are too many eyes and ears—but Terry can't help himself.

Jack attempts to walk past him but Terry calls out tauntingly, 'Hey, pretty boy, how's your girlfriend?'.

Snarling, Jack launches himself across the space between them and they crash to the deck, pummelling each other furiously. The fight is broken up quickly by a corporal assisted by a couple of soldiers.

The pair is fronted to the regimental sergeant major. The RSM is thinking of an appropriate punishment when Major Hammett, who has heard about the fracas involving one of his men, steps forward.

'RSM, may I suggest that these two might want to get the shit out of their livers by engaging in a boxing match? Queensbury rules, of course.'

The RSM thinks this is an excellent idea. It will give the troops some entertainment as well.

Quickly the bout is organised. The navy PTI supplies the gloves, some ill-fitting mouthguards, and protective head gear. There is space on the deck, and a crowd of soldiers gather, excited to witness something out of the ordinary. Money exchanges hands as they bet on the likely winner. These guys are amateurs, so it is not likely that they have much experience in the ring. The fight will be more of a brawl, which the crowd wants. None of that dancing and hugging that the professionals carry on with.

The PTI marks out a ring area with chalk. No-one moves to assist Terry, who is not popular. Major Hammett speaks quietly to Jack as he is gloving up.

'Private Martin, you are both evenly matched in size and weight. I don't know if you can fight or not, but let me give you a tip: watch his eyes, they will telegraph his moves. Keep on your toes, and keep circling. Don't stop. Good luck.'

The referee is the PTI. He calls Jack and Terry to the centre of the makeshift ring and issues instructions. There are to be a maximum of six three-minute rounds, with a minute break in between. Terry stares malevolently at Jack through his head gear. Jack stares back expressionlessly. The pair separate and go to their corners.

The PTI blows his whistle to signify the start of round one.

Jack circles warily, watching Terry closely. Terry is not moving, instead standing and taunting Jack. Jack realises that Terry obviously believes he is the better fighter based his experience earned on the streets of Newcastle. Jack reminds himself that he is a product of the same environment. He has had his share of scraps in his teenage years, but has had only one major fight previously. This was when he was eighteen, and some boofhead picked on him at a local pub. Although the other guy was bigger, Jack was stronger, and put him on his ass a couple of times before the boofhead's mates pulled him away.

When Terry arrogantly turns his head to shout something to the crowd, Jack seizes his chance. He swings with a left and catches Terry on the side of the face. Terry instinctively covers up and ducks, and Jack's follow-up right misses the mark. Terry's insolent smirk is wiped off his face. He attacks.

Jack does his best to cover up and weave during the remainder of the first round, but Terry catches him a couple of times with heavy blows—one very low, which earns Terry a sharp reprimand from the PTI.

Rounds two and three are similar to the first: Jack lands a few blows, but he receives more from Terry. However, Terry seems to be tiring. Jack's superior fitness from the combat training is starting to show.

Jack lands a solid uppercut on Terry's jaw early in the fourth, and for the first time Terry is back-pedalling. Jack pursues him, but lacks professional fighting skills, and is unable to nail him again before the bell ends the round.

Both adversaries are breathing heavily now, and both have streaks of blood on their faces. Jack's left eye is closing, but he can see enough to go on.

Round five is more even. Jack is on the receiving end of a couple of good shots as Terry uses hidden reserves to attack once more. Jack is tiring fast, but manages to hit Terry with a well-timed right cross. The noise of the crowd swells as the end of the fight looms.

The pair stands wearily for the last round. Terry seems to be more tired than Jack, but the blows that Jack has absorbed are beginning to tell on him.

The PTI draws them to the centre of the ring and gets them to touch gloves.

'You're cactus, pretty boy,' Terry wheezes unconvincingly. Jack doesn't reply, trying to conserve his energy.

The last round starts, both of them moving much slower now. Suddenly Terry launches a savage right cross. Jack sees the blow coming but can't get out of the way. It strikes him on the side of the jaw and his world goes briefly black. Next thing he knows he is on the deck, the PTI standing above him, counting him out. He sees out of the corner of his good eye Terry leaning in triumphantly, his mouth in an ugly sneer. Somehow Jack gets to his feet, staggering a little, before regaining his footing. The crowd is screaming for blood, but Jack, dodging and weaving clumsily, manages to evade Terry's swings. Jack's mind slowly clears.

Terry swings again, but this time Jack is ready for him. He drops slightly and Terry's fist whistles past his head. Mustering all his strength, Jack lashes out with an uppercut, which catches Terry squarely on the chin. As if in a dream, Jack watches Terry's knees buckle, then he is on his knees, shaking his head in an effort to clear it, spitting out blood onto the deck. Jack staggers back, trying to conserve what little energy he has left. Anticlimactically, as the count reaches eight, the bell rings. The fight is over. Terry makes an almighty effort, and regains his feet, swinging at Jack after the bell. But the PTI grabs Terry and effortlessly pins his arms until the fight goes out of him. Drawing Jack in, the PTI raises both their hands and declares the bout a draw. The crowd drifts away, satisfied with the stoush and the result.

After taking their gloves off, the PTI makes Jack and Terry shake hands, which they do reluctantly. They regard each other with undiminished loathing, but they are both spent for the moment—although Jack knows that this is not the end of their personal battle.

*****

HMAS Sydney is joined by *HMAS Parramatta* off Singapore, and the two ships turn north. *Parramatta* is to act as escort to counter the illusionary threat offered from Chinese submarines off the coast of Vietnam, and to provide naval gunfire support whilst at Vung Tau. 1RAR's preparation picks up in earnest as the ships steam closer to Vietnam.

Jack turns twenty-one just before the ships arrive in Vung Tau. He has been old enough to drink, to fight in a war and perhaps to die. Now he is old enough to vote. Another of life's little ironies.

*****

Chapter 23

The morning of April 9 dawns early in the tropics. In February of 1968 the Year of the Horse has been succeeded by the Year of the Monkey.

Jack, in full kit, leans over the rail of *HMAS Sydney* as it steams into Vung Tau harbour and drops anchor. Slightly ahead, he can see the destroyer *HMAS Parramatta* on escort duty. The evening before, the ship's captain announced on the broadcast system that it is *Sydney's* tenth visit to Vung Tau in support of the Australian war effort since 1965. As well as Jack, the ship is carrying about four hundred and fifty soldiers from 1RAR, and will take 7RAR home as their tour of duty has finished.

HMAS Sydney drops anchor and the call comes for the troops of 1RAR to prepare for disembarkation. They will be ferried ashore using the ship's landing craft. As Jack lines up with the other young men he spies Lieutenant Colonel Phillip Bennett, 1RAR's commanding officer, standing to one side, watching his men as they climb onboard one of the landing craft. Jack doesn't envy the colonel's responsibility: he has well over six hundred troops under his command, including one hundred and thirty who have previously served in Vietnam. The word is that Bennett is a veteran of the Korean War, where he was wounded and also mentioned in despatches for bravery. Jack thinks he should know a thing or two about war.

During an earlier briefing held in the South China Sea, Jack and his fellow soldiers learnt that an advance party of about one hundred and fifty 1RAR troops is already in country. The main body onboard *HMAS Sydney* will join them at Nui Dat—the Australian base in Phouc Tuy Province—about twenty-five kilometres north-east of Vung Tau, and about forty kilometres south-east of Saigon. The officer giving the briefing has stressed its location is ideal, away from population centres but close to Vietcong base areas. This news causes an uneasy murmur from several National Service soldiers, but this is quickly silenced by the officer.

As Jack and a group of men are ferried ashore, he notices navy frogmen in the water checking the hulls of both warships for any signs of submerged attack. Towering above him, the deck of *HMAS Sydney* is covered in military equipment and stores waiting to be offloaded.

A deafening roar interrupts his observations and he swings around in time to see *HMAS Parramatta's* 4.5 inch guns booming out, targeting suspected Vietcong positions in the hills nearby. Watching the shells impact in the distance, Jack is nervous and constantly checks his weapon. He is not consoled by the fact that many others are doing the same. But not all—the old hands are more nonchalant. They know the real war is further afield.

Five days into the trip north, the troops had been shown a newsreel about the Tet offensive a few months earlier. Elements of the Vietcong and the North Vietnamese Army had launched a surprise attack during the Lunar New Year—a time when a ceasefire traditionally operates. The communists referred to it as Tet, Year of the Monkey.

Chapter 23

The newsreel described widespread attacks by around eighty thousand communist troops right across South Vietnam, which initially caused confusion and panic amongst the allied forces. But within days the communists were beaten back, suffering heavy casualties. This brought a cheer from the men watching.

Jack and his fellow troops were informed about battles like Khe Sahn and Hue, where the fighting had been protracted and bloody. They were told that 7RAR and 2RAR had been involved in fighting in Saigon and nearby countryside. This put the troops who haven't yet faced combat on edge. Jack was no exception.

It takes about five hours for the disembarkation process to be completed. Jack, now stripped to the waist in the heat and humidity, sips from his water bottle as he watches *HMAS Sydney* weigh anchor and gradually fade from sight over the horizon, heading back to Sydney. He blinks away the sweat and puts the ship out of his mind.

It is finally time to move. Jack swings his heavy pack onto his back and, with his rifle in hand, trudges towards the waiting trucks. He is in a section of eight men, one of three sections in a recon platoon, which include a radio man and a medic.

Jack is a member of a four-man fire team, a brick, led by Corporal Harry 'H' Jameson. Jack is the designated sniper in his brick. The platoon is part of Delta Company, a force of just over one hundred men.

The platoon climbs into a truck and prepares to depart on the journey to Nui Dat. Jack glances out, and sights Terry Bannister walking past. Their eyes meet, and reflect mutual hate.

*****

Chapter 24

Nui Dat, the Dat, becomes 1RAR's home away from home. It is situated in the middle of Phuoc Tuy Province near Route 2, a road that cuts the province north to south. The base sprawls out from a low hill, with a barbed wire perimeter over twelve kilometres in length. The surrounding countryside out to five hundred metres has been cleared to provide unimpeded lines of fire in case of an attack by Charlie.

The Dat is a noisy place. The din of air operations by helo and fixed-wing planes is constantly in the background. Dull percussions from intermittent artillery and mortar fire in support of operations in the province add to the racket.

1RAR is housed in one of several miniature villages inside the compound. As well as tents, the village contains a canteen, store, post office, cinema, helipads, a Salvation Army tent and a chapel. Some chairs and furniture fashioned from artillery ammunition boxes have been left by their predecessors, and these are quickly claimed by the old hands.

The latrine system is not flash, but Jack learns that, compared to being in the field, it is relatively luxurious. The only danger comes from the occasional snake, and practical jokers who periodically stuff a smoke grenade down the latrine chimney. Jack is on the receiving end of such a practical joke. Onlookers laugh themselves silly when Jack comes scampering out, trying to wipe his eyes from the noxious yellow smoke whilst simultaneously pulling up his pants.

After completing a token sentence in what passed for the lockup in the Dat, Terry is assigned to a support role. His day consists of mundane tasks: painting, road repairs, latrine duty, and a host of other menial jobs. The army has a slang term for this: BOHICA—bend over, here it comes again. He quickly grows bored with the humdrum routine, but is careful not to show it. He has no wish to be assigned to combat duties.

Radio broadcasts out of Australia and constant mail deliveries are a welcome diversion from the everyday soldiering tasks. Parcels arriving from the Australian Forces Overseas Fund are welcome as well. The troops love the Anzac biscuits, confectionary, and salted peanuts that come in the packs.

Terry is delighted to receive a letter from his 'Uncle Duke', who cryptically tells him to expect a new assignment. He will be contacted by someone in the army within a few weeks. Terry can put up with this tedious crap for that long—you bet.

The army loves routine, and the Dat is no exception. Everyone is up at first light, and rostered patrols scout the perimeter and further afield. The troops take their malaria tablets, and then breakfast follows at about seven-thirty. Inspections, briefings, assigned work, lunch, and more work ensue. Then it is time for more rostered patrolling followed by a beer or two or maybe three, dinner and a movie.

They get up the next morning, and do it all over again.

Harry 'H' Jameson, the corporal of the brick that Jack is assigned to, is regular army and is on his second tour. Jack, who holds H in awe, is well aware that he is a bit of a legend in the Royal Australian Regiment from his first time in Vietnam, in 1966. As a lance corporal in 6RAR, H and his company were involved in the Battle of Long Tan, one of Australia's heaviest actions to date. The VC attacked in force but, after fierce fighting, withdrew with heavy casualties. Although wounded, H saved the lives of several Australian troops during the firefight, and was subsequently awarded the Distinguished Service Order for his bravery.

Like the others in his brick, Jack has heard all about H's record. Promoted to the rank of corporal subsequent to Long Tan, he quickly lost a stripe after being involved in a brawl with civilians back in Australia in 1967.

The brawl is now part of army folklore. Enjoying a quiet drink in a pub, H and some soldier mates had been subject to a deal of verbal abuse from a group of drunk yobbos. H and his friends weren't too fussed about being called army wankers—this is common enough—but when the yobs used the term 'baby killer', this was a bridge too far. H and his mates went on the offensive.

Thirty minutes later military police from their base placed them under arrest. Three yobs were on their way to hospital. The bar was in a shambles. H had a black eye and a gash on his cheek, but he was grinning. The army's reputation was upheld.

The base commanding officer, pompous and old school, was not amused and ordered that H be demoted, but the regimental sergeant-major had a different view and whispered quietly 'well done' in his ear afterwards.

This incident earns H as much status amongst the troops as the gong. For Jack and his fellow brick members, H being their leader is definitely bragging material.

Now a corporal again and posted to 1RAR for a second Vietnam tour, H is careful to make sure that the troops in his brick know what to do on patrol. And what to expect. He drills his soldiers thoroughly, to the point they can sense exactly what each will do in the most likely scenarios.

Jack and the brick practise for long periods at the Dat's rifle range. Jack thinks they resemble something out of a Wild West show as they march to the range, festooned in bandoliers of ammunition. Jack's chest swells with pride when H comments favourably on his shooting skills.

Absorbing H's constant stream of information, Jack now knows as well as anyone in the brick the reasons why they are in this particular province, as well as the terrain where they will patrol. Whoever controls the province controls the port of Vung Tau, which is vital to resupply for the Australians. The topography is ideally suited to the guerrilla warfare favoured by the VC. The terrain in some parts is flat and open, suitable for farming. Small villages and settlements dot the landscape, with a lot of rice fields where the locals tend the crops. There are isolated mountain areas, particularly to the north, covered in dense vegetation. These provide cover for VC supply routes and bases. This is from where the most likely threat will emanate.

But a lot of the province is covered in thick rainforest and long grass. Wheeled vehicles find it difficult to penetrate, and visibility is limited. The VC also likes to operate in this heavy undergrowth.

Jack learns from H to be thankful it is the dry season, otherwise their patrol would face the extra challenge of being caught in heavy tropical downpours, further restricting visibility and making patrolling uncomfortable. The noise of the rain also makes it difficult to hear properly. The VC move stealthily, and it is difficult enough to detect them at the best of times.

H has drummed into Jack and the others not to trust the locals. The VC and their predecessors, the Viet Minh, have controlled the area for many years, since before the French colonial occupation. The villagers are more likely to favour the VC than the corrupt

South Vietnamese Government.

Delta Company attends a lecture on the size and composition of enemy forces. Jack learns that the VC and North Vietnamese Army together make up the National Liberation Army. The North Vietnamese are much better trained and equipped for major confrontations, and the VC engage in most of the guerrilla warfare.

H disabuses Jack of any grandiose notions he has about being the brick's designated sniper. He warns him: 'Don't think you're gunna be doing any John Wayning out there in the scrub, Jack. Your job is to lay down suppressing fire if we meet any VC, not to hide in some hole wearing a ghillie suit and shoot them from a kilometre out. You won't see the little bastards until they're about ready to piss on your foot'.

Chastened, Jack takes H's advice to heart.

Delta Company is routinely rostered for patrols of the perimeter and occasionally further afield, searching for signs of the elusive Charlie. The patrols carefully avoid the mined areas in close to the Dat, sewn by sappers to help secure the base.

H tells them that the VC regularly infiltrate the minefield and painstakingly dig up M16 'Jumping Jack' and toe popper mines planted by the Australians. They are then used by the VC to protect their bunker systems. Jack silently vows to be very careful to watch where he steps when on patrol.

Jack has overcome the initial nerves experienced during his first time outside the wire. Well aware that H has to babysit three green Nashos, the patrol members follow his detailed directions. Once past the cleared area, the patrol moves carefully through the countryside, avoiding marked tracks, with H reminding them constantly in a low voice what they need to do and what they should watch out for. H knows that the boys are scared, nervous, and can easily do something stupid, so he keeps a tight rein on them.

H instructs them to lock and load their weapons just outside the perimeter, so that they are ready to do battle if necessary. From bitter experience, H makes sure that their weapons are pointing outwards towards the threat, as he has no wish for a friendly-fire incident. That would spoil his whole day.

They patrol for several hours, but see nothing apart from some peasants working the rice fields and some water buffalo. The locals ignore them, intent on doing what they have done for centuries. The brick sets up an ambush in a copse of trees adjacent to a well-worn track, but again no VC reveal themselves. It is frustrating, but Jack learns in time that not encountering VC is good news for his chances of survival.

Back at the Dat, Jack realises that he stinks of sweat and fear. He has survived his first patrol, and is thankful. Under H's steady influence, the brick members are no longer virgins. However, he doesn't join in with his brick members when they express their relief by shouting and hollering. H notices this and files it away.

Despite the incessant patrolling done by 1RAR from the Dat, Charlie is nowhere to be found.

*****

Chapter 25

Answering a summons, Terry reports to the base administration centre. It is midafternoon at the beginning of May, and 1RAR has been at the Dat for about three weeks. Terry is heartily sick of the place.

The clerk hands him a message, scrutinising Terry as he takes it. 'You must have friends in high places, Bannister.'

Terry scans the contents. It is an order for him to report immediately for temporary duty to a unit of the Australian Army Service Corps based in Saigon. Terry has never heard of them. He asks the clerk about the corps.

'Oh, them. These buggers look after stuff like transportation and air despatch. I think they're part of the Ordnance Corps, which is headquartered at the Bien Hoa airbase in Saigon. But someone told me that the supply guys are at Tan Son Nhut, another airbase nearby. I hear they are even responsible for the mail. Perhaps you will become a postie,' the clerk jokes. Terry is not amused.

Terry reads on. The order is signed by a Captain Williams.

He stares distractedly at the clerk, mystified, but suddenly excited by this. Is it the news he has been waiting for? The clerk addresses him again.

'Pay attention, soldier. There's a tilly leaving the Dat soon for Saigon. You've got an hour to get your gear together. You'd better hop to it. And sign this order, in triplicate. You know the army loves its paperwork. Take a copy with you, in case you get asked by someone where you're going.'

Terry needs no second invitation and hurries off to pack his gear.

The utility truck, nicknamed tilly, is packed to the rafters, but Terry manages to squeeze himself in the back, jammed between several crates of supplies. The tilly follows Route 2 north, the driver motoring along as fast as the poor state of the road will allow. Although there is little danger from attack, one can't be too careful. This suits Terry just fine, and he ignores the uncomfortable ride. He is on his way out of the Dat to do God knows what, but whatever it is, it will be in Saigon. He can picture the lovely local females in their slinky dresses.

About an hour later the truck enters the outskirts of Saigon. Terry peers out, fascinated. The buildings are a mixture of Buddhist and French influence. There are many stately structures intertwined with peasant-style humpies. The truck enters the central part of the city and heads for a large air base. There are a lot of military aircraft scattered on the runways and taxiways—mostly US, but also what he thinks are South Vietnamese Air Force.

The driver of the truck pulls up at a control point and the guards scrutinise their credentials. Terry shows them his orders. He is directed to a small building near one of the taxiways, thankfully not far from where the truck drops him off. Carrying his gear, he strides towards the building and enters it.

An Australian Army Ordnance Corps grunt is sitting at a desk, typing. He glances up as Terry stands in front of the desk.

'Private Bannister reporting for duty. This order says I'm to report to a Captain Williams. He around?'

The soldier shakes his head. 'He's knocked off for the day, mate. He'll be back tomorrow, probably. You can meet him then.'

Terry regards him with astonishment and growing anger. 'Where the fuck do I go until then, *mate*?'

The soldier is unfazed. He points behind him.

'There's a spare bunk in the other room. You can get your head down there tonight, and the captain will sort you out tomorrow. There's some C-rations that I pinched from the Yanks in a cupboard—and coffee. The ablutions are next door.'

With that, the soldier returns to his typing, leaving Terry standing there.

I ought to punch your head in, he thinks savagely. But he has learned a few lessons of late, and it is no use shooting the messenger. Hefting his pack, Terry moves into the next room and settles in for the night. At least it is better than sleeping in a tent.

Short, pudgy, rat-faced and with an uninspiring bearing, Captain Bungy Williams greets Terry the next morning. Glancing at the two clerks in the office who have turned up shortly before, he suggests that he and Terry walk over to the canteen for breakfast.

Terry examines his surrounds as they trudge through the air base. There is a lot of activity occurring with transport planes being loaded, unloaded and coming and going.

The Captain tells him that the base, Tan Son Nhut, is mainly used for command and control; the operational air base, Bien Hoa, is nearby. The US military runs Tan Son Nhut. Williams heads a small detachment of Australians that liaises with the Americans over air and sea transportation as well as more basic things like mail deliveries to and from the diggers in Vietnam. Terry asks the obvious.

'So, what am I doing here, Captain? How do I fit in?'

'Well, Terry—I may call you Terry?—it seems that your mates back in Sydney have pulled a few strings. You'll be based here for the length of your time in Vietnam.' Seeing the expression of consternation on Terry's face, the officer laughs.

'Don't worry, Terry, your mates are my mates too. As you'll find out, you're about to become involved in one of the sweetest little rackets going. Have you heard of Air America? Not really? Well, this base is a major hub for their activities, and we're a small part of it. Come on. Let's get some food. I'll tell you all about it. And by the way, call me Bungy, but not in front of the others. And don't talk to them about anything I'm going to tell you. This is strictly for your ears only.'

The canteen is a revelation to Terry. Designed by the US to be a home away from home for their troops, it is filled with every imaginable consumable good. Clothes, candy, books, fast food, postcards, electrical equipment—it has the lot. He is in seventh heaven.

They each take a tray and proceed to pile their plates with food. They find a table, sit down and tuck in. The food, although a bit starchy, is pretty good. Terry is hungry, and wolfs it down.

Finally satiated, Terry leans back and considers Bungy, who is still stuffing his face. Not the most impressive specimen he has ever met, but who is he to judge? Still, this seems to be a nice safe place to spend the war. He concludes that this will suit him just fine.

But his newly gained optimism is soon shattered.

Without warning, a series of explosions erupt somewhere in the air base. People jump up, alarmed, and mill around in confusion. There is a pause, then someone screams out, 'It's the Vietcong. They're attacking the base'. This is almost correct. It is both the VC and elements of the North Vietnamese Army acting in concert for maximum effect.

Although this is not an offensive of the same scale as Tet, it is as savage in terms of the fighting. The communists are attempting to influence the upcoming Paris peace talks between Hanoi, Saigon and the USA. These are designed to negotiate peace in Vietnam and end the war, and Hanoi wants maximum leverage. Saigon is about to feel the impact of an assault for the second time in a few short months.

Bungy turns white. *Oh shit*, he thinks, *the bastards aren't satisfied after Tet, they're back for another go. I'd best be off to my bolt hole. It's well stocked with food and drink, and the young girl who looks after it will tend to all my other needs if I pay her enough.*

He grabs his cap. 'Terry, I've got urgent business elsewhere. You stay here. I'll get back to you.' With that, Bungy scurries out thc door and runs towards the office as fast as his stubby legs will carry him.

Fucking Rupert, Terry thinks savagely, *useless as tits on a bull. At the first sign of trouble, he flies the coop. Still, that's not a bad idea. I might do the same.*

Terry moves swiftly to follow Bungy. However, he is no sooner out the door than a US air force sergeant calls to him to stop.

'Hey, buddy, where the fuck do you think you're going? In case you don't know, there's a war on, and that war has just come to visit us. Again. Come with me. We need to get us each a big gun and join in the fight.'

Terry's attempts to convince the sergeant that he shouldn't be involved fall on deaf ears.

'You're in uniform, so you fight. I don't give a flying fuck what sort of uniform you are wearing. Stop arguing or I'll have you arrested for desertion in the face of the enemy.'

Terry has no choice but to comply. He curses his luck.

*****

Equipped with an American M16 rifle and half a dozen thirty-round magazines, Terry moves with a small group of USAF security police towards the northern perimeter of the airfield. Mortar explosions ring out from all sides, some at the airfield, others further away. Smoke billows everywhere, and Terry is frightened out of his wits.

Suddenly, a couple of Yanks stop, crouch, and begin to fire their weapons into the smoke. Terry follows suit, blindly, although he can see nothing to shoot at. But if the others are doing it, he will too. He doesn't know if he hits anything, but doesn't care.

There is a lull in the fighting a few hours later. Terry and the others slump to the ground behind some cover, eyes tearing from the smoke, nerves stretched to the limit.

Finally the VC withdraws from Saigon, with heavy losses. Terry returns to his bunk and sleeps for eighteen hours straight.

*****

Chapter 26

Bungy Williams turns up late in the afternoon of the next day, bringing his clerks with him. He acts as if nothing has happened. Of course, for him it hasn't, but he encounters one very pissed-off Terry, who is convinced he has been left to rot.

Terry takes Bungy aside and threatens to beat the shit out of him, but Bungy is unperturbed.

'I'm too important to hang around and risk being killed,' he states nonchalantly. 'If something happens to me, the whole organisation falls on its ass. I'm the man with the corporate knowledge; I know how all the pieces fit together—and believe me, there are lots of pieces.'

Terry is not placated. 'Well, it's about bloody time you told me.'

'Okay, let's go over to the canteen and have a few brews. Unfortunately, they stock only American piss, but I'm sure you could use a drink. I hope those VC mongrels don't come back like they did the other day. It's a long story, and I'm just the one to tell it.'

After establishing that Terry knows Michael Hand, Bungy tells him about the connection between Michael Hand and Bernie

Houghton.

'It started when the two Americans met up here in Saigon in the mid-60s. Mike was a Green Beret, part of the US Special Forces, and he won a couple of medals for bravery earlier on in the war. He then somehow got involved with the Central Intelligence Agency who recruited him to work for them. His job was to train hill tribesmen in Laos, called the Hmong, for combat against the VC. Air America, run by the CIA, supplied them with weapons and other stuff, and Mike was the contact point.

'In the meantime, Bernie was freelancing in Vietnam, making a buck through selling war surplus material and catering to the needs of the US servicemen—women, booze, dope, whatever they wanted. And they wanted plenty.

'In 1967, Bernie arrived in Sydney and opened the Bourbon and Beefsteak in Kings Cross, as well as several other bars nearby—Texas Tavern and Harpoon Harry's. These three establishments catered specifically for US servicemen and their booze, women and drug needs.'

Terry breaks into the monologue.

'How could Bernie, a Yank new in town, set up shop in the part of Sydney most controlled by organised crime?'

Bungy smiles cagily. 'It must have been through connections, people like Lenny Macpherson and Perce Galea, who both had legitimate and crooked business interests in Kings Cross'.

'Where do you think the money to set this all up came from?'

Bungy is cautious in his reply. 'Well, I think Bernie was being bankrolled by the CIA, but I have no idea why.'

Terry is dubious; Bungy seems to know everything else.

The penny suddenly drops for Terry.

'The only way I can see this happening is if the CIA is involved in a massive drug-running scheme, using Air America as the first transportation link in the supply chain. And I reckon you're the link in Vietnam to the distribution network that ships the drugs to Australia. What I can't understand is why the CIA would be involved.'

Bungy grins. 'Perhaps it helps to finance their dirty work elsewhere.' This somehow rings true to Terry, and he wonders at the audacity and complexity of the operation.

'So how does the pipeline work?' asks Terry.

Bungy has the grace to look uncomfortable.

'This may shock you Terry but, amongst other things, they use the bodies of GIs killed in the war to transport the drugs. The bodies are sent back to the States in sealed caskets, so there's no check done.'

Terry is astounded. He thinks that is absolutely disrespectful to the guys who have died for their country. He thinks of the grieving relatives of the dead soldiers. They would never know that it is more than just the remains of their loved one coming home in a casket.

Bungy continues: 'Mate, there are heaps of Military Assistance Command Vietnam flights every day in and out of Saigon, some of which are used to transport the caskets. But those MACV flights also contain tons of other stuff, drugs included, in their cargo'.

With more prompting, Bungy reveals the whole logistic chain link to Australia. Terry isn't sure if Bungy is relieved to tell someone, or whether he just wants to boast about the simple elegance of it.

'Well, Terry, it all starts with this unit, which has the responsibility of coordinating all Australian air freight movements and all Australian Navy shipping movements of freight leaving Vietnam. You know the *Vung Tau Ferry* is a frequent visitor to Vietnam. It too is regularly used for illegal shipments. The freight is sealed up here in Saigon, and no-one onboard the *Sydney* or any aircraft knows what is in the cargo.

'Once it arrives in Australia, customs people on the take turn a blind eye to any specially marked crates being offloaded—or alert the network if any raids are planned. It's an easy matter for a crate or two to go missing.'

As he tries to digest these revelations, Terry asks Bungy how long he has been in Saigon and how long he will stay. Bungy nods in approval at the query.

'Good question. I got here nearly a year ago, and set this all up. And I've just volunteered to stay on for another year. Queen and country and all that bullshit. The brass loves that sort of macho stuff. So, I'll probably just outlast you here, given your tour of duty will be about twelve months.

'Terry, I'm sure you have been told this before, but now you're completely in the loop it would be very wise of you to keep shtum about this. Believe me, if you open your mouth the guys who operate here will do things to you that you can't even imagine in your worst nightmares. And when they've finished, no-one will ever find the pieces.'

*****

Terry sits in the canteen after Bungy leaves, sipping on his beer. It is Bungy's final statement that has completely captured his attention. He gets up and buys another beer then returns to his seat, seeing with fresh eyes the US aircraft landing and taking off. He goes over every bit of the story that Bungy has told him. He is sure of one thing: he will need to be very careful—but if he can survive his posting to Vietnam, he will be in a very good position indeed when he returns to Australia.

*****

Chapter 27

Just before the mini-Tet offensive commences, based on intelligence reports, 1RAR is ordered to deploy outside Saigon to interdict suspected VC incursions against the South Vietnam capital.

H strides into the tent where Jack and the others live and directs the brick members to grab their gear and report to him in ten minutes. When one of the brick asks H what is going on, he responds: 'Fuck knows, fella. I'm almost as low on the totem pole as you grunts. But something is going on, and we're obviously gunna be part of it. Oh, and we are now operational, so be ready for anything'.

They quickly form up and H guides them to a waiting helo, which is burning and turning, ready to launch. Other diggers follow. When the chopper is full, it takes off, dust streaming over the ground from the downdraft of its rotor blades. It turns and heads north.

About fifteen minutes later the helo lands in a paddock. The soldiers alight and fan out, crouching, guns ready to fire. H motions the brick to follow him as the chopper ascends into the sky and disappears into the distance. Jack's heart is beating hard, his mouth is dry and his attitude is taciturn. He responds only to H and ignores his fellow brick members. They head out into the unknown.

*****

The infantrymen of 1RAR patrol their assigned area for the next week. Apart from some minor skirmishes, the patrols do not encounter the VC in any strength. Jack feels increasingly frustrated as word spreads about the VC attacks on Saigon.

He expresses his irritation to H, who replies nonchalantly: 'Charlie must either have by-passed us, or snuck in another way. I understand you and the other guys are impatient to get amongst them, but I'm sure we'll get our chance. The buggers have to come back out, and they're sure to be in a hurry. The Ruperts are saying that Charlie is getting a real caning in Saigon, but the cheeky bastards even attacked the American Embassy. I bet that got the Yank's attention'.

Jack settles back into his makeshift hoochie to await further developments. This doesn't take too long.

H rouses them the next day. 'Come on, get your gear. We're off.'

Along with two US army brigades, 1RAR and 3RAR are ordered to move to an area known by the Americans as 'the catcher's mitt'. The Australian troops are to occupy an area labelled by the Australian brass as Surfers. Obviously someone in the planning staff likes the beach.

It wouldn't do Jack's nerves any good to learn that the combined forces are to act as bait to lure suspected North Vietnamese forces and the VC into the open, but the commanding officers of 1RAR and 3RAR doubt the intelligence assessments that warn of increased North Vietnamese movement in the area. After all, based on faulty assessments, they have just sat on their bums for a week waiting in vain for the enemy to appear.

However, for a change, the intelligence is correct. There is a looming threat from crack North Vietnamese troops who are moving towards Saigon to mount a fresh offensive, and area Surfers lies directly in the line of advance of the North Vietnamese Army seventh division, located only about nine kilometres to the east. The North Vietnamese watch from concealment as the US and Australian troop build-up continues throughout the day.

After waiting for hours for the choppers to arrive, Jack and his brick are finally airlifted to a sector within Surfers, called Coral. Another sector, called Balmoral, is to the immediate north. The terrain is low-lying, flat and mostly cleared. There are patches of scrub and a few stunted trees scattered through the region.

The insertion is, from the start, a shambles, as US helos are diverted from carrying Australian troops to ferrying their own soldiers. It is, in the vernacular, a SNAFU—situation normal, all fucked up.

Coral and Balmoral are set up to provide fire support to the infantrymen in 1 and 3 RARs. Standard army doctrine states that, whilst the infantry patrols an area, they are backed by artillery, mortars, and machine guns in case they run into trouble.

The looming Battle of Coral/Balmoral is about to enter the history books as one of the most intense bouts of fighting undertaken by Australian troops in the Vietnam War.

*****

Chapter 28

Such is the disorganisation associated with the logistics of setting up Coral that it is late afternoon before 1RAR in its entirety arrives at the landing zone. The LZ is a scene of confused chaos. Trying to impose some degree of order into the turmoil, Colonel Bennett directs that his infantry companies immediately move east to set up a defensive perimeter. This is done at speed in order to beat darkness that is rapidly approaching and which would leave the troops out in the open. As a result, the defences are poorly prepared. They will have to do, but there are large gaps in the perimeter as a consequence.

As Delta Company makes its way to its allotted defensive position about fifteen hundred metres out from the hastily prepared headquarters, Jack can hear the boom of artillery in the distance. H tells his brick that they are most likely American guns.

Heads turn as the company passes the bodies of two long-dead enemy soldiers in the remnants of grey uniforms. They sit eerily in an upright position, as if still on guard. Jack is acutely aware that this is the real thing, finally. There are men out there who want to kill him. This realisation creates butterflies in his belly. One of his brick is literally shaking with fear, which earns a sharp rebuke from H.

Reaching their allotted position, Delta Company is ordered to dig in. Their nerves aren't helped by a sudden downpour that hits soon after darkness, adding to their discomfort. They know that the rain will make it harder for them to see and hear Charlie, if he comes calling.

Back in the headquarters area of Coral, defensive preparations are not completed by the time the sun goes down. The immediate perimeter is not yet protected by barbed wire, and there isn't time to lay Claymore mines as an extra layer of defence. Although the artillery and motor platoons have dug weapons' pits to a reasonable depth, the platoons lack sufficient protective troops. These are scattered out in the scrub.

The rain comes down in sheets, filling the pits with water, making everyone uncomfortable. Despite the lack of preparation, the troops are expecting small pockets of enemy to attack.

About midnight the rain finally stops, but under the cover of the downpour, large numbers of the enemy have snuck stealthily past the scattered diggers in the outer defensive perimeter, and have quietly dug in within several hundred metres of the inner defences. They await the command to attack.

The only action out in the scrub comes in the early hours of the morning, in the midst of Delta Company. An enemy patrol is engaged by one of the company platoons, and the twinkle of gunfire lights the sky in the immediate vicinity. Then the enemy retaliates with rocket-propelled grenades, and the sky is briefly lit up like a mini New Year's Eve celebration.

Jack hears a distinctly Australian voice screaming in agony in the darkness, and shudders. The atmosphere is tense, unsettling and ethereal. Jack is scared stiff. It is like ghost hunting in the inky blackness. Someone fires their SLR blindly into the night until a harsh voice commands the shooter to stand down.

The platoon commander calls in the contact to headquarters, and almost immediately the artillery opens fire at targets past the outer perimeter, further adding to the noise and the light show. Helicopter gunships appear overhead and fire blindly into the scrub. A dustoff helo lands nearby, ready to evacuate the wounded.

Abruptly, the night falls silent again.

As the nearby firefight erupts, H whispers for his troops to renew their scrutiny of the darkness, even though their night sight has been temporarily destroyed by the firing. Jack needs no urging, adrenalin surging through his body, his nerves stretched tight. But nothing moves out in the darkness, so the brick lies there, waiting ... waiting.

The communists attack the inner perimeter in strength and quickly overrun some of the inner defensive positions. In the pits, desperate hand-to-hand fighting between the diggers and the enemy erupts. M60 machine guns spew deadly fire at the attacking foe. The crump of hand grenades adds to the uproar.

Unable to resist the temptation, Jack turns and stares in astonishment at the sound and light display. He shouts out in disbelief. 'Oh fuck, the bastards are behind us. How did that happen?'

Savagely, H orders him to shut up and keep searching for the enemy. The fuckers might be going to launch an attack against Delta Company. H is worried, the NVA is behind them and who knows what might be in front of them. He prays for daylight to be able to see what is going on, but dawn is still some hours away. *Those buggers*, H thinks in reluctant admiration, *they've cut the defensive line in half. We could all be in big strife here.* Anxiously, the brick members scan the darkness for any sign of the enemy.

Ignoring H's order, Jack can't help but glance back at the battle. Despite the distance, the racket is thunderous as the sounds carry in the night air. Helos wheel over the action, spitting death into the enemy ranks.

Jack is mesmerised when something resembling a spaceship suddenly appears overhead. It is brightly lit and illumination flares shoot out from it above the battlefield, further adding to the eeriness of the melee. A rain of bullets disgorges from its mini guns.

In wonder, Jack asks, 'What the fuck is that thing?'.

'It's a Spooky,' H replies, 'a specially converted C47 Dakota. Death from the sky. Isn't it bloody awesome?'.

One of the platoon commanders radios in to headquarters, asking if they need assistance. The commander pauses briefly, and then tells him no, there is enough confusion without having any accidental blue-on-blue encounters. They are to stay put.

Finally, the communist forces are beaten off, and at first light they melt back into the countryside, dragging their wounded. Coral has survived—just.

A kilometre out, Jack and the rest of Delta Company warily settle back in their shallow trenches and try to snatch a few winks of sleep. H tells his brick that they will almost certainly be patrolling soon.

In the morning all the infantry platoons are recalled and move back inside the inner perimeter. H takes the brick on patrol, but they don't venture too far. Everywhere there are signs of Charlie and his northern comrades. Discarded items of equipment and a few dead bodies litter the area, but of the main body of the enemy, there is no sign.

This continues for another two days before the communists attack again in force with around eight hundred troops committed to the assault. But this time the combined forces are ready. The perimeter is heavily fortified. Wire and mines lay in the path of the enemy. A wall of fire from the ground hits the enemy advance and helos and Spooky aircraft spit a destructive rain of fire from the sky.

For the next four hours mayhem ensues. The communist forces come up against Alpha, Bravo and Charlie Companies of 1RAR, who engage them in pitched battles. Delta Company is spared much of the onslaught. Again the enemy withdraws at first light. Coral has been held.

Jack doesn't know whether to feel relieved or cheated. H has no such worries. He and his brick are in one piece, and that's fine with him. They patrol again the next morning. Expecting to see a large number of dead communists, Jack is mystified when there are only a few bodies in the kill zone. H explains that the opposition has a habit of taking their dead and wounded with them as they withdraw. That way, no-one knows how many troops they have lost.

For the next few days 1RAR patrols area Surfers but, apart from a few minor skirmishes, no real contact with the enemy occurs. Although tired, the troops are determined to engage with them, but the communists have other ideas.

Jack eats some C-rations and considers the situation. He has, as yet, not been directly involved in a real firefight and still doesn't know how he will react. Will his training kick in, or will he go to custard? Jack timidly confides his fears to H, who is surprisingly supportive.

'Jack, I'll tell you something I've never told anyone before: when I was involved in that crazy fight at Long Tan, I initially had exactly the same feelings. The waiting was the worst, but when the shit hit the fan, in all the excitement I forgot to be scared. I'll bet it will be the same with you. Now, eat your tasty rations, and don't forget to clean that rifle of yours. We don't want our ace marksman to have a jam at the wrong moment. We're depending on you, mate.'

A few days later 3RAR is ordered to move north to Balmoral, five kilometres from Coral. This time the insertion is done by the book, with ground troops securing the sector before the remainder of 3RAR and supporting heavy guns are moved to Balmoral.

Bravo Company, 1RAR, is directed to escort several Australian Centurion tanks from Coral to Balmoral to further bolster the defences there. As they pass a series of concealed enemy bunkers, the enemy attacks with machine-gun fire, pinning the troops down. The tanks move forward and lay down suppressing fire until Bravo Company can withdraw.

The communist commander decides to attack Balmoral, and about four hundred enemy soldiers engage the defensive perimeter in the early hours of the next morning. After heavy fighting, the NVA again withdraws.

Delta Company, accompanied by Centurion tanks, is instructed to clear the bunker system from whence the enemy attack on Bravo Company originated. Delta Company moves north, and pauses whilst several Canberra jets drop bombs on the bunkers. When the jets have finished their bombing runs, the troops move off again, anticipating an engagement with the communist forces.

As they near the location of the bunkers, enemy machine-gun fire rings out. The Centurion tanks engage the communist forces in a frontal assault in the first Australian combined infantry and tank assault since World War II.

The Centurion tanks wreak havoc with the bunker system, firing shell after shell into them, and then crushing them under their tracks. The infantry moves behind in a mopping-up operation.

The bunkers are cunningly concealed amongst thick vegetation, and visibility is limited to ten metres or so. Enemy soldiers pop up out of hidden positions and fire at the advancing diggers. The fight quickly becomes a small group struggle as the men of Delta Company spread out through the dense foliage.

Jack is moving forward with the brick when suddenly an enemy soldier appears in front of him, as if by magic, from a concealed tunnel entrance. His AK47 is tracking straight at H, who hasn't yet seen the communist. As if in slow motion, Jack sees H's head turn—too late. Instinctively, Jack aims and fires with deadly accuracy, killing the soldier before he can pull the trigger.

'Thanks, mate, I owe you one,' H grimaces at Jack, the fear of a near miss clearly etched on his face.

Jack's mind is in a whirl. He has killed a human being, but he doesn't have time to dwell on it. The enemy are everywhere. It's kill or be killed. Jack presses on, eyes sweeping from side to side, ready to react to any threat.

The fight rages for about four hours before Delta Company is ordered to withdraw and return to Coral. Aerial reconnaissance reveals that the bunker system forms part of a larger enemy base, and the hundred or so diggers are not a large enough force to engage what could well be over four hundred enemy soldiers.

During the battle, Jack hits at least two further enemy troops, but doesn't know whether they are dead as they instantly disappear back into the bunker system. Delta Company has suffered no casualties.

By the end of May the communist troops, their commanders deciding that direct confrontation is not achieving the objective, quietly move out of area Surfers and calm returns. At the end of the first week in June the infantrymen of 1RAR are ferried by Chinook helicopter back to the Dat. The Battle of Coral/Balmoral is over.

Back at Nui Dat, Jack sits wearily besides the members of his brick. For the first time in a year, he takes a good hard look at himself. He realises that up until the last few weeks he has been able to force his emotions down so that he has not thought about the reasons why he is here. In a moment of insight he comprehends how stupid and juvenile he has been in trying to escape something he should have faced up to like a man.

Yes, Susie betrayed him, but maybe he put pressure on her that she wasn't ready to handle. He should have just backed off. Now he's caught up in a senseless war that seems to have no ending. And he's been an asshole to his mates in the brick. They deserve better. Bluey and Mal and even silly Andy haven't done anything to him, apart from watch his back. And H—that bloke has got Jack through that last firefight and trained him up so that he is able to react without thinking. It's about time he woke up to himself. He's alive and kicking. Someone with a future. He needs to stay alive so that he can go back to uni after this is over and get on with his life.

Jack stands up and calls to his mates. 'Hey guys, let's go and get a beer. It's my shout. Come on, H. I'm fucking thirsty.'

Surprised, the others rise and walk with him to the amenities' tent. H is all smiles. It would seem that Jack has overcome whatever demons possessed him.

Jack has changed. His normal friendly self has returned, replacing the surly and quiet man he had become. The nerves have largely gone. He has now killed, for Queen and country. He has been blooded, and his life has changed forever.

*****

Lieutenant Colonel Bennett joins his company commanders in the officers' bar for a few drinks before the evening barbeque. As they consume cans of beer, the chat turns into an informal debrief on the Coral/Balmoral fight. They are pleased that the battalion has acquitted itself well under heavy enemy assaults. Bennett announces that he will pass on his congratulations to the troops at tomorrow's parade.

Talk drifts onto the war in general. Bennett asks his senior officers what they think about the progress in achieving their objective. One of his officers, his tongue perhaps loosened by one beer too many, states flatly that he doesn't think the war is going too well at all. Whilst the victory at Coral/Balmoral can't be discounted, the officer observes that, in reality, all they have done is defend, in the main. In most cases, it is the enemy that has dictated the terms of battle.

The other officers exchange worried glances. Has their colleague gone too far? But Bennett, taking a swig from his beer, keeps quiet. Privately he agrees with this realistic assessment. He recalls there is a term used to describe this conflict: asymmetrical warfare. It means simply that small mobile forces, using guerrilla tactics, pit themselves against larger, more traditional and cumbersome armies. *It is like an ant taking on a bull. The VC and the North Vietnamese are the ants, and we are the bull. And the ant is winning.* He also remembers the history of the last twenty or so years of conflict in Vietnam. Ironically, the VC's predecessor, the Viet Minh, was trained by US Special Forces who were part of the Office of Strategic Services. The Viet Minh managed to chase the French out after decimating them at the Battle of Điên Biên Phú. Bennett recalls another fact: the OSS is the forerunner of the CIA.

Back in Australia, Bennett's thoughts are shared by others. An army lieutenant colonel named Peter Gration, later to become the chief of the Australian Defence Force, has anonymously written an article that is widely publicised. He claims the war cannot be won and in fact needs to be scaled back. This shocks but does not deter the hard liners in Canberra, who continue to bleat the party line that victory is inevitable. Maybe that's why politicians don't fight wars.

*****

Chapter 29

It is mid-June in Saigon. Terry becomes actively involved in another type of death. Using drug labs the locals in the Golden Triangle, overseen by imported chemists, convert opium into heroin. H, horse, smack, tar, brown, shit, junk—whatever it is called, it can kill as easily as any weapon.

At the air base, Bungy introduces Terry to several Americans who step off a small plane that has no markings. They are dressed in bright civilian clothes and wear dark wraparound sunglasses. They look relaxed but somehow menacing. Bungy tells Terry they work for The Company—in other words, the CIA.

They deliver a large package to Bungy and then get back in their plane and take off quickly. Bungy nonchalantly carries it into his office and closes the door. He puts the package on his table and turns to Terry, a satisfied smile on his face.

'This is the real thing, Terry. It is ninety per cent pure smack. You don't get much better than that. This has been refined by Hong Kong Chinese chemists working in Laos. They call it Number Four, or China White. It runs rings around anything else available. It's the duck's nuts.'

Bungy expands on his explanation. 'It will be broken down when it reaches Oz, most likely diluted heavily with all sorts of crap. You don't want to know what they will do with it. But by the time it is sold on the street the purity level will be way down. That way, the profit margin is enormous.'

Terry smiles. This is great news. He imagines his bank balance in Australia skyrocketing whilst he is six thousand kilometres away in another world.

Bungy decides that Terry cannot keep on living in the warehouse from which they operate. As Bungy's partner, he deserves better, much better. Terry has no problems at all with this logic. He collects his stuff and Bungy drives him into District 1 to the Tu Do precinct, the red-light centre of Saigon. They pull up at a rundown-looking building and Bungy gestures for Terry to follow him inside.

There are several girls hanging around the entrance, dressed in skimpy dresses. Bungy speaks to a woman standing at a counter in a mixture of pigeon Vietnamese and English. She is dressed in a graceful Vietnamese silk ao dai, or dress. She looks to be about forty-years-old, but is still quite beautiful. Terry cannot understand much of the conversation, but they are obviously negotiating. The pair haggles for a while before the woman smiles and bows slightly, obviously pleased with the outcome. Bungy beckons to Terry.

'Mate, this is Hong, which means Rose in Vietnamese. She is the mama san of this brothel. You will be living in a room upstairs. The place has everything you will need: hot and cold running women, Aussie beer, and the food these girls can cook is to die for. Enjoy. I'll pick you up in the morning at 0800. And, by the way, everything is paid for, so don't be shy.'

Bungy goes to leave, but remembers something and turns back to Terry, grinning slyly.

'Mate, there is a very high incidence of VD in these parts, so make sure you wear protection. Otherwise you'll be up for a very painful course of medication to fix you up. See Hong if you haven't got any rubbers. See ya.'

With that, he departs, leaving Terry with Hong.

Terry greets Hong politely, shaking her hand gently. He calls her Rose, which she seems to like. Rose escorts him upstairs and shows him to his room. It is fairly basic: an old double bed, a wardrobe, a wash basin and a mirror on the wall. But it is clean and it has a small balcony that overlooks the street. Terry can imagine sitting on the balcony, sipping a cold beer, taking in the sights, sounds and aromas of the local area. He is happy.

Rose shows him where the ablutions are. Again, they are basic but clean. In the hallway outside, several girls gather, giggling and chattering away in high-pitched voices. They sound like canaries.

Smiling, Rose asks him, 'Which girl you like?'.

Terry considers, and then points to the smallest one. She seems to be no more than sixteen, with beautiful long straight hair that falls to her waist. She has a pretty, pixie face and a slim but shapely body. She smiles shyly when he selects her and takes Terry's hand as they walk back to his room. Terry is salivating in anticipation.

*****

Terry loves the streets of Saigon: the incessant hustle and bustle of hordes of locals and people of all nationalities going about their business; the exotic sights and sounds of the red-light district after dark. He is invisible amongst the scores of westerners who congregate in bars and eating houses, sampling the delights of the mix of French-Indochinese food. Everyone converses intently to each other, heads close together, plotting, scheming, for who knows what purpose. There is a constant air of mystery and intrigue and danger. Terry discovers pho soup and loves the salty taste of the broth as well as the fresh rice noodles. And it isn't too filling, he realises after consuming a large bowl.

Chapter 29

His work with Bungy takes up only about half of each day, so he is mostly free to wander around Saigon in civvies. Bungy has arranged for Terry's army pay to be forwarded to the office, but this fortnightly pittance is nicely supplemented by crisp new US currency that Bungy supplies each week. Bungy says it is to cover expenses. As a result Terry has plenty of cash to indulge himself. He employs a cyclo rickshaw driver from one of the scores that hang around on the corner of his street. The guy cannot speak English but this doesn't matter. Although small in stature, he can keep going for hours, and Terry lounges in the front seat whilst the driver peddles furiously behind him. Terry pays him peanuts, but the driver seems to be happy with the amount.

In his travels Terry passes the massive US Embassy, with remnants of shell damage from the Tet offensive. He is impressed with the headquarters of Shell Oil, across the street from the embassy. The building has magnificent Corinthian columns at its entrance.

Terry enjoys the marketplaces, where everything imaginable is traded. He becomes used to bartering, and takes pleasure in haggling with the local traders. He is amused by the antics of the Vietnamese police—the White Mice—as they determinedly shake down the locals. *Everyone's on the take here*, he reflects.

On the same street is the presidential palace, which houses the current South Vietnamese president, Nguyen Van Thieu, reportedly as corrupt as his predecessors. Security is tight around both this building and the US Embassy.

Saigon is also chock full of Buddhist temples. Xa Loi Pagoda—known as the Temple of the Buddha's Relic—is one of the biggest. It is not far from the central market and Terry, who is not in the least bit interested in religion of any kind, cannot understand why such large crowds of locals flock there. *Typical peasants*, Terry thinks dismissively, *forever believing that the big statue of that fat smiling guy with the funny ears will keep them safe. Those Buddhists are as crazy as those nutters who worship in churches back home. Didn't some mad monk set himself on fire somewhere around here a while back? What was his game? Protesting about the Catholics in the South Vietnamese Government giving the Buddhists a hard time? What a lot of crap.*

On Tu Do Street, right near where Terry lives, stands the popular Caravelle Hotel, a squat multi-story building designed by French and Vietnamese architects. Although it is a popular drinking hole and place to stay for westerners, it is also home to the Australian and Kiwi Embassies, as well as several US media outlets. Terry likes to have a drink or three at the rooftop open-air bar, which has a great view over the city. Everyone who is anyone drinks there, and he and Bungy occasionally meet at the bar to discuss business.

Terry has tried the rooftop bar at the Rex Hotel, also in District 1, but he doesn't like the media scrum that descends each afternoon to listen to what they call the 'five o'clock follies'—the presentation of misleading and inaccurate drivel on the progress of the war invented by the US Public Affairs Office. Terry isn't interested in the bullshit, he just wants a quiet place to drink. He prefers the Caravelle bar.

Tu Do Street and its surrounds teem with action—not just after dark, but all day. Terry has seen the most beautiful girls parading this area, on the lookout for a mark. Saigon, the town on the make.

Terry's main role is to act as the go-between for Bungy and the guys who arrive regularly in light aircraft. The size of the parcels averages around ten kilos. Terry asks Bungy exactly how he goes about getting this freight back home. Bungy doesn't seem to understand the question.

'No, I don't mean whether it's an aircraft or a ship,' Terry clarifies. 'How do you know which one to use, and when?'

'Terry, there are some things I'm just not prepared to tell you. It's not because I don't trust you—far from it; you are in this as deep as I am, so I don't think you're likely to sign your own death warrant—but it comes down to the need-to-know principle. If you don't know, you can't tell.'

Seeing the crestfallen expression on Terry's face, Bungy throws him a bone. 'Mate, how about you take a trip down to Vung Tau in early July. It's a great spot for a bit of R and R, not that you're exactly overworked. There are a few guys down there you should meet. Mind you, a couple of them are White Mice, so you need to be a bit careful around them, but there is a Yank there who runs a bar called the G Spot. He's ex-US Army and he's part of the business. He sells a lot of shit to GIs on R and R. His name is Walter. Walter Kowalski.'

*****

Concerned with Terry's treatment of her girls, Rose asks him not to damage them too much, as it is bad for business. If they are hurt, they cannot work as much and thus earn as much. Terry has developed a taste for rough sex, and whilst some of the girls play along, others don't. Regardless, it all adds to Terry's depraved enjoyment.

Arrogantly, Terry ignores Rose. Frustrated, she decides to complain to Bungy and he turns up unannounced soon after and hauls Terry over the coals.

'For fuck's sake, Terry, you're on a bloody good wicket here. I'm not averse to a bit of slap and tickle myself, but you're going too far. Tone it down. The last thing either of us wants is to draw unwanted attention to ourselves.'

Terry apologises, and promises not to do it again. But he is angry that Rose has ratted on him. *I'll fix her at some stage*, he promises.

Bungy is not convinced by Terry's apology. *He can be a bit of a loose cannon unless he's kept in line*, Bungy thinks. He makes a mental note to keep a closer watch on Terry's extracurricular activities in future.

*****

Chapter 30

Jack's platoon is given three days' short leave in Vung Tau. The army calls it Rest and Convalescence, R and C. Jack is very happy and he shares this with his mates.

'We're gunna have a shitcan full of fun while our money lasts, boys. I hear that there are more bars in the place than you can poke a stick at.'

'And there's miles and miles of pussy,' Andy adds. 'I haven't seen a beautiful woman in I forget how long. Bluey, even you with your ugly moosh is gunna get lucky. Oh man, we're gunna party.'

Mal, ever the practical one, chips in, 'I reckon we should drink that Tiger beer. It tastes like it's been strained through Jack's jock-strap, but it's the cheapest. That will help to make our hard-earned dollars go further'.

Jack turns to H, who has been silent up till now.

'H, do you know any good spots to get up to a bit of no good?'

H grins slowly. 'Boys, I know them all.'

Before they leave the Dat that morning they get a lecture on the evils of venereal disease. They are shown horrible pictures of guys who have caught syphilis or gonorrhoea and who have left it untreated. This deters them, but only momentarily. Andy puts it into perspective.

'That's what French letters have been invented for.'

They all take large handfuls from the padre who is present at the lecture. He shakes his head sadly.

The Vung Tau military base occupies a huge expanse of land. This place is one big sand dune. It includes a hospital and an air base, but for the four diggers, importantly, it contains around one hundred bars, as well as a couple of beaches. One even has surf lifesaving patrols, manned by volunteers, usually soldiers from the Second Australian Army Ordnance Depot who are based there. They belong to the Phuoc Tuy surf club. The accommodation for the diggers is basic, but they don't care, they're not here to sleep.

Australian and US troops line the streets and festoon the bars and whorehouses. H takes the guys to one of the better-known places, the Blue Angel, but there are no angels here, only a lot of sinners. Almost before Andy can down his first beer, a girl grabs his hand and implores him to go off with her.

'You numba wun boom boom,' she says in comical English. 'You wanna fuckie?' Andy needs no second bidding.

Jack and the others resist for several beers before succumbing to the charms of the girls. Jack has made up his mind that he is here to have fun. He has lost any vestige of longing for the past to change, and Susie is now firmly out of the equation.

'What you name, soldier,' a pretty girl with huge eyes asks him.

'I'm Jack. What's your name?'

She smiles. 'Who you want me to be? Wife? Girlfriend? What name you like?'

Jack is persistent. 'Just tell me *your* name, and I'll buy you some Saigon Tea and we'll discuss how much.'

'Me name My. It mean pretty.'

'Yes, you are, My. Let's have a drink, eh?'

*****

During the next twelve hours, the four mates shag and drink themselves to a standstill. Wearily, they gather on the beach for a dip and to lie on the beach and snatch a few hours' sleep. Then they shave, shower, grab some food and do it all over again.

On the afternoon of the second day the group hits the beach to recover from another big night out. They have a quick swim to cool themselves off and to let the warm salty water seep into their alcohol-soaked pores. Then they lay back on the beach and talk a lot of shit to each other, then doze, then chat some more.

Jack decides to have another swim. As he nears the water he notices a young Caucasian woman with blonde hair, wearing a brief bikini, lying on an inflatable air mattress about twenty metres from the shore. The wind is blowing the air mattress slowly but steadily out to sea. The girl must have sensed this because she suddenly sits up and tries to paddle back towards the beach. In her haste she upsets the air mattress and overbalances into the water.

Immediately Jack can see, by the way she is struggling, that she is a poor swimmer. He dives into the warm water and is next to her in a few powerful strokes. Although she is in no real danger, the water is over her head and she is beginning to panic.

'Hey, lady, calm down, you're okay. Just grab the handle and I'll give you a tow back in.'

The girl stops thrashing about and Jack pushes her back onto the air mattress, getting an eyeful of a shapely bottom as he does so. The girl clings on as Jack side-strokes into shallow water, pulling her along behind.

As she climbs shakily to her feet, Jack looks her over. About five feet six inches tall, attractive, short hair, maybe in her early twenties. He takes the initiative, lying slightly to build his case.

'Jeez, I haven't seen a white woman for six months, and no-one as pretty as you for years. You need to be a bit careful on those things. They aren't designed to go surfing on. My name's Jack, what's yours?'

The girl pauses to catch her breath, and responds. 'I'm Jenna, and thanks for helping me.'

'My pleasure, Jenna.' Jack decides that a bit of flattery won't go astray. 'Now that's a beautiful name.'

Holding the surf mat defensively in front of her with one hand and combing her short hair with the fingers of her other hand, Jenna replies seriously: 'Yes, it means fair-haired in Welsh. My ancestors come from there'.

Jack notices, for the first time, that she has brown eyes.

'Well, Jenna, what say we go and get a cold drink? All this exercise has made me thirsty.'

Jenna's smile lights up her face, and Jack is entranced by her, but she then dashes his hopes.

'Sorry, Jack, but my fiancé wouldn't like that too much. Nice pick-up line though—as good as I've heard for a while. No offence, but you're about the tenth guy today that has tried to chat me up.'

Jack smiles back. 'Okay, Jenna, I give up. But can I ask you a question?'

'I suppose you are entitled to one question, seeing how you just saved my bacon. What do you want to know?'

'What are you doing here?'

As he speaks to her, he registers that her skin has a lovely brown glow. He suddenly has an irrational urge to touch it. Jenna seems unaffected by his gaze.

'I'm a nursing sister attached to the Australian Air Force Nursing Corps. I'm based at the hospital. I've been here six months, and I've got another six months to go before I go back to Sydney and get married.'

'Oh,' says Jack, deflated by this news. 'They keep you busy at that hospital?'

'Very. And speaking of which, I've got to get back and clean up.

I'm on duty in an hour.' Jenna turns to go, and gives him one of those smiles again. 'Good luck, Jack. Stay safe.'

As she walks off, Jenna thinks that Jack is a nice young man, and attractive—even with an obvious hangover. *Stop that*, she scolds herself. *Phillip is waiting for you back home. Don't get distracted. Think of the wonderful time you'll be having in six months.*

But there is a tiny seed of disquiet in her mind. Phillip's letters haven't been as frequent in the last month or so, and they seem more formal, less light and breezy than they have been. *Maybe he's just too busy. After all, he is in the final stages of his medical internship. He's probably just working his cute little bum off.*

Back at the hospital, Jenna prepares to go on shift. The 1st Australian Field Hospital has expanded to over one hundred beds, and it is well equipped with an intensive care ward and facilities for triage, surgery, X-ray, pathology, dentistry, physiotherapy and psychiatry. It even has a dedicated VD ward. Jenna is currently working in the triage section, where the injuries are prioritised and treatment provided accordingly.

It is exhausting although rewarding work, but the nurses that go to Vietnam are woefully underprepared for what they will face. There is no training beforehand and no-one tells them what to expect. For Jenna, the first month was a nightmare until she became used to the system. And the injuries sustained by the troops during the Tet offensive have tested the resources of the medical staff. Still, miracles are performed daily, and new and radical surgical techniques are developed as the blowtorch of war is applied to the medics in Vung Tau.

Dressed and ready to go, Jack is already forgotten as she walks into the triage area.

*****

Jack walks back up the beach to the cheers and jeers of his mates.

Andy yells out: 'Do any good, Jack?'

Smiling, Jack shakes his head. 'No, mate, she's taken. Some lucky son of a gun back in Oz is marrying her at the end of the year.'

As his mates commiserate with Jack, H spies an impromptu game of beach volleyball being played between Aussie and US soldiers further up the beach. The group trudges through the sand to watch and to barrack for the Aussie team. It is obvious that there isn't a lot of skill on display, save for one big black guy who moves with athletic grace. He has to be at least six feet three inches tall, with ropey muscles and black tight curly hair.

The game is over but Andy, whose hearing has been slightly damaged by the noise of a mortar round landing near him in the recent firefight, speaks loudly and tactlessly. 'Shit, the black guy moves like a chicken strangler, but he's a bit big for that.'

The black guy hears him and walks towards them. He speaks softly but menacingly.

'What did y'all call me?' This is spoken in an accent unmistakably from the Deep South.

'Easy, mate,' Jack replies, 'my friend here is actually paying you a compliment. We Aussies call members of the SAS—they're the Australian equivalent of your Special Forces—chicken stranglers. My mate thinks you are that good'.

The American's attitude changes instantly, and the menacing expression is replaced by a guileless smile. *It's almost as if this guy has drawn a veil over his face*, Jack thinks.

'Hey man, the only chicken I know is good ol' fried chicken that my dear mammy makes. Hell, I ain't no Special Forces. I'm in the 388th Transportation Company. We're based here in Vung Tau. I'm just a support guy. My name's Eugene Trumper. Most folks call me Gene.'

Jack puts out his hand to shake.

'My name's Jack, and the loud-mouthed guy is Andy. The others are H, Bluey and Mal.'

'Pleased to meet y'all,' replies Gene, shaking hands with the four Aussies. 'Say, Jack, didn't I just see you in the water with a darn pretty girl? She your girlfriend?'

Laughing, Jack explains what has transpired. *This guy doesn't miss too much*, Jack notes.

Gene frowns briefly. 'Pity, Jack, she is a real looker. A bit skinny for my taste, though. Not like my gal Rita back home in Georgia. She's got curves on her curves. Say, you guys want to see a picture of her?'

Gene pulls out his wallet and extracts a black-and-white photo of Rita posing in a bikini. He is right; she has a voluptuous figure and is very attractive. Her dark skin glows in the sunlight. She is leaning forward suggestively, her generously sized breasts pushed out.

'Wow, Gene, she's hot,' Andy says in admiration.

'Yeah, she's a real hot tamale is my girl Rita.' Gene is serious for a moment. 'But she's got brains as well as beauty. Rita's working at a drugstore so that she can save enough money to study law. I said to her "Rita, that's a great idea, honey. Then you might be able to keep my black ass out of jail someday". That Rita, she just laughed.' Gene addresses the diggers. 'Y'all got girlfriends?'

The four shake their heads and stand there, envious of Gene. Jack breaks the silence. 'Tell you what, Gene, by way of apology for his big mouth, Andy here is going to buy you a drink. It must be beer o'clock by now. How about it?'

Gene agrees and the new friends move off the beach. Gene suggests that they go to a nearby bar called the G Spot because he knows the beer there is not watered down like in some places. As they walk, Jack is again struck by an odd feeling that there is something not quite right about Gene, but he can't put his finger on it.

After several beers, the talk turns to the differences between the USA and Australia.

'Hey guys, I hear y'all got so many kangaroos in your country that they just go hoppin' down the main street of town.'

H replies. 'Well, Gene, I'll let you in on a little secret. 1RAR, that's our battalion, has a kangaroo mascot, and he is kept in our base in Nui Dat. Everyone has to take turns to feed him, even the CO.'

'That true?' demands Gene, wide-eyed. The burst of laughter from the Aussies tells him that they are taking the piss. 'You guys,' says Gene, 'you're such jokers. Say, you got any black people in Australia?'.

'Yep, Gene,' Andy replies, 'There're called Aborigines. And believe it or not, Bluey here is part Aboriginal. Can't you tell, from his red hair?'.

Gene stares at Bluey in disbelief. 'You joshin' with me again? This guy ain't black. He can't be.'

Bluey replies seriously. 'It's true, Gene. There have been a lot of interracial marriages in Australia, and I'm the product of one. My grandmother is black and my grandfather is white. But he has, or had, red hair and freckles, which I've inherited.'

'Fuck me sideways,' exclaims Gene. 'That happened in the States, especially where I come from, there'd be a lynchin' party goin' on. Say,' a thought strikes Gene, 'that Lionel Rose dude who won the boxing title against that Japanese guy a few months ago, he any relation to you, Bluey?'.

'No,' Bluey laughs. 'That'd be the same as asking you if you're related to Martin Luther King.'

Quick as a flash Gene comes back at him. 'How do you know I ain't?' Seeing the expressions on their faces, he laughs. 'Of course I ain't, you crazy Aussies. Come on, drink up, it's my round. What you call it—shout? Well, I'll shout. Bartender, bring us some more beers, quick, these boys are real thirsty,' Gene commands in a loud voice.

The drinking session continues, the group having a good time. Jack watches Gene surreptitiously. *He's scoping this place out*, Jack realises, as he notices Gene casually glancing around several times. Jack wonders what he's really up to. Is he casing this joint?

But Jack is none the wiser when the group finally separates and the Aussies and the Yank go their separate ways. The diggers need to get some sleep; they return to Nui Dat tomorrow. Back to the war. They are determined not to think about it.

As he walks to his quarters, Gene reflects on his meeting with the Aussies. *They seem to be nice guys*, he thinks, *and they fight this goddamned war differently to us Yankees. They know better than to blunder around the place making a lot of noise, giving the VC plenty of warning. The Aussie troops also stay off trails, and love to ambush Charlie, something that Charlie isn't used to. And those SAS guys, they're almost as good as the good ol' Delta boys.* He has seen Jack eyeing him curiously, but Gene is confident that his cover has held up. Jack's suspicions are correct, there is a lot more to Gene than meets the eye.

*****

The next morning Jack sits next to H in the back of the truck that is transporting them back to Nui Dat. Jack quietly asks a question.

'You ever think about what we are doing in this country, H? I mean, the locals don't seem to want us around, do they? And we don't seem to be too successful in getting rid of the VC.'

H sighs and responds in a low voice.

'Jack, I try not to think about it, cos I know it will do my head in. I know you're better educated than me, but believe me, stop thinking about it if you can, otherwise you're not gunna be concentrating like you need to. And that can kill you.'

*****

Chapter 31

Soon after arriving in Vung Tau, Terry walks into the G Spot bar. The place is crowded, not usual for early evening. He is dressed in his cams so that he may blend in, but most guys are wearing shorts and sandals and are shirtless. *This is a pretty casual place*, he thinks.

He moves to the bar and tells a Vietnamese guy serving that he wants to speak to Walter Kowalski. The bar tender says nothing, but goes into a back room. After a minute or so, a white guy comes out. Big across the shoulders, the guy appears to be in his early forties, and is slightly overweight, although his height allows him to carry it well enough.

'Yeah, who are you?' the guy asks with a distinctly Brooklyn accent. He stares at Terry suspiciously.

'My name's Terry and I'm an associate of Bungy Williams. He said to come down here and meet up with you.'

'Describe this Bungy guy for me,' Walter asks cautiously.

'Short, fat, and ugly. And he loves smoking fucking awful-smelling cigars.'

Walter smiles for the first time. 'I'd say that's a pretty good description of Bungy.' He lowers his voice. 'You can come to a meeting in a couple of hours with some other guys. Have a few beers and some food while you're waiting. I'll give you the nod when it's time.'

Neither Walter nor Terry notice the big black guy sitting quietly nearby, nursing a beer. Gene Trumper's face reveals nothing. He finishes his beer and ambles nonchalantly out into the evening. Once outside, Gene positions himself in the shadows where he can watch the front and rear exits of the bar. He waits patiently for the pair to appear.

Terry and Walter emerge an hour or so later and head for the wharf area. Gene shadows them, as silent as a ghost, and easily counters their amateurish attempts to evade a tail. The pair enters a warehouse near the docks. It appears deserted, but then Gene notices a light come on inside. He creeps up alongside the building, searching for a window. There is one on the side, and he carefully sidles up to it. He crouches and peers inside. The two white guys are talking with two Vietnamese guys dressed in police uniforms. He recognises the two White Mice. Gene knows they have some connections to drug dealing here in Vung Tau, but to date he has not connected them to the guy who runs the G Spot. *And who is the other dude?* Gene wonders. *He sounded Aussie when I heard him speak in the bar. What's his story?*

Gene cannot pick up what they are saying, as the window is closed. All he can hear is the murmur of voices. As he straightens further in an attempt to hear better, his foot brushes a piece of tin, which falls to the ground. The noise is not loud, but it is enough for the four inside to stop talking, their heads swinging towards the direction of the sound.

Quickly Gene drops to all fours, and hastily scrabbles away into the shadows. He pulls a can of beer out of his pocket, and dowses himself liberally with the fluid, then sprawls untidily on the ground.

Chapter 31

The four rush outside the warehouse to check out the noise. They are confronted with a seemingly exceedingly drunk black guy singing to himself, trying to sip on a can of beer.

Walter bends over to examine him, but quickly recoils from the strong smell of alcohol. The black guy smiles at him with a vacant gaze, and offers him a drink, hand shaking. Disgusted, Walter turns to the other three dismissively.

'It's okay. It's just some useless drunk nigger. He's so out of it he probably doesn't even remember his name. I've seen him before, and he's usually sauced to the back teeth. He's harmless.'

None of them see Gene's eyes momentarily narrow in anger at the derogatory description of him. He quickly allows his eyes to glaze over again.

'Come on, let's go,' suggests Terry. 'Our business is finished anyway. It's time for a drink, Walter.'

The four split into two groups, the Caucasians heading back to the bar. Gene is left lying there, but not for long. He athletically regains his feet and heads off in a different direction. It won't be good to be seen by them again tonight. He has some thinking to do about this latest development.

*****

Chapter 32

Back in Nui Dat, Jack settles into the normal same old, same old, routine. 1RAR are told by Colonel Bennett that their role has reverted to concentrating on their local province. This is part of a move by the high command towards a policy of Vietnamisation. This means that the South Vietnamese Army will be gradually given more and more authority and command over the war effort, but before this can happen locally, Phuoc Tuy Province must be cleared of VC. Intelligence has Charlie hiding out in thick jungle in a hilly area in the west of the province. The area is known as the Hat Dich.

Jack's platoon patrols regularly out of the Dat and only twice encounters the VC, but the contacts are fleeting, and Charlie disappears before a proper engagement can occur. This is frustrating to the troops, who are growing increasingly tired of chasing shadows.

Jack spends a lot of time at the range, practising with his rifle. His skill level develops to the point where he can regularly hit the centre of the bull's eye at a distance of three hundred metres. He learns to control his breathing and relax his body until the rifle sights are steady. Jack earns the praise of the sergeant who runs the range.

This gets back to H, who also praises Jack. Jack in turn is pleased and more than a little proud. To be praised by someone of H's status is heady stuff indeed. Never mind that soldering won't be Jack's career; it is the here and now that is important to him.

Jack and the rest of the brick enjoy the occasional short leave in Vung Tau, but even that doesn't help much to break the boredom of routine. Jack does not encounter Gene or Jenna during these leave breaks, and time passes slowly for him and the others with little happening in the way of action to break the tedium. It's weird—when he's in the thick of the action he's so wired with the adrenalin pumping that all he wants to do is get it over and done with, but when the stand-down periods get too long, all he wants to do is to get back into hunting Charlie. Perhaps he has become addicted to the adrenaline rush. He shares these feelings with his mates, and is not surprised to find they agree with him.

There is something else they agree on—they are all heartily sick and tired of Vietnam as the months pass without being exposed to any further danger. Jack constantly asks himself what the fuck he is doing here. What is the army doing to win this bloody war so they all can go home? But the answer is not apparent.

In his more positive moments, Jack writes long letters to his parents, trying to convey the conditions here but downplaying anything that might cause them to worry unnecessarily. Jack finds himself writing a letter of apology to them, saying that he is sorry to have caused them such heartache and that his actions were immature and unthinking. He asks for their forgiveness. Their enthusiastic reply makes him happy.

In one letter he outlines his plan to go back to university when his Nasho stint is finished, although he is unsure whether it will be in Newcastle or somewhere else. Jack declares he wants a fresh start, so Newcastle may not be the best option. The response to this from his parents indicates sadness, but they seem to understand. Henry writes in a pleased tone that Jack seems to be back on track in his life.

Jack has an unusual request of them. Can they find any books that cover a newly emerging computing language called BASIC? He has heard from some guy that this is going to be all the rage, and he wants to learn a bit about it. Henry volunteers for the task. After some searching, which culminates in a visit to the Newcastle University bookshop, Henry is finally successful. Several weeks later Jack receives a parcel from home. Inside it is a thick text on BASIC programming. He is over the moon, and immediately begins to devour its contents.

Even though the army censors do their best to limit any material that criticises the war from reaching the troops, this doesn't always work. Jack and his brick members read Australian newspapers that have been smuggled in via resupply missions. Several stories report on the high level of casualties inflicted on the allied forces during the Tet offensive, which comes as a shock to Jack. The press have taken the opportunity to criticise the way the war is being fought, deriding the claim by the authorities that the war is being won. Several newspaper editorials are openly anti-war in their sentiment.

For Jack, this is unsettling, and adds to his sense of unease and discontent. Here they are in Vietnam, fighting a war that seems to be growing very unpopular back home. What is the point of it all?

*****

Back in Saigon, Terry recounts to Bungy the circumstances of his Vung Tau visit. Bungy is suspicious of the encounter with the American soldier. Despite Terry's assurances that Walter said there was nothing to it, he is a bit worried and his voice betrays this.

'Mate, I have it on good authority that the powers that be are on the trail of the drug shipments, even though certain faceless men with influence are working hard to throw these investigations off the scent. There is growing pressure from the do-gooders to rein in the drug trade, and the MPs and other civilian law enforcement agencies are starting to act. Sooner or later the shit is going to hit the fan, so we'd better be careful, eh?'

Bungy intends to have an umbrella ready if this happens. He doesn't let on to Terry, but he has a plan B and a plan C set up—just in case. Terry will have to look out for himself. Bungy has no compunction about leaving Terry to be the bunny if things go pear-shaped. With Bungy's connections in this shithole of a country, it has not been too hard to obtain false papers, including a passport. He will be gone the moment anything happens that might implicate him.

In any event, Bungy has plotted further ahead than his time here. He may not be God's gift to womankind, but he is no mug. He has no interest in being posted to a dead-end job in an army base near some one-horse town, as is likely. When he gets home, he intends to quietly resign from the army. He has already had words with the guys back in Sydney. His logistical knowledge and expertise will be of great value to them as the drug distribution network grows larger and more complex.

As long as he is careful and minimises the risks, he is confident that he'll be okay. Terry can figure things out for himself.

*****

Chapter 33

In December 1968 Lieutenant Colonel Bennett briefs the assembled 1RAR troops on the latest intelligence concerning higher levels of VC troop movements in the Hat Dich area. 1RAR is to be committed to the area as part of a large allied force to locate and destroy VC and any North Vietnamese Army forces they encounter. They will be supported by tanks, armoured patrol vehicles and artillery. Two other Australian Army Regiments, 4RAR/NZ—an ANZAC force—and 9RAR, will join them later, along with SAS patrols. This is a big operation, and Bennett tells his troops that they should be proud that 1RAR has been chosen as the vanguard of the Australian forces. Not many of the soldiers share his enthusiasm.

In early December Jack, along with the rest of the recon platoon, is airlifted by a US Army Chinook CH-47 helicopter to a sector codenamed Dyke. Jack can't work out whether it is named after a dam or a lesbian. Not that it matters.

The platoon is fully laden with equipment, ready to fight. Jack, like many others, is nervous and excited. He is glad that the humdrum routine has changed, but he is edgy about going into a known enemy stronghold. Still, 1RAR will have all manner of firepower with them, and that made a big difference at Coral and Balmoral.

Jack peers out of one of the windows in the large ungainly helo as it transits north. *It's a way different view from up here*, he reflects. He can see for kilometres, rather than a few hundred metres, at best, on the ground. He thinks he'd rather be up here than down there. At least he can see what's shooting at him. He studies the interior of the helo. It is huge, with space to carry a large load of equipment or troops, or both. The cabin is about fifteen metres long and ends in a ramp at the rear, which currently is in the closed position. Jack is told by one of the diggers onboard that the Chinook's nickname is Hook, and the pilots are called Hookers. He smiles at the thought.

As Dyke is only about twenty kilometres north-west of Nui Dat, the troops are on the ground and have secured the perimeter before midday. Alpha, Bravo, Charlie and Delta Companies then commence a recon mission to seek out the enemy. But they find nothing apart from some freshly killed game, probably by the VC.

Charlie Company engages with the VC during the following days, but once again the enemy disappears. The troops fret that this will be another busted flush.

H tells Jack and the others in the brick that Colonel Bennett has ordered them to move to another area, ironically called Diggers' Rest, a few kilometres north of Dyke. Once there, Jack's brick and the rest of Delta Company continue to patrol in search of the elusive VC. Proceeding cautiously through the thick scrub, they find a number of abandoned bunkers, but no enemy. Jack is not the only one wondering where the hell Charlie is.

Major Hammett orders his troops to establish an ambush site near a narrow trail. The soldiers dig in. Jack is scrutinising the foliage around him, trying to see any sign of the VC, when shots ring out nearby. Before they can react to this, a fusillade of bullets hits their position. There is the distinctive sound of AK-47s firing at them. Jack and his mates duck and then return fire, but they can see jack shit in front of them.

Suddenly Jack sees a VC stand in front of him and aim a rocket-propelled grenade at the trench he is in. Jack instantly fires, and his round strikes the enemy soldier in the chest, but the VC has fired off the grenade round as he is hit and it streaks towards them. Jack and the others duck as the high explosive warhead misses the trench and instead hits a tree behind them, exploding in a shattering roar. Immediately Jack feels a savage burning sensation in his back as he is struck by white-hot shrapnel. In pain, he slumps forward in shock and disbelief.

'Oh shit, I'm hit,' he cries. H is immediately by his side, screaming at the others to continue firing in the direction the grenade shell came from. H kneels beside him and puts down his rifle.

'Easy, mate, let's have a look.' H gently examines Jack's back. 'Soldier, you are one lucky son of a bitch. Your pack has absorbed most of the impact. I'll just take the bloody thing off. It's cactus anyway. No, not you, the bloody pack.'

Jack laughs despite the pain, and winces as H gingerly removes the pack.

'Yep, although there's plenty of claret flowing, I reckon you're gunna be okay. I don't want to examine you too closely in case I hurt you more, so I'll just press on where the worst of the blood is coming out. Andy, let the platoon commander know and call for the medic, will you? And, all of you, keep your bloody heads down.'

Jack cannot be moved until the platoon commander is reasonably sure that the VC has gone. This takes about fifteen minutes. Jack can feel the blood trickling down his back, but H says that the flow seems to be slowing as he keeps the pressure on the largest of the wounds. His back is hurting a lot now, and Jack bites his lip to keep from crying out.

Chapter 33

Finally they get the all clear and H and Bluey half carry, half drag Jack out of the shallow foxhole. Then H grabs his shoulders, Bluey his legs, and they carry him, face down, out of the thick undergrowth to where a dustoff helicopter is waiting in a small clearing, its blades whirling. Jack is carefully lifted, still face down, into the helo. H and Bluey then back away and wait for the helo to take off.

Onboard the chopper, a medic gives Jack morphine for the pain, even though he has not made a sound after being wounded. He remains conscious as the helo immediately lifts off. It rapidly ascends, then turns and heads for the 1st Army Field Hospital in Vung Tau.

H watches the helo disappear, then turns back to the remains of the brick, who have followed on behind.

'Come on, guys, we're got some VC to hunt. Jack will be okay. He'll be back with us before you know it.'

They turn and disappear into the bush, forcing Jack out of their minds.

It is two weeks before Christmas.

*****

The dustoff lands on the pad near the hospital amongst a cloud of dirt and sand. Strong hands grab Jack and place him on a stretcher. The morphine kicks in, and the pain recedes somewhat. A delicious lassitude creeps over him. He is dimly aware as the medical orderlies carry the stretcher into the hospital and then place him on a gurney.

Expert hands gently cut his clothing from his back. The triage nurse examines him quickly, noting the multiple wounds. She wipes the blood away in an effort to see the extent of his injuries. Most of the wounds are small, but she has no idea how far the shrapnel has penetrated. She checks his vital signs: blood pressure elevated; pupils dilated—probably because of the morphine—pulse fast but not racing. She makes a judgement call.

'This one needs surgery, but I don't think his injuries are life threatening.'

She places a temporary dressing over the area and quickly inserts an IV drip into his arm. Jack is largely oblivious to this. He feels disconnected from his body, as if he is floating.

Thirty minutes later Jack is wheeled into the operating room. Someone places an oxygen mask over his face. His IV line is used to inject a knockout drug and Jack is quickly unconscious. The surgeon probes the wounds, extracting half a dozen grenade fragments from his back. They are not deeply embedded, so he is on the operating table for only a short period. Jack is stitched up and the procedure finished. The surgeon moves on to the next operation.

Jack hears voices in his dreams. They seem to be calling his name, over and over. What sort of dream is this? Irritated by this noise, he slowly opens his eyes. A pretty female face stares at him. She knows his name. How?

The nurse says kindly, 'Welcome back, soldier. You're in Recovery. You've just been operated on. Are you able to speak?'.

Jack manages a few garbled words as he slowly becomes more alert. He becomes aware that the nurse is bending down and that he is lying on his stomach. There is pain in his back, but it is dull, muted.

The nurse asks him if he would like a drink. Jack realises he is parched and nods his head. She feeds him some cool liquid through a straw, then says: 'You just rest up, now. You have to stay here for a while so that we can check that you're recovering okay'.

Jack asks haltingly, 'Wha … what happened? Where am I?' Then he remembers the explosion and the pain in his back, but nothing after that.

'You've been wounded. You're in the army hospital at Vung Tau.'

'Am I gunna be okay?'

'I'm sure you will be, but the doctor will tell you all about it when he sees you. You just relax and enjoy the view.'

What view? Jack thinks. *I can't see much at all, stuck upside down.* But he puts his head down on the pillow and closes his eyes.

Sometime later he hears an authoritarian voice. Awkwardly, he cranes his neck and sees a guy dressed in a green surgical gown heading his way. He is accompanied by the nurse that he spoke to earlier. Jack presumes he is the doctor.

'Ah, Private Martin. How do you feel?'

'Uh, okay, Doc, sort of. A bit of pain, but not too bad. What's the verdict on my back?'

'You are a very lucky individual. You were hit by fragments of an exploding RPG shell, but they don't seem to have penetrated too far. You've got nothing vital damaged, but it's going to take a while for the wounds to heal.'

'How long, Doc?'

'Oh, a couple of weeks I should think. With a bit of luck, you'll be out of here for Christmas. Well, I've got to see other patients. I'll see you on my rounds later. Nurse, he can go into the general ward now. Make sure he gets pain relief as required.'

The doctor leaves Jack's bed and moves on.

Soon after Jack is wheeled out of Recovery, down a long corridor, and finds himself in a ward with a large number of other wounded soldiers. He is lifted gently onto a bed. He is asleep quickly.

*****

Jack wakes up, moans and slowly moves his head around. The ward is quiet and dark, with only subdued lighting coming from what appears to be the nurses' station. A flashlight beam moves towards him as a nurse gets up to investigate the noise. Whispering, she asks him if he is okay.

'Hurts … thirsty,' he gasps.

The nurse goes away but soon returns with some fluid that Jack drinks thirstily. Whilst he is slurping the liquid she does something to his IV line. Jack feels a cool sensation pass through him and the pain ebbs away slowly. He closes his eyes and is out again, not feeling the nurse as she checks his blood pressure and pulse. After noting these on his chart, she quietly moves away.

*****

In Australia Jack's parents are surprised and dismayed to receive an urgent telegram addressed to them. Henry tears it open, his heart in his mouth. He reads from it aloud to his wife in a quavering voice.

> *IT IS WITH REGRET YOU ARE INFORMED THAT YOUR SON 25790341 PRIVATE JOHN HENRY MARTIN SUSTAINED MULTIPLE FRAGMENT WOUNDS TO THE BACK ON 13 DECEMBER 1968 IN PHUOC TUY PROVINCE VIETNAM AND WAS ADMITTED TO 1 AUSTRALIAN FIELD HOSPITAL VUNG TAU VIETNAM. IF HIS CONDITION WHICH IS SATISFACTORY CHANGES ANOTHER PROGRESS REPORT WILL BE FORWARDED TO YOU.*
>
> *ARMY HEADQUARTERS*

Gladys collapses to the floor in shock, sobbing. Henry stands by numbly, trying to digest this news. After a while he helps Gladys to her feet and hugs her, thinking, with some degree of relief, that at least Jack is alive.

*****

The next time Jack opens his eyes, daylight is streaming through the windows. There is a deal of background noise as the healthier patients chatter to each other. With difficulty, Jack moves his head to one side.

A voice speaks close to him. 'G'day, mate, how are ya?' It is a soldier in a pair of pyjama pants sitting on the next bed, with his arm bandaged from wrist to shoulder.

'I … I'm a bit bloody sore,' Jack replies.

'I'm not surprised, mate. You should see your back. You look as if someone has used you for a pin cushion. You've got holes everywhere. My name's Duchy, Duchy de Ward, Charlie Company, 1RAR, by the way. You from 1RAR?'

'I'm Jack Martin, Delta Company. And you don't exactly look fighting fit yourself.'

Duchy laughs. 'Mortar fragments almost took my arm off, but the quacks here worked a miracle. I'm told I might lose some movement in the arm, but at least it's still attached. What about you?'

'RPG round exploded behind me. At least I didn't get shot in the ass.'

Duchy and Jack exchange friendly banter for a while until Duchy notices Jack has become noticeably pale. He calls out in the direction of the nurses' station, 'Hey nurse, my mate Jack here needs a bit of TLC'.

Jack is again topped up with pain killers and he settles into a light slumber.

He awakens to the sound of crockery and cutlery banging against something. It appears to be late afternoon, and Jack suddenly feels hungry. He realises that he hasn't eaten for some time. He manages to attract the attention of the orderly serving what he thinks is dinner and asks if he can have some. The guy checks Jack's chart and, satisfied, places a plate of food on a table near Jack's head. Before Jack can ask him how he is going to feed himself in his position, the guy is gone. Jack eyes the food and calls out for Duchy to help him, but he isn't there. Jack gives a frustrated sigh and tries to move his left hand to pick up a fork. The sudden pain makes him drop it. Jack curses.

He hears a female voice that is somehow familiar, say teasingly in his ear, 'Temper, temper, Jack.' Jenna moves into his line of vision, dressed in a grey tunic with an apron over it. She looks cool and collected, and quite beautiful despite the unattractive garb she wears. Jenna fetches another fork and proceeds to feed him slowly. He notices the name tag on her uniform—Jenna Davies. *This isn't exactly how I intended to meet up with her again*, he thinks abstractedly. Despite his injuries, again he has an urge to touch her skin.

'I think your injuries require a bit more than vinegar and brown paper,' Jenna says lightheartedly. 'It seems that someone took a distinct dislike to you.'

'But I got the bastard,' Jack replies, then, seeing the expression of distaste on Jenna's face, he adds, 'I mean, it was him or me. And it seems like it was him and me'.

Jack decides to change the subject. 'How's that fiancé of yours?'

Jenna's face clouds over for a second, then she replies with a false cheerfulness, 'Oh him. He found someone else. He obviously couldn't wait twelve bloody months.'

Jack can see the bitterness in her eyes.

'Jeez, I'm sorry, Jenna. I was only trying to steer the conversation away from me and that VC. But I think I've put my foot right in my big mouth. Sorry.'

Jack looks so contrite that it makes Jenna smile. It transforms her face, and Jack just stares at her in wonder.

'That's okay Jack, you weren't to know. So, let's get back to you.' She picks up his medical chart. 'It would appear you are going to have a rest in here for a bit.' The nurse in her comes to the fore, and she asks in a concerned voice, 'how's the pain?'.

'My back is a bit sore,' Jack admits.

'Hold on, I'll fix that very soon. Then, I've got to get back to my rounds. I'll see you a bit later.'

*****

Chapter 33

Over the next two weeks Jack's wounds heal slowly and the pain gradually eases until it only hurts when he moves. After a week he is able to rest on his side and is allowed to walk around slowly.

Jenna visits him when she can and they talk about everything but the war. She is due to return to Sydney in the New Year and intends to apply for a nursing position at the Prince of Wales Hospital in Randwick. She hopes they will jump at her, given her experience here. She wants to rent a flat in nearby Bondi. Jenna loves the crazy range of architecture found in the buildings near the beach, and the laid-back lifestyle of the Eastern Suburbs. She acknowledges she is not a good swimmer, but she intends to take lessons.

Jack likes it when they talk. Although the nurse stuff reminds him a bit of Susie—perhaps it is the fact that both are beautiful—the two women are chalk and cheese. Jenna is stable, sensible, and seems to know what she wants to do. She has her head set firmly on her shoulders, and seems to be very practical. Compared with Susie, she is very together.

Jack tells her about his desire to complete his studies at uni and she quizzes him on his reasons for choosing computing. She seems genuinely interested, and Jack is pleased with her attention. Jenna tells him she would like to study nursing at university at some stage, when such a course becomes available. Jack manages to hold her hand for a short period of time, until Jenna has to go elsewhere.

This is so different from being back with 1RAR, Jack thinks. He almost wants to be able to stay in hospital longer so that he and Jenna can talk more, but the time is drawing near when he will be discharged and have to report back to Delta Company. Jack doesn't really want to go back into harm's way. He secretly envies Duchy, who has been sent home for further treatment on his arm. But this is the army. What he wants doesn't come into consideration.

*****

Chapter 34

In mid-December Bungy excitedly tells Terry that Mr Michael Hand himself will be visiting Saigon in a week or so. Terry is not so thrilled with the news.

'Bungy, is something wrong? What is he here for?'

Bungy dismisses Terry's fears.

'Mike's coming here to have a meeting with some of the Air America guys in Saigon, but he also wants to visit Vung Tau. Apparently he and Walter Kowalski go way back. He will only be here for a few days, just before Christmas, then he's off to who knows where. Now, Terry, let's talk about the Saigon meet. You know the hotels. Which one would be suitable for him to stay in? Oh, and we need a place for a quiet get together at, say, fifteen or sixteen hundred hours?'

Terry ponders this question. 'You want somewhere not too noisy, right?' Bungy nods.

'Well, what about the Majestic? It's got nice views over the river, and there's a cosy little lounge bar on the top floor. I would have said the Continental, but there are too many nosy journos staying there.

The Majestic is classy, and the bar I've got in mind is pretty private and it won't be busy then. The action starts around sundown, and I'd imagine the meet will be well and truly over by that time?'

'Sounds good, mate. I'll leave that to you, and I'll arrange the Vung Tau visit. Here's five hundred bucks to cover expenses. Make sure Mike gets a good room and we get a good table. And have some women on tap for afterwards, eh? I'll let Mike know about the arrangements.'

Two days before Christmas, the man in question lounges comfortably in a business-class seat onboard the weekly Qantas 707 V-Jet service to Saigon. He sips on a whiskey and soda, smoke from a Lucky Strike curling into the air, as the plane starts its descent into Tan Son Nhut airport. Michael Hand obligingly obeys the stewardess' request to fasten his seat belt, and the plane lands smoothly on the tarmac. Is has been several years since his last visit, and over five years since he first came to Vietnam, but he can remember it like yesterday. He remembers the VC attack on the US Special Forces compound at Dong Xaoi.

It was June 1963 and the VC 9th Division was ordered to attack the town of Dong Xaoi, strategically located at the junction of National Highway 1 and several other important roads that run through Phouc Long Province, about 100 miles north of Saigon. There were about a dozen US Special Forces troops based in a compound in the town. Michael Hand was one of these.

Michael and the other SF troops were soon engaged in a major conflict as the VC attacked in force and targeted the compound. After a fourteen-hour pitched battle, and despite heavy casualties, the VC overran the compound, but not before Michael Hand escaped—probably the last American left alive. He fought a rearguard action that earned him a Distinguished Service Cross, which ranks only second to the Medal of Honor in the USA. When the fighting around Dong Xaoi finished, one hundred and twenty-six VC bodies were found in the Special Forces compound. Michael remembers with grim satisfaction the dead VC soldiers piling up against the barricades.

Michael was recruited by the CIA shortly afterwards, and was soon closely involved with Air America operations.

The plane taxis to the terminal and stops. The announcement by the aircrew that the passengers can now disembark interrupts his reminiscences. He unbuckles his seat belt and stands up. He has only a carry-on bag with him and, after walking down the boarding steps onto the taxiway, he is soon inside the terminal. Customs and passport control are quickly dealt with.

Outside the arrivals hall is packed, but he spots Bungy Williams and his offsider Terry, whom he remembers vaguely from some time before in Sydney. Bungy greets him warmly and Terry, after shaking hands, takes his overnight bag as the pair escorts him to a waiting vehicle. Terry drives, watching and listening to the conversation between Bungy and Mike, who lounge in the back seat of the car.

'Good flight, Mike?'

Mike replies with a Bronx accent. 'Yeah, Bungy. A lot more comfortable than a military aircraft. And plenty of booze, too.'

The pair proceeds to discuss the city and how much it has changed over the past few years. Terry is disappointed. He thinks he might find out some more details of the purpose of Mike's visit. He'll just have to wait.

Mike is dropped off at the Majestic to book into the suite Terry has arranged for him, and to freshen up after the long haul from Sydney via the Philippines. Bungy and Terry will return midafternoon. As Terry drives away, Bungy casually tells him that he will not be sitting in on this afternoon's meeting. Instead, Terry is to keep an eye out to see if anyone is taking an undue interest in the gathering. Terry is disappointed, and lets Bungy know it.

'Terry, Terry, just relax, will you? Someone has to make sure that no-one is snooping around. This is a very sensitive and important meeting. Hopefully, out of it may come bigger quantities of dope, and that means more money for you and me. So chill out, mate, okay?'

Terry is only slightly mollified. He would very much like to be part of the inner circle, but he realises he will have to bide his time.

Terry ushers the two American guys he regularly meets at the air base into the bar. They are wearing the same gaudy clothing as always. Bungy and Mike rise to meet them. Mike, dressed in a casual silk shirt and trousers, embraces them warmly. They seem to be old friends. Bungy orders drinks from a waiter hovering nearby.

Terry discreetly moves away and sits at the bar, glancing from time to time at the four as they talk and sip their drinks. He also scrutinises the bar and doorway carefully, but no-one seems to be taking any interest in the meeting. He takes a mouthful of beer, using the mirror behind the bar to surreptitiously check for anything unusual. All is quiet.

He glances back once again at the four. There seems to be an argument taking place, and heated but hushed words are exchanged between the three Americans. Bungy is giving off worried vibes. Terry's interest is piqued. What is going on? He resolves to quiz Bungy once the meeting is over.

After an hour the four stand up and shake hands. The two Air America guys depart and Mike leaves as well.

Terry crosses to Bungy and asks, 'Will I get the girls now?'

Bungy shakes his head. 'No, mate, something has come up. Mike, you and I have to get down to Vung Tau toot sweet. There's a problem there. Let's go and get the car while Mike changes into something a bit more appropriate. I'll fill you in as we walk.'

As they fetch the car Bungy informs him that one of the White Mice has been seen in the act of passing information on to the American MPs. The crew in Vung Tau have him in the warehouse and are interrogating him vigorously. So far he hasn't talked, but it's only a matter of time. They need to find out what information he's imparted so that they can limit the damage, if possible.

The three are largely silent during the trip to Vung Tau. Terry can see that Mike is fuming, so he wisely keeps his mouth shut. They drive as quickly as possible through the early evening, and arrive at the outskirts of Vung Tau as the sun drops below the horizon.

*****

Jack's wounds are almost healed and he is allowed out of the hospital for a few hours at a time, as long as he stays away from alcohol. He decides to take in a Christmas show at the Peter Badcoe club. He has heard the singers there are first-class. He promises the duty nurse that he will be back before 2100, well before the base curfew of 2200.

Jenna is on duty, which is disappointing. He would have liked to ask her to go with him. He is unsure whether she would accept. He senses that their relationship hasn't progressed to a point where she is likely to interact with him socially. And their association probably won't go much further, with her departing for home in a week or so. Still, he is gleefully contemplating the prospect of getting out of the confines of the hospital for a few hours.

As he dresses, he thinks of his mates. He hopes they're okay. He hasn't heard much about the fighting at Hat Dich, although several wounded 1RAR soldiers have been brought into the hospital in the last week. He is reluctant to talk to them. Most of them are hurt a lot worse than he has been, so he decides to leave them alone.

Oh well, I'll be back there with the boys in a few days, he thinks, as he walks out of the hospital. It is a bit of a distance to the club, but Jack is enjoying the exercise. His back is only slightly sore now. The way to the club is mostly lit, but he decides to take a short cut past some warehouses, just for the heck of it.

*****

Chapter 34

In the warehouse, the informant is strung up by his wrists, his feet clear of the ground. He is gagged and has been beaten severely, and blood runs freely from several nasty gashes on his head and torso. Mike, Walter, Bungy, Terry and two White Mice stand in front of him. Another two White Mice are outside, keeping watch.

Terry stares in fascination as one of the Vietnamese police hits the informer again in the face, grunting with the effort. Walter urges the White Mouse to inflict maximum pain, but not to the point where the informant cannot speak. Mike watches impassively at the beating. Bungy looks sick, and turns his face away. *Weak prick*, Terry thinks, watching dispassionately as Bungy vomits on the floor.

'That's enough,' commands Walter, walking up to the badly beaten man. 'You ready to talk yet?'

The man says nothing, and tries to spit blood on Walter, who sidesteps.

'Hit him again. But this time, aim for his balls. If he doesn't talk, he'll never fuck anyone again.'

The man emits muffled screams as the assault continues.

Suddenly there is a shout from outside. One of the White Mice guarding the warehouse has spotted something.

'Take care of whatever that is,' Mike calls to Terry, 'this guy will talk soon, and then we can get out of here.'

Terry rushes to the warehouse door. A couple of the Vietnamese police are chasing a big guy down an alley, their guns drawn. As the big guy passes under a light Terry thinks he recognises him. He thinks it is the drunken soldier who was near the warehouse several months ago. Terry sprints after the fleeing man and the police who are chasing the black guy. *We've got to get him before he can raise the alarm*, Terry thinks anxiously.

*****

Gene creeps along the wall of the warehouse, keeping to the

shadows. He hears muted cries from inside, but as yet can't see what is going on. It sounds like someone is being tortured. He has followed Walter Kowalski to the warehouse and caught a glimpse of several figures getting out of a car and entering the building. There is something big going down, and he needs to find out what it is. He sidles up to the window.

A shout from behind him penetrates the silence of the night. He has been spotted. *Fuck*, thinks Gene, *that's blown it. I've got to get out of here and get help*. Gene doesn't waste time turning around, instead he sprints away from the warehouse, dodging and weaving.

*****

Terry rounds a corner and stops, hidden in the shadows. The two smaller White Mice are struggling with the big black guy. Shoot him, Terry wants to scream at them, but instinct makes him stay silent. Terry can see that the policemen are reluctant to fire for fear of one hitting the other. Suddenly, the black man uses his superior strength and shoves one of the Vietnamese violently against the other, who falls backwards, striking his head hard on the ground and losing his grip on the gun he is carrying. Before the other policeman can bring his pistol to bear, the big guy is off. Leaving his stunned partner on the ground the policeman again takes off in hot pursuit. Terry quickly scoops up the loose gun on the ground and chases after them.

At the next corner Terry can hear the sound of ragged breathing. He stops and peers around, concealing his body in the darkness. The policeman has finally cornered the black guy, who is backed up against a wall, frantically searching for a way out. The policeman stands well back, having learnt his lesson from the earlier skirmish. Deliberately, he raises his pistol, aiming at the black guy's head. His face contorted into a ghastly smile, the policeman starts to pull the trigger.

Chapter 34

Without warning a shape of a man flies through the air, striking the policeman from the side, sending the gun flying out of his hand. The newcomer immediately strikes the policeman a heavy blow to the jaw, knocking him to the ground. The stranger calls out urgently, 'Gene, this way, quick'.

Terry is stunned. He knows that voice. *What the fuck has Jack got to do with this? What's he doing here?*

*****

Cutting between two old warehouses, Jack suddenly hears the sound of running feet and laboured breathing. Without warning, in front of him appears Gene, his face a mask of despair. He has not seen Jack. Jack is about to call out to him when Gene turns and backs against a wall, his attention focussed on something or someone up a side alley. A figure appears, armed with a pistol, his attention fully on Gene. He raises his pistol and points it at Gene.

Jack doesn't hesitate.

Gene turns at the sound of his voice and recognises Jack as he tackles the policeman. The Vietnamese thug, although winded, is quickly on his feet, and recovers the gun and points it at Jack. Moving fast, Gene takes a couple of paces and strikes the policeman savagely in the face with all the force that his two hundred pounds of bulk can bring to bear. The shot goes wide as the Vietnamese crumples like a rag doll, his jaw hanging loosely.

Jack starts to bend down and pick up the gun, but Gene urgently calls out: 'Leave it, Jack. Let's go'. He leads Jack in a race down a side alley, completely unaware they are about to pass in front of Terry, who crouches and takes aim. As the pair runs past, the black guy slightly in front of Jack, Terry fires twice. He sees Jack stumble, but the big black soldier quickly grabs him and pulls him into the shadows.

Unfortunately for Terry, the noise of the first shot has attracted unwanted attention. Shouts are heard from nearby, and a group of soldiers runs into the alley, abruptly stopping when they hear the next two shots. They fan out and cautiously move forward, and Terry, still hidden from sight, is forced to retreat to avoid being flanked. He turns and runs madly away, followed by the soldiers at a slower pace, conscious of the fact that whoever is in front of them may be carrying a gun.

Terry is in full-on panic mode. He has to get out of here, and fast. He sprints back to the warehouse, where he sees Bungy and the others standing beside the car. They have heard the shots and are ready to flee. The informer is dead, the damage inflicted on him so severe that his heart has given out. Acting quickly, Walter has instructed the other two White Mice to get rid of the body.

Terry jumps into the car, closely followed by Bungy and Mike. Walter takes off on foot, aiming to return to the G Spot by another way. In a tense voice, Mike commands Terry to drive out of Vung Tau as quickly as possible without attracting too much attention, and to head back to Saigon. Terry takes a circuitous route, but there is no sign of trouble. The soldiers are still back in the group of warehouses, and the MPs have not yet turned up. They are soon on Highway 56, speeding away from the unholy mess left behind.

*****

Gene notices Jack stumble as shots ring out. *Shit*, he thinks, *he's been hit*.

One of the shells from the Smith and Wesson Model 38 that Terry fired has struck Jack in the lower right-hand side of his gut, slicing through the intestinal wall and the intestinal cavity before exiting out Jack's lower left side. Due to its relatively low speed, the .38 bullet doesn't expand as it passes through Jack's body. The exit hole is only slightly larger than the entry. The bullet has not struck any vital organs, but it has perforated Jack's lower intestines. This is serious.

Gene has no idea how badly Jack is injured, but he takes no chances. He hoists Jack onto his shoulders and awkwardly runs as fast as possible towards the hospital, shouting out for help as he does. He is dimly aware that he is not being chased, but he doesn't slow down. Gene risks a glance at Jack's face. He is grimacing in pain and shock, but says nothing. Jack's eyes are glazing over. Gene can feel blood on his back from the gunshot wound and this spurs him on.

Some soldiers, alerted by the shots, run up to him. They help carry Jack through the night and they soon reach the hospital. They rush Jack inside where they are directed to the triage section. Gene is screeching at the top of his voice for a doctor. Jack has now lapsed into unconsciousness, his head lolling forward. Blood continues to spurt uncontrolled from the entry and exit wounds.

Jenna is the duty nurse in triage. Alerted by the shouts, she rushes to the small group of men who push their way through the door, carrying someone.

'Put him over there on that bed,' she commands. Jenna notes that the injured man, whose face she cannot yet see, is dressed in civilian clothing. She addresses the men in a clipped, authoritative tone. 'What's happened to him? Is he in the military?'

A large black man in a blood-soaked uniform answers her, his voice chock-full of exhaustion and anxiety.

'He's been shot, Ma'am. He's an Aussie soldier. And he just saved my life. Please help him. It's my buddy, Jack.'

Jenna's eyes dart back to the injured man, astonishment and shock on her face. *Jack? It can't be. He's at the concert. It must be another Jack.* She crouches down to check his face and her worst fears are confirmed.

She wants to sit down and weep but her professionalism kicks in. She quickly examines the bloody wounds. She instructs the big soldier, 'Hold this pad here, and one of you others hold the other pad there. And press firmly on them to try and quell the bleeding. I'll get the doctor'. Jenna races out, calling out urgently. A small team of medics responds quickly.

Minutes later Jack is in the operating room, being prepped for emergency surgery. Jenna is back in the triage room, accompanied by the big American. He turns to her, recognition dawning in his eyes. Now a little calmer, Gene says quietly to Jenna, 'You know Jack, don't you. I remember you from the beach, months ago, when you met him. I asked him if you were his girlfriend'.

Jenna's poise leaves her all at once, and she bursts into tears. 'Jack, oh Jack. What happened to him? And who are you?'

Gene comforts her, placing his arm gently around her shoulders and leading her to a chair. She sits and looks expectantly up at him.

'Ma'am, as I said, he saved my life. Some bad guys were chasing me and were about to shoot me when Jack jumped them. I've got no idea where he came from. As we were getting away, one of them shot Jack. That's what happened. As for me, let's just say I was in the right place at the wrong time. It's okay, I'm on the right side of the law. But hey, now I've got to get things moving before those bastards get too far. There's gunna be some arrests made very soon, and I hope someone tries to escape. You okay if I leave you now?'

Jenna listens in disbelief to the story. As he goes to leave, she asks him, 'What's your name, soldier?'.

'Gene, just call me Gene. Tell Jack I'll be back as soon as I can.' With that, he hurries out the door, his face set with determination and anger.

Jenna shivers. *I wouldn't want to be the men he is after*, she thinks. Her thoughts return to Jack. He appears to be seriously wounded, but at least he's in the best hands here. She wants to check on him, but knows she can't leave the triage area.

*****

Chapter 35

Back in Saigon, Terry and Bungy drop Mike off at the Majestic Hotel. It is late evening and Mike is calmer now. 'Bungy, we've got to shut down this operation temporarily. I'll leave that to you. I'm on a Cathay flight to Hong Kong first thing in the morning. Someone will contact you. And Terry, you saw nothing and you know nothing. Capisce?'

Terry nods numbly. It has totally gone to shit, and so quickly. Bloody Jack, what's his game? Better not let on he knows him or anything about him, or someone might jump to the wrong conclusions. Besides, maybe he has gotten rid of Pretty Boy for good.

Bungy gets Terry to take him to the centre of Saigon. Bungy doesn't intend to hang about. He will head for his safe house, collect his false papers, and make his escape into Cambodia. Bungy tells Terry that he will meet him at the air base in the morning. Of course, he has no intention of doing this.

Terry drives back to his room in Tu Do Street. He cannot sleep, and commands Rose to send a girl to him. He is rougher than usual, and the girl leaves afterwards, quietly sobbing in pain. Still his mind will not rest. He will have to sort things out with Bungy in the morning.

But when he arrives at the Supply Corps office on the morning of Christmas Eve, he is arrested by several burly MPs who have been there since dawn. The MPs remain at the office for most of the day, with Terry in handcuffs. Bungy is nowhere to be seen.

Terry is taken to the Military Correctional Establishment at Vung Tau that evening. The Provosts put him in a holding cell prior to interrogating him. Terry is determined to say nothing. He is kept in the cell overnight.

On the morning of Christmas Day he is paraded before a warrant officer, who is seated in a chair in front of a table in a room with a mirror running across the wall behind the WO's chair. The WO is a tough-looking individual with a scar running diagonally across one cheek. When he smiles, the scar makes his face appear lopsided and a little evil. The WO smiles malevolently at Terry, but Terry is not afraid.

The WO is pissed off that he has to do this on Christmas Day. His plans to have a nice lunch with a few beers are shot to pieces, but this has precedence.

'Well then, Private Terry Bannister, we're going to have a nice little chat. A chat about drug running, and what happened in that warehouse. I'm going to ask you some questions, and you're going to answer them. Truthfully. Now, I know the answers to these questions, so it isn't much point lying to me. It will only go badly for you.'

Terry scrutinises the WO. *I bet he's bluffing*, he tells himself. *Unless they have found the body of the dead Vietnamese, they have diddly-squat.* He decides to try it on a bit.

'Well, if you know the answers, why ask them then?' Seeing the WO's face flush red with anger, he quickly continues. 'But why have

I been arrested? I'm only a driver. I don't know anything about any drugs. Maybe you should talk to my boss, Captain Williams. He'll vouch for me.'

'I'd like to talk to your captain, but we haven't been able to find him—yet—but, believe me, we will. And when we do, I'm sure he'll vouch for you all right. He'll tell us all about your little operation, and the part you've been playing in it. It's only a matter of time.'

The WO lays a few more cards on the table.

'Your mate Walter Kowalski is helping our American friends with their enquiries into what happened here the night before last. You know what happened, don't you, because you were there. And our South Vietnamese allies are having a cosy chat with the White Mice that were guarding the warehouse—though I doubt the soon-to-be ex-policemen are calling the chat "cosy". I'm sure you are aware that the South Vietnamese use methods that are a little ... unorthodox.'

The WO smiles that smile again, and Terry suddenly becomes uneasy, but he decides that there is no point in talking. He's not a grass, and he's not starting now. He decides to continue playing dumb, but deliver a version that is as close to the truth as he is prepared to admit.

'Sir, I'm just the driver. Sure, I admit I was there. I was driving my boss and a friend of his so that they could go to a meeting. But I didn't see anything. When the meeting finished, I drove them back to Saigon. The captain said he'd see me yesterday morning, but he never turned up. That's all I know.'

The WO regards Terry thoughtfully, then leaves the room. He goes next door where Gene, dressed in the uniform of a US Army captain, is watching Terry through the one-way glass. He is a member of the Eighth Military Police Group (Criminal Investigation) and has been on secondment in Vung Tau for the past eight months as an undercover operative.

The WO provost asks him: 'What do you think, Gene? Did you see this guy?'.

Gene pauses, studying Terry. He has recognised Terry from the earlier encounter a few months before, but he can't place him at the scene of what obviously has been a murder. When US and Australian MPs searched the warehouse after Gene raised the alarm, there was no body, although there was plenty of blood on the floor. Apart from that, the MPs found no evidence of drugs. The place was clean. Gene is momentarily tempted to tell a lie and say he has seen Terry at the warehouse—he wants to strike back at the gang who shot Jack—but reason prevails. Terry is almost certainly small fry in this operation, and Gene wants the big boys.

'I think he's lying through his teeth, but no, I didn't see him. So, if none of the guys in custody identify him, and we don't find his boss, or the mystery guy who says he was with them, all we have are suspicions.' Gene frowns. 'He's got priors, hasn't he?'

'Yep, but that's not going to help much here. From his file, he refused to talk back in Australia when he was last arrested and, between you, me and the gatepost, he withstood a fair bit of unofficial "encouragement" to make him spill the beans. So, you're right, unless he is identified—or he talks, which is unlikely—we've got fuck-all on him.' The WO kicks a chair in disgust and frustration.

'Well, I need to visit a buddy in hospital and then return to headquarters at Long Binh to get on with the interrogation of Walter Kowalski. But I doubt he'll talk, either. As he is a civilian, if he doesn't talk, all we can do is kick him out of the country. And I'll bet that those White Mice won't get a chance to open their mouths and squeal. The South Vietnamese police won't want too much more shit to hit the fan in their ranks. There already is enough flying around to paint most of Saigon brown. Everything will be covered up and papered over, so I wouldn't rely on anything coming out of that source, unfortunately. Good luck with your guy. Sweat him good. Let me know if anything changes. I'm going to concentrate on the missing guy, as well as Kowalski. See if you can get your guy to tell you where he dropped his boss and the other fella in Saigon. Maybe that might give us a lead.'

The WO returns to the interrogation room to quiz Terry some more, and Gene leaves the 2nd MCE and heads for the hospital. *God, I hope Jack is okay*, he prays.

When Gene arrives at the hospital, Jack is in intensive care. Gene isn't allowed in, but he sees Jenna coming out, dressed in a surgical gown. She spots Gene and approaches him, smiling tiredly.

'How is he, Ma'am?' Gene asks nervously.

'Please call me Jenna.' She takes a deep breath and releases it slowly. 'Jack is still very sick, but he'll live, unless there are any complications. The bullet missed all the important organs, but nicked a few pieces of his small bowel, and they had to be repaired, otherwise he would definitely have died from infection. But he's not out of the woods yet. Once he is stable enough to travel, he'll be flown back to Australia for further treatment, probably in Sydney at the Military Repatriation Hospital. Even if that is successful, he'll take a fair while to recuperate.'

Jena pauses, and then says: 'His war is finished, Gene. And I'm glad. Being wounded twice in a period of several weeks is not going to do him very much good, physically or emotionally. But he's a tough cookie, and hopefully he will come out of this without too much damage, apart from the scars on his back from the shrapnel and those from the latest wounding'.

Gene gazes at her with hurt in his eyes. 'Can I see him?' he asks quietly.

'Sorry, there's too much risk of infection. Only immediate kin and medical staff go in there.' Jenna adds, impishly, 'And I don't think you'll fool anyone into thinking you're his brother.'

Despite himself, Gene chuckles. 'I guess you're right, Jenna.'

Sizing her up, Gene asks shrewdly, 'Would I be right in saying that you care for Jack, just a bit?'

It is her turn to smile. 'Yes, I do, a little. As you know, it's hard not to like Jack, but I doubt anything will come of it. He has a long and painful road ahead, and although I'm returning to Sydney in the New Year, I doubt our paths will cross.'

Gene regards her thoughtfully. 'Maybe you could visit him, seeing as y'all will be in the same town?'

'I may just do that, Gene.'

Gene bids her farewell, asking her to tell Jack that he has called. Before he leaves, he hands Jenna a letter for Jack. Jenna accepts it and puts it in her pocket. She will deliver it later.

*****

Henry and Gladys read the second urgent telegram with despair. *Jack has been injured again? And seriously hurt this time. How could that be? Surely he can't have been sent back to the war so soon?* Henry calls the Department of Army in Canberra, but as it is the holiday period between Christmas and New Year, no-one in authority can help him. He hangs up, frustrated, not knowing where to turn. He and Gladys wait for further news, praying that it won't be what they fear most.

*****

The WO provost provides Gene with the location where Terry dropped off the mystery man. Terry has told him that, but nothing else. Gene is not surprised. Everyone seems to have the fear of God put into them. Captain Williams' room has been raided, but nothing incriminating was found. Gene is pretty sure he has not left Saigon by plane. There is no record of anyone fitting his description passing through immigration. He seems to have vanished into thin air.

A uniformed Gene, accompanied by an MP in the tunic of the army of the Republic of South Vietnam, enters the Majestic Hotel and strides to the reception desk. He flashes his ID and politely asks the receptionist to show him the guest register. She tells him that she will need to check with the duty manager. Gene waits patiently until she returns with a small, officious-looking man who speaks to Gene in English with a slight French accent.

'How may I help you, Sir?'

Gene hates the guy on sight, but holds his temper. 'I need to see your guest register.'

The manager replies in a haughty tone, 'That information is confidential, Sir'.

Gene loses it. 'Look, fella, I'm investigating a serious crime, and I have no time to debate the issue with you. Either you co-operate, or you can deal with my friend here.'

The manager's face pales, and he is suddenly obsequious. 'No, no, Sir, I'm sorry, I must have misunderstood.' He reaches down and picks up the register. 'Here it is, Sir.'

Gene examines the book, searching for names of males who have stayed in the hotel over the past few days. There are several that might be the guy. One name sticks out for some reason. Michael Hand. A US citizen. Booked in on December 23, and out the next day. He's gone, at least from the hotel.

Gene searches his memory for the link. He grunts in surprise as an image springs into his mind of a US Special Forces operative being decorated for valour some years back. Then he frowns as he remembers something else—something that may well stop the investigation dead in its tracks. Wasn't Hand seconded to MACV-SOG? Gene's heart sinks. The Military Assistance Command, Vietnam—Studies and Observations Group, is a rival to the Green Berets, Gene's former unit. Gene calls it the Dark Side. SOG, with links to the CIA, is well resourced and has the favour of the US Joint Chiefs of Staff over the Green Berets. Gene knows that trying to take this investigation further is going to be very complicated, and maybe impossible.

Sighing, Gene disconsolately hands back the register to the simpering manager and leaves the hotel, dismissing the ARVN MP. Gene will check through his sources, but he has little hope of getting anywhere. He knows from experience that the CIA is a law unto itself.

Then he brightens a little. *At least we've put a big dent in the drug pipeline.* But he knows that the war on drugs, like the other war taking place here, is ultimately unwinnable.

*****

Jack slowly returns to consciousness. He peers down at his body. There are tubes everywhere, and he feels drowsy and very sore. He has dressings in several places on his lower torso. He remembers the fight, and shudders as he relives the feeling of the bullet striking him.

He moves his head slowly to the right. Jenna is sitting on a chair, studying what appear to be medical notes. She senses his movement and her eyes move to meet his. She smiles.

'Hello, Jack, please don't try to talk. Just conserve your strength. Nod if you're thirsty.' Jack nods. Jenna feeds him some water through a straw. 'How is the pain? Bad?' Jack nods again. 'We'll fix that.' When Jack is more comfortable, Jenna talks to him again.

"Your mate Gene called by yesterday. He said that you saved his life. He wanted to thank you, but he wasn't allowed to come into intensive care. That's where you are, Jack. But Gene left a letter for you. When you're a bit better, you can read it.'

Jenna stops talking. She can see Jack is sleeping. She gets up, leaving the letter on his bedside table. She will come back when she has finished her next shift.

When he awakes, Jack feels a little better. He notices the envelope next to him, and slowly reaches over and picks it up. He tears it open and starts to read what is written. The handwriting is difficult to decipher, but he is determined to find out what it says.

> Hey Jack,
>
> I just want to say thanks, buddy, for saving my life. I don't know where you came from, or what you were doing there, but I guess that doesn't matter. You were in the right place at the right time, that's what's important for me.
>
> I'm real sorry you got shot, but we are after the guy who shot you, and he and his buddies are in our sights.
>
> I owe you everything, Jack, so I'm going to come clean with you.
>
> I am not a support guy. I'm an MP and I've been working undercover in Vung Tau for a long time, looking for the source of the drugs, heroin really, that my countrymen like to use so much. I suspect that it is making its way to your country, too.
>
> Jack, what I said to you guys about not being Special Forces isn't true either. This is my second tour of 'Nam. During my first tour I was a Green Beret. I got shot during a black op up near the DMZ in 1966, and I was declared medically unfit to continue as a Special Forces soldier.
>
> So I joined the Military Police, and here I am.
>
> So, Jack, you get well, you hear? If there's ever anything I can do for you, you let me know. I'm going to keep tabs on you, so you'll be able to find me. I've got friends in lots of places, so you better behave, you hear?
>
> Your friend,
>
> Gene

Jack reads it again, then sits back, exhausted. He's pleased that he has been able to keep Gene alive, but is the cost worth it? He feels like shit, much worse than his first lot of injuries. All he can do is rest and wait to hear the verdict on his condition from the medical staff.

This comes the next day. A doctor checks him over and seems happy with the results. The doctor speaks to Jack.

'Private Martin, Jack, may I call you, Jack?' Jack nods. 'Thanks. I'm going to bring you up to date with the next steps in your medical treatment. You are aware that you have been shot in the abdomen and that the bullet perforated your bowel?'

Again Jack nods, and the doctor continues.

'Well, speaking in layman's terms, we've been able to do a patch job on you, but you're going to need more sophisticated surgery than we can give you here. So, in a day or so, when you're a bit stronger, we'll put you on a medivac flight back home. It will be a fairly long trip as you'll have to be checked and cleared on the way, at a hospital in Butterworth in Malaysia. When you get to Australia, you will be admitted to the Concord Repatriation Hospital in Sydney. The medical team there will take care of you after that. Any questions, Jack?'

Jack asks anxiously: 'How long will it take before I'll be able to rejoin my mates in 1RAR? We've become a real team, and the brick won't be at their best if they're down a man for too much longer'.

'Jack, I'm sorry to tell you this, but I don't think you'll be taking part in any further action here in Vietnam. Your injuries are going to take months to heal, and I doubt that you will receive a medical clearance to resume the sort of full-on activity required to serve your country in a war zone.'

The doctor holds up his hand to forestall Jack's next question.

'Let me be clear. It's very probable that you will make a complete recovery in due course and be able to lead a normal and full life. I can't guarantee that you won't have to go through a few medical hoops first, but with a bit of luck and a lot of good medical care, you'll be ready to take on whatever challenges you might come up against. But those, in all probability, won't include active military service. If that disappoints you, so be it. But I would have thought that, as a National Serviceman, you have plans for after your period of service is concluded. The likely outcome of this is that you will be able to get on with what you intend to do with your life. So just relax and concentrate on getting well. My staff will make the necessary medivac arrangements. You'll be told when it will happen.'

The doctor moves away, leaving Jack to come to terms with what he has just been told. His first reaction is to feel guilty at letting down H and his mates, but a large part of him feels only relief at being no longer a part of the killing machine.

Jenna visits him again and gives him the news that he will be flown out of Vung Tau the next morning. She seems a little sad, so Jack tries to cheer her up, not realising that she is sad about him leaving.

'Come on, Jenna. Just think of Bondi and all those bronzed men on the beach. And the food. And the absence of dustoffs to spoil your day. I bet you'll get a great flat with a view of the ocean. Or perhaps ocean glimpses. I hear that the rents can be a bit high down near the beach.'

Jenna gives a sigh of exasperation. 'Oh, Jack, sometimes men can be so thick.' She bends and kisses him on the cheek. 'Goodbye, Jack, get well. Perhaps we'll run across each other at some point.' With that she walks quickly away, hiding her face so that he cannot see her tears. *Damn you*, she thinks. *I think you've got to me, and that's the last thing I need. It's too soon after Phillip.*

As she disappears, Jack is at first mystified by her behaviour. Then the penny drops. *My God, does she fancy me*? he wonders. He lies back on the bed, suddenly feeling better about his situation.

First thing the next morning Jack is transferred to the Vung Tau Army Airfield, where he and other injured soldiers are carefully loaded onboard a RAAF Hercules C-130 transport plane from 37

Squadron for the flight to Malaysia. A doctor accompanies the injured. After a two-and-a-half-hour flight, the aircraft lands at RAAF Butterworth in north-west Malaysia.

Jack spends several days in the hospital at Butterworth before being given the green light to be loaded onto a Hercules for the fifteen-hour flight to RAAF Richmond, an airbase nestled beneath the gateway to the Blue Mountains, to the west of Sydney. On arrival, he is transported by ambulance to the Repatriation General Hospital at Concord, about ten kilometres west of the Sydney CBD. He is admitted, and once his condition is checked, he is scheduled for follow-on surgery.

It is early January 1969.

*****

A third telegram arrives and Henry opens it with trembling hands. He reads it to Gladys, and they grab each other and dance a little jig, tears in their eyes. Jack is coming home. They try not to think about the state he might be in. Their son, their flesh and blood, is alive; that is what matters most. Henry is determined not to be fobbed off by the army. He will call and call until he gets more details about Jack's return.

*****

In Sydney, a few days previously, Michael Hand met Bernie Houghton for a drink at the Texas Tavern in the Cross. After leaving Saigon, after a brief stopover in Hong Kong Michael flew on a Pan Am flight to the States for a brief conflab with some CIA contacts at Langley, Virginia, before flying back into Sydney. Both he and Bernie are disappointed that the drug operation out of Saigon and Vung Tau has been disrupted, but they know it will recommence once the heat has died down.

Michael hands Bernie a newspaper cutting from *The New York*

Times. It is a short article filed in Saigon concerning the discovery of a decapitated body of a white man found on the South Vietnam–Cambodian border a week previously. He has been identified by his fingerprints. It is Captain Bungy Williams.

'Pity,' grunts Bernie. 'He could have been useful back here. Still, he's in no position to talk now. That's a bonus.' He pauses and asks Michael, 'What about Terry? Have you heard anything?'

Michael emits a short laugh. 'Yeah, he's in custody in Vung Tau. But he hasn't said anything, and he won't, I'll bet. He may be a bit uncontrollable, but he ain't stupid.'

The pair discusses Terry for a short time. Michael sums it up: 'I'll keep an ear to the ground to see what happens to him. I'll keep you posted'. They then turn their conversation to other pressing matters—Terry forgotten for the moment.

*****

In Vietnam, 1RAR will be replaced at Hat Dich in early January 1969 by the ANZAC Battalion 4RAR/NZ and will enjoy a well-earned rest back at Nui Dat. 1RAR will continue to rotate in and out of Hat Dich until their tour of duty ends in February 1969. There are no further injuries in H's brick of soldiers. H heard that Jack has been injured again, severely this time, and has been airlifted out, but the circumstances are shrouded in mystery. H is perplexed by this turn of events, but no-one can enlighten him.

Relieved by 5RAR, the 1st Battalion departs Vietnam in mid-February, onboard *HMAS Sydney* once more, but this time the atmosphere is relaxed and drowsy, with much sunbaking and plenty of beer issues. They cross the equator heading south, and King Neptune finally visits them, amongst much laughter and frivolity.

That evening, Lieutenant Colonel Bennet joins his officers for beers on the quarterdeck of the troop transport. Although the atmosphere is festive, he is saddened by the human cost of their tour of duty. 1RAR has paid a high price—31 killed and 165 injured. *And for what?* he thinks. Sighing, he sips his beer and watches the spectacular sunset as the ship steams through the Indonesian Archipelago.

In the lower decks of the *Vung Tau Ferry*, the navy brig has a customer. Terry is being transported back to Holsworthy, to the military jail, to await trial. His state of mind is the complete antithesis of the soldiers who are anticipating the familiarity and safety of home. But he has stuck to his story, and the MPs cannot budge him.

*****

Chapter 36

Jack is lying in bed in the Concord hospital in late January 1969 when a nurse ushers in his parents who rush to his side, his mother weeping and his father trying to keep himself composed. Henry has finally been able to track down where their son is, miraculously breaking through the army bureaucracy.

Jack appears drawn and pale, but Gladys and Henry see that he seems to be on the mend. Gladys anxiously questions Jack about his condition. Jack smiles wanly.

'Well, Mum, since I got here a few weeks ago I've had two operations. After the first one, something called peritonitis, which I was told is a pretty serious infection in the stomach, almost took me out.' He grins. 'But the second emergency operation, plus antibiotics, seems to have worked.'

Henry asks him: 'How did this happen? How did you get injured twice?'

Reluctantly, Jack tells his story, to the disbelief of his parents. They are aghast at the tale. It is bad enough for him to have been wounded in battle, but to get caught up in a fracas involving drugs, corrupt policemen and God knows who else is almost beyond comprehension. But when he tells them that he is likely to be discharged from the army medically unfit, they smile for the first time. At last there is some good news.

With gentle encouragement from the duty nurse, Gladys and Henry leave Jack to rest. They will return regularly to see him for however long he remains in hospital.

*****

At the end of February 1RAR marches proudly through the streets of Sydney. There are cheers from onlookers but also quite a few jeers from anti-war protesters. The troops mutter derisory comments as they see the long-haired hippy types screaming out meaningless slogans. Get them in uniform and put them in a war zone; that would change their attitude quick smart.

The MPs have a devil of a time after the march rounding up celebrating diggers as they roust them out of pubs along George Street. Most soldiers struggle to comprehend they are back in a land of prosperity and peace. Their bodies are here, but their minds are still in the heat, humidity and killing fields of Vietnam.

A few weeks later Jack, who is now well enough to be out of bed and is enjoying the sun on the balcony of his hospital ward, hears footsteps approaching. He spies H striding towards him, a broad grin on his face. Jack is astonished. How did H find him? They embrace awkwardly, H conscious of the dressings on Jack's belly.

'So, Jack, this is the life, eh? Sunbaking out here, not a care in the world. But, mate, you could have chosen an easier way of getting here. Yes, I heard all about your escapades. You're the talk of Delta Company. The buzz is that the president of the United States is coming over here to personally pin a medal on that scrawny chest of yours for saving one of Uncle Sam's finest.' H grins, pleased to have invented the story.

'Bullshit, H. You just made that up.' Jack smiles too, appreciating

H's humour.

'What's the story on the recovery, Jack?'

Jack gives him the lowdown and H whistles as he hears about Jack's brush with death.

'Shit, mate, that's three lives you've used up. You'd better stay out of trouble from now on.'

Jack nods in agreement.

'Tell me, H, what happened after I got carted out of the jungle? How are the guys?'

H fills him in on the details of the rest of the operation at Hat Dich, and subsequently.

'The brick members are fine. The other three Nashos have just about done their time. Andy is going back to his father's butcher business in Narrandera; I reckon it's almost as dangerous as Vietnam. Bluey is returning to Melbourne to resume a career as a boilermaker. And Mal, the strong silent one, is thinking of joining the army permanently. I will miss them all.' Jack agrees. H concludes his catch up. 'So the battalion's back in Holsworthy, shining boots and doing all the useless things that troops do when they're not fighting wars.' H's expression becomes serious. 'It's a bit difficult to handle, frankly. I miss the action, but I don't—you know what I mean?'

Jack does indeed know exactly what he means. He asks H quietly, 'So, mate, what are your plans?'. H regards Jack pensively. 'Ah, I'm buggered if I know, mate. My hitch in the army is up in a few months, and I don't think I'm gunna sign on again. I'm a bit over all this soldiering stuff, to tell you the truth. But I haven't got a clue what I would do in civvy street. Maybe I could grow my hair long, smoke some dope, and become a protestor. Those guys seem to pull the chicks.'

Jack laughs at the absurdity of that idea.

'Come on, H, a guy like you can do anything his heart desires.'

He tries to lighten things up a bit. 'Shit, man, maybe you could become a mercenary. I hear they make pretty good money.'

H pretends to consider this. 'Yeah, maybe I could.' The mates stare at each other, and simultaneously burst into peals of laughter. Jack grabs at his stomach. 'Oh God, I hope those stitches hold. I haven't laughed so much in ages.'

H stands up and shakes Jack's hand.

'Well buddy, I'd better be getting along. I don't want to waste too much of this short leave hanging around crocks like you in hospital. I need to find me some friendly senoritas to party with. I'll be seeing you, Jack, take care.'

H goes to leave but Jack stops him.

'Wait, H, we should keep in touch. Tell you what, I'll give you my parents' address and when you've figured out what you are going to do, drop me a line care of them. I probably won't be going back to live at home, but they'll pass on your letter.'

Jack gets a piece of paper and writes on it and gives it to H. Jack gives him a wicked grin.

'See ya, H, remember those condoms.'

H's smirk says it all.

*****

Terry is paraded before the commandant of the Holsworthy Army Base. The MPs have thoroughly briefed him on Terry's case. Despite being almost certain that Terry has been involved in murder, drug running and a host of other crimes, they do not have the evidence to back this up. The commandant realises that he doesn't have much choice.

'Private Bannister, this is the second time I have had the misfortune to have you standing in front of me. Your appalling record speaks for itself. Last time I offered you a choice—Vietnam or a custodial sentence. It would seem that the Vietnam option was a mistake on the army's part. In the past twelve months, you have probably been up to a considerable amount of illegal activity. This cannot be condoned. Therefore, I now sentence you to serve the remainder of your time in National Service behind bars in the Military Corrective Establishment. After that, you will be dishonourably discharged.' With disgust written on his face, he turns to the WO provost. 'Take him away.'

As the MPs lead Terry away, the WO provost walks beside him and whispers in his ear: 'You're not going to enjoy the next few months one little bit. Your last stay here will seem like a picnic compared to what I've got in mind for you'. Terry does not acknowledge the words; he won't give the WO the pleasure of seeing him scared, but inside he is very afraid indeed.

*****

BOOK THREE

THE STALKING HORSE

Stalking Horse

1. Something that is used to hide someone's real purpose.

   The Free Dictionary

2. A person, thing, or expedient used in a deceptive manner, to achieve some hidden purpose; a pretext or ruse.

   Wiktionary

Horse: Heroin.

Nugan Hand Bank

The Nugan Hand Bank was an Australian merchant bank that collapsed in 1980 in sensational circumstances amidst rumours of involvement by the Central Intelligence Agency and organized crime.

Wikipedia

Chapter 37

Jack is sitting on his bed, writing a letter to his parents. Late in summer, it is warm outside and although a light breeze blows in from the balcony, the temperature isn't much cooler inside. Jack is wearing only a pair of pyjama bottoms. The dressings covering his wounds are gone. He has several puckered scars, which are still raw and red, to show for his adventures. He has been told that the colour will fade in time.

He hears voices at the nurses' station and turns his head in that direction. Jenna is standing there. She is wearing a short sleeveless dress covered in white, yellow, pink, and blue flowers. There is a white band in her hair, and she wears white boots that reach her upper calves. A pair of sunglasses hang from her neckline. Her appearance is casual but very elegant.

Jenna is deep in conversation with the duty nurse. They glance in his direction and Jenna waves and blows him a kiss. The duty nurse says something that makes Jenna laugh. Jenna walks towards him, hips swaying.

'Hello, Jack, I must say you are showing a vast improvement over the last time I saw you.'

Jenna kisses him on the cheek. Her scent is subtle but very feminine and Jack, who is now feeling his oats, has to constrain himself from kissing her back on the lips.

'Hi, Jenna, you look absolutely amazing. This is the first time I've seen you wearing anything but that drab uniform. Apart from your swimmers, that is.' Jack takes the chance to check her out again. 'H'mmm.'

She smiles and says archly, 'Yes, I'd say you are definitely on the improve'. She studies his body. 'And you don't seem to have lost much muscle tone,' Jenna adds in a mischievous tone, trying to wind him up. 'I won't tell you what that nurse said to me about you.'

Jack decides that two can play this game.

'You mean Sarah? Isn't she pretty? She's been very helpful to me, very helpful. She's got amazing talents.'

But Jenna plays a straight bat to this.

'Oh, that's excellent. She told me that you've been very sick. We nurses can do wonders at times, even with difficult patients like you.'

'Difficult? She said that?'

Jack has an indignant expression on his face, until he realises that Jenna has beaten him in the one-upmanship stakes. He grins shamefacedly.

'You got me there.'

Jack decides he would be better off changing the subject.

'So, how are you? Did you get a job at that hospital in the eastern suburbs? Are you living at Bondi?'

She sits on the side of the bed, her hand close to his leg. She can feel the heat of his body. It is a nice feeling.

'I'm quite well, thank you for asking, and yes to the other questions. I'm employed as a nursing sister in the Accident and Emergency Ward, A&E we call it. My trauma experience was a big factor in them hiring me. And I managed to find shared accommodation several blocks back from the beach, within walking distance to work. I share with another girl—she's a hairdresser, great fun—and a very nice guy who is something in banking.'

Jenna notices, with amusement, the change in Jack's face when she mentions the banker.

'Yes, it's a pity he's gay. Such a handsome chap.'

Jack's face brightens.

'You got any guys hanging around?'

So much for subtlety, Jenna thinks.

'No, there's just little old me.' She smiles at him demurely, and flutters her eyes innocently. 'Why do you ask, Jack?'

'Well, perhaps you might like to go out one night for a drink when I get out of here. I've decided to stay in Sydney and go to uni, if I can get in. The army's going to kick me out, which I'm now feeling not too bad about at all, and hopefully I'll be discharged from this rest home in a few weeks. So maybe we could get together. What do you say?'

Jenna crosses her legs, watching Jack's eyes being drawn magnetically to the point where her dress meets her thighs.

'I think that can be arranged.' She pre-empts Jack's smile. 'But on one condition—I want to take our friendship and any relationship that might come with it very slowly. I subscribe to the old maxim "Once bitten, twice shy". Okay?'

Jack is in full agreement. He has no desire to repeat the mistakes he made with Susie. But Jenna is very cute ...

When Jenna leaves, Jack resumes writing his letter. It is to the head of the Department of Electronic Computation at the University of New South Wales. Jack is not telling untruths about Sarah the nurse. She has helped him find out these details. Jack is enquiring about how he might enrol in this field of study in the following year, 1970, but first he has to find a job in Sydney and save some money to pay for his tuition and living expenses. He doubts the army will provide any assistance.

Chapter 38

Jack sits nervously in the lobby of the building, waiting to be called in to a job interview. He is in IBM Australia's Sydney head office in mid-July, and is dressed neatly in a shirt, tie, long trousers and polished black shoes. Jenna has helped choose his attire and he is thankful for her dress sense. If left to his own devices, he would have chosen something more casual. As he glances around him, he sees most other men are in similar attire, apart from a few weird-looking types who seem to have no dress sense at all.

Jack has applied for a relatively low-skilled job in the company. He knows he is capable of a much higher level of work, but he needs a foot in the door, not to mention some money. Although he has a reasonable amount in savings from back pay from the army and his previous stash, he doesn't want to go through this reserve too quickly on everyday necessities, otherwise he will have nothing left to pay for uni fees and text books. That is, assuming he gets into uni. He won't know until later in the year, but he has to plan ahead if he's going to accomplish his ambitions. And now he is fit again, he wants this very, very much.

As Jack waits he thinks back to his discharge from both the hospital and the army, several weeks earlier. The former was more notable than the latter, by a long shot. Several of the nurses and his doctor bade him a cheery farewell from the ward, and handed him a framed photo taken of him sunbaking on the hospital balcony. To remember the good part of being there, they said to him.

The army, however, was different. A pasty-faced civilian from the Department of the Army met him at the front desk of the hospital and wordlessly handed over his military discharge papers. The only thing he said in the five minutes it took to complete the formalities was that someone from the Department of Veterans' Affairs would be in contact via his next-of-kin to discuss any welfare benefits that might accrue from his injuries. Jack is not going to hold his breath on that.

Jack's reverie is interrupted by the sound of his name being called by a slightly pudgy man in his early thirties. Jack gets up and walks over to the guy, who regards him with an air of bored indifference.

'Jack Martin?' Jack indicates the affirmative. 'Come with me, this way please.' The pudgy guy makes no attempt at small talk as they move towards an office a few paces away.

This doesn't appear too promising, thinks Jack, *maybe I'm wasting my time.* The guy motions for him to sit on a chair in front of a desk. The man plonks himself down behind it and swings on a swivel chair.

He picks up a folder and starts to examine it. He speaks in a bored tone. 'My name's Robert Walters. Tell me a bit about yourself, Mr Martin. And not the usual stuff, that's all in here.' The guy continues to read Jack's application and still hasn't looked at him.

Stuff this, Jack thinks. *I'd better get his attention or I'll be back outside in a couple of minutes.* He straightens his back and speaks in an even, measured, confident tone.

'Mr Walters, I've done some research on your company and your competitors.' Jack silently thanks Sarah the nurse for helping here. 'I considered applying for jobs with the Burroughs Corporation, as well as General Electric and Honeywell, but my investigations have led me to the conclusion that IBM is number one, and the rest are just making up the numbers.'

Jack watches in satisfaction as the man glances up sharply, suddenly interested in what he is saying.

The man drops the folder and sits back in his chair. 'Go on.'

Jack continues. 'I believe the key success factor with IBM lies in the introduction of the System/360 a few years back. As I understand it, the S/360 has revolutionised the way computers operate, and it has permitted IBM to bring to the market a wide range of scientific and commercial applications. It's modular, isn't it? So customers can purchase a smaller system and have the confidence that they can expand their usage without having to buy a new mainframe.'

Jack can see that he now has the guy's complete attention, so he concludes, 'And it runs rings around its competitors'. This latter statement isn't necessarily correct, but Jack feels that a bit of buttering up won't go astray. Still, he feels he should not be too much of an ass-licker. 'But, I've also heard that the operating system isn't too flash.'

Robert is stunned. *My God, this young guy seems to have a better handle on our business than half the people employed here.* Robert is suddenly suspicious. *Is he a plant? Is one of our rivals trying to get him into the company? I wouldn't put it past a couple of them. They hate how we've wiped the floor with them in the past couple of years.* He decides to ask some pointed questions about Jack Martin's recent activities.

'Mr Martin, I'd like to delve a bit deeper into your employment history. You don't seem to have any experience in computing, apart from some university study? What have you been doing in the past few years?' Robert stares at Jack, expecting to hear some fairy tale.

Jack gives him a brief account of what he's been up to since the beginning of 1967, briefly mentioning university, then National Service, ending with an abbreviated version of how he sustained his injuries. Worried that the guy might see him as unfit to work, Jack hastily adds, 'But I'm just fine physically now. And I really want to work here. I hope to resume studying next year and I want to major in computing science.' He regards Robert apprehensively. Has he blown his chances?

Robert sees Jack with fresh eyes. Although he is a middle manager in what many would view as a nerdy occupation, he secretly admires the action hero genre. In a modest attempt to emulate the breed, he has become a Weekend Warrior, a member of the Army Reserve. *Crikey*, Robert thinks, *this youngster has been to Vietnam and has been shot at—maybe even knocked off some of those Vietcong—all I've done is been on a few camps, and shot at a few targets, and not very well.* Robert suddenly wants Jack Martin to work in IBM, and particularly to work for him. Maybe he'll tell him a few stories. He'll be the envy of his Army Reserve mates.

Robert makes a quick decision. 'Mr Martin. Jack. Please call me Walt. The job you applied for is probably a bit beneath your dignity.' Seeing Jack about to protest, Walt hurries on. 'What say you come and work on my team? We're involved in developing and integrating some cutting-edge applications for some of the big names in Australian business. You'll start at the bottom, but I would think that a person of your acumen will find himself moving up the ladder pretty smartly. When can you start?'

Jack is ecstatic at this unexpected bonus. Almost too late, he remembers his university ambitions. 'Gee, thanks, Mr Walters … err … Walt, but I have to factor in the possibility of university next year. If that causes a problem, I'm afraid I'll have to decline your generous offer.' Jack is crestfallen, fearing that he's blown his chances.

Seeing Jack's disconsolate expression, Walt hastens to put his mind at ease. 'Jack, let me see if I can't arrange some sort of cadetship for you. That just well may kill two birds with one stone. Have you considered studying at university part-time?'

Jack considers this. Walt's solution might well work. He too makes a decision. 'Walt, that sounds terrific. I'll have to double-check with the university, but I seem to recall from this year's handbook that part-time study is offered in the department that teaches computer science.' He adds: 'If it's okay, can I suggest that I start Monday? That will give me a few days to sort some things out'.

Walt beams. 'Done, Jack. I'll hand you over to the personnel team in a moment so that they can take you through the paperwork. Now, we like to pay a bit over the odds here, we find it keeps our people motivated to stay with us. How about you start at, say, seventy dollars a week?'

It is Jack's turn to smile. *That's pretty good money*, he thinks happily. *Enough for me to live on, and afford some accommodation that's within public transport travel to Jenna's place and here. I think I know just the spot.*

Walt and Jack shake hands on the agreement.

*****

That evening Jack invites Jenna out to dinner to celebrate. They meet at a cafe in Bondi. Jack is staying temporarily in cheap lodgings near Central Station in order to conserve his savings. She is a knockout, even dressed casually in jeans and a T-shirt. Jack excitedly recounts the events of the interview and the outcome, and Jenna hugs him and congratulates him. She smells good, he thinks. Jenna recognises the look on Jack's face.

'Jack, don't you go and get any ideas about me. I told you that I want to take any relationship that might develop very slowly, so I'm not about to jump into bed with you, if that's what's on your mind. So take a deep breath, and relax. Your tongue is hanging out so far that it is almost on the table. Come on, let's talk about where you're going to live.'

Jack begins to talk enthusiastically. 'Well, I was thinking of the Randwick area. Hopefully I can find some shared accommodation like you. It's close enough to the beach and I can walk to uni if I get in, or even ride a pushbike. And the public transport is reasonable for me to get to work as well. And it's close to you.' Seeing Jenna's face, Jack hastily adds: 'I only say that because I'm volunteering to be your swimming coach. You could train in the ocean baths at Bondi beach'.

Jenna smiles gently. 'That's a good idea. When do we start? And how much will it cost?'

Jack bites back the retort that instantly comes into his mind. 'Oh, just buy me a beer or a glass of wine every now and then. And we can commence your conversion into Dawn Fraser the Second just as soon as I find a place to live.'

They order their food and settle back to enjoy the meal. Jack steers the conversation to Jenna's past. He is curious to know more about her and Jenna is happy to talk about it. Her parents live in Katoomba in the Blue Mountains, where she was born and raised. They both work in a family business; her father is a dentist and her mother manages the dental practice. She has a younger sister, still at school, and an older brother, who is an accountant. Jenna has always wanted to be a nurse and did her training at the Nepean Hospital in Penrith, where she worked until she was persuaded by one of her mentors to apply to nurse in Vietnam because it would most likely give her experience she wouldn't easily obtain anywhere else. That certainly proved to be true.

Jenna gives Jack a light kiss on the lips after the meal. They go their separate ways, both full of hope for a future that appears to be rosy right now.

*****

Chapter 39

In Kings Cross, Terry Bannister is entering into a very different employment agreement. He sits in Bernie Houghton's office at the Bourbon and Beefsteak Bar, sipping on a cold beer. He is five kilos lighter than he was, courtesy of the friendly staff at the MCE in Holsworthy. And he has a couple of new scars on his body for his trouble.

His mood is savage, but he is very much in control of himself. He has reflected long and hard on the events and circumstances that led to his incarceration, as well as his attitude. There is nothing like a few months of semi-brutality to make you see the error of your ways. Terry has resolved never again to be the mug and the patsy that he has been. And for keeping silent through all the rough treatment, he is well and truly due some favours. He is here to collect, but he must be cunning and play the long game. And he is determined to never go behind bars again.

Terry turns to face Michael Hand, who is also in the office. Terry keeps his voice respectful, but he has a point to make.

'Mr Hand, it's good to see you. It must be, what, six months since out last meeting in Saigon and Vung Tau? A lot of water has passed under the bridge since then. I hope that water has been nice and clean for you because, as you know, it hasn't been for me.' It is obvious to Michael that Terry wants recompense for his time in jail.

Michael decides to ignore Terry's implied criticism. 'Yes, Terry, the water has been very beneficial for me and my associates. Things are on the up, in lots of areas. You might say business is booming. So much so, I'm thinking of going into the property business. There's a lot of money to be made in that game.'

Michael takes a sip of his drink. 'Speaking of money, you'll find that your bank account has grown appreciably over the period that you were … out of circulation. But I've got even better news for you. I'm going to need a troubleshooter in my new business venture, and I want to offer you the job.'

Terry, who isn't sure what a troubleshooter is or does, asks cautiously, 'What specifically would I be doing?'

Michael has a sardonic grin on his face.

'Well, in a nutshell, you would be supporting my business associates and me to achieve our aims, using whatever means necessary to make the other party see it our way. I don't want to go into specifics—those will depend on how much persuasion is required—but I think you get my drift.'

Terry nods watchfully. 'And what sort of money would this troubleshooter job pay, Mr Hand?'

Michael exchanges a glance with Bernie. 'I think we can start you on a retainer of two hundred dollars a week, plus expenses. We can review that amount, depending on performance. And I hear you might need a new car. How about I throw in a sign-on bonus of four thousand dollars so that you can get something that takes your fancy?'

Terry doesn't know what a retainer is, but the weekly payments sound just fine to him. He'll be earning over three times the average weekly earnings, not to mention a large cash bonus as well. And he knows just the type of car he wants. Terry leans over to shake Michael's hand.

'You've got yourself a deal, Mr Hand. And don't worry about performance; for that sort of money I'll guarantee you will be well satisfied with any troubleshooting that is necessary.'

Terry leaves Bernie and Michael to discuss business. He intends to have a drink with Dozer. Hell, maybe several. It's time to celebrate. In his mind he has already purchased the latest six cylinder Torana GTR XUI—the Peter Brock Special can do the standing four hundred metres in under sixteen seconds—and he'll have change left over to get it properly accessorised. *That's the way to negotiate*, he thinks happily.

*****

Chapter 40

The eighth decade of the twentieth century has dawned bright with promise, technologically at least. Although the Vietnam War lingers on like a slow-acting cancer, elsewhere things are on the up. Apollo 11's lunar module has successfully landed on the surface of the Moon in mid-1969, and Neil Armstrong has taken the first steps on this alien world. Humankind is astonished, and the West celebrates whilst the kingpins in the East fume.

Although it is not widely known, the digital flight computer system used in the lunar and command modules has only a small amount of hard-wired memory and uses primitive integrated circuits for processing basic commands. But it works, and it works beautifully. Notably, the IBM S/360 has been used extensively in the Apollo project for complex number crunching.

Jack is well aware of all this. His work at IBM has given him access to all sorts of esoteric information on computers and computing. With Walt mentoring him closely, Jack has come on in leaps and bounds and is now an integral part of the small team that Walt uses to problem-solve tricky customer challenges.

His studies at the University of New South Wales are almost mundane by comparison. Jack has been successful in enrolling in the obscurely-named Department of Electronic Computation at the uni for 1970. Jack regards this strange name as typical academic highbrow nonsense, and most of his classmates agree.

Walt has delivered on his promise to get Jack a cadetship, and his uni fees and other costs are covered by his employer. Thankfully, he has been granted exemptions by UNSW for the first year subjects he undertook at Newcastle University, so this year he is studying several computer programming subjects that are allied to the department's S/360 computer. Jack is very happy because he is learning how to write software. The logic of computer programming appeals to him. He is able to quickly pick up the cryptic skill of writing computer code. As the department's only computer is heavily booked and students have very limited time to use it, Jack can't wait to use his newly acquired knowledge at work, where there is plenty of access. He isn't too interested in the academic applications; he is more focused on commercial gain.

However, early on he is frustrated at the seemingly inefficient method of obtaining an output from the simple academic-style programs he writes. The steps involved in obtaining a result are tedious. He firstly has to write the program by hand on a specially marked page. The information on the page is then transcribed onto a block of rectangular cards, one for each instruction in the program. If there is an error in the program or the page, or the cards are incorrectly transcribed, then the program won't work, and the only way to know whether he has been successful is to come back later to collect a printout of the results after the program has been run on the mainframe. If there is a problem, everything has to be rechecked, with the process being repeated until success is achieved. It is such a pain in the bum. Jack wishes there is a better way of doing this. He thinks the procedure, called batch processing, is in urgent need of review. He is not alone.

Soon after being discharged from hospital Jack makes the journey north to Newcastle to visit his parents and to retrieve his beloved motorbike. The bike will come in handy to ride to university and to work, and parking is a cinch. It isn't too flash when it rains, but apart from that it is the perfect form of transportation around the busy eastern suburbs.

Gladys and Henry are reconciled to Jack making a new life in Sydney; after all, it is only a couple of hours' drive. But Gladys still sheds a tear when he drives off, waving as he accelerates away.

Jack has also been able to find a shared flat in Randwick, not far from the main street. His flatmate is also a uni student, although he doesn't seem to spend a lot of time studying or attending lectures. Will Cochrane is the son of a very well-to-do barrister who is funding his son's rather extravagant lifestyle. There is usually a party at the flat every weekend, with lots of attractive and available females in attendance. Will is a bit of a pothead, but doesn't take offence when Jack declines to share a joint with him.

The party girls are friendly and willing, particularly after a few drinks, and Jack has had several one-night stands as a result. The girls in question invariably go off happily the next morning, with a casual kiss and wave goodbye. Things with Jenna are progressing in an unhurried way, so Jack has no compunction in enjoying himself with other girls. It is only sex, and there is nothing serious yet going on with Jenna.

This situation changes gradually as Jenna finds herself becoming more emotionally attached to Jack. Jenna slowly comes to the view that Jack may be suitable husband material. He is loyal, dependable, honest, hardworking, and although he loves a social drink, he doesn't get carried away. He seems to show no ill effects from his spell in Vietnam, even with the trauma he went through. They have started having sex, which she finds she enjoys very much. He has a great body, even with a few scars. Moreover, he doesn't seem to have a wandering eye. These are attributes she finds hard to resist, and she suggests that they live together. Jack is more than happy to agree, and they find a suitable apartment in Coogee.

For Jack, it doesn't much matter that the fireworks in bed that he previously experienced with Susie are more muted with Jenna. He is contented. Jenna is a wonderful partner—kind, considerate, understanding, and sexy enough. She knows her mind and is not afraid to speak it, and Jack respects that. She is enjoying the wide mix of thrills and spills that crop up during each shift in A&E, and her ability to cope with the weirdest and most wonderful cases that turn up. She regularly has Jack in stitches of laughter with accounts of chaos and mayhem caused by the tide of human flotsam and jetsam that make their way to the hospital.

Jack doesn't have much success when he tries to explain to Jenna what he is doing at work and at uni. If he gets too technical she just crosses her eyes comically, sticks her fingers in her ears, and chants 'la, la, la …' until he translates the jargon into English. To her horror, Jenna realises that she now knows quite a few basic computing terms.

That is enough information for her. Although she is impressed with the names of the IBM team's commercial clients, she isn't the least bit interested in what he does for them, or how he does it. The only time she is a bit excited is when he cites an example of using databases for inputting and extracting patient information. She gets that, but doesn't want to know any more about the nuts and bolts.

As Walt's friendship with Jack grows, he invites him to do some practice shooting at the Malabar Rifle Range, in the southern suburbs of Sydney. It has been renamed the ANZAC Rifle Range by the army and Jack feels right at home. Walt is proud of his Sportco Model 44, a bolt-action single-shot target rifle that takes a 7.62 mm calibre bullet. Walt's rifle has a foresight element box screwed to the pistol grip, and Parker Hale Model 5C rear target sight and an adjustable eye piece for an optical lens. Jack likes the feel of the weapon.

Walt is keen to see what Jack can do, and asks, 'Why don't you have a couple of warm-up shots with the rifle on the 300-metre range, Jack?'.

Jack dons some earmuffs and prepares to fire. After two test shots Jack checks the target and finds that the rifle pulls slightly to the left and shoots a fraction high. After he adjusts it, Jack fires the next three rounds into the centre of the bullseye. Walt is impressed, particularly as he finds his own accuracy, whilst not up to Jack's standard, has improved when he too uses the rifle afterwards.

Walt says: 'Why don't we try the 600-metre range, Jack? I've never done it, but I'm willing to have a go if you are'.

This idea excites Jack, as he has not previously fired a rifle that has the range and accuracy over distances longer than 300 metres. Walt has a go, and gets a couple of rounds onto the target, but nowhere near the centre ring. It is Jack's turn. He settles down on the firing mound and carefully brings the target to bear through the sights. He slows his breathing and squeezes the trigger. After ten shots he and Walt check the target. Walt is amazed.

'Fuck me sideways, Jack, you have put all ten shots into the centre ring, and three of those into the X inside the centre ring.'

Jack recalls the countless hours spent at the range in the Dat. It has obviously paid off.

Jack's accuracy has attracted the interest of a senior member of the local rifle shooting association, who is practising nearby. He asks Jack to consider joining the association and, with Walt's urging, Jack agrees.

Jack takes Jenna to Newcastle to meet his parents. They get on well, and Jack is pleased and relieved. Jack avoids the surf club, partly out of embarrassment, but mainly because of the bad memories. Jenna reciprocates with her parents and her siblings. Jack loves Katoomba and finds Jenna's family easy to get on with.

*****

In early 1971, during a break at uni, Jack and Jenna take a couple of days off work and hire a car and drive north to the Central Coast. They stay at the Florida Hotel at Terrigal, right across the road from the beach. During dinner in the restaurant the first night he surreptitiously takes an engagement ring out of his pocket. On cue, the pianist plays a drum roll, which stops all conversation in the dining room. Jenna is almost speechless when Jack goes to one knee in front of her and pops the question. But she recovers quickly and, kissing him, mouths the word 'yes', much to the delight of their fellow diners, who cheer them both. Their lovemaking is particularly vigorous that night.

They decide to tie the knot in December 1971. Jack will have completed his second year studies by then, and Walt has agreed to his suggestion that Jack finish his last year of uni via full-time study. His salary will drop a little, but Jenna is earning enough to cover the gap. Besides, as a newly married couple they won't be out and about too much anyway. But in exchange IBM requires him to sign an agreement to remain with the company for three years after he graduates. Jack signs.

Jack gets in contact with H, who is working as a security contractor in Sydney, and asks H to be his best man. H agrees, proud to be asked. Jenna's sister will be her bridesmaid. After much discussion, which includes input from both sets of parents, the wedding will take place in Katoomba. It will be a small wedding, with no more than 50 guests, including family. Jenna is very excited, and is busy planning the event, aided by her mother and Gladys. Jack is happy to let them loose on it; he just wants to get it over and done with.

*****

With the women busy planning the wedding, Jack is able to concentrate on his work and study. He has become interested in the field of relational databases, their applications in particular. He is intrigued with the concept of storing similar types of information in tables in order to speed up access to the information the user is interested in. A special computer language called Structured Query Language has been developed for this purpose. Jack believes that relational database management using SQL is the coming thing, and he wants to be in at the start. Walt gives him free rein; after all, the clients will be the beneficiaries, and a happy client means more business.

The Department of Electronic Computation at the university is more into developing an academic-style data system. This is interesting stuff, and Jack can see its potential for commercial applications, but to Jack the real bonus is the invention by one of the staff of a new high-level computer language that runs so much faster on the 360/S than the IBM-equivalent software. However, when he suggests through Walt that head office back in the USA consider this—after all, it is freeware, and thus available for use by anyone—he is met with a brick wall of indifference from head office. Doesn't he know that all technological advances must come from the USA, not from some little country like Australia? Jack is frustrated, but there isn't too much he can do about it. This frustration grows slowly but steadily.

*****

Jack and Jenna's wedding goes off without a hitch. Although tradition dictates a church wedding, Jack is not interested. He feels that it would be hypocritical; neither he nor Jenna is a church goer, nor are their parents. Jenna backs him, and they elect to have the wedding ceremony using a celebrant on the cliff tops near Leura, close to Katoomba.

Chapter 40

The day is blessed with perfect weather, and they tie the knot in a simple but moving ceremony. Jenna and her sister are radiant in pink, and Jack and H, dressed in snappy hired suits, look handsome in their formal attire. Afterwards, they celebrate the wedding breakfast at the historical Carrington Hotel. H makes an amusing speech recounting some funny moments from Vietnam, and everyone gets mildly tipsy and enjoys the dancing.

Jack and Jenna stay at the hotel that night in the bridal suite and consummate their marriage. Jenna wears some very sexy lingerie and this inflames Jack's lust. They emerge exhausted but very happy for a late breakfast, then catch the train back into Sydney and head for the airport for a flight to Coolangatta. They have booked into a hotel in Surfers Paradise and arrive midevening, hungry and tired. The newly married couple spend a blissful week relaxing at Surfers, swimming and sunbathing at the beach in the morning, enjoying lengthy lunches and lovemaking in the afternoon, and then taking in the nightlife in the evening.

All too soon, they have to return to Sydney. The honeymoon over, the married couple settles contently into marital life. They notice that not much has changed at all in what they do, except that now they are officially together.

Jenna, who keeps her maiden name for professional reasons, is now very experienced in the A&E department at the hospital and is considering her future in the health arena. Jenna is contemplating moving into a management role as the years of doing shift work are taking their toll. She would very much like to have a normal day job so that she can be home in the evenings to be with Jack. But any decision on her future will have to wait until Jack finishes his final year of studies.

Jack throws himself into academia, determined to elicit the maximum benefit from both the theory and practical. He learns about mathematical methods to mimic real-world situations such as movements on the stock market. He can't get too excited about this, it appears to be quite limited, unable take into account the human factors of greed and fear, the real drivers of stock prices. He revels in database theory, where his real interest lies.

He is not surprised when the university decides to introduce a new name—Department of Computer Science—to his area of study. This makes more sense than the old one, everyone agrees.

*****

Chapter 41

Michael Hand is away overseas for much of the first half of 1970, so Terry is mostly left to his own devices, save for the occasional job for Bernie. Dozer has been promoted from being a bouncer at the Bourbon and Beefsteak to running security for Bernie's network of businesses. Dozer tells Terry that the previous occupant of the position has mysteriously disappeared after being caught with his hand in the till. Dozer, with a wicked grin on his face, denies any knowledge of his predecessor's fate. Terry imagines that his demise wouldn't have been pleasant. Dozer invites Terry to train at the gym he frequents in Woolloomooloo, a nearby suburb. Over time, Terry slowly increases the weights he can lift, politely but firmly refusing the offer of steroids from gym members to help increase his muscle mass.

He finds a small one-bedroom flat to rent in Potts Point, just near the Cross. From a tiny balcony off the lounge/dining area, there is a limited view of Rushcutters Bay where yachts belonging to the rich and famous are moored. The flat is in a quiet area, even though it is only a couple of blocks behind the strip joints in Darlinghurst Road.

It even has a single car lock-up garage for his Torana. It suits Terry just fine.

With plenty of time on his hands, Terry also begins to jog and swim to further his fitness. By the middle of the year he is able to run around six to eight kilometres and swim a kilometre. After a few months, Terry finds that he can usually run at just over the four-minute klick pace, which leaves him quietly satisfied.

All the exercise sees him very fit and losing a few more kilos. Terry feels this is not a bad thing, as after his incarceration and before this training he had become a bit pudgy. And he has plenty of spare cash for new clothes. It is only a walk of several kilometres into the Sydney CBD, and he enjoys purchasing the latest fashions in the multitude of shops that line the bustling streets.

The new Terry has learnt to largely temper his more unusual sexual desires, but as he becomes increasingly familiar with the Cross and its bizarre range of occupants and visitors, he finds there are enough girls that are willing participants in his deviant behaviour.

But his pride and joy is his bright red car. He treats it so much better than his women; no whips and rough treatment for the XU1. He has shod it with shiny mag wheels and high-performance tyres and it looks very hot. It does attract the attention of the local cops, but many of them are on the take from the Kings Cross nightclub owners and leave him alone.

Now he is in the money he makes a call to an aunty who lives in Cronulla and invites himself for a visit. Aware of Terry's behaviour as a younger man, she and her husband greet him warily, but he quickly puts them at ease. He has a financial proposition for them—in exchange for Terry paying them a weekly fee for their trouble, will they take his younger sisters in, care for them and ensure they are properly fed, clothed and attend school? Of course they will; the girls will be company for their fifteen-year-old daughter, and the money will be put to good use.

Happy with this arrangement, Terry travels to Newcastle and collects his sisters. Mary is at first reluctant, but Terry won't take no for an answer, so she and her sister, Maureen, pack up their meagre possessions and accompany him to their aunt's place. Terry gives the aunt strict instructions about how his sisters are to cope with school, boys, and a change in lifestyle. His aunt is in full agreement with his desires for them.

Terry visits them every second Sunday and takes them out for a few hours to the beach, for lunch or to a movie. The girls have settled well into the quiet suburban life in Cronulla and seem happy. Mary, in particular, seems to have changed considerably in the better environment. Terry is pleased that he is able to do something positive for them.

In mid-1970 Michael returns from Vietnam, where he has been fundraising for the new company. Terry learns that the company, called Australian and Pacific Holdings, has a large number of shareholders, several of whom are old Air America buddies of Michael's. Terry wonders about the deal: is the CIA really backing Michael? This seems improbable, but Terry doesn't discount it. The other scenario he comes up with is that the company is backed by a consortium of Michael's mates, some of whom happen to be the veritable cowboys that are, or were, employed by Air America. Whatever the truth, Terry isn't about to mouth off about these theories.

Even though he enjoys the large amounts of spare time, Terry is getting a bit toey. He is therefore happy when Michael calls him to a meeting in the company offices. There Terry is introduced to a new face, a charismatic, slightly overweight Aussie named Frank Nugan who, according to Michael, will be entering into a few property ventures with him and Bernie. Terry's troubleshooting role is to include these deals.

Impetuously, Terry speaks out. 'But, Mr Hand, I don't seem to be doing too much of this troubleshooting. How will this deal be different?'

Michael regards him with a cool smile.

'Terry, my company now has the capital necessary to start purchasing a range of properties in inner Sydney in the first instance, and possibly further afield in due course. And Frank here's expertise is in taxation and financial advice. He'll be helping with the acquisitions.' Michael pats Frank on the arm in welcome. Then Michael frowns.

'But we may have a problem; these properties are in demand and there is interest being shown by some rival entities. Those entities may need some persuasion that it would be in their best interests to turn their attention elsewhere. So, I want you to accompany Frank on a visit to the guys in charge to see if you can't get them to change their minds. And Bernie has given the okay for you to take Dozer along—just in case. No offense, Terry, but Dozer projects a hell of a lot more menace than you or Frank.'

Michael gives Terry two names and addresses.

'Oh, and Terry, let Frank do most of the talking. You just keep shtum and learn from him. You'll be amazed how a lawyer like him can gild the lily with his fine words.'

The trio make their first visit midafternoon that day. The guy, in his late fifties and sporting a large belly, takes one look at Dozer and meekly agrees with Frank's erudite suggestion that he might wish to find some other properties to invest in.

The second visit late in the afternoon of the same day doesn't go as smoothly. This guy is younger, and very aggressive. When he hears Frank's proposition, he screams obscenities at them and is not at all over-awed with Dozer's bulk. Frank starts to retort, but before he can say anything he may later regret, Terry steps in and calmly suggests they leave. The guy is still hurling abuse as they depart his suite of offices. Terry hands the receptionist a plain white card that contains just a telephone number, and no address.

In the early hours of the morning a couple of days later the guy is awakened from a sound sleep by his wife shouting in alarm. He rushes out of his very nice home in the up-market suburb of Vaucluse in Sydney's eastern suburbs to find his brand spanking new Mercedes-Benz 280SE sedan well alight in his driveway. By the time the fire crew has doused the flames, the car is a burnt-out shell.

The phone, whose number is on the card, rings the next morning. Terry picks it up but says nothing. It is the formerly aggressive guy who has suddenly changed his tune. In a trembling voice far removed from the belligerence shown two days before, he swears that he will not bid for the properties and pleads for him and his family not to be harmed. Terry hangs up without a word. The message has been delivered, and received. He and Dozer have done the job required.

Michael is pleased with both the outcome, and the way Terry handled the problem. He figures that, with a quick churn of the properties he will pick up at a knock-down price, the company will make a tidy profit of several hundred thousand dollars. His shareholders will be happy, and his management fee will net him at least fifteen per cent of the profit. Not bad at all.

Frank is impressed with Terry as well. He takes Terry out for a drink at a nearby bar to celebrate their success. After a half-dozen schooners, he impulsively takes Terry into his confidence.

'You know, Terry, I don't really need to do this sort of work, although I like it.' He pauses, and then continues. 'Have you ever heard of the Nugan Group? No? Well, my brother Ken and I run it. It's based in a town called Griffith, in south-west New South Wales, and we're in the fruit and veggie business.'

Terry is not particularly impressed with this bit of information. Fruit and vegetables? This bloke's nothing but a farmer. Terry makes a non-committal grunt in response. Frank laughs when he sees Terry's reaction.

'I bet you think I'm some mug who hangs around with the big boys and runs a Ma-and-Pa outfit out in the sticks. Well, let me tell you, our business will turn over a bit under four million bucks this year.'

Terry is impressed. He would never have dreamt that so much money could be earned this way. He decides to quiz Frank some more.

'So why *are* you hanging around with the big boys?'

Frank scans his surrounds to see if anyone is within earshot. The beer is starting to take effect and he leans towards Terry, slightly over-balancing as he does so.

'Whoops,' he apologises, 'never could hold my grog. You see, Terry, Michael told you that I have some skill in taxation and financial advice. That's true'. Frank drops his voice to a whisper. 'But what he didn't say is I'm good at hiding the money trail. Real good.'

'I see,' says Terry thoughtfully. He decides to take a gamble and ask pointedly: 'So, Frank, what's the story on that little bit of business we did this week? I get the impression that Michael will do very nicely out of it'.

Frank touches the side of his nose in a conspiratorial gesture.

'He sure will. But there's more to come, you just wait and see.' He sits back and takes another pull on his beer, smiling smugly.

'What are you grinning at, Frank? How come you know so much? Is it you who is giving Michael the inside story on these properties?'

Frank regards Terry wistfully and shakes his head.

'No, I wish I could claim to have the information, but it isn't me.'

'Then who is it?'

Frank gazes at him seriously.

'Terry, even though you have proved yourself to me, it's not worth my while to divulge that. Let's just say that it comes from a very well-known public figure, and leave it at that. Anyway, that's enough shop talk. Let's have a few more beers and you can tell me a bit more about yourself, eh?'

During the next eighteen months Frank, Terry and, where necessary, Dozer do the necessary persuading that enables Australian and Pacific Holdings, acting on hot tips from the mysterious benefactor, to churn a large volume of commercial property all across New South Wales, making very large profits. Everyone benefits, and by the end of this period Terry's weekly cash 'retainer' is now at over $400. Terry and Dozer only have to resort to appropriate levels of controlled violence three more times, each of which produces the desired result.

*****

Chapter 42

In November 1972 Edward Gough Whitlam, leader of the Australian Labor Party, wins the Australian federal election and becomes the 23rd prime minister of Australia. Campaigning on a slogan of 'It's Time', Gough wins a narrow majority in the lower house. One of the first acts of the Whitlam government is to order home all Australian troops in Vietnam. Gough's government then abolishes university fees and declares that the song *Advance Australia Fair* will replace *God Save the Queen* as the national anthem. He also recognises Red China. Times are a'changing indeed.

On hearing the election news in the South China Sea, the captain of *HMAS Sydney*, Lawrence 'Red' Merson, is somewhat saddened but also relieved. He reasons, with some justification, that the current trip, the 25th to Vietnam, will be the last for the *Vung Tau Ferry*. He is correct. *HMAS Sydney* is to be decommissioned in July 1973. Red is not entirely mollified when he and his crew tow the disabled freighter *Kaiwing* from Vung Tau to Hong Kong over a four-day period in heavy seas generated by an approaching typhoon. He is, however, happy to receive the captain's share of the salvage money generated from this adventure.

Gough Whitlam's decision to abolish university fees is met with glee by Jack, even though it will be too late to impact on his study. Walt however thinks that Gough is a left-wing radical who will bring nothing but trouble to the commercial world. He is partly correct.

Gough and his socialist government commit the unpardonable sin of disrespecting the US establishment, condemning US actions in Vietnam and tacitly supporting a union ban on all US shipping entering Australian ports. In an act of political retaliation, the US president, Richard 'Tricky Dicky' Nixon, deliberately delays issuing the customary invitation for the new prime minister to visit the White House by about six months. The Australian-US relationship is teetering at an all-time low and Nixon is considering reviewing the previously strong alliance. US interests in Australia, including IBM, are worried about the impact that this contretemps may have on business.

The private sector likes stability and surety so that capital investments can achieve a reasonable return. This applies not only to legitimate business, but to the darker side of the ledger. A US company, Bally Machines, that makes and sells poker machines has an Australian subsidiary, Bally Australia. There are unproven allegations of a link between the US Mafia, Bally and its subsidiaries—including Bally Australia—and Abe Saffron, a Sydneysider known as 'Mr Sin'. Abe Saffron owns a string of nightclubs and hotels in Sydney and is a mate of Lenny McPherson and a business colleague of Bernie Houghton. None of these shady characters is too happy with the Whitlam Labor government's attitude to organised crime; they much prefer the laid-back approach of Bob Askin, the premier of New South Wales.

*****

Chapter 43

In April 1973 the annual autumn horse racing carnival is held at the Royal Randwick racecourse. The premier event is the Sydney Cup, run over 3200 metres. Terry has been invited to the race meeting by Bernie, who is a keen punter. Bernie gives him some advice.

'Wear your best bag of fruit, Terry, we'll be in the member's enclosure, and there are sure to be lots of important people attending.'

So Terry has his almost-new dark-green suit dry-cleaned for the occasion. He chooses a long-collared white shirt and a paisley tie to wear. He checks his appearance in the mirror. 'Not bad,' he nods approvingly. He checks his money clip. Yes, a thousand bucks. That should be enough to get through the day.

Bernie picks Terry up in his silver Jaguar XJ-6 and they drive to the racecourse. As well as a suit, Bernie is wearing a pork pie hat. *Not for me*, Terry thinks, *that's for old guys like Bernie.* Of course Bernie has a car pass and he parks in the members' car park. The pair alights and walks to the member's enclosure. Whilst Bernie pauses to greet friends, Terry glances around. It is a glorious April day in Sydney, sunny and with the temperature in the mid-twenties. There are lots of beautiful women wearing the latest fashions—after all, it is one of the top days on the racing calendar. Terry smiles appreciatively. *If only I can back a few winners.*

Using the pass that Bernie provides him, Terry enters the member's area. The place is packed with the rich and famous. Terry spies several VIPs, including the recently retired police commissioner, Norman Allan, who is deep in conversation with Lenny McPherson. Standing near them is the well-known punter and nightclub owner, Perce Galea. As Terry watches, Perce turns and warmly greets none other than the premier, Bob Askin.

Seeing Terry staring at Galea and Askin, Bernie takes him by the arm and moves in their direction. The premier and the punter pause their conversation as Bernie and Terry approach, and both smile and shake Bernie's hand vigorously. Bernie introduces Terry to them.

'Pleased to meet you, Mr … uh … Premier, and you two, Mr Galea,' Terry manages to gulp out.

Askin speaks first. 'Call me Bob, Terry. I'm just a working-class man at heart. Never could stand those highfalutin titles that people put on me. So, you're a friend of Bernie's, eh? Well, good luck to you, young fella.'

Askin sees someone waving to him and says to Terry and Bernie: 'Sorry, got to go. I enjoy a good punt, but politics is a business, and business calls'. As he leaves, Askin says to Terry, 'If you want a tip, just ask my old mate Perce here. He knows all there is to know about this meet. See you later'. Then he is off to work the room.

Perce Galea regards Terry affably and smiles. 'A tip, eh? Well, I'll give you two. Miss Personality in the third race, and Apollo Eleven in the Sydney Cup. You'll get better odds on Miss Personality, but my mail says that Apollo Eleven is a red-hot special. So, take my advice and get on both. Now, I need to catch up with my mate Bernie for a private chat. Maybe I'll catch you later, and you can buy me a beer out of your winnings.'

Terry hastily moves off, watching Perce move to Bernie's side and chat quietly about something which is obviously serious, judging by the expressions on their faces. Terry would love to know what they're talking about, but he has other pressing matters to attend to, namely getting the best price on the two tips as quickly as possible. Who knows if a late betting spree might bring in the odds on either or both of them? Terry wants to place his bets right now.

He moves out into the betting ring, where the on-course bookies are located. Several are only taking bets on the next race, the second on the card, but a few are showing the odds for the whole race meet. The best odds he can see are eight to one for Miss Personality, and fives for Apollo Eleven, but with different bookies. But how much to bet on each? He decides to wager three hundred dollars on the first horse, and five hundred on the second—both on the nose. That way, if they are beaten, at least he has a couple of hundred left to try and get his money back.

Terry carefully folds the two lots of cash and puts the second bundle into his suit pocket. He approaches the first bookie and successfully places his bet. Then he does the same for the second bookie. Terry notices that, as soon as his bets are laid, the prices shorten by half a point. *Bloody bookies, always looking after number one*, he thinks. He double-checks his tickets for accuracy. *Time for a beer*, he thinks.

Before long the horses parade for race three. Taking his beer out into the stand, Terry is very nervous as he watches them. Miss Personality is a beautifully groomed brown mare with impressive musculature. She is sweating slightly but seems calm enough. Her jockey is wearing emerald-green colours. *A bit like the colour of my suit*, Terry notes. *Maybe that will bring me luck.*

The horses move into the barriers and suddenly they are racing. Terry screams out in excitement as the field starts to spread out. Miss Personality is travelling well in third place at the halfway mark, and with two hundred metres to go, has moved into second. It is then that the jockey gives the horse its head and the mare bounds forward, passing the frontrunner and wins going away. Terry has shouted himself hoarse with excitement. *You little beauty*, he thinks in joy.

After calming himself down, Terry collects his winnings. *Fantastic. I've won two thousand, four hundred dollars; I'm fourteen hundred ahead on the day, and the Sydney Cup is still to come.*

He goes into the member's dining room and eats a light lunch. Sipping on a beer, he spots Bob Askin doing the politician's thing with a group of punters. As he watches Askin doing what he does best, for some reason he thinks back to what Frank Nugan said to him some months back about a high-profile public figure providing him and Michael with inside property information. *Surely it couldn't be Bob Askin? No, no way*, Terry concludes; *that's just too incredible to be true*.

Terry is calmer for race five, the Sydney Cup. He has a feeling that his horse is going to win. He realises that this is foolish, but he can't shake it off. He knows that 3200 metres is a long way, but that doesn't matter. He sits in the stands and watches the race unfold. Apollo Eleven not only wins convincingly, but sets a new course record in doing so. Terry quickly calculates his winnings. When he picks them up, they will be a further two thousand, five hundred dollars, bringing his total winnings to nearly five grand. *Shit, what a good day!*

Terry's attention is drawn to a small group of women screaming ecstatically in the nearby public stand. *They must have backed the winner as well*, he thinks. *Good on them.* As he is about to get up and go to collect his money, he suddenly recognises one of the females. *Shit*, he realises, *it's that Susie sheila from Newcastle. What the fuck is she doing here?*

At that moment Susie glances in his direction. The smile of

pleasure on her face is instantly replaced by a frown. Then the penny drops. She rushes over to the wall between them and screams angrily: 'You bastard, I remember you. I've a good mind to get the coppers up here for what you did to me'.

Terry freezes for a moment in astonishment, but at the sound of her voice he quickly recovers. He pleads in a placating tone, 'Susie, that was a long time ago'. In a lower voice, he adds: 'And I'm sure that, if you think it through, you won't want the cops to hear how you did drugs, and what you let me do to you. Besides, it's really just your word against mine'.

Susie is about to reply but wisely shuts her mouth. The hatred for him is written all over her face. Suddenly a voice interrupts their argument. It is one of her girlfriends. 'Susie, who is this delicious man? Have you been hiding him from us?'

Susie decides not to make a scene. 'He's an … a … a guy I used to know in Newcastle a few years back.' Susie seems lost for words, so Terry smoothly jumps in.

'Yes, Susie and I go back a ways.' Despite his better judgement, Terry decides to take a risk. 'Susie, why don't you and your friends have a celebratory drink with me? I've just backed the winner and I'm in a mood to celebrate.' Terry looks expectantly at Susie, anticipating that she will tell him to piss off.

To his surprise, she doesn't. Instead, she says meekly: 'Why don't you invite us in to the members for that drink, Terry? We're celebrating too. You're not the only one who backed Apollo Eleven. By the way, this is Maggie, and the one coming over to us now is Deborah'. Susie indicates to the other girls in the party of three.

Terry is taken aback, but decides to go with the flow. He wants to find out what she's up to.

'Yeah, sure, I'll just arrange a couple of passes from a mate, and I'll meet you at the entrance. Oh, and hi, Maggie and Deb. See you in ten minutes, okay? I've got to pick up my winnings.'

Maggie, ever the social climber, gushes a response.

'Oh, Terry, that would be great. We've got to get our money, too. We each put five dollars on Apollo Eleven to win at four to one. Deb fancied the beautiful shade of peach that the jockey is wearing, and we've won sixty dollars between us. We're so happy.'

Terry deduces that peach must be orange, because that's the colour of the jockey's top. 'Right oh, girls, I'll see you soon.'

Terry strides inside to find Bernie. He spots him talking to Perce Galea. Terry thanks Perce profusely for the tips, promises to buy him that beer, then pulls Bernie aside briefly and asks him for a favour. Bernie happily gives him three guest tickets. Terry then collects his money from an unhappy bookmaker before moving to the entrance where the three women are waiting. Susie's friends giggle nervously. Susie, though, is calm; the previous look of hatred towards him no longer apparent. Terry studies her. *She's up to something*, he decides.

Terry orders a bottle of champagne and five glasses, plus a beer for Perce. He escorts the women to where Perce and Bernie are standing and introduces them to the men.

'Ladies, the well-groomed one here is Perce Galea. He is the proud owner of a number of nightclubs in the Cross. The Texan gentleman is Bernie Houghton. Bernie owns the Bourbon and Beefsteak as well as the Texas Tavern. I'm sure you've heard of them?'

Both Maggie and Deb giggle again and make appreciative noises, but Susie says nothing, just smiles slightly. Ignoring Perce and Bernie, Susie says directly to Terry: 'Well, it would seem that you have moved up in the world. I hear you ended up in Vietnam. And here I was hoping that you might have been killed over there, but instead, you pop up here. And it appears you have friends in high places, Terry'.

If Terry is stung by this, he does not show it.

'Yes, you're right, Susie. And I must say you are looking a damn sight better than when I last set eyes on you.'

Terry is pleased when he sees that, from a flash of hatred on Susie's face, his barb has struck home. He realises that the other four are staring at him and Susie in confusion. He smiles, and pours the champagne.

'But all that is water under the bridge. What say we get on with enjoying the rest of the afternoon, eh, ladies?'

Terry hands out the glasses and raises his in a toast.

'To Apollo Eleven.'

Relieved, the group, apart from Susie, echoes his toast. Instead, she regards him solemnly, thinking hard.

After several bottles of champagne and the revelation that the women are all nurses and have the weekend off, Bernie suggests that the group take the party back to Kings Cross, where they can have more drinks and perhaps a meal at the Bourbon and Beefsteak. Deb and Maggie agree enthusiastically, and even Susie seems content for this to happen. Perce begs off, pleading another engagement, so the five leave the member's enclosure and head for the car park. Settling them into his car, Bernie drives the group along Anzac Parade and Victoria Street to Macleay Street.

The women are in the back of Bernie's Jaguar. Susie can see that Bernie is checking out Maggie's long legs as she tries unsuccessfully to prevent her very short dress from riding up. *I'll stop that*, Susie decides, and places her handbag on Maggie's knees. Susie sees the flash of annoyance cross Bernie's face as he is deprived of the view. Oblivious to this, Maggie prattles on about how much she is impressed with the XJ-6. Outside the club, Bernie parks illegally and escorts the other four inside, leaving the doorman to park his car in the private garage.

The group settles into a booth in the bar area and Bernie signals for more champagne. The women protest weakly that they shouldn't drink any more but Bernie ignores this. Terry can tell that Bernie thinks he may do all right tonight with Maggie, and that won't happen if the women are sober. He lets Bernie go; he has Susie on his mind.

For her part, Susie continues to think furiously. *I need to get something on this prick, but what? Maybe I should just play along for a while longer, then if nothing presents itself, I'll get my girlfriends out of here before that old fart tries something. They deserve a lot better than what happened to me.* This thought takes her back to Newcastle, and the past few years …

*****

By the late 1960s, Susie had grown tired of the anti-war scene and decided to do something more in terms of nursing. After talking it through with some of her mentors, she became interested in nursing for children under the age of five—what is called mothercraft nursing. Although she had no desire to have babies of her own—at least not for some time—her maternal instincts made this choice an easy one. She contacted an organisation named Tresillian, who provided training for nurses in this field. They offered her training at a home in Petersham, an inner west suburb of Sydney, which she accepted eagerly.

Susie was not upset to leave Newcastle. For her, it was always a stepping stone to another destination. Besides, she had almost no emotional ties to the town after Jack. Although she had toned down her behaviour after that dreadful night, she still liked to party, and wasn't put off by the thought of drugs. Apart from the consequences, which she would not forget for a long time, she loved the buzz that the cocaine gave her. She would take something similar, in the right circumstances. But these hadn't, as yet, arrived.

She moved to Sydney in 1971 and found a bedsit in nearby Newtown. There she met Deborah and Maggie, both nurses doing their training. The trio became firm friends. Susie loved working with the babies and young kids, and their mothers. Tresillian didn't discriminate over whether the mother was married or not; the welfare of the child was the overriding factor. The work was extremely fulfilling and she felt a real buzz when mothers left feeling more confident and better equipped to manage their precious little bundles of joy.

As Tresillian was affiliated with the women's hospital in Randwick, the three nurses, on graduating from their training, were successful in obtaining work there. Susie moved into a flat with her girlfriends in Maroubra, a few kilometres to the south of the hospital, a short bus ride to work. All three girls liked to party and the trio had a lot of fun outside work.

*****

As the champagne flows, Susie decides to take the bull by the horns. She leans over and speaks to Terry in a low voice, fighting the disgust and revulsion she feels for him. *Keep calm*, she tells herself.

'Terry, can I talk to you for a moment, alone?' She wills herself to look directly into his face.

Terry regards her with suspicion, and replies, 'Sure, Susie, let's go into one of Bernie's private rooms'. Seeing the expression of fear and hostility that suddenly appears on her face, he quickly adds, 'No hanky-panky, I promise'.

Susie takes a deep breath and agrees, and they walk through a doorway and down a corridor. Terry opens a door and they enter the room. Terry's voice is harsh with distrust.

'What do you want, Susie?'

She wills herself to be brave.

'I'd really appreciate getting my hands on some good stuff, Terry. I'm sure with your contacts here you can get some for me. But understand this: there are to be no strings attached. You're not getting me to do anything like what you did before. No way.' Seeing the hesitation on his face, she adds: 'Come on, you owe me—big-time—and you know it'.

Terry suddenly smiles, and it chills Susie to the bone.

'Why, sure, I'll get you something. Have you ever tried heroin?'

Susie is doubtful. 'I'm not sticking any needles in my arm.'

'You don't have to do that. You can smoke it, just like grass. And I guarantee it will have a similar effect on you to that coke I gave you before.'

Susie remains apprehensive.

'How much would I need to smoke to get a buzz? And don't lie to me, I have used it before.'

Terry knows she isn't telling the truth, otherwise she wouldn't have asked him. And he thinks he knows the way to get Susie out of his hair once and for all. She has had a fair bit to drink, and this will be her first time on horse. All she needs to do is smoke an amount that is larger than a few grains of pure China White and there's a good chance she will overdose.

'Okay, I won't bullshit you. I'll give you enough for a couple of pipes worth. You know how to use a pipe, yeah? Good, but I'm warning you, only do a teaspoon full at a time.'

Terry leaves Susie in the room and goes to find Dozer. He knows the club has a stash of horse on hand for the more well-heeled customers who want to get high. The China White is normally diluted before it is provided to the punters, but Terry fills a small plastic bag with undiluted product.

He returns a short time later with a small package. Susie says nothing, but is over the moon. All she has to do is go to the police and tell them that Terry gave it to her, and he'll be done for dealing.

As they move back to the booth, Terry whispers in her ear.

'Now, Susie, don't you be going off to the cops with this and try to fit me up. Just so you know, Bernie and his pals have connections that go all the way to the top in the police, so you'll just be wasting your time. Here's some free advice, bitch, take that horse and piss off. And don't come back, otherwise you might regret it.'

With that Terry smiles coldly and heads away from the bar, disappearing out of sight. Susie, furious that Terry has gotten the better of her, hurries to the booth and demands that the girls leave right away. But Bernie insists that they have another bottle of bubbly, and Susie can't convince the others to leave before this is drunk.

The trio bid farewell to an obviously disappointed Bernie and teeter out onto Macleay Street. Susie hails a cab; they have won enough to treat themselves to a quicker ride home than the train and bus. Maggie and Deb giggle their way through the trip, well under the influence of the copious amounts of alcohol they have all consumed. Susie knows she is drunk, but her anger overrides this. *The bastard has screwed me again.*

Once back in their flat, Susie pleads a headache and retires to her room. She pulls the package out of her handbag and opens it. It contains a small glass pipe, a piece of steel wool, and a small plastic bag of white powder. She recalls that a guy she met at one of the anti-war protests told her how to use the device.

Her ire, coupled with the alcohol, clouds her judgement and she makes a hasty decision. *Fuck that prick, if I can't get him arrested, I might as well enjoy this.* She quickly walks to the kitchen and gets a teaspoon. Back in her room, she carefully measures out a small amount of the powder and puts it in the pipe. She doesn't believe Terry about the quantity of drug to use, so she figures that if she uses a lesser amount it will be okay. Susie then puts the steel wool into one end of the pipe and pours the powder into the other end. She takes out a cigarette lighter and slowly heats the pipe, careful not to burn her fingers. She draws the vapour into her lungs.

Nothing happens for a minute or so, then the drug reaches her brain. She feels waves of pleasure hit her, and she feels deliciously drowsy. She lies down on the edge of her bed and closes her eyes. She is oblivious to the incredible danger she is in; the drug, in concert with the alcohol, acts as a further depressant, and the impact on a first-time user will be much worse than a seasoned druggie. As she slips into oblivion, her breathing slows from the impact of the drug on her brain stem, to the point that she stops breathing. Susie is within moments of death.

She lapses into unconsciousness and falls from the bed. Her girlfriends hear her hitting the floor. Despite being pretty drunk, they had noticed Susie's unusually quiet state in the cab and now wonder whether to knock on her door to see if she is okay. They rush into her room and find her lying insensate. They are not able to detect any breathing, and her pulse is very erratic. Maggie rushes to the phone to call the ambulance whilst Deb commences CPR on Susie.

The ambos arrive within five minutes and quickly establish that she has overdosed on heroin as the packet of China White is on the bedside table. They immediately inject Susie with an antidote drug called Narcan. Within a couple of minutes Susie is awake and breathing by herself, but she is extremely disoriented. The ambos place her on a trolley and into the ambulance. Accompanied by Deb, she is rushed to the Accident and Emergency Department at the nearest hospital, the Prince of Wales. It is about nine o'clock.

Deb explains to an attractive blonde nurse about what she thinks has happened to Susie. The nurse, whose name tag reads Jenna Davies, listens attentively whilst taking Susie's pulse and blood pressure. She asks for Susie's full name, and confirms with Deb that she seems to have taken an overdose of heroin.

Jenna asks, 'Has she been drinking?' Deb, embarrassed, replies in the affirmative. With an understanding smile, Jenna asks her to relax and to provide as much background on the incident as possible. Deb is unable to shed much light on it, but she is able to state that, to her best knowledge, Susie is not a regular drug user.

Jenna gets one of the doctors to check Susie. He suggests that she remain in hospital overnight so that the nursing staff can monitor her. He explains to Deb: 'Sometimes the Narcan wears off quicker than the drug she has taken, so it's best that she stay here for the next twelve or so hours. We don't want her relapsing'.

Deb leaves a conscious but very dazed Susie in the hands of the A&E team and goes out to the reception area, where Maggie is waiting anxiously. Deb updates Maggie on Susie's condition, and the pair decides to go home and get some sleep. They will come back in the morning and hopefully collect Susie. They have some pointed questions to ask her.

Susie gradually improves overnight and manages to sleep, despite the growing level of noise and mayhem as A&E is inundated with all sorts of trauma victims. Jenna girds herself for another extremely busy shift. At least the time passes quickly.

Jenna finishes her shift the next morning and goes home, tired and very pissed off with the moronic behaviour exhibited by some people who turn up at A&E. *I can't believe the stupidity of some of them*, she thinks, exasperated. *Still, I'm off now for twenty-four hours, and Jack is waiting at home for me. The problem is, he'll be raring to go, and all I want to do is fall on the bed and sleep for a week.*

Jack is indeed up and about when she walks through the door of the apartment. He kisses her affectionately and asks about her shift. Jenna replies tiredly: 'Bloody mayhem, as usual. People keep on finding newer and more bizarre ways to hurt themselves. The usual mix of fights, cut feet, drug overdoses—you name it. The only one I feel sorry for is a girl about our age who overdosed on heroin, but she isn't a user. She must have had some major problem to try that. What a pity, and such a pretty woman, dark hair, great figure—Susie, I think her name is'.

Jack stiffens. *Susie?* His mind immediately returns to Newcastle, and dark thoughts cloud his mind. He makes no connection other than the name.

*****

Chapter 43

Susie is discharged from the Prince of Wales hospital on the Sunday morning and is strongly advised to rest for a few days before returning to work. The doctor provides her with a medical certificate. She is having periodic mental flashbacks that generate minor panic attacks. Physically, she is okay. Maggie and Deb want to hop into her as they drive her back to the apartment, but her fragile emotional state holds them back. Susie senses their anger and frustration, and promises to tell all once she is feeling better. The other girls settle for this compromise, and pamper her silly for the remainder of the day.

The next day they go to work, leaving Susie alone. She has called in sick and spends the day thinking about her life. This near-death experience has shaken her to the core. *And it is my fault*, she realises. *I made those choices, and I'm responsible, even though I'm pretty sure that bastard Terry tried to kill me.*

Susie slowly comes to the realisation that she needs to change her outlook on life. Sure, it's okay to party, but in moderation. And drugs are a no-no. *Stick to alcohol if you want a buzz, but don't overdo it.* Her mind turns to her work. *You love the infant welfare business, and why is that?* she asks herself. *It's because you are helping to save and nurture life, not destroy it.*

She thinks of the poor souls who have become addicted to drugs. *Who's helping them?* she wonders. A thought-bubble forms in her mind. *What's the name of that guy in the Cross who has started the Wayside Chapel? Ted somebody or other?* She suddenly remembers something, and grabs the weekend newspaper. There is an article on the Wayside Chapel and its founder, the Reverend Ted Noffs. She scans it avidly. *Yes, he's making a difference in helping drug addicts in Kings Cross. He's not pedalling religion to them, he's operating a drug referral centre and has attracted business and private support. Addicts can get advice, support and counselling.*

Susie sits back, reflecting on what she has read. *I wonder if he needs any help?* she asks herself. *I'm a nurse. Surely I can do something?*

Admittedly, I don't know too much about drugs, apart from the affects they can have on you. Maybe that might be the way to go. Susie is suddenly happy that she has thought of a way to do something positive. *And,* she thinks, *maybe I can help give Terry and his cronies a black eye this way. Perhaps I can act like a flea, and give them an itch that will cause them a lot of irritation.*

She makes a cup of tea and sits down to nut out the angles. She is feeling much better now.

When the girls arrive home that evening, Susie has prepared a chicken kiev dinner for the three of them. Maggie and Deb are delighted by her appearance—she seems to be aglow with excitement. They sit down to enjoy the meal. Susie declines the offer of a glass of wine. As they eat, Susie gives them the whole story about her involvement with Terry, warts and all. Her friends are goggle-eyed with shock and horror at her experiences, but they are amazed at her persona; she is relaxed and calm as she recounts the torrid tale. It is as if she is relieved to get it off her chest, finally.

Susie tells them what she has decided to do. They are worried that she might be over reacting, but Susie smiles and says: 'Don't be silly. I'll do this in my spare time. I'm not going on some mad crusade. I'll need to work to pay the bills. If they'll have me, I'll do this on weekends, and if I seem to be going overboard, I give you permission to pull me back into line. I really value our friendship, and I won't do anything to spoil that. And, let me apologise for the other night. I'm really embarrassed about my senseless behaviour. You two don't deserve to be put through anything like that again'.

The girls kiss and embrace. Her friends can see that Susie is determined to go through with this. They offer her help and support, but after talking it through they reluctantly agree that she has to do this on her own. It is not their fight; it is hers.

*****

Chapter 44

In 1973 Michael Hand and Frank Nugan announce that they are opening an investment bank in Australia, to be called the Nugan Hand Bank. Terry learns that Bernie Houghton has a financial interest in the venture. This announcement surprises even Terry, who by now is well used to the trio setting up outrageous but very lucrative deals. He wonders what they are up to this time. He doesn't have long to wait to find out. A few days later, Michael summons Terry to a meeting with him, Frank and Bernie, in a private room in the Bourbon and Beefsteak.

'Hi, Terry,' welcomes Michael, 'beer?'

He pours Terry a cold beer from a bottle of Tooheys draft. Terry sips it appreciatively. Michael continues.

'Buddy, you've heard about our latest venture? Yes? What do you think about it?'

Terry is slightly taken aback to be asked such a direct question. *What is going on here?* He replies frankly, 'I honestly don't have an opinion, Michael, and I don't know too much about banking'. Terry has, by now, moved to a first-name basis with the three guys. He pauses for another sip of beer, then says, 'But I'm sure you've got your reasons, and knowing you three, I've no doubt that the venture will result in some big bucks being made'.

Michael smiles coldly in agreement.

'Indeed, Terry, as you are aware, the R and R business has quietened down considerably now that Nixon has pulled more troops out of Vietnam. Lucrative property deals are still around—and will continue as long as the present state government is in power—but we've decided that we need to expand our operations in a way that maximises our returns, while still using our contacts to leverage off.'

Michael pauses for a sip of beer, then leans towards Terry purposefully.

'Now, we want you to take a broader role in our new venture than what you do presently. We're very happy with your work—very happy indeed. We envisage that you'll be a busy boy, and you'll be doing a lot of travelling, inside and outside Australia. We intend to set up some branches of the bank offshore, and you'll be playing a part in that.'

Seeing Terry about to say something, Michael holds up his hand.

'No, we don't want you involved in the physical set up, Terry; more to do with facilitating our customers in doing deals with the bank. You've shown you have a talent for that, and we want you to put that talent to good use in a more sophisticated setting.'

Michael smiles at Frank. 'Also, there will be a fair amount of liaison required between Frank's family company in Griffith and the bank.'

Seeing Terry's confused expression, Michael adds: 'Let's just say that there will be an increasing number of shipments of goods that will be transported from the country not only to Sydney, but to the other Australian capitals and overseas. We need you to assist in the management of the distribution, so you'll need to make sure your passport is current. And in recognition of your increased workload, your remuneration will increase significantly'.

Michael beams at Terry's smile of gratitude. Terry, for his part, has a million questions but knows better than to ask them now. He thinks he can find out the specifics from a source in the room.

Bernie and Michael leave to attend another meeting. Terry decides this is a good opportunity to get some alcohol into Frank in the hope that he will spill the beans. He knows that Frank loves Scotch whiskey, and when he has had a few, he becomes very garrulous.

*****

His mission accomplished, Terry leaves Frank to his own devices and strolls down to the park near his apartment. He sits on a bench in the shade of the large fig trees and idly watches the passing parade, lost in thought. What Frank has revealed is dynamite.

Frank has let him into the world of sleazy high finance. The new investment bank will take deposits from a wide range of depositors. Many of these will be legitimate, seeking only a fair return on their invested dollars, but some will have bigger sums of money and larger gains in mind, and the new bank can discretely accommodate them. Frank has provided an example of the deal for this type of investor.

In return for a guaranteed hundred per cent return on investment over a six-month period, the client has to invest a minimum of twenty thousand dollars. Frank and Michael will take this money, deduct a few thousand for overheads, and then use Michael's and Bernie's long-serving connections in the Golden Triangle to procure horse to that dollar value, arrange for it to be shipped to Australia via the usual channels, and sell it to a distributor for around five times the cost of the heroin. The distributor pays on receipt of the product. That way there is little to no risk to the bank, and the bank doesn't even use its own money. After paying the investor forty thousand dollars on an original investment of twenty thousand dollars, the bank makes a profit of around fifty thousand dollars.

The distributor has to arrange for it to be placed on the street, but based on the street value of horse the distributor will make around five hundred thousand dollars. So everyone in the chain wins. Any attempt by the distributor to cut out the middle man and go directly to the source is likely to come up against tribesmen in the Golden Triangle who are still living in the Stone Age and are inherently suspicious of new faces. Any new people going in there seeking to cut a deal will most likely end up in small pieces.

Michael's role will be to target his pals and other US Armed Forces people in the first instance, while Bernie and Frank go after some bigger guys. With Michael's contacts it is likely he will snaffle a few big customers as well.

Full of whisky, Frank brags that the bank intends to open a branch in Hong Kong in due course, and hints of plans for a few more, in places that Terry will never think of. Michael will handle that side of the business.

Terry's role will be to help Michael overcome any impediments that might be placed in the bank's way. Terry savours Frank's final comment. 'We're gunna get big, mate, very big, and you're coming along for the ride. I think we should have another drink to celebrate, eh? Man, I love this Scotch.'

*****

For the next two years Terry accompanies Michael on numerous overseas trips to promote the Nugan Hand Bank. Michael, at first, seems to concentrate on small investors from the US Armed Forces scattered around Asia and the Middle East. Michael and Terry travel often to Chang Mai in Thailand, as this is the gateway to the Golden Triangle. Michael seems to know every ex-Air America operative in the area, and it is obvious to Terry that a lot of drug deals are being done—not that he cares.

Terry loves Asia. The girls there are much more compliant,

and cheap, and he is free to satisfy his urges, even with very young females. If Michael knows what he is up to, he doesn't let on. Michael is almost entirely focused on business, but occasionally he disappears for a day or so, returning with a satisfied glint in his eye.

After twelve months or so of travelling Terry and Michael begin to meet with Americans who Michael describes as members of 'The Company', which Terry takes to mean the CIA. Deals involving large sums of US dollars are made with just a handshake. Terry is impressed with the range of contacts Michael has. His network is extensive, and there seems to be endless sums of money available. Terry and Michael carry this in bags, just like an ordinary tourist would carry their holiday clothes. They are never checked.

The bank's activities start to really warm up in 1975 when, in quick succession, branches are opened in Hong Kong, the Philippines, Hawaii, and in Chang Mai. Surely it must be purely coincidental that the Chang Mai branch is located in the same office suite as the US Drug Enforcement Agency office? Bernie and Michael somehow convince former very high-ranking American military officers to head up operations in these locations. There is even an office in Washington, DC.

By this stage tens of millions of dollars per year are channelling through the Nugan Hand Bank, a lot of it being used to finance drug deals. Michael, Frank and Bernie are becoming very rich very quickly. They move their headquarters to a prestigious Macquarie Street address in the Sydney CBD. Before long, Bob Askin joins them in their offices. Mr Askin has retired as premier of New South Wales to avoid being thrown out of office by the Liberal Party for being a naughty boy. Bob, always the good friend to the trio, acts as a referee when they want to recruit recently retired US Admiral Earl 'Buddy' Yates as president of the bank. Buddy takes the job.

Frank, always the flamboyant one, uses his new-found wealth to purchase a few toys. He buys a roomy mansion with its own private beach on the waterfront in the very upmarket Sydney suburb of Vaucluse. He takes to driving a top-of-the-range gold Mercedes 450SL sports car. Although married, he lives a playboy lifestyle and loves to punt heavily on the horses. He is now consuming up to a bottle of Scotch a day. Frank's face appears regularly in the gossip columns of the Sydney tabloids. This doesn't go down too well with Bernie and Michael, but Frank is unrepentant.

The trio, with Terry, meets in the Cross and Michael and Bernie suggest Frank tones his behaviour down a bit. He responds angrily.

'Hey, guys, everyone is making a lot of money here. What's the point of having it if you can't show off a bit? I do my job—and bloody well—and you know it. Who else do you know that can launder money like me? I'm the best, and don't you forget it.' He continues in a more conciliatory manner. 'Okay, I'll keep my head down a bit, but the people I associate with in business expect me to show off, and that in itself attracts more customers. They all want to be like me.'

Terry isn't too sure about that. His personal preference is to keep a low profile and operate under the radar as much as possible. With the success of the bank, he has amassed quite a considerable amount of money. Acting on tips, under an assumed name, he has quietly purchased several properties in Elizabeth Bay and Potts Point and they are providing a steady rental income, as well as the promise of an excellent capital gain. Under the Whitlam government, inflation is increasing rapidly, but interest rates are being kept artificially low. This has created a property bubble, and Terry is capitalising on the fact that median housing prices in Sydney have almost doubled since 1970.

He is the proud owner of a two-bedroom apartment in Rushcutters's Bay, in the name of his alter ego, Anthony Bishop. The real Anthony Bishop is long dead, and Michael's connections have obtained for Terry expertly forged identity documents in this name.

Chapter 44

Like his last apartment, it is quiet, even though it is only about 500 metres behind Macleay Street. It has great views extending east over the park and the yachts moored in the marina, to Darling Point. He has the latest model colour TV set in his lounge. A transvestite he knows who works in the Cross has put him onto a very attractive female interior decorator and she has transformed the previously dowdy decor of the apartment with the latest in chic. She nimbly evades his not-so-subtle advances and instead presents him with a bill that makes him think he is in the wrong game.

Terry is present in 1975 at a meeting in the Macquarie Street offices when Michael announces that he has been approached by a couple of his buddies in The Company to help out in fighting communism in Africa, to 'give the Russians, who are backing the local communists, a bloody nose'. Of course, he will not be involved in the actual fighting; at forty Michael feels is too old for that. Terry privately doesn't agree with him—Michael appears to be as fit now as when he first met him in the late 1960s—but concurs with Michael's logic that it is much smarter, and more profitable, to supply the arms rather than use them.

Michael informs them that he is off to meet with some anti-communist rebels in a country named Angola. The deal is simple: the bank will purchase the necessary firepower and arrange for it to be shipped via air into the country for use by the rebels. The Company will pay the bank, and if the bill is double the cost price, who cares? Michael wants Bernie and Terry to arrange for the arms purchase and the shipping, once Michael finds out what the rebels want.

This is done, and Bernie and Terry place an order through one of Bernie's arms dealer contacts for ten million rounds of ammunition and three thousand rifles and machine guns. Out of the Angola deal the bank pockets a cool $US30 million. The arms business is extremely profitable.

Over the next few years, the same arrangement is repeated in Somalia, the former French Republic of Guinea, and Nigeria, but these ventures do not all go as well as expected. In Angola, the anti-communist forces, called the FNLA, equipped with the arms supplied through the bank, attack the capital Luanda but are repelled by the communist forces. They flee in disarray, leaving much of the armament behind.

In oil-rich Nigeria, which is receiving Soviet military aid, a decision is taken by the USA not to invade the country, even though intelligence sources suggest that the Soviets would not choose to become further involved. Instead, arms are purchased through the channels set up for Angola to support anti-communist sympathisers. But despite this, the Nigerian government remains hostile to the USA. When the Nigerian President is assassinated in 1977, suspicion falls on the USA, which is suspected of engineering the murder.

*****

On the evening of November 11th 1975, Terry is invited to an impromptu celebratory party at the Bourbon and Beefsteak. He, Bernie and Michael are in the country for a change. A lot of important people turn up. Bernie, Michael and Frank host the glitterati of Sydney. Frank is already half drunk.

The partygoers include a veritable who's who of politics, media, law enforcement and crime: Bob Askin; Abe Saffron; Jack Rooklyn, the President of Bally Australia; Perce Galea; Fred Hanson and Norman Allan, present and former New South Wales police commissioners, along with a few federal and state politicians and king-makers. Even the chief of staff of Rupert Murdoch's *Australian* newspaper makes a brief appearance.

The champagne is flowing freely and everyone is in party mode. Terry knows that the celebration is for the dismissal of the Whitlam government by the governor-general, John Kerr, that day. He can understand that the Liberal Party politicians would be delighted, but why are the rest so jubilant? He keeps his ear to the ground as he sips his champagne. Before long, he has gathered a few titbits—something about a large slush fund being raised to use against Gough Whitlam and the Labour Party in an effort to unseat them. Well, if it is true, it has worked a treat, even though the dismissal has triggered a constitutional crisis. Gough's radical reformist but left-leaning agenda is stopped in its tracks. Terry marvels at the ability of the high and mighty to have a role in manipulating the demise of a federal government that they despise.

A week or so later, the Nugan Hand Bank roadshow resumes its travels around Africa and Asia.

*****

Chapter 45

Jack's parents, along with Jenna, attend his university graduation ceremony in late March 1973. His rented gown and mortar board give him a distinguished air. The family watch with pride and joy as he mounts the steps to the platform, doffs his headdress, shakes the hand of the dean of faculty, and accepts his degree.

They go to lunch in a local restaurant in Kensington to celebrate. Despite feeling an enormous sense of relief that he has finally finished studying, Jack is slightly worried about his father. Henry seems to be a little short of breath, but when Jack asks him about this after the meal, Henry dismisses it as nothing. Jenna, always the nurse, has noticed it too. Jack makes a mental note to check with his mother later. Maybe Henry should see a doctor.

His Distinction Grade Point Average has the head of computer science urging Jack to do an honours year, but Jack is having none of that. The academic tries to throw him a carrot: a new operating system called UNIX has just been developed, written in a language called C. It may well revolutionise the computer world as it permits multiple programs to be run simultaneously. Jack is very interested in this concept, but he figures that he can learn about it just as easily outside the university environment.

At the office, Jack mentions UNIX to Walt, whose concern is obvious. It appears that head office is uneasy about this latest software development, as it has the potential to degrade the high level of control enjoyed by IBM over the business market. UNIX can run on relatively inexpensive hardware and is easily adaptable to a variety of machines, which means that the company has an entirely new set of competitive challenges to face. Jack is intrigued. He resolves to find out more about this new language.

Jenna is also relieved that he has finished studying, but for another reason entirely. She thinks she is pregnant. Her period is well overdue, and she has been feeling nauseous in the mornings lately.

Without telling Jack, she visits the doctor who confirms her suspicions. She is just under two months gone. The baby is due before Christmas. Jenna is overwhelmed with joy, but this is tempered with the realisation that her own aspirations to study will have to be put on the backburner for quite a while.

Over dinner that evening Jenna tells Jack the news. She is slightly apprehensive: how will he take it? To her delight, Jack is over the moon with happiness. He dances her around the room before suddenly stopping, concerned that he might harm the baby. Jenna laughs at his silly concerns. Jack sits her down, anyway. Then the questions come tumbling out.

'When is it due? Do you know what it is? What will we call it?'

'Whoa, you're off like a startled rabbit,' Jenna laughs. 'It's due in mid-December, and I hope it's not late, otherwise the poor child will miss out on having two lots of presents. No, I don't know whether it's a boy or a girl; and what we call it will depend on whether it's a boy or a girl. But we've plenty of time to choose names.'

She gazes at him tenderly.

'What I'm most concerned about right now is morning bloody sickness. Judging from what I've heard, that's going to last for another couple of months, but I'm over it already. Still, I'm only twenty-seven, so no doubt I'll be able to handle it.'

Jenna leans over and hugs Jack.

'But, I'm sure a lot of TLC will help.' She holds up her hand. 'And that doesn't necessarily mean just sex, Jack—although a girlfriend told me that she got very horny during the middle stages of her pregnancy. We'll have to wait and see how I go.' Seeing the disappointment on Jack's face, she adds: 'Jack, I'm not feeling sick at the moment. What's say we celebrate the news in bed?' Jack is in full agreement.

They abandon their dinner and move quickly to the bedroom. Their lovemaking is tender and deeply satisfying.

*****

Jack never does get to ask his mother about his father's health. In mid-April he receives a phone call at work from the police. Henry has had a massive heart attack at a bus stop on the way home from work. He died instantly.

Jack is struck dumb. How could this be? His dad is only in his mid-fifties. He should have lived for a lot longer than that. Jack sits silently at his desk for a long time, staring at nothing, until Walt happens by and spots the stricken look on his face.

Ever reliable, Walt takes charge. He instructs Jack's secretary to call the hospital where Jenna works and tell them the news—Jenna's pregnancy is no secret and he hopes the hospital will break the sad news to her gently. He then leads Jack out of the office and into a taxi. Jack moves like a zombie.

Jack is sitting on the lounge sipping a stiff drink when Jenna hurries in. Wordlessly she goes to him and they hug. Jack breaks down and cries, Jenna joining him. Walt decides it is time to make himself scarce.

After writing a short note, which he places on the table, Walt silently shuts the front door of the apartment and leaves them to mourn. After about thirty minutes Jack summons the resolve to call his parents' house in Newcastle. An aunt, whom he knows slightly, answers the phone. Whispering, she offers him her condolences and tells Jack that his mother has been sedated and is now asleep. The aunt and a neighbour will care for her until he can make the journey home.

Jack distractedly reads the note from Walt. It, too, offers condolences and advises Jack that he can take as much time as he needs to attend to what needs to be done. Jack is grateful that he has a friend like Walt. Jenna helps Jack pack a small bag and calls a cab to take him to Central Station to catch a train to Newcastle. She will follow the next day after she has a routine check on the baby's progress.

Feeling wrung-out emotionally, Jack arrives at the family home late that evening. Neighbours are there on a watching brief. His aunt has gone home. She will be back tomorrow.

Gladys is awake as he quietly knocks on her bedroom door and enters. Her face is in shadow from the weak glow of a bedside lamp, but Jack can see that she has been crying. He goes to her side and she hugs him fiercely. He mutters words of sympathy as she clings to him. She looks as bad as he feels.

Finally, she lets go of him and he sits on the bed. They talk in halting tones about Henry. She recounts a fuller story of his last moments. He had just alighted from the bus on the corner of Hunter and Darby Streets when a passenger getting off behind him saw him clutch at his chest, and then sink to the ground. He did not say a word. Passers-by attempted CPR, but to no avail. The ambulance arrived within minutes, but Henry was pronounced decreased on arrival at the hospital.

Jack stays with his mother until she sleeps. He goes into the kitchen and pours himself a glass of whiskey, and downs it in one gulp. For some reason he feels guilty that he hasn't often told his dad that he loves and respects him, particularly for when he supported Jack's impetuous decision to join the army. And it's too late now. He realises that his father will never know his grandchild. He bends his head and quietly weeps.

The next morning mother and son sit together and speak to the local Anglican minister who has come to visit. Jack's parents aren't particularly religious—and Jack regards himself as an agnostic after what he has seen in Vietnam—but the padre doesn't seem to mind; he focuses on the practical and downplays the spiritual side of things. They discuss the secular aspects of death: the funeral; who will speak; what music will be played; who they will use as a funeral director. When it is all sorted, the minister departs to organise things.

Jenna calls. She is catching the midday train. Jack arranges to pick her up at the station in his parents' car. Jenna and Gladys embrace when she arrives at the house. Weeping, Gladys is able to admire her baby bump. Even in death, life must go on.

The funeral is held at the parish church three days later. The hall is packed with mourners, including his parents' relatives and friends, Jack's surf club and Newcastle uni mates, and others that Jack does not know but have somehow been touched by Henry's life. Jack has to overcome a great surge of emotion to speak, and he breaks down several times, but manages to get though the eulogy. Jenna and Gladys cry softly throughout the service, but are proud of Jack for having the strength to do what he does.

Jack asks all present back to the house for a wake. Some come, including Wally, his old sweep hand. They don't stay long, wanting to allow Jack and his mother to continue to grieve privately. Jenna busies herself with the washing-up and clearing away the remnants of the food. The trio are wrung out, and retire to bed early. Jack finds it difficult to sleep, and he suspects his mother is the same.

Gladys slowly but surely gives up on living after Henry's passing. She is listless and won't eat properly, despite neighbours checking on her regularly. Jack and Jenna visit as often as possible, but Jenna finds the ride on the back of the motorbike is becoming more difficult. Gladys doesn't seem interested in talking or doing much of anything. All she does is hold a photo of Henry in her hands and stare at it fixedly. She even takes it to bed with her. Gladys slowly loses weight and her skin takes on a grey pallor. Even the prospect of a grandchild won't bring her out of her depression. It comes as no surprise to anyone when she dies quietly in her sleep in November, just over seven months after her husband.

Jack buries her in late November. Hopefully, she is reunited with Henry. Only the impending birth of his child keeps Jack on track. He has lost his parents, and there is a big hole in his life. He mourns them but some part of him feels that this is a bit two-faced. He hasn't had a lot to do with them since his decision to become a Nasho. They have always been patient with him, and not overly critical of his decisions. Jack feels that he has not reciprocated their unconditional love, and this is disquieting, as he can't now do anything about it. He confides in Jenna, and she hugs him in sympathy.

'Maybe,' she suggests, 'they would want you to pour that love into us as a family'. Jack makes a vow that this will happen.

His mother's will is read a few weeks later. Jack is the beneficiary of the family estate, which includes the house and car, and a few thousand dollars in cash. The car is welcome because of the imminent arrival. Whenever Jack drives it, he feels the spirit of his parents alongside him.

In mid-December, Jenna's waters break and Jack drives her at a controlled but furious pace to the hospital where she is booked in. For the next twelve hours he paces the waiting room, thinking unthinkable thoughts, until a nurse finally puts him out of his misery.

He has a daughter, and mother and child are well.

Jack is bursting with manly pride as he is ushered into the maternity ward where a very tired and drained Jenna awaits, a tiny bundle in her arms. Wordlessly, Jenna holds his daughter up for him to see for the first time. All Jack can see is a fine down of blondish hair and a face that resembles a prune, all screwed up, tiny cries issuing forth. Wisely, he does not say this to Jenna.

He carefully takes her from Jenna and gently tucks her in his arms. He notices an awful smell and is alarmed, and asks Jenna is something is wrong. Jenna giggles out a response: 'It's just poo, silly. You'd better get used to it. You're going to be changing a lot of nappies over the next few years'.

Jack isn't convinced that this is the best idea, but he doesn't want to rock the boat, and remembers his vow of unqualified devotion to Jenna and the child. *If that is what it takes, I'll do it,* he promises. He tries not to gag as Jenna shows him how to clean his daughter's bottom and put on a new nappy. He is glad when it is over. He thinks he'd rather face the VC.

After a few minutes, the nurse shoos Jack out of the ward, telling him his wife and baby need to rest. He can come back at visiting time. At the appointed time he and Jenna's parents, who have rushed into town from the Blue Mountains, coo over the baby, almost entirely ignoring Jenna, who lies back in bed, watching them contentedly.

The proud parents name their daughter Natalie Julia Davies Martin. It is a bit of a mouthful, but it satisfies all the stakeholders, even Jenna's grandmother whose name is Julia.

H goes out with Jack for a celebratory drink to wet the baby's head. H's contracting business is doing well, but he is still without a permanent girlfriend. Although he has his fair share of casual encounters, he has not yet found the right one. Jack chides him that he will soon be over the hill; H is now thirty. The pair part after consuming a few too many drinks, drunkenly vowing eternal friendship.

Chapter 45

Jenna and Jack quickly realise that their lives have changed forever with the birth of Natalie—or Nat, as they like to call her. Neither of them gets a lot of sleep for the next six months, but Jenna takes the brunt of the onslaught of a crying, pooping, eating, demanding and growing baby. Despite their fears that she is either dying of some mysterious disease or somehow abnormal, Nat grows like Topsy, and eventually starts to sleep through most of the night. That is, until the teeth start to come after about ten months, and she reverts to a demanding, attention-seeking bundle that threatens to destroy their already frayed nerves. Jenna's mother is wonderful throughout it all, offering sensible, and what mostly turns out to be accurate, advice on how to deal with the myriad challenges they face with a rapidly developing baby.

Not surprisingly, their social life withers and dies. The baby is everything. Even so, despite their unconditional love for Nat, now and then they long for the time, usually around seven in the evening, when she goes down to sleep—hopefully for the night. Their sex life is also impacted, much to Jack's chagrin, but he understands that Jenna is utterly focused on the baby, and his needs come a distant second.

Jenna finds that her thought processes have been transformed from the outside world to the baby world. She knows that it is a consequence of her mothering instincts kicking in, but it is as if nothing is as important as whether Nat has eaten well or slept properly, or her poops are the correct colour. She finds herself just sitting in wonder, watching her daughter as she plays on a mat with a soft toy, or tries to roll around on the floor. And when she smiles at Jenna, it is so amazing that tears come to her eyes.

Jack, being a male, is rapt in his daughter, but he knows that life has to go on. He is the sole breadwinner. The hospital is prepared to allow Jenna a month of leave without pay, but with no provision in New South Wales for paid or unpaid maternity leave—similar to that introduced by Gough Whitlam several years earlier for commonwealth employees—Jenna is forced to resign from the hospital.

Although the death of Jack's parents leaves a dark hole in his heart, ironically, it has helped the family financially. The family home is sold in early 1975 for just under $150,000—a larger sum than he expected. One of his former football coaches, who is a Newcastle real estate agent and has handled the sale for mates' rates, told him that the old working-class neighbourhood is being rejuvenated by young people wanting to live in the inner city. Housing prices have been pushed up by the demand. The sale proceeds have been placed in the bank, and Jack and Jenna adopt careful budgeting to minimise the top-up needed from their capital to meet the increased household expenses.

Jack's work is beginning to really bother him. Although Walt is still as great as ever, their work relationship is increasingly tested by company decisions. The winds of change in the computing business are blowing much quicker now—even though the Australian economy isn't doing too well—threatening the team spirit he loves. The software revolution is now well ahead of improvements to the hardware, and the pace of progress in both is accelerating. Jack feels strongly that the traditional business model is no longer applicable, but head office back in the States seems to have its head stuck firmly in the sand. Jack has plenty of ideas, and he wants to build on them. His frustration is rising, but he knows he can't do anything rash just yet. The family needs the money he is earning.

*****

In April 1975 the combined forces of the Vietcong and the NVA rapidly advance on Saigon. Most of the US forces have already pulled out, and the ARVN fight a desperate rear-guard action to prevent being overrun. South Vietnam refugees stream southward in a vain attempt to avoid the marauding communists. But they are unstoppable, and victoriously enter Saigon in late April amongst chaos as panicked high-ranking South Vietnamese officials, US citizens and other foreigners try to clamber over each other to board the few remaining US helicopters departing the now-empty US embassy compound.

Jack numbly watches this all unfold on television. He feels a mixed bag of emotions: anger, sadness, frustration. *The bloody war has all been for nothing*, he thinks savagely. *How many people killed, and for what? It's a bloody disgrace.* Jack's mind turns to the fate of a young Vietnamese navy officer whom he had briefly met on leave at Vung Tau in 1968. He can't remember his name. *If he's still alive, the poor bugger probably won't be for much longer*, Jack thinks sadly.

But this is not the case. The officer, Binh Nguyen, has risen through the ranks of the Vietnamese navy and has reached the rank of lieutenant commander. Binh has command of a former US coastguard frigate and is very much aware of the fate awaiting him and his crew if they are captured by the communists.

His frigate is anchored near a small island just north of Vung Tau. He has been trying to call his younger brother, whose nickname is Ba—for second born—on the radio. He finally gets through. Ba, a lieutenant who has only just been awarded his flying wings, is based at the Tan Son Nhut airfield in Saigon. Binh can hear the sound of firing in the background as the communists attack the airfield. He urges Ba to fly his Huey to the frigate as soon as possible.

Needing no second invitation, Ba obeys his older brother and, dodging small-arms fire as he races at low level south towards Vung Tau, lands unscathed on the ship's stern. Although the frigate has precious little fuel, Binh sets sail immediately and heads at maximum revolutions into the South China Sea to avoid capture. The frigate has well over five hundred navy personnel and their families on board. Binh prays for good weather.

The US 7th Fleet is standing off the South Vietnamese coast, awaiting orders to sail. Binh is heading towards this heavily armed armada of ships, hoping that his vessel can be refuelled by one of the oilers. He is very relieved when he receives an order from the Americans to come inside the cordon, to safety.

Not long after, Binh is contacted by Captain Diem Do, who is in charge of a fleet of over thirty South Vietnamese navy ships, with nearly 30,000 people crammed onboard. They are doing exactly the same as Binh's frigate.

The Binh brothers and the crew and families join the remnants of the South Vietnamese navy and sail east with the 7th Fleet to a major US navy base at Subic Bay, just north of Manilla, the capital of the Philippines. Off Subic Bay, the thirty-five South Vietnamese ships are ordered to ditch all weapons, including Ba's helo, as well as all ammunition, into the South China Sea. They are then allowed to steam into the US navy base.

Nguyen and Ba are eventually resettled in Florida. Ba resumes flying helicopters. Ironically, Ba returns to Vietnam in 2008, posted to the country in the employ of the US Department of Homeland Security. He is in his mid-forties. It is a different country when he returns, but in Saigon, now called Ho Chi Minh City, it is almost as if the war never happened.

Nineteen seventy-five seems to be cursed. South Vietnam has fallen, and later in the year the Whitlam government is sent packing. Gough Whitlam is to be soundly defeated in the forthcoming federal election, despite an outpouring of public outrage about the method of his government's dismissal.

*****

Chapter 46

Susie Adams walks into the Drug Referral Centre in Rushcutters Bay and cheerfully greets the other volunteers. It is part of the Wayside Chapel. The offices are not flash; the organisation is very lean as there is little spare money for new furniture or anything swank, but the clients don't care.

Several months earlier, Ted Noffs had welcomed her with open arms, and was not in the least concerned when she told him that she had no experience in helping addicts. She confessed that she had occasionally used drugs and had even overdosed, and Ted declared that was all the experience she needed to be able to relate to the tormented souls that come to the centre. Her nursing experience also helps her to relate to clients, and before long she is providing counselling and advice on where to go to receive expert help for drug problems.

Susie loves the work, but is often in tears when she hears the stories that people tell her. There are a lot of indigenous people using the centre, and she becomes all too familiar with their tales of abuse and disadvantage. She meets people like Charlie Perkins, who works in the Office for Aboriginal Affairs and is an outspoken indigenous activist. Charlie is a straight shooter, who is not afraid to take on the establishment.

Ted introduces her to a woman named Juanita Neilson, who is associated with the Wayside Chapel, and edits and publishes a community newspaper called *Now*. Juanita is vocally opposed to drugs, vice, organised crime and the stand-over tactics often used in the Cross to allow commercial redevelopment of older homes in the area.

Juanita is a slim, attractive and stylish woman who sports a distinctive beehive hair style. Juanita seems to know where a lot of skeletons are buried, and she isn't afraid to reveal them publicly. Susie is secretly envious of Juanita: her beauty coupled with her clothes sense, her out-there attitude, and her money. Susie learns that Juanita is the heiress to the Mark Foys retail fortune, and uses her wealth to fund the newspaper.

The two women become good friends. Juanita has no airs or graces, and she appreciates Susie's efforts to contribute to alleviating, in some measure, the social and physical problems caused by drugs. Besides, they have something in common; Juanita is a Novocastrian. Being ten years older than Susie, Juanita treats her like a younger sister.

Susie feels very contented. Her nursing work is extremely fulfilling, and the extra-curricular activities she is involved in are equally rewarding. Her girlfriends are pleased; Susie is happy and energetic. Deb thinks all Susie needs now is a man. Make that three. One for each of them.

*****

In early 1975 Frank Theeman, a crony of Abe Saffron, attempts to construct an apartment complex in the Cross and has been instrumental in evicting tenants from houses in Victoria Street, a few blocks from Macleay Street. The fix is in as bouncers and thugs from the nearby nightclubs, led by an ex-cop named Fred Krahe, physically throw people and furniture out on the street as the police stand by and watch. There is a public outcry, and Juanita leads the push through her newspaper *Now*. Support for the anti-development movement comes from an unlikely direction; the Builder's Labourers Federation, a union itself not averse to a bit of thuggery, slaps a green ban on the site, stymieing demolition progress. But the developers are not to be outdone.

Juanita disappears in July after visiting one of Abe Saffron's clubs to discuss advertising prospects with an employee. Conspiracy theories abound: Theeman has had her killed for opposing his development plans; she has been murdered because she is about to publish an expose on vice, corruption and illegal gambling in the Cross. Theeman, Saffron and Krahe are amongst the suspects, but nothing is ever proven. The truth remains as elusive as her remains. The development project is eventually completed, with the BLF hamstrung by the courts.

Ted Noffs and Susie are devastated by the news. Susie, in particular, had been increasingly worried that Juanita was overstepping the boundaries. Her earlier experience with Terry had exposed her to the sleazy side of the world of vice and drugs that exists in Kings Cross. Susie feels helpless; it doesn't matter which way she turns, the bad guys are ahead of her and others who are trying to make this area a better and safer place.

Susie, although shaken to the core, remains resolute. She will continue to be the flea in their ear. But she will be very, very careful.

*****

Chapter 47

Jack has received an invitation for him and Jenna to attend a lavish party on Christmas Eve 1975 at a work colleague's apartment in Potts Point, just down from Kings Cross. They both would love to go but what would they do with Natalie? Jenna's overjoyed parents come to the rescue and volunteer to mind their granddaughter for a few days, if the three of them will come to an early Christmas lunch in the Blue Mountains. Jenna and Jack accept with alacrity.

While Jack, Jenna's parents and Jenna's siblings eat a sumptuous meal of turkey, chicken and pork with all the trimmings, and feed Nat titbits in her high chair, Jenna springs a surprise. She tells the gathering that she wants to go back to work part time. Jack's immediate reaction is surprise, but he is also a little annoyed. Jenna has not discussed this with him. Not that he minds particularly, although he is interested in finding out what Jenna's plans are for Nat, but she could at least have said something to him. This is a family matter, and she should have discussed it first with him.

Jenna, ignoring Jack's hurt expression and her mother's

immediate objections, declares that a girlfriend will babysit Nat for the periods in the day when she is at work. In a quiet voice that hides his irritation, Jack asks for more details.

'You've met Angela, Jack. She and I go to the same baby health clinic. Her son's name is Peter—remember?'

'I think so,' replies Jack doubtfully, 'but isn't she …' Jenna cuts him off before he can complete his thought.

'If you're thinking what I think you are, Jack Martin, then yes, she is a single mother.' Jenna turns to him aggressively, 'and what's that got to do with it, eh?'

Jena's mother tries to come to Jack's rescue. 'Darling, I'm sure Jack just meant …'

Again Jenna breaks in. 'Don't you start, Mum. Angela is a lovely girl. It isn't her fault that that mongrel of a bloke who knocked her up didn't stay around.'

Jenna's brother and sister sit and watch the sparks fly with increasing delight. Jenna is obviously fired up. Jenna's sister glances over at her dad. He seems to feel the same way, wearing a little smile as he watches his elder daughter in full swing. Jenna continues, staring defiantly at Jack.

'Now, if you and Mum will take a deep breath and have a drink of wine to calm you down, I'll tell you how this is going to work. I've talked to the hospital, and I'll be starting on night shift initially, as that's when they most need nurses. If I need to sleep during the day after a shift, Angela will bring her son to our apartment and look after Nat. She lives nearby, so it's only a short walk for her. All you've got to do is to get up to Nat in the night if I'm not there. Surely that's not too much trouble?'

Jack has no objections to this arrangement, but doesn't like Jenna's tone. He's not sure what is going on, but he doesn't appreciate her making decisions unilaterally. He feels ignored by her. Jack replies stiffly.

'Fine, Jenna, it would seem that you've got it all sorted out. I'll just act like a good little husband and do what I'm told.'

Staring at Jenna angrily, he grabs his glass and exits the room. He stomps his way out into the garden, leaving the group sitting with their mouths open.

After a short while his father-in-law, Malcolm, joins him, wine bottle and glass in hand. He sits beside Jack and takes in the view. Eventually, Malcolm starts talking, more to himself than Jack.

'Women. Can't live with them. Can't live without them. That's what I've learned in these past thirty-plus years of wedded bliss. You think you've got them figured out, and then they go and do something you never thought they would.'

Malcolm takes and sip of wine and refills Jack's glass.

'Jenna has always had a bit of an independent streak. I remember when she came home and told us that she was going to Vietnam. We tried to talk her out of it, but she wouldn't listen. And off she went. But you know what? Something wonderful happened over there. She met you. And now you have a beautiful daughter, and my wife and I have a grandchild that we love to bits. Don't let a little difference of opinion come between you, Jack. You've both got too much skin invested in this game to falter now.'

Sipping on his wine, Jack considers these wise words. 'I understand, Malcolm, but she could have at least discussed this with me beforehand.' He stares morosely into his wine glass.

Malcolm sighs. 'You're probably right, Jack. But she didn't. I bet she's regretting that right now. Perhaps she was worried that you might not agree?'

Jack is angry. 'I've got no problem with what she wants to do. I'm just pissed off at the way she let that cat out of the bag.'

'Why don't you tell that, then?' Malcolm rises and motions for Jack to join him. 'Let's go inside and have some of that marvellous plum pudding that Jenna has made.'

Later that evening, in the privacy of Jenna's old bedroom, Jenna and Jack have a heart-to-heart discussion. Jack apologises for walking out earlier, and tells her how he feels about the way she divulged her plans. Jenna kisses him and apologises for the way she has broken the news. As Nat sleeps innocently in the cot, the pair makes languorous but silent love. Jenna giggles quietly to herself at the realisation that it is the first time she has done this in her bedroom.

Leaving Natalie in the care of her grandparents, Jack and Jenna drive back into Sydney for the few days before Christmas Eve. They are both looking forward to the party.

*****

Chapter 48

Terry is invited to a Christmas Eve party at the Pink Panther nightclub in Kings Cross. The Pink Panther is owned by Abe Saffron, who also owns a brothel located above the strip club. Terry gets to the club about ten o'clock and greets the doorman by name and climbs the narrow staircase to the first floor. He crosses the room where the strippers gyrate, ogled by drunken punters who wolf-whistle and make obscene comments to the girls. Terry ignores this, and is admitted by another bouncer to a private room where about forty guests drink and socialise. The noise is almost deafening in the confined space, but no-one takes any notice.

After chatting for an hour or so to a few well-known identities, including the police commissioner and several politicians, Terry takes a moment to glance around the room. There are as many women as men, and he recognises several of the women, one of whom works in the Pink Panther. She is a stunningly attractive girl who goes by the name of Crystal, which is probably fake—not that Terry cares. On a whim he decides to try to chat her up.

If Crystal is flattered by Terry's banter, she doesn't show it. They have a few drinks but Terry can see that, unless he tries something else, he is not going to get anywhere with this woman. He leans in close and says quietly to her, 'Crystal, do you fancy a toke of something?'

Terry immediately senses that he now has Crystal's attention. She replies, 'Why, have you got some gear?'.

Terry grins. 'Not on me, but I can get my hands on some smack if you're interested.'

'Okay, I'd like that,' she responds, smiling at last.

Terry is confident that he's snared her. 'Why don't I get it and then we can go back to my pad and have our own party?'

But Crystal is cannier than Terry thinks.

'By all means you get it, Terry my lad, but there's no way we're going to your place. I've heard about what goes on there. Believe me, I'm no prude, but I don't do kinky.' Seeing Terry's expression, Crystal softens the blow. 'I tell you what, we can go to my room instead. It's only next door, in the Savoy Hotel. It's a bit of a dump, but it's comfortable enough, and I know enough people there who will come running if I don't like what you're trying to get me to do.'

'Okay,' Terry says, 'I'll get the smack and some booze. Wait here. I'll be back in a couple of minutes'.

Terry is back in less than five minutes, and he and Crystal leave the party. Crystal takes him next door to the Savoy and she embraces Terry, kissing him hard, as they enter the lift to take them to her room on the fourth floor.

Once in her room, Crystal grabs a couple of glasses and, while Terry pours them a drink, she rolls some of the smack into a smoke. She asks, 'This is good shit, right?'

Terry nods, 'It's the best around. China White'.

Lighting the cigarette, Crystal smiles and begins what is called 'chasing the dragon' as she waits for the rush to start. Terry watches her expressionlessly, sipping on his drink. Crystal is slightly defensive: 'I can handle this, Terry. I don't inject the stuff, and I only use it occasionally. But, God, it gives me such a high'. Terry is sceptical. Once someone starts using heroin, then they keep on using. But it is not his concern; all he wants from Crystal is sex anyway.

After about fifteen minutes Crystal starts to remove her clothing, telling Terry that she is feeling warm and sexy. He watches as she sheds her dress and dances around in her panties and bra. The bra is next to go, revealing a particularly fine pair of breasts that stand out proudly, the nipples already hardened. Then her panties come off, and Terry gets a good look at her *mons venus*. She has almost no pubic hair, and her pussy lips can clearly be seen.

Terry is instantly hard, and quickly removes his clothes then grabs her and begins to run his mouth down from her neck to her breasts and then lower. She writhes in pleasure as his tongue plays with her clit. He pushes her back on the bed and enters her, thrusting hard as she moans beneath him, her fingers clawing his back.

*****

Reg Lyttle is angry and upset. His boyfriend, Warren, has done the dirty on him and left Reg in the lurch. Despite searching everywhere throughout Christmas Eve and into the early hours of the morning, Reg can't find Warren.

Reg cuts a rather sad figure as he lets himself back into the rear entrance of the Savoy Hotel at about five in the morning. Reg is employed as a cook, a job he is lucky to get with his record. Born in Newcastle twenty-four years' previously Reg, after being sent by his parents to a boys' home at age four, has a history of arson. He likes to burn things, and he loves publicity.

Inside the back door Reg spies a pile of newspapers. His eyes light up, and soon the papers do as well. Reg leaves the fire and goes to his room in the Savoy.

In a matter of minutes the flames spread across the ground floor, rendering the old creaky lift inoperative, and race up the carpeted stairs. Thick smoke billows upwards through the hotel.

*****

Terry awakens with a start. For a moment he doesn't know where he is, and then he spies the comatose naked figure of Crystal next to him on the bed. He smiles in memory: a good night indeed.

Then Terry realises what has woken him. He can smell smoke—lots of smoke. Throwing on his pants, he runs to the door and opens it. Outside is bedlam. People are running everywhere, some screaming, some naked, all in a panic. The smoke is thicker and he can hear a roaring sound. Someone screams out, 'Fire, fire'. Terry is suddenly very afraid.

He rushes to the stairwell but he can see the flames advancing upwards. *Shit*, he thinks, *there's got to be another way out*. Forgetting Crystal and her wellbeing instantly, Terry runs upstairs to the fifth floor. But there is no way out that he can see. Then he thinks of the fire escapes. *Where the fuck are they?* Terry shouts to a guy, asking him about the fire escapes, but the man yells back that they are blocked off by the fire and smoke.

Terry is desperate, he doesn't want to die in some stupid fire. There must be another way out. He runs along the corridor, peering into rooms. Suddenly he hears loud voices. He follows the sound and finds himself in a room at the back of the hotel near the end of the corridor. Here people are climbing out through the window.

Terry rushes to the window and leans out. Three people are edging gingerly along some pipes towards the next building, amid shouts of encouragement from scantily clad women in that building who are hanging out of windows to help. Terry realises it must be the back of the Kingsdore Motel, the brothel above the Pink Panther.

Terry notices a guy climbing towards him, but he is obscured by the smoke. *What a mug*, he thinks, *some hero trying to rescue people. He'll not get any help from me. It's everyone for themselves.*

Terry doesn't hesitate. Out the window he goes, only to be pushed back by the guy coming in. 'Get the fuck out of my way,' Terry snarls, and then stops, astonished—Jack Martin has just climbed in the window.

*****

The party that Jack and Jenna attend is held on the roof of an apartment block overlooking Woolloomooloo and the navy base. Hosted by one of the multinational computer companies, the who's who of the computing world are in attendance. Jenna is thankful that the conversation is about anything other than computers.

Earlier, Jenna was a bit worried about Nat, but a phone call to the Blue Mountains put her mind at rest. Jenna's mother declared that Natalie was having a great time, conveniently omitting the fact that she was on her second bowl of ice-cream. Some things are best kept quiet.

With Jenna in a relaxed mood, the pair dances, chats and drinks sparingly until just before sunrise. Not-so-fond memories are rekindled for Jack when he gazes out over the navy's Garden Island Dockyard. He quietly describes for Jenna the scene nearly eight years' before when he and most of 1RAR boarded *HMAS Sydney* for the trip to Vietnam. Jenna points out an aircraft carrier in the dry dock and asks, 'Is that the *Sydney*?'.

'No,' replies Jack, I think that's the *Melbourne*. I seem to recall that the Whitlam government sold the *Vung Tau Ferry* for scrap a few years ago.'

'Oh,' said Jenna, 'are they similar?'.

'Well, that one down there has an angled flight deck and, from memory, *Sydney's* was straight. I think it's like that so that jet aircraft can land.'

That is the limit of Jenna's interest and she starts chatting about the Sydney CBD skyline. Jack is pleased to change the topic of conversation.

Bidding their hosts farewell as the first streaks of dawn lighten the eastern sky, Jack and Jenna decide to stroll through the Cross to catch a bus.

They are halfway up Darlinghurst Road, chatting contentedly about their evening, when they hear a commotion ahead. Smoke and flames are billowing from a building in front of them. People are running everywhere, screaming and yelling. Someone jumps from a window to escape the flames and crashes to the pavement. There is no sign, as yet, of the fire brigade, although there are several coppers on the scene.

Jack's attention is drawn to a woman leaning from a window of the building next door, screaming: 'Help, someone help, please. People are trying to escape from next door. They're at the back, on one of the upper floors. Will someone help?'

Jack doesn't hesitate. Urging Jenna to say where she is, Jack runs to the open door of the Pink Panther and takes the stairs to the top floor two at a time. A group of women in various stages of undress cry out to him, motioning him into a room where people—faces and bodies blackened from smoke—are climbing in the window.

Jack looks out. There is a man climbing along a pipe towards him, gingerly holding on to what are obviously hot pipes. Jack grabs him and pulls him into the room. The man gasps out, 'There are still plenty of people next door,' then collapses to the ground, exhausted.

Jack climbs out the window, shuffling carefully along one pipe, holding on to another above, which is bloody hot. He climbs in the first window, thrusting some guy out of the way.

*****

At the sight of Jack, Terry's mouth opens and he speaks before realising what he is saying: 'Jack? What the hell are you doing here, pretty boy? I thought you got finished off in Vung Tau'.

Jack turns on Terry, an astounded expression on his face. Putting aside the shock of finding Terry here, he screams out: 'How do you know about Vung Tau, Terry? Were you there?' Jack's eyes narrow, and he bellows angrily. 'Did you shoot me, you prick?'

Instead of answering, Terry suddenly pushes Jack, who stumbles and falls to his knees. Before Jack can recover, Terry is out the window, climbing along the pipe work to safety.

Jack is tempted to follow Terry, but he hears shouting coming from outside the door. The smoke is now very thick, and as Jack emerges into the corridor he can see flames licking at the ceiling, highlighting two people, a man and a woman, the man dragging the female along the floor. 'In here,' Jack shouts, and the guy limps towards him.

Jack quickly sizes up the situation. The fire is close, and he doesn't see any way that anyone else in the building can escape this way. It's time to get the two people, and himself, out.

Coughing hard as he breathes in smoke, Jack screams above the roar of the flames into the man's ear: 'You go out the window, mate. Climb along the pipes. People will help you. It's not far. I'll bring the woman because I'm in better shape than you. Okay?'

The guy needs no further encouragement. He climbs out the window and slowly clambers to safety, urged on by the shouts of encouragement from the women next door.

Jack checks the woman. She is barely conscious, with a bloody graze on her forehead, and covered in soot. He thinks hard. How is he going to get her to safety? His gaze settles on a venetian blind cord hanging in a window, and he pulls on it until it breaks free. There is enough to tie him and the woman together, face to face. He accomplishes this by lying her down and straddling her, pulling the cord under her body and around his. He pulls himself upright and props up her inert body as he carefully manoeuvres both of them out of the window. There a shock awaits. The lower pipe has burnt through. His escape route has been cut off. They are trapped. Jack sags to the floor in despair.

*****

Chapter 49

Jenna waits anxiously across the road from the burning Savoy Hotel for ten agonising minutes before deciding to find out where Jack has gone. She rushes into the Pink Panther and tries to climb the stairs but is pushed back by a man who tells her that it is too dangerous to enter. Frustrated, she makes her way to the rear of the premises and finds herself in a laneway behind the buildings. There she watches in fascinated horror as several people scramble to safety from the building on fire. They must be nearly twenty metres above street level. One slip and they will be dead or seriously injured. There is no sign of Jack.

Terry Bannister hurries down the stairs through the Kingsdore Motel and then the Pink Panther before exiting through the rear into a narrow laneway. Panting with fear and very glad to be alive, he gazes up to where a man is inching his way along the pipework to safety. It is not Jack. As the man climbs into the window in the motel, Terry sees one of the pipes suddenly burst into flames. About ten feet of its length drops into the laneway below as onlookers scatter out of the way. Terry smiles jubilantly—Jack's escape path is blocked. He turns and strides briskly away. His slip of the tongue will surely come to nothing now.

Jenna sees the pipe fall and gasps in terror. Is Jack in there? Her worst fears are confirmed a few moments later when she sees his head poke through the window. He appears to be holding up a woman. Then he disappears. Jenna slumps to the ground, sobbing.

Jack looks around the room desperately for an alternative way out. But there is nothing apart from a bed and mattress in the room. He has a crazy idea: maybe they can jump out of the window on top of the mattress. That might cushion their landing. *Risking severe injury is better than just staying here and being burnt alive or succumbing to the acrid smoke*, he thinks. Suddenly, the door to the hallway starts to catch fire and Jack's mind is made up. Struggling with the semi-conscious woman, he pulls the mattress off the bed and staggers to the window, steeling himself to launch them out.

Suddenly, there is a shout from the adjacent building. Jack leans out and spots a fireman hanging out of the nearest window. In his hands he holds a rope. He shouts to Jack: 'Hey, mate, grab this when I throw it. Then tie it around you and that other person and I'll make it secure at this end. Then you'll have to jump, and we'll lower you to the ground. You might lose a bit of skin, but that's way better than the alternative'.

Suddenly hopeful, Jack drops the mattress and gives the fireman the thumbs up, then catches the rope as it sails towards him. Swiftly tying it around him and the woman and knotting it securely, Jack shouts that he's ready.

'Okay, mate, jump when you're ready. We've got you from this end,' shouts the fireman.

Gathering himself and, despite the dead weight of the woman, Jack launches himself out of the window. He and the woman fall about ten feet before the rope jerks tight, slamming them into the wall, but Jack is prepared for this, and manages to turn in the air and stretches his legs past the woman's body, buffering them as they strike the wall. What little air Jack has left in his lungs is cut off by the rope cutting into him, but within thirty seconds they are lowered to the ground to be met by a couple of firemen and an ambulance man. The rope is released, and Jack is able to draw in shuddering breaths. One of the firemen cuts the nylon cord attaching Jack to the woman, and she is lowered gently onto the ground where the ambulance man begins to work on her.

Jenna is suddenly next to him, screaming with joy and relief, and they embrace fiercely. All around there are scenes of chaos as police, firemen and members of the public run in and out of the smoke. Jack recovers quickly and motions for Jenna to follow him.

'Where are we going, Jack?'

'We're going to find a guy named Terry Bannister. He was up there in that building and he said something to me that leads me to think he knows who shot me in Vung Tau. It may even have been him. I want some answers from the mongrel.' Grimly Jack searches through the faces and the smoke for Terry.

After thirty minutes of fruitless searching, Jack has to stop. Exhaustion replaces the earlier adrenaline rush. He staggers, and Jenna grabs him.

'That's enough, Jack,' she says firmly, 'it's time to go. That guy you are after is well gone. Come on, let's go home'.

She leads Jack away, soothing his angry demands for answers. She can't see that Jack is going to be able to find this man, and anyway, she will do her best to discourage him from looking further. What's done is done, and there's no point going back.

*****

In Katoomba the next evening Jack and Jenna watch the news on TV and are aghast to learn that, of the sixty or so people inside the Savoy Hotel when the fire started, fifteen have died and twenty-five are seriously injured. Sometime later, they learn that police have arrested Reg Lyttle. Lyttle is eventually sentenced to life imprisonment.

Chapter 50

Midway through 1976, Jack comes home from work and sits Jenna down in the lounge room. She has done a night shift the night before and is relaxed and refreshed after a good sleep. The part-time work arrangement is working well; the babysitter is great and Nat is happy and loves to play with the little boy. Jack has hardly seen Angela. Jenna tries to work as many weekend shifts as possible, and the extra pay is a bonus.

Jack has a proposition of his own. He asks Jenna how she would feel if he was to go it alone in the business world. He has had enough of 'working for the man', especially when that metaphorical man seems to be heading in a direction he doesn't want to go. He is bursting with ideas and, given that the shift-work situation is working well, Jack feels that now is the time—particularly as he can mostly work from home. Jack humbly asks Jenna what she thinks of this proposition. He is elated when she throws her arms around him and urges him to go for it.

Jenna presses him for details, so he outlines his plan.

Unbeknown to Walt and Jack's work mates, Jack has been researching business opportunities from where, he believes, demand will come in the future. He is now well versed in UNIX software and, with his by-now considerable experience in working in systems integration, he feels that the opportunities lie in fields related to database management and communications. Jack is keen to explore the potential for applications that will help to manage activities such as hotel reservations, communications networks, or even running a bank's financial systems, all through automated processes. This is cutting-edge stuff, but Jack is confident that he can develop the software and systems to do such things, if only customers will pay him to do it.

'Therein lies the rub,' he reveals to Jenna. 'I need to have some tools to show potential customers, and the development of the tools requires money. I hesitate to ask this, but what do you think of the idea of using some of the money we have in the bank to finance my ideas?'

To Jack's delight, Jenna is all for it, although she does have one caveat—he must not spend any more than forty per cent of their capital on the project. Jack eagerly agrees.

Energised, he starts to plan the details of how he will achieve his goal.

The pair has a mutual acquaintance who runs a successful business advisory service in Sydney. Jack meets with Bob Ward, and Bob likes his ideas. Sensing an opportunity, he quickly agrees to help Jack develop a business plan and provide specific advice as required, in exchange for Jack fixing a problem he is having with his computer system at work. And Bob wants the option to buy in if the business starts to thrive. Jack is ecstatic; the barter system is alive and well.

Jack has one further problem to resolve. He needs access to at least one minicomputer, and preferably a second of a different brand. He invites Walt out for a beer and breaks the news about his intentions.

Walt is disappointed but not surprised. He has known that Jack is probably not going to hang around for much longer; he is good at reading the little signs that signify Jack's unhappiness at work. When Jack asks him for a favour, Walt is cautious. Jack explains the access issue to him, and what he is after.

Cannily, Walt puts a counteroffer: Jack can have access at no cost, but he must agree to provide Walt with a free license for the company to use any software he develops. Jack considers this carefully. Would he be giving too much away? Mulling it over, he cannot see any alternative.

Finally, he agrees. Without access he is stymied before he can start. He chides Walt for his hard-line position, although he knows that Walt has him over a barrel. He consoles himself with the thought that it is not necessarily the software tool that will make the money, but the skill of the person using it.

After they shake hands on the deal, Jack decides to ask a leading question.

'Mate that solves one half of the equation for me. Who do you know that might give me access to another brand of minicomputer under similar terms and conditions?'

Walt smiles at Jack. He knows exactly what he is getting at.

'I suppose that I could give my old mate Barry Turner from DEC a call. The PDP-11 should fit the bill. He owes me a favour or two, even though, officially, we are competitors.'

Walt leans forward, smiling admiringly.

'Jack, I'm proud of you. You really have learned how to bargain.'

*****

Bob Ward meets Jack to talk about his business plan. Bob starts the ball rolling.

'Do you know, Jack, this systems integration stuff you're into sounds a bit like systems theory, which I seem to recall is a part of a field of study called Organisational Behaviour. In essence, it is about how the parts of the organisation, people, structures and technology, interact with each other. Do you see a parallel with your work?'

'Yeah, Bob, but I'm more interested in the technology side of the organisation, in particular computers and software, and how they interact. So I suppose it's a sort of a subset of this stuff you are talking about.'

'Okay, I get the picture. Let's get on with this business plan.'

After several sessions, they finalise the plan. Jack is impressed with the content. He has almost all the business tools he needs, but there is one more thing he has to acquire. He calls a friend and orders an Altair 880 kit from the USA. The Altair 880 is a new portable device that is being called a microcomputer. Jack has heard it initially was a mongrel to use because the software was complex, but a guy named Bill Gates has recently written a simpler software version and it is now wildly popular. And $US400 won't put too big a hole in the budget.

It takes a month for the microcomputer to arrive in Australia and another week before it is released by customs. He installs it in the lounge room of the apartment, swearing like a trooper as he tries to figure out what bit goes where. Finally, it is ready, and Jack gets down to business.

For the next three months he writes code, trials programs, and rectifies errors. By Christmas 1976 he has several programs that he has tested, retested and trialled on dummy databases. Jack is ready to put them to work. All he needs are some customers, but that may prove to be the biggest challenge.

Once more the family celebrates Christmas with Jenna's family in the Blue Mountains. Natalie is now two years old, and has entered the Terrible Twos. Her blonde hair has grown to the point where Nat now fashions it in a short pony tail—when Nat allows it to be brushed. Nat is a little ball of energy that can walk quite well and talk—well, sort of. Her favourite word is 'no'. However, she is amenable to bribery and corruption, and Jena and Jack shamelessly resort to this method of controlling Nat. Her grandparents are equally blatant, and everyone gleefully admits that she is spoiled rotten.

At least she sleeps right through the night, so the married couple have some respite after bed time. They are both happy, but Jack knows that the New Year will be make or break for his business aspirations.

Nineteen seventy-seven doesn't start well. Jack takes his programs to business after business, but none of them want to be the guinea pig. If only Jack has a track record, they say, over and over, completely ignoring his previous high-quality work for them with IBM. Jack begins to wonder if someone in the industry has put the word out on him, but he is unable to confirm his suspicions.

By March, Jack feels the weight of despair settle on his shoulders. He cannot continue for much longer. He is about to resign himself to going back to Walt, cap in hand, although the thought fills him with frustration. Jenna is very supportive, but she sees the toll this is having on her husband. She privately wishes him to stop, but she will not voice her concerns. At least, not yet.

Then a miracle happens in the form of a phone call from H late one afternoon while Jack and Jenna are in the lounge room with Jack going over his presentation for the umpteenth time.

H is upbeat. 'Hi Jack, how's it going?'

'Bloody awful, H, to tell you the truth.' H knows about Jack's struggles, so Jack doesn't need to amplify this.

'Well, I've got some news. You'll never guess who I bumped into in town today?'

'H, I'm not really in the mood for guessing games right now,' Jack says in a tired voice.

'Jack, stop being a sook. It is Gene, the American Gene, and he wants to catch up with me and you and Jenna. Tonight. Can you get a babysitter at short notice?'

Buoyed by this revelation, Jack places his hand over the handset and whispers to Jenna, 'Can Angela babysit tonight? Can you find out?' Jenna nods and motions for Jack to keep an eye on Natalie, who is playing with some toys on the floor.

Jack resumes his conversation with H. 'Bloody hell—Gene. I can't believe it. What's he doing in Sydney?'

'He told me he's here on business. And he's got his wife with him. Remember the picture of the girl he showed us in Vung Tau? Well, he married her, and she's three times as gorgeous in the flesh. Rita really is a hot tamale.'

Jack ignores H's appreciative description of Gene's wife. 'What sort of business is he in?'

'My sort. He apparently owns a large security type company that is involved in all sorts of secret squirrel stuff, and he's planning to expand Down Under. That's why he wants to talk to moi, me being such a successful businessman.' H immediately realises his mistake. 'Ah, mate, sorry, I didn't mean it to come out like that.'

Jack knows his friend is sincere. 'Forget about it, H. Hang on, here's Jenna.' Jenna nods an okay. 'Yep, it looks like we're good for a babysitter. Where and what time do we meet Gene?'

H names an upmarket restaurant in the CBD and tells Jack that they are to meet at seven-thirty in the bar. Jack hopes that the bill won't be too steep; his reserves are running low. *By God, it will be good to see Gene again.* Jack tells Jenna the story and they rush to feed and bathe Natalie and dress her in pyjamas before Angela arrives.

Jack drives the car, which is starting to get on in years, into the city. He manages to fluke a park near the restaurant. They arrive on time and head for the bar. Jack has dressed carefully; he wants to make a good impression on the American. Jenna is stunning, as usual, in a figure-hugging sleeveless dress, in keeping with the warm evening.

Gene spies them as they walk in and hurries towards them. He grabs Jack in a bear hug that nearly crushes the air out of him, and more politely bids Jenna hello with a peck on her cheek. He ushers them to the bar. H is already there, and sitting next to him is Rita. *H is right*, Jack thinks, *she is a real looker.*

Gene introduces Rita to the pair. Rita smiles and immediately envelops Jack in a warm embrace. Jack is startled and Jenna laughs. Rita examines his face and in a grave southern tone drawls, 'Thanks, Jack, for saving my man'. Then she smiles, and adds impishly, 'But maybe a bullet in his ass, instead of your back, might have made him a bit more humble'. Everyone laughs, and the ice is broken.

Drinks are called for and consumed as they catch up on the past few years. After a second round, the maitre d' appears discretely at Gene's side and informs him that their table is ready. The Australians are impressed when the maitre d' escorts them to a private dining room.

They enjoy a sumptuous meal accompanied by fine wines and top-shelf beers. After a couple of beers Jack asks for a glass of red, preferably shiraz, and the wine waiter appears soon after with a bottle of 1959 Lindeman's Bin 1590. Jack knows this wine is highly rated by the experts and that it will cost a small fortune. Seeing the expression of incredulity and then concern on Jack's face, Gene laughs and says, 'Relax, man, the meal and the drinks are on me tonight'.

As he enjoys the delicious wine, Jack sizes Gene up. He must be in his mid-thirties by now, but still appears to be pretty fit. He certainly looks prosperous, and he is wearing a very expensive suit. Rita is dressed to the nines. Jenna sees him staring and leans over and whispers that it is a creation by some well-known French designer. Jack has never heard of the name, but the dress is something else.

Chapter 50

After dinner, Gene suggests that the men return to the bar for a nightcap whilst the women powder their noses and compare notes. Jack chooses a Drambuie and savours the smooth fire as it slides down his throat. Gene and H are drinking bourbon. Gene turns to Jack.

'H probably hasn't told you about our conversation earlier today. I'm in Australia on the lookout for opportunities to set up here. I think that H and I might be able to do some business.' H beams at Jack, and nods in agreement.

Gene continues. 'H attempted to explain to me earlier today what you are trying to do with this computer stuff. I don't pretend to understand about it, but I'm prepared to listen, if you've got some time tomorrow. You might not want to hear this, Jack, but I always pay my debts.'

Jack is not sure where this conversation is going, but begins to protest about the debt bit. Gene stops him.

'Hear me out, Jack. If there's any way I can help, I will. Rita was right, you saved my ass. And she loves that ass of mine, you'd better believe it.' Gene laughs heartily. 'Drink up, you guys. Time to go to bed. Jack, I'll see you at my hotel—it's the Hilton, just down the street—at, say, ten in the morning. Okay? Good.'

Excitedly, Jack explains to Jenna what has transpired as they drive home. He has an idea related to Gene's business that might just work. If he has to pull an all-nighter, that won't matter. He has to develop something to show Gene in the morning.

At ten the next morning Jack opens his car door in the underground car park of the Hilton hotel in George Street. He has called ahead and Gene, clearly mystified, has reserved a car space for him. Jack is met by one of the hotel porters who helps him carry his microcomputer to the elevator and then to Gene's suite on the fifth floor. The pair places it on a desk and Jack plugs it in and starts it up. Gene tips the porter and watches Jack play with the machine.

Jack looks like shit, he thinks. *I bet he's been up all night.*

Jack asks, 'Tell me about the way you run the administrative side of your business, Gene. What I want to know specifically is, do you use paper files?'

'Hell, yes. The number of clients my company has, and the number of cases we work on, would amaze you. I'll fill you in on how I got started later. But tell me, what is this thing?' He points to the computer.

Jack's expression is serious. 'Before I answer that, do you have any problems storing and accessing all those files?'

'Hell yeah, Jack, but why do I get the feeling you already know that?'

Jack smiles and replies: 'I took an educated guess. This thing in front of me is called a microcomputer. It's just a dumb machine really, but it has a set of operating instructions, a bit like an army drill sergeant, but a bit more sophisticated in how it does things. I've developed a database management program that might help you and your business. In layman's terms, that's a system that allows you to not only efficiently store a shit-load of data about people, objects—you name it—but more importantly it enables you to interrogate the data—like you did with those baddies in Vietnam—so that you can get answers to almost any question you might have. Here, let me give you a demonstration'. Jack rapidly types commands into the computer, and soon a string of data appears.

For the next thirty minutes Jack shows Gene how it works, using a set of dummy data that he made up the night before. Gene whistles in surprise as he sees what can be stored and what information comes out.

'Jeez, this thing is so good, I'll bet even Rita could understand it.' Rita, who has just entered the room, punches Gene hard on the arm. 'Ouch, woman, that hurt,' he jokingly complains.

Rita pretends to punch him again. 'I've got more brains than you give me credit for, Gene my love.'

'But I didn't marry you for your brains, girl, I married you for your …' Gene doesn't get the chance to complete the sentence as Rita picks up a chair and pretends to swing it at him.

Gene becomes serious. 'Jack, this system you have here, how much would it cost to buy and run?'

Jack is thoughtful. He doesn't want to scare Gene away … and he is a buddy … and he needs some runs on the board that he can tell others about … He decides to take a punt.

'How about I do this at cost, Gene? To tell you the truth, I can use the business, and hopefully I can leverage off you. All you need to pay for is the computer, and let's say five hundred bucks US for my time to set it up. Your people can input the data. So, your capital outlay would be less than a grand. If you want more machines, then you pay for them, and I'll set them up for, say, three-fifty US a pop. That will include user licenses.' Jack hopes he hasn't appeared too greedy, as Gene regards him pensively.

Gene thinks aloud. 'Now, I've got offices in seven US cities, not counting my head office in Washington DC, and I'll probably set up an office here in Sydney and one in Melbourne. That makes ten at this stage, so my outlay will be, what, a tad over thirty-five grand US, plus wages for the staff who do the input? I'm paying them anyway, so we won't count that. I'll have to throw in some airfares and some accommodation and meals for you for your travels, but all that will be a tax deduction, and that's good.' Gene has another thought. 'Say, Jack. I don't suppose there is some way you could connect all those machines up so that they could talk to each other?'

Jack is struck by the idea. *Maybe Gene has stumbled onto something here*, he thinks. He replies, 'Not at the moment, Gene, but that's a bloody good suggestion. You've given me something to think about'.

Gene considers this, and then smiles at Jack. 'I reckon your brain will figure something out, buddy. The "nice to have" option can wait, but do I like the package you're offering? I think you've got yourself a deal.'

Gene sticks out his hand to shake on it. Jack is eager, but he holds back momentarily. Is Gene just doing this as payback, or does he really want the system? Then Jack thinks, *why do I care what reason he has?* He mentally calculates his fee. Over three thousand five hundred US for … what? … less than a month's work. Jenna will be over the moon. Jack grabs Gene's hand and shakes it vigorously.

Gene invites Jack to lunch in the hotel's dining room. As they chew on a couple of steaks with the trimmings, Gene gives Jack the summary version of what has happened after Jack flew out of Vietnam.

'We never did get to the bottom of your shooting. There was some Aussie guy involved, but we couldn't pin anything on him, and there were a lot of untouchable guys I couldn't get anywhere near.' Gene looks away, the memory obviously painful.

'Anyway, I got a bit tired of chasing drug dealers and, when I returned to the States at the end of '69, I resigned my commission in the army. I went from being a captain with lots of kudos to a civilian nobody. That was initially a bit tough.'

Gene shrugs in memory of the feeling. 'But I had a few contacts, and before I knew it I was working for one of the biggest private security firms in the USA. I won't name names—anyway that isn't relevant. I learnt quickly; my background and experience helped, and I made plenty more contacts. You'd be amazed at the variety of things private security firms, particularly big ones, are involved with in the States and elsewhere in the world.'

Gene can see that Jack wants to say something, and pauses. Jack jumps in: 'You mentioned an Aussie bloke a few moments ago. His name wasn't Terry Bannister, was it?'

Gene regards Jack with astonishment. 'How do you know his name?'

Jack's face turns angry. 'He and I go way back. I had a run-in with the bastard a year ago, and he let slip about Vung Tau. I'd like to get my hands on him, Gene.'

Gene slowly shakes his head. 'I'm sorry, buddy, but if he's connected to the sort of people I think he is, getting to him won't be easy.'

Jack sighs and studies the table, obviously frustrated with this response.

In an attempt to cheer him up, Gene changes tack. 'Anyway, let's get back to business. I'll take an educated guess here about why you struck out on your own. Like you, I didn't want to go on working for someone else, particularly in a large bureaucracy—too many rules and regulations—so I started my own business. I called it Trumper Risk Management. I'm a bit more specialised than the big boys. I stole a few clients, and hired my own guys. And here I am.' Gene smiles at Jack, who smiles back.

Jack puts his thoughts of Terry aside for the moment and asks curiously, 'What exactly is your specialisation, Gene?'

Gene grins and recites what is obviously a well-used statement. 'Like the company name says, I'm in the risk management business, Jack. My guys and I help our clients to identify internal and external threats, develop options to manage the risk, and if necessary help in implementing the resulting strategies. That's the spiel I give to the client. What we actually specialise in is human threats; the rest of the risk stuff I subcontract out. That's where H's experience will come in handy here in Australia. I've come to the happy conclusion that clients are willing to pay big money when their personal safety is in danger, whether that danger is real or not.'

His throat dry from all the talking, Gene pours himself and Jack a cup of coffee. As he sips the brew, Jack speculates on Gene's employees. 'The people you hire, they'd have to be pretty well trained in unarmed combat, weapons use, and stuff like that.'

'Right on the button, Jack,' Gene responds. 'I use ex-Special Forces guys mainly, and I'll be interviewing some ex-SAS guys later today. What did you guys call them in 'Nam … "chicken stranglers"?'

Jack laughs. 'You remembered. Yep, and for my money they're up there with the Brits and the Yank Special Forces. I'd say you'll be well served by hiring them, as long as they're not too crazy.'

Their talk turns to the logistics of Jack travelling to the States. Once an outline itinerary is agreed, Jack makes his departure.

When Jenna arrives home, Jack pulls out a bottle of iced champagne and breaks the news to her. She shrieks with delight, and they dance around the kitchen in celebration.

*****

Chapter 51

In Sydney, during 1977, Frank Nugan asks Terry to lend a hand with a problem he is having in Griffith. By now, Frank's family company is turning over in excess of nine million dollars a year but, despite this, he is not happy. When Terry agrees to help out, Franks confides in him.

'Now mate, you will be working closely in Griffith with an ex-cop named Fred Krahe who's doing some facilitating for the bank.'

Terry, well aware of Krahe, is suddenly more interested in the problem.

'What seems to be the trouble with your company, Frank?'

'Let's just say that the fruit packing shed in Griffith occasionally holds more than merely fruit and vegetables. I've got a mate named Bob Trimbole who is in the Indian hemp growing business. It's bloody high quality stuff, and we transport it out of there to where it needs to go. The problem is, there are some busybodies sniffing around this arrangement, and Fred is helping to ensure that they don't get too close. Once he has sorted things out down there, your job will be to make sure that the shipments arrive at the right place at the right time, and the right people collect them.'

Terry is pensive, thinking about Fred Krahe. There were plenty of whispers about him being on the take when he was a cop, and his penchant for gambling and womanising. He also has a menacing reputation as a stand-over man, and it is rumoured that he has been involved in more than one murder whilst he was a cop. Terry decides that he will need to be very careful around this guy.

Over the course of two days, Terry drives his Torana to Griffith via Canberra, where he spends a night. He visits the Australian War Memorial late that afternoon. Of course, there is nothing about Vietnam in the displays.

As he drives, he notices that the countryside is still quite lush from the heavy rains over the past several years, but what Terry enjoys most about the road trip is getting his performance vehicle onto the open highway and letting it rip. Terry is thrilled when the car reaches 190 on a long straight out in the middle of nowhere.

He arrives in Griffith midafternoon on the second day and books into a local hotel. Griffith is a regional service centre for the state's Murrumbidgee Irrigation Area—one of the most productive agricultural regions in Australia. A good proportion of the population is Italian working class who have been migrating from the Old Country since the First World War, but particularly after World War Two. They are skilled farmers, and with the plentiful water available as a result of the MIA project, fruit and vegetables flourish. But this is not the only harvest that is proliferating. Indian hemp is the new cash crop.

Bob Trimbole is the son of an Italian immigrant. Soon after declaring bankruptcy in 1968, his panel-beating business is mysteriously destroyed by fire. All records of the business are lost, to the dismay of the tax office, but this setback doesn't deter Bob. In 1972 he opens a restaurant in Griffith named the Texas Tavern, and sells it in 1973 to Guiseppe Sergi, who is Bob's brother-in-law, and is related to another Trimbole associate, Tony Sergi. It must be a coincidence that one of Bernie Houghton's nightclubs in the Cross has the same name, but Terry doesn't think so; he has long ceased to be amazed at the tentacles that Bernie and his mates have spread across the Australian landscape.

Bob has fortuitously come into an appreciable amount of money and has built a very upmarket house, complete with pool, for him and his family. The locals have nicknamed it the 'grass castle'. Bob also has a link to Bally Australia through interests in poker machines—not that this information is in the public domain. Terry learns all this from his new mate, Fred Krahe, over a few beers and a meal in a restaurant in Banna Avenue.

Fred is a heavy-set man, slightly overweight, with a pug nose and several double chins. He eats quickly and without polish. His eyes are dark and project menace. *I'm glad I'm on his side*, Terry reflects.

'Frank told me that you are attending to some problems he is having down here,' Terry says tentatively, hoping that Fred will tell him more.

Fred is happy to talk. 'Yep, there are a few people that are giving him and Trimbole a bit of grief. There's one bloke in particular, a real pain in the ass. He's a do-gooder, they're the worst kind. His name is Mackay, Donald Mackay. This Mackay geezer thinks he's running the bloody place.'

Fred finishes his steak and wipes his chin. 'Mackay tried to enter the world of politics a while back but came up against one of Trimbole's mates, a guy named Al Grassby—another Gyppo. Al and Bob Trimbole are both members of the Calabrian Mafia and our friend Mackay hates them both. My mates in the cops have told me that this Mackay fella is a secret informer about where the marijuana is grown around here. The problem is, Bob is using Frank's warehouse to store his crop, and Mackay might know about it—or at least suspect it.'

Fred checks to see that no-one is within earshot. 'And my cop mates tell me that Mackay is trying to big-note himself in connection with some really large harvests that Bob and Tony Sergi are involved in. They're in some place called Coleambally, about fifty kilometres from here, as well as another flyspeck down near the Victorian border close to the Murray River. The word is that the street value of these crops is around ninety million dollars. That's a whole lot of cash in anyone's book. So Bob and Tony are not at all happy, and Frank is ropeable. This Mackay guy has pissed them off in a big way.'

Terry listens with incredulity. *Shit, that sort of money is way bigger than anything he has been involved with since the bank started. No wonder Frank has gotten Fred involved.*

Fred pauses for a pull of his schooner. 'But they've got another problem. The auditors of the family business have turned up some really sus transactions that involve a lot of money paid to Trimbole and Sergi. The bloody auditors are smelling blood, and they need to be discouraged from pursuing that line of enquiry. And the same applies to a couple of the company shareholders who have got cold feet because of these transactions.'

Terry wants to know what Fred plans to do. Fred acts cagey, and will only say that Donald Mackay will be taken care of very soon, and that he and Terry need to lean on the auditors and the recalcitrant shareholders. Terry shudders when he thinks of what might happen to Donald Mackay. Terry doesn't want to know what role Fred will play in this, but the intimidation of the others is very achievable, and well within Terry's capabilities. With Fred at his side, surely it will be a doddle.

In mid-July 1977, Donald Mackay, after enjoying a few drinks with friends at a local pub in Griffith, disappears from the car park. Blood is found on his vehicle and on the ground, along with several spent shells from a .22 calibre weapon. He is never seen again, despite an extensive search by police and volunteers.

The prime suspects, Trimbole and Sergi, have watertight alibis. The disappearance makes the national and international news but, as time passes with no sign of Donald Mackay, people lose interest. The drug crops are harvested and transported to Sydney, from where most of it heads to the huge US market, with the remainder spread across Australian capital cities.

Soon after Mackay's disappearance, the auditors for Frank's family company resign after a rigged board meeting. But Terry and Fred, much to their astonishment, fail in their attempt to fully silence the vacillating shareholders. Because of the intense public interest in Mackay's disappearance, they are unable to do more than make empty threats to the shareholders. These are not only ignored, the pair is threatened with legal action. Terry observes a sense of defiance growing in the local community, and he convinces Fred to back off. A court case will later will heard in connection with the Nugan Fruit Company and Frank's attempts to conceal the secret accounts. But that is in the future.

Fred and Terry return to Sydney, their assignment over. Terry is not the only one who is infuriated about the lack of success with the shareholders. Frank is both angry and worried. For the first time he feels exposed. A shadow has fallen over him and he is afraid it may grow darker. To him, the enormous profits the bank will reap are not supplying the satisfaction he is expecting. He is already so rich he could never spend it anyway—although he has every intention of trying—but the impending threat takes him out of his comfort zone for the first time in a long while.

For Terry, these events mark the beginning of the end of what he has come to call the golden years. In the game of snakes and ladders, he has been up the ladder big-time; now he has the uncomfortable feeling that he is about to go down a very long snake. Who knows what will be waiting for him at the bottom?

*****

Chapter 52

Terry locks the door to his apartment and strolls up towards Kings Cross. It is a beautiful day: warm, a slight breeze, not a cloud in the sky. He is feeling content. The bank is going great guns, and the money continues to roll in. Terry has gotten over his sense of impending doom and is back to feeling positive.

As he walks along he suddenly notices Susie Adams standing in the doorway of a drug centre. She spots him as he crosses the street to avoid her. Her initial expression of alarm is replaced by a sneer; her pretty face transformed into an ugly mask.

As Terry goes by Susie cries out, 'Keep on walking, Terry, you prick'. Terry angrily turns to her to retort but just then two Aboriginal men appear beside her at the drug centre door. They wear the tough look of boxers and regard him with hostility. She flashes a smile of triumph. Terry turns away and continues to walk uphill, quietly fuming. That bitch; he will find some way to get her.

Terry asks Dozer about the drug centre. Dozer gives him a look of disbelief.

'What do you want to know about that place? They're just a bunch of losers. Druggies, all of them. And that Ted Noffs—he's just a do-gooding God-botherer.'

'I saw a girl there this morning. Attractive, dark hair. You know her?'

'Oh, her. I think she works there as a volunteer.' Dozer smiles lasciviously. 'She's a looker, all right. I wouldn't mind doin' the horizontal mamba with her.'

Terry smiles coldly: 'Do me a favour, Dozer? Keep an eye on her for me, will you? I want to know everything about her. Where she works, where she lives, the whole deal. If you do that, who knows, you might well get your wish.'

Dismissing Susie from his mind, Terry bids Dozer farewell and leaves to catch a cab to a nearby Holden dealer. He wants to find out more about the newest Torana to hit the streets, the A9X. With its five-litre V8 motor, Terry is convinced the car has his name written all over it.

His intuition is correct. The A9X two-door SS hatchback is every bit as exciting as he thought it would be. Terry haggles enthusiastically, but ultimately unsuccessfully, with the salesman to bring down the asking price. Eventually Terry capitulates and orders a new Flamenco Red-coloured four-speed manual with dealer-fitted air conditioning, a sunroof, a window demister and a radio. He writes a cheque for one thousand, two hundred and fifty dollars—ten per cent of the agreed price.

*****

Chapter 53

When his stint in the States finishes mid-1977, Jack finds himself very busy. He completes the installation of software and hardware in Gene's new Sydney and Melbourne offices and is inundated with orders. The word quickly spreads about the capabilities of the programs and it is like a switch has been pulled; everyone wants his products.

Jack's determination to find and confront Terry about Vung Tau slowly fades as his business takes off. He is too busy to even think about Terry, let alone search for him. And what would he do if he found him? He has no proof of Terry's involvement in his shooting and, more importantly, if Gene is reluctant to pursue it because of Terry's links to high-placed shadowy figures, then what chance does Jack have? His angry thoughts about Terry get lost in the noise of Jack's expanding business.

After a few months, Jack finds it necessary to hire a secretary to field enquiries and orders. Jenna astutely ensures that the woman, although well qualified, is suitably middle-aged and dumpy. She doesn't want any temptations placed in front of Jack.

Chapter 53

By the end of the first twelve months of operation Jack's firm, which he names Martin Business Solutions, has a turnover of forty thousand dollars, and forward orders for the next three months alone are certain to exceed this total. He hires extra analysts and, as 1978 draws to a close, the business expands to include a staff of six. Turnover for the 1978-79 financial year is projected to be upwards of one hundred thousand dollars.

Jack leases an office in North Sydney in the newly developing Technology Park, and a new Ford motor car. The banks seem to like him and are willing to take a punt on his business, so he is also able to obtain a largish loan to purchase a house for the family.

After a lot of searching by Jenna, they choose a three-bedroom dwelling on the lower North Shore of Sydney Harbour with a safe backyard for Natalie to play in. The leafiness of the surroundings make the house feel like it is miles from the hustle and bustle of the city. Jenna loves it and Jack only has a fifteen-minute commute to work.

In early 1979 Natalie departs for her first day at school looking so cute in her uniform. The tears shed come mainly from Jenna; Natalie is raring to go. Jack is too busy at work to accompany Jenna, and Jenna is none too happy about his absence.

Perhaps unsurprisingly, the frenetic pace of his business expansion starts to take a toll on the couple's relationship. Jack is hardly ever home before dark, and often puts in twelve-hour days as well as spending half of the weekend at work.

Jenna grows increasingly frustrated about being left to cope with the household chores and raising a very active five-year-old. They begin to argue, leaving both of them upset and angry. Jenna pleads with Jack to slow down, but he either can't or won't. In the excitement and challenge of the business expansion, Jack seems to have forgotten his vow about the family coming first.

Jack is over the moon about the latest project involving the installation of specialised software onto the hardware of a major bank. It will not only permit the bank to speed up its financial transactions, but trial a communications link from the bank's computer workstations to its minicomputer. Jack, with the aid of a communications wiz he now employs, has built on a concept that has originated in the USA, called the ethernet. It is a way of linking computers via coaxial cable so that they can talk to each other—but only over a short distance to date. The technique has a new name: networking. If it works, Jack's business will be heading towards the big-time.

The mounting tension between Jenna and Jack explodes one Saturday evening in late March 1979. Jenna has cooked a special roast meal in an attempt to patch up the strains showing in their relationship but, although he promises to be home on time, Jack is late as usual, working desperately to get the network in and the software working before the bank's Easter shutdown.

Jack walks wearily into the house just after nine o'clock. He realises he has again missed his daughter's bath and bedtime story as he sees Jenna sitting in the kitchen sipping on a glass of wine, an almost empty bottle in front of her. She doesn't look up or greet him; she just sits there. Jack can see that she is upset and angry, and attempts to mollify her.

'I'm really sorry, Jen, but it's a crucial time in the project, and I just had to get something finished today.'

Jenna, however, won't be placated. Staring blankly at the kitchen table, she quietly says: 'The thing is, Jack, everything is crucial to you. Everything but your wife and your child. I'm fed up with all this bullshit. I've asked you—begged you—to slow down and spend some time with us. I thought family came first. That was what you promised me.' She dissolves into tears and buries her face in her hands.

Jack hugs her to him.

Chapter 53

'Jen, I promise ...' He doesn't finish the sentence; she pushes him away and, sobbing, stumbles out of the room.

At the doorway Jenna turns and, in a voice made harsh with rage, says, 'If you want your dinner, you'll have to get it out of the garbage'. With that, she flees to their bedroom and slams the door. Jack runs after her, but stops when he hears the agonised sobbing coming from inside. He decides to back off and leave her alone for a while. *Maybe she'll calm down*, he hopes optimistically. Jack returns to the kitchen to find something to eat.

An hour later he quietly opens the bedroom door and tiptoes in. The light is off, and all he can see is Jenna's shape in the bed. He undresses and silently slides in next to her, tentatively placing an arm over her shoulders. But Jenna squirms away. They lie in the dark, listening to each other's breathing, the tension between them a palpable thing.

Jack wakes the next morning to find Jenna's side of the bed empty. He throws on a pair of shorts and searches for her in the garden, but there is no sign of Jenna or Natalie. Worried, Jack returns to the house. He finds a note propped up on the kitchen table. He opens it and begins to read.

> Jack,
>
> I have decided that we need a break from each other, at least until you agree to cut back drastically at work and spend a proper amount of time with us. I know your pride and reputation are on the line, but I can't continue to live like this. I have aspirations too, and I've put mine on the backburner for way too long.
>
> Although I don't really want to, I have taken Nat to my parents' place. I can just imagine the lecture I'll get from my mother, but at least I will be talking to someone.
>
> Call me if you agree to my terms. If you don't

> agree, then perhaps the break may have to become permanent. I hate making threats and I don't want this to happen, and I suspect neither do you. You need to know that I am determined to follow this path, and pleas from you won't change my mind.
>
> Jenna.

Jack is stunned. Has it really come to this? He is suddenly angry. *Jenna doesn't mind the money that is coming in. How does she think that happens? I can't just sit around all day and hope contracts fall out of the sky like magic. I can't walk away from this job; there's too much at stake. Why can't Jen hang on for six months more? By then, word will spread about this networking concept and I can afford to back off a bit and hire some more people to handle the extra work.*

A thought strikes him. He hurries outside to find the driveway empty. *Shit, she's taken the car. Damn her.*

Then the indignation fades as Jack imagines a life without Jen and Nat. This is too much, and tears well into his eyes. He slumps to the floor and sobs. He does not know what to do. After a while he showers and shaves and dresses. *I'll just go to work today by taxi and I'll call her tonight. Surely we can work things out?*

Jack calls his in-laws' house that night. His father-in-law answers and is sympathetic, but Jenna will only talk to him if he agrees to back off at work. Jack hangs up without another word. He is determined not to give in to what he sees as emotional blackmail. He can be just as pig-headed as her.

The pair remains separated. Jack pays a brief visit over the Easter break to Katoomba to see Jenna and Natalie. Jenna refuses to talk to him. He leaves in tears, the feel of his daughter's arms around his neck indelibly imprinted on his mind.

*****

Chapter 54

Nineteen seventy-nine starts with a bang for the Nugan Hand Bank. The Organisation of Petroleum Exporting Countries, OPEC, has increased oil prices to record high levels, and the member countries—Iraq, Iran, Kuwait, Saudi Arabia and Venezuela—are overflowing with petro dollars. In Saudi Arabia, billions of dollars of ambitious new infrastructure is planned and construction is quick to follow. The labour force is Asian and most of the management teams come from the USA. Wages and contract fees are enormous and paid in cash, but there is a major practical problem with this arrangement: what to do with the Saudi riyals they are paid in? There are no western-style banks and, under Muslim law, no interest is allowed to accrue on deposits.

Bernie Houghton and Terry enter from stage left. The ever-urbane Bernie offers a foolproof scheme to make depositors money by investing in secure bonds. He will convert their Saudi money into US dollars and issue their clients with certificates that they can redeem at a later date. Well over five million dollars US in cash is deposited into the bank's coffers. Bernie and Terry carry anything from briefcases to plastic bags stuffed full of money.

By mid-1979 the Nugan Hand Bank's global turnover exceeds a

staggering five hundred million dollars. New offices are opened in the Cayman Islands, a tax haven, as well as Singapore and Taiwan. Everyone is in the money, and Terry's earlier fears seem to have come to nothing.

But the same can't be said for Frank Nugan. He is facing fraud charges over the dodgy dealings and falsified accounts of the family company. On the outside, Frank is the epitome of a very successful businessman—the press has claimed he is the richest man in Sydney, and his lifestyle certainly reflects this—but Frank is a very worried man, and the anxiety eats at him like a cancer.

Terry, although by now very well off, continues to keep a low profile. His only sign of extravagance is his new SS A9X, one of only one hundred that are released to the public. It has the same basic specifications as the car Peter Brock drove to victory at the famous Bathurst one thousand kilometre race in 1978. Terry thinks that Brockie, in his A9X, will be unstoppable in this year's event at the iconic Mount Panorama circuit.

The day-to-day management of the bank's activities in Sydney is undertaken by a small team picked by Michael, Frank and Bernie. This team is generally given cart blanche to run the administrative functions such as recruitment, hiring of specialists and the newly developing science of information technology. The trio provide the overarching policy direction and, behind closed doors, scheme to put the money to uses that advantage them. If the team members are aware that the bank's operations are sometimes not quite kosher, they are careful not to speak of this.

Automation of banking functions is a topic of increasing interest in the banking world. There is too much scope for error or fraud in human processing of large sums of money. No self-respecting bank manager wants any whiff of fraud to waft into the public arena.

When George Horner, the bank's security manager, hears on the grapevine about a guy named Jack Martin's success with one of

Australia's leading transactional banks, he is curious. A self-admitted computer illiterate, he is keen to find out more about newly emerging ways of using computers to speed up bank operations. He invites Jack in for a chat, and by the time Jack leaves he has an agreement to trial his system in Nugan Hand's Sydney office. None of the three senior partners are consulted on this decision—after all, it is only a trial.

Things remain tense between Jack and Jenna, despite neither of them really wanting the stand-off to escalate further. At Jack's suggestion, and to Jenna's parents' relief, she agrees to move back into the house on the condition that Jack lives elsewhere. Jack arranges to rent a small flat a few streets away on a short-term lease. Jenna is happy to allow him access to Natalie—about the only thing that Jack is pleased about.

Determined to do her own thing, Jenna enrols part time at the New South Wales Institute of Technology's Kuring-Gai campus and starts a Bachelor of Business degree. The campus is not too far from the house, and Jenna finds a reliable and experienced sitter to mind Nat when she is not in school.

As the pair settle into an uneasy truce of sorts, Jack is increasingly distracted by the unsatisfactory domestic situation, but he has no choice other than to put in the hard yards at work; fame and fortune possibly wait just around the corner. He hopes that maybe, then, Jenna will reconsider; under those circumstances, Jack would certainly be prepared to meet her more than halfway. There is a saying: money can't buy you love, but Jack knows that real money can make life very cruisy if you've got it.

The problem, as he sees it, is that he is almost, but not quite, there. He needs money to take the business to the next level. He makes a snap decision and goes to see his bank manager with a written proposition.

'How can I help you, Jack?'

The bank manager likes Jack and his style. He listens as Jack outlines his plans and examines the documentation Jack brings with him. He is impressed with the detail and the prospects.

'So, you want a business loan to expand. How much do you think you'll need?'

Jack takes a deep breath and says quietly, 'I reckon two hundred thousand dollars would do it'. He watches the bank manager's face nervously.

The man says nothing as he considers the request, reviewing the documentation before him. Finally he speaks.

'Hmm. So taking into account the one hundred thousand you have in your housing loan, if this business loan was to be approved, you'll be in debt to the tune of three hundred grand. You sure you can handle that?' His tone of voice suggests that he is doubtful.

Jack answers positively. 'I wouldn't have asked if I didn't think I can service the debt. The projected income figures you've got in front of you show this to be the case.'

Revealing nothing of what he is thinking, the bank manager advises Jack that he will talk to his senior people and get back to him. Jack spends a nervous week waiting for news. Then he receives the news he has been waiting for: he has the loan, subject to a few terms and conditions. Jack is excited but anxious. *It's all or nothing now*, he thinks.

*****

Gene is back in Sydney for a lightning visit and he and H meet Jack for a quick drink. H has filled Gene in on Jack's domestic situation, and Gene knows better than to lecture Jack. When Gene tells Jack that he will do anything to help him, Jack is touched, but there is nothing his friend can do. Jack changes the subject and informs Gene about his latest work. Gene is very interested, and wants Jack to install the software at his offices, but Jack reluctantly has to put him in the queue. He resolves to jump Gene's company several places to repay the original favour.

Chapter 55

Jack receives an anguished call from Walt.

'Jack, I don't know what to do. I've just found out that my youngest son, Chris, is hooked on drugs. He's living in some dive at the back of the Cross. Jenna's a nurse; maybe she can give me some advice. My wife and I are going crazy with worry. Can you speak to Jenna for me, please?'

Jack doesn't want to add to Walt's burden by disclosing that he and Jenna are currently living apart. Instead he offers his sympathies, and quickly puts in a call to Jenna. Luckily she is at home. He recounts Walt's tale of woe to her.

'That's terrible, Jack. Poor Walt, he's such a nice guy. I can't imagine what he and his wife are going through. I'm no expert on drugs, but I do know that there is a drug referral centre near King's Cross. Perhaps Walt could take his son there. They would be better placed to advise Walt than I am.'

Jack thanks Jenna and, after enquiring after Nat, hangs up. He calls Walt back. Walt sounds even worse than before. Jack relays Jenna's suggestion. Walt is enthusiastic but Jack can't help but think that Walt is grasping at straws. When Walt asks Jack to go with Chris and him, Jack initially hesitates and then agrees. He owes

Walt, and he has a narrow gap between contracts. They agree to pick Chris up the next day, Saturday.

*****

Terry keeps running into Susie near his apartment and up in the Cross. She seems to be everywhere: in anti-drug rallies with that Ted Noffs and his trendy hangers-on; protesting on street corners, cunningly with a few well-built males accompanying her; and just standing on the steps of the drug centre and staring at him in hatred as he passes by. He resents her being around; she is diminishing his enjoyment of his regular haunts in the Cross. More importantly, she is attracting the attention of important people, including Bernie Houghton, who don't want the status quo upset.

Terry, Dozer and Bernie meet one evening at one of Bernie's clubs. Bernie is thoughtful.

'You know that dame from the drug centre, don't you, Terry? Well, she is becoming a real pain in the ass. My associates don't want anyone upsetting the apple cart, but the way she's going, a few apples might get spilt. That's not good for business. Got any ideas about what to do with her?'

'I know what Dozer wants to do with her, Bernie. Me, I've already done it. Whatever it is, we would need to be discreet. Maybe a snatch job. What about stashing her in that old warehouse down in Walsh Bay where some of the merchandise is stored from time to time? It's quiet and there's usually no-one hanging around there. Then Dozer can teach her a real good lesson.' Terry smirks at Dozer, who nods eagerly.

Bernie agrees and Terry and Dozer plan to grab Susie. Dozer has some good intelligence; she normally volunteers at the drug centre on Saturday mornings. She invariably walks back up to the Cross via a back lane just near the centre, which is a short cut to the bus station. Dozer will do the snatch there.

*****

Chapter 55

Walt picks Jack up from Central Station midmorning and they drive to Kings Cross. Jack waits while Walt enters a decrepit-looking building to get his son. After ten minutes Walt comes back out alone. Chris is heavily asleep or unconscious, and Walt can't budge him.

It takes Walt and Jack over an hour to rouse Chris sufficiently so that they can get him out of the dingy bedroom he lives in. Jack half carries Chris down the stairs, wishing he was in better shape—all he has time for these days is work and the occasional shooting practice. He realises that he needs to get fit again. Soon, he promises himself, as they drive off with Chris lying in the back seat. He stinks of vomit and who knows what else.

Walt and Jack manhandle Chris into the drug referral centre and plonk him untidily on a chair. Whilst Walt talks to the receptionist, Jack decides to get a breath of fresh air. The smell of Chris is all over him.

Jack walks to the door and opens it. As he breathes the outside air deeply into his lungs, he notices an old white van pull up. He can't see the driver's face—it is obscured by a dark knit cap and the driver is facing the other way—but the guy somehow looks a bit dodgy. *What a neighbourhood*, Jack thinks disgustedly as he looks away.

Just then a door opens at the side of the drug centre and a familiar figure walks out. Jack gives a gasp of recognition. Susie glances up at the sound, and sees Jack. Startled by his sudden appearance, she begins to run away from him, down an alley, a panicked expression on her face.

Jack cannot believe his eyes. Susie. What is she doing here? Why isn't she in Newcastle? Instinctively, he follows her, crossing the street and entering the alley.

As he does, he sees a large, muscular guy dressed in dark clothes with a beanie pulled well down over his face grab hold of Susie and clamp a large hand over her mouth. She kicks and struggles, but the guy is way too strong for her.

Alarmed, Jack lets out a shout, 'Hey you, let her go'. The guy turns around and spots him. Unease shows on his face, but he immediately turns Susie around and clubs her across the face with a huge fist. She slumps to the ground. The big guy faces Jack as he runs towards him, Jack screaming out loudly for help.

Jack has almost reached him and then he slows, bracing himself for what will probably be a hiding. His opponent is way too big for Jack to stand a chance in an even fight, but he has to try. The big bloke grins savagely and then beckons Jack on. Jack feigns left and quickly throws a right, hitting the big man on the chin, but his adversary just shakes his head and growls. He swings a massive haymaker at Jack, who just manages to dodge it. Jack thinks quickly. Time is on his side; he's just got to delay the guy until someone hears the commotion. With this, Jack resumes shouting at the top of his lungs.

This produces a result, but not the one Jack is hoping for. He hears a vehicle roaring up behind. Jack, hoping it is someone to help him, turns slightly. The big guy takes advantage of the distraction and unleashes a savage left hook that catches Jack on the side of the face. Instantly, Jack knows he is in trouble as he staggers backwards, only to be struck a glancing blow on the left side of his body by the approaching vehicle. He goes down, reeling in shock and pain, as the white van he has seen earlier rushes past. It comes to a screeching halt adjacent to the big bloke who jumps quickly into the front seat. The van then accelerates down the lane, fishtailing as the driver puts his foot down hard. In a few seconds, it vanishes around a corner.

Jack lies there in disbelief. He hurts all over, but his left side seems particularly painful. He feels blood trickling down his side. Suddenly Susie is next to him. She has a small gash on her jaw and some blood on her face, but she seems to be otherwise okay.

Susie gasps as him, 'Jack, are you all right? Where the hell did you come from?' She pauses, suspicion on her face. 'You haven't been following me, have you?'

Chapter 43

Pain shooting through his hip, Jack grimaces: 'No, I haven't been following you. I was helping a mate whose son has a drug problem, and suddenly there you were. My side hurts a lot. I think we'd better call the cops and get me to a doctor'.

Susie looks stricken.

'No. No cops, Jack. I think I know who tried to kidnap me. If I'm right, believe me, the last people you want to talk to are the cops. There is too much corruption in this place and, besides, I've already been warned off once. I guess they really mean business this time.'

Susie asks if he can walk. Jack thinks so. She helps him to his feet. Jack can see the after-effect of her near miss. Her eyes are wildly staring and she is shaking.

Jack's side is on fire and the blood continues to seep out of somewhere on his torso. Susie gathers herself and says: 'Come on, I'll get you back to the centre. There's a doctor there. He's a really good guy and he can examine you. Then I'll tell you all about what I think is going on'.

Back at the centre, with Susie giving the orders, Jack is taken straight into the doctor's office. Walt, holding his son upright in the chair, stares at him with an astonished expression. Jack ignores him. Explanations can come later.

As the doctor examines him, Jack sees that Susie is now reacting to the full impact of the attack. She slumps in a chair, sobbing quietly, then shudders and suddenly throws up into a wastepaper basket.

Stripped to the waist, Jack feels the doctor's gentle fingers probing his left side. He winces as the doctor finds a sensitive spot. The physician comments: 'It is pretty obvious that you've had some trauma here, judging by these scars. Am I correct in assuming that they are the result of a gunshot wound?'

'Yep, in Vietnam about ten years ago. The bullet went in on the right side and out where you're touching. Peritonitis nearly took me out.'

The doctor straightens and moves to the sink to wash his hands.

'Well, it looks to me like you've damaged the muscle sheath already weakened from the bullet passing through it. It's a painful injury, and it's going to hurt for a few weeks until it heals. My advice is don't aggravate it by exercise or any sudden movement. Just let it repair itself. I'll apply a surgical dressing; you'll need to change it daily, and keep it dry.' He addresses Jack and Susie. 'I don't suppose you two are going to tell me what happened, are you.'

Susie stares at him. 'Doc, you're familiar with this neighbourhood. I don't think you need—or want—to know. Can we leave it at that?'

The doctor nods silently. He has other people to attend to, and if Susie doesn't want to tell him, it's no skin off his nose.

'Just clean out the bin, will you? There are enough unpleasant odours around here from our clients without you adding to them.'

Jack walks stiffly out into the waiting room, with Susie following. Walt and Chris are nowhere to be seen, thank goodness. Susie washes out the bin and places it outside the doctor's door.

'Come on, Jack,' she says, 'let's find somewhere safe to have a chat'.

*****

As the van careens through the back streets, Terry punches the steering wheel in rage. Jack fucking Martin. He has a very bad habit of turning up at the wrong time, like Superman, except he's not super in any way, and he certainly can't deflect bullets.

Terry glances at Dozer, who is obviously reflecting on his lost opportunity to bang the lovely Susie. 'Dozer, I know that prick that got in the way back there. He's name is Jack Martin. He's from Newcastle, and he was a Nasho, like me. Let's put the feelers out; someone must know of him. This means we now have two scores to settle. And settle them we will.'

Chapter 56

Sitting in a quiet cafe in Darlinghurst, Jack listens silently to Susie's story as they each sip a coffee. She starts at the night Terry gave her the drugs, way back in 1968. Jack is hostile and disbelieving at first, but as the tale unfolds, he begins to realise that Terry is utterly evil. Susie concludes by voicing her suspicions about Terry and the nightclub owners in Kings Cross. She also suspects that the big guy works for an American named Bernie Houghton, the owner of the Bourbon and Beefsteak. She is pretty sure she has seen him there. The word on the street is that the lot of them are connected to drugs.

Jack sits back, his brain working furiously.

'If they know how to get to you at the centre, they probably know where you live and where you work.' He pauses, and stares into her eyes, his face softening. 'Oh, and Susie, now I know the truth about Terry, I'm really sorry about the way I treated you back in Newcastle after the … well, you know.' He pauses, embarrassed, and Susie smiles and pats his hand. He feels the familiar electricity of her touch. Careful, he thinks, stay on message.

He resumes his thought. 'I think you're in real danger from those blokes. What can we do?' If Susie notices the use of the word 'we', she doesn't react. 'If you like, I've got a couple of mates who will know exactly what to do. It's their business. Let me call them.'

H arrives within twenty minutes and they climb into his car. Jack introduces him to Susie, and H gives Jack a knowing look. Jack says quickly, 'Mate, she's an old friend, from before Jenna's time'. He glances quickly at Susie to see how she will react to Jenna's name.

Susie coolly returns his look, and smiles. 'It's okay, Jack. I saw the wedding ring on your finger. Women notice that sort of thing.'

Jack doesn't know why he says it, but the words slip out. 'I'm separated, Susie. Things didn't work out between me and my wife.' He mentally kicks himself. *You're digging a bigger hole. Just shut up.*

H cuts in. 'Let's not start a discussion on the merits of marriage, Jack; first things first. We need somewhere for Susie to stay for a while until I do a bit of scouting around. What about your flat?'

Jack is initially taken aback at the suggestion, but then warms to the idea. *Those goons are not likely to have identified me*, he thinks, *so Susie will be safe there as long as she keeps her head down.*

'Good idea, H. Can you drop us off there?'

Susie protests that she has no clothes or toiletries or anything a girl needs to suddenly relocate. H blunts her objections. 'You can buy something, Susie, there are a few shops near the flat. Just make sure you buy and wear some sunglasses to hide that pretty face. I'll advance you five hundred bucks. Gene will pay; he owes Jack a few favours.' H grins at them both, and starts the car for the trip north over the Harbour Bridge.

Once Susie has purchased a few essentials and the pair is ensconced in Jack's tiny flat, H departs to 'check out a few things'. Susie eyes the flat. 'Not a lot of room here, Jack,' she says.

'Ah, no, but, it's okay, I'll sleep on the lounge. You take the bedroom. You want a cup of tea or a drink?'

Susie asks for a whiskey and water. Jack mixes the drink and grabs a beer. He sits down on the couch beside Susie, careful to keep a decent gap between them. Susie sips her whiskey and regards Jack.

'Tell me about your wife. Do you have any kids? And how did you get shot?'

Jack gives her a potted version of the past ten years of his life. She winces when he recounts how he was injured in Vietnam and his suspicions about Terry. Susie's eyes are full of sympathy when he tells her about the marital difficulties. She notices that his eyes glisten with tears when he mentions his wife and daughter. *They obviously mean a lot to him*, she thinks. She is a little sad as she imagines what life would be like with a partner and a child.

They have another drink and Susie suggests that they prepare a meal. Jack finds some steaks in the fridge and some tomatoes, lettuce and carrots for a salad. Susie searches his cupboards and finds a bottle of shiraz. She smiles at the memory and says to him: 'I see you haven't changed your taste in wine, Jack Martin. You'll be pleased to know that I've developed a liking for red wine too. How about we open this?'

The food cooked and eaten, they wash the dishes and then Jack pours the last of the bottle into their glasses. They have talked a lot about their lives over dinner. Jack is a little tipsy, and Susie appears to be as well. The wine has relaxed them both, and they settle back onto the lounge. Jack, emboldened by the alcohol, thinks he detects a come-on look in Susie's eyes and, no longer the inexperienced youth, he leans deliberately towards her and kisses her lips. She throws her arms around him and returns the kiss passionately. They frantically shed their clothes and, without delay, he enters her. She gasps in pleasure as they couple. Susie comes quickly, and Jack groans in pleasure as he ejaculates soon after.

They slowly disentangle. Jack is obviously embarrassed, but Susie laughs.

'Jack, Jack, please don't read too much into this. You know me. I like a good time, but I'm not so good at long-term commitment.

I like you, and that little episode was terrific, I'm sure you'll agree, but you're a married man, and even though things between you and your wife are strained, I believe you'll work it out. Your daughter needs her father. This was only sex.' Susie turns away so that Jack cannot see the look of sadness in her eyes.

Jack's feeling of guilt is relieved. *Thank goodness*, he thinks. *Things might have gotten very complicated very quickly.*

*****

Chapter 57

Terry and Dozer confer about Jack. Using Fred Krahe's contacts, Dozer has managed to trace Jack through his business. Terry thinks hard. Perhaps that snatch attempt was not the smartest thing to do. The memory of the shit-fight that occurred after Juanita Neilson disappeared is still fresh in his mind. *Maybe I should have a chat to Frank about this. There must be a way to kill two birds with one stone.*

Smoking a fat cigar, Frank listens to Terry's story.

'You say that Bernie wants to get rid of the woman, but this guy Martin is now in the frame? You're right about the kidnap attempt—that was a bad idea. And Fred's contacts say that no-one contacted the cops afterwards? She must be running scared, which is good, as she'll keep her head down now. Anti-drug campaigning will be the last thing on her mind.'

Frank switches his attention to Jack. 'Now, this Martin guy …' Frank has a thought, 'what sort of business is he in? You don't know? Well, I think we should find out right now'.

He buzzes his blonde secretary who sashays into the office.

'Mandy, I want you to get one of the team to do a check on a guy who runs a business—what's it called, Terry, Martin Business Solutions? This is urgent, Mandy. I want to know what type of business it is and what shape it's in. And I want to know in under an hour.'

Frank and Terry watch admiringly as Mandy's shapely bottom sways out of the room.

'A great girl with great assets,' Frank smiles appreciatively.

Terry and Frank make small talk while they wait. Terry thinks Frank is starting to display signs of ageing; he has large bags of skin under his eyes, and his face is puffy and unhealthy looking. *Too much of a good thing*, Terry reflects.

Frank resumes talking about Jack.

'The same thing applies to this Martin fellow as the girl. We don't want another investigation like with Donald Mackay going on. The repercussions are still being felt around here, particularly by me.' Frank looks unhappy for a moment.

Mandy is back in just over thirty minutes. Without a word, she places a folder on Frank's desk. Frank thanks her, opens it and begins to study it. When she has left his face transforms into a chilling smile.

'Well, Terry my lad, it would seem that we might just have something to stop your Jack Martin dead in his tracks, without resorting to violence. What do you know about credit ratings?'

Terry doesn't know what he is talking about. Patiently, Frank explains.

'It seems that Mr Martin has a large amount of debt, possibly in order to finance a planned expansion of his business. His work has something to do with computers, and by all accounts he's pretty good at it. But his debt is his Achilles heel.'

Frank pulls out a page from the folder, examining it closely.

'Anyone who applies for a loan through a bank or finance company gets a credit rating. Our Jack Martin's rating is good at the moment, but he is on toast with the level of debt he holds. What do you suppose would happen to him if his credit rating is downgraded?' Frank grins wolfishly, then answers his own question. 'The bank that he owes money to will demand he repays the debt immediately. If he can't—and from the information I have here he won't be able to—they will foreclose on the loan. That means he will lose his house, and his business, and will have no choice but to declare himself bankrupt. He will be in so much shit he will drown in it.' Triumphantly, Frank puffs his cigar, the smoke billowing into the air.

Terry is exhilarated. Good old Frank. This will surely take his nemesis out of the frame, then he will be able to go after Susie at his leisure. He asks a final question. 'You can arrange this, Frank?'

'Consider it done, mate.'

Frank walks Terry out of the office suite and shakes his hand at the entrance to Macquarie Street building. Neither of them notices a shadowy figure take a long-range photo of them from concealment across the street.

*****

H examines the photos his operative has taken over the past day or so of the likely players in the kidnap attempt. The pictures are of four men who seem to be linked. He has been able to identify two of them: he recognises Bernie Houghton's face; he also thinks he has found out the identity of the big guy—his name is Anton Kocher, aka Dozer, and he works for Bernie. The other guys he doesn't know, although he thinks he has seen the older one before somewhere. But they will have to wait; he has a plane to catch, to the USA. Gene has summoned his managers to a meeting about a huge contract the company has won. It will impact not only the USA but Australia as well.

*****

Chapter 58

Jack receives a call from his bank manager two mornings later. He is apologetic, but he needs to see Jack right away. *Is something wrong*, Jack worries? *There surely can't be*. Jack is so close to achieving his dream he can taste it.

The bank manager's secretary ushers Jack into his office. He comes straight to the point.

'Jack, I'm sorry to tell you that your credit rating has been downgraded, and the implication is that you are now considered a high financial risk by the bank.'

Seeing the expression of absolute shock and alarm on Jack's face, the manager hurries on.

'As a consequence, the rules say I have to ask you to pay back the loans you have with us immediately,' he pauses and regards Jack sympathetically, 'but I know you and like your style, so I'm going to give you two weeks' grace. You'll have to find the money somehow, or we will be forced to foreclose on your mortgage and take your house. And of course, you'll need to find the money to repay the business loan.' He is aware of the incredulity plastered on Jack's face, but he can't waver. 'I'm sorry, Jack, I really am, but I'm putting my head on the chopping block here by giving you even that amount of time. Get back to me as soon as you can about the repayment.'

Numbly, Jack shakes the manager's hand and walks with him out of the office. Jack's brain is struggling to process this shocking news. *What the fuck? What has happened? It can't be my projects or my work.* Jack comes to a sudden realisation. *Someone has done a job on me. But how do I find out who it is?* Although his mind is in turmoil, he manages to put a question to the manager. 'Can you tell me how this has happened?'

The bank manager shakes his head apologetically.

'Sorry, Jack, I don't know, but even if I did, I still couldn't tell you. I don't make policy, I just implement it.'

Jack has no idea how he arrives back at his office. Once inside, with the door closed, he is struck by an overwhelming urge to scream in disbelief. He flings the paperwork on his desk onto the ground in frustration and anger, then he does the first thing he thinks of—he calls H. *Maybe H can use his contacts to find out, somehow, what is going on?*

But his mate isn't available; his office tells Jack that H is overseas in the USA. Jack thinks that H is most likely with Gene. He calculates the time difference between Sydney and Washington DC. It is ten here, that makes it six the previous evening there. Gene hopefully is still in the office.

He places the call. The phone rings and rings, then he hears the international call pips as someone picks up.

'Hello,' a female American voice says.

Jack asks desperately, 'Can I please speak to Gene Trumper?'.

The woman replies formally: 'Sir, the office hours are from nine to five. Can you call back tomorrow, please?'

Jack speaks hurriedly, worried that she will hang up on him.

'I'm Jack martin, a close friend of Gene's, and I'm calling from Australia. I need to speak to Gene. It's extremely urgent.'

'Oh Mr Martin, why didn't you say it was you straight off,' the voice responds in a friendlier tone. 'Hold please while I check if he's still here.'

Jack waits anxiously. Suddenly, he hears Gene's deep voice on the line.

'Jack, my man, what's up? H is here with me. He's on speaker.'

Jack lets loose. 'Some bastard here in Australia has gone and stuffed my credit rating. As a result, my bank wants me to pay them the three hundred grand that I owe them, and they want it within two weeks.' Jack's voice wavers. 'If I don't pay by the end of the first week in December, I'm done.'

Gene angrily replies: 'What the fuck? It sounds like someone is trying to stuff you up. Tell you what, I can't do much about the money, unless you want me to loan you the dough, but I sure can find out who stiffed you. Hold on a second while I talk to H'. Jack waits as his mates confer. Gene is back quickly. 'Okay, here's the plan: you get off the line and let me and H make a few calls. I'll be back to you ASAP. You in your office?' Jack confirms he is, and then hangs up.

*****

Jack sits impotently and waits for the return call, trying to think what this is about. He is fuming. *Can this be related to Susie somehow? But how could they know of his involvement? If they do, then who would have had the connections to engineer this? Surely this whole mess can't just be related to drugs; someone has gone to a lot of trouble to set this up.*

But no answers come to mind. This puzzle has to be unravelled somehow, but for the moment he doesn't have a clue.

His confusion is interrupted by the ringing of the phone. Jack snatches up the handset. 'Yes?' he says.

'Jack, old buddy, you certainly have kicked over a hornet's nest down there in Australia. I've got H on an extension. Now Jack, is an organisation called the Nugan Hand Bank one of your customers?'

'Yes, I've just finished doing a trial installation of some new software there. But what do they have to do with the price of eggs?' Jack is mystified by this revelation.

'Man, I love those Aussie sayings,' Gene chuckles. But then his voice turns serious. 'Well, someone at that bank, most likely high up, has put in an adverse credit report on you. That's why your credit rating has been downgraded.'

Jack is incredulous. 'But I don't know anyone high up in the Nugan Hand Bank. The only bloke I've been dealing with is their security manager, and he loves me after what I have been able to do for them.'

Gene has more information to disclose. 'Jack, have you ever heard of a guy named Frank Nugan? He's one of the founders of the bank.'

'Most people have heard of that bloke—he's as rich as Croesus—but I've never met him.'

Then Gene delivers the hammer blow. 'H has shown me a photo taken a couple of days ago outside the corporate offices of the Nugan Hand Bank. Frank Nugan is in it, and with him is none other than your old pal Terry Bannister.'

Jack suddenly feels very cold. He slumps back in his chair. 'Terry? How the fuck is he associated with the Nugan Hand Bank?'

Gene hears the frustration and panic in Jack's voice.

'Take a deep breath, Jack, and calm down. I'm going to tell you a story. I'll keep it brief, because the full version would take a while. The Nugan Hand Bank was started by two guys, one American and one Australian. The American's name is Michael Hand. He used to work for the CIA in Vietnam, and I'm pretty sure he is still involved with them. The other guy is Frank Nugan. He's a lawyer by trade, but he's also got a reputation for being involved in really tricky stuff like money laundering. You with me so far?'

Jack mumbles that he is. He still can't see the connection.

Gene continues. 'It's been long rumoured that the Nugan Hand Bank has been involved in drug running out of the Golden Triangle in Asia, maybe for the CIA, maybe not. That's where a guy named Bernie Houghton comes in. He's another American who runs a few shady clubs in Kings Cross. Bernie Houghton and Michael Hand are probably the conduit to drugs coming out of Asia. But here's the kicker: remember a guy named Donald Mackay who mysteriously disappeared a few years back from some town in New South Wales? Well, there seems to be growing evidence that his disappearance is somehow linked to marijuana distribution by the company belonging to none other than Mr Frank Nugan. And your not-so-favourite buddy Bannister is linked to all of them. How do you like them apples?'

Jack thinks fast. 'So those bastards trashed my credit rating to try to shut me down. I guess I should be grateful that they didn't take a more permanent approach to get me out of the way. Shit, if I wasn't so angry, I could almost admire their deviousness. But, how come you know all this?'

Gene pauses, and then replies: 'If you ever repeat this, I'll deny it and then come over there and bust your ass. One of my biggest clients in the States is the FBI, and they do not like the CIA. That goes back aways, but I'm not getting into that now. Anyway, a few FBI guys I know have been on the trail of covert payments made by the CIA through that Aussie bank. They know all the players. So there you go'.

Jack absorbs this information, then he says dispiritedly: 'At least we now know what is going on. But that doesn't mean that there is any way to stop it. I'm still stuffed'. Jack sits disconsolately back in his chair.

Gene tries to cheer him up, but knows he is fighting a losing battle. Jack is up against some real heavy hitters.

'Jack, H will be on the next plane back to Sydney and I'll be there in a day or so once I get a few things sorted out. Hang in there, buddy, we'll think of something.'

Jack cannot concentrate on work now. *What is the point?* he thinks, *my dream is over*. His thoughts turn to Jenna and Nat. *I've really fucked things up for them. Jenna is never going to talk to me again when she finds out about this. She'll have to go back and live with her parents, and she will hate that. I'll be bankrupt and have to go back to Walt with my cap in hand, begging for a job.*

He sits up. *Walt. Shit, I've forgotten all about him and his son.* Jack sets his problems aside for the moment and picks up the phone to call Walt.

'Hi, Walt, it's Jack. Sorry to have run out on you like that last Saturday. How's Chris?'

Walt replies in a happier tone than he had on their last meeting.

'That place is terrific, Jack. They got Chris into a rehab program. He's made the big switch from heroin to a drug called methadone, which is supposed to reduce his dependence on that bad shit. He's got a long way to go, and we're trying not to get our hopes up too much, but there may be some light at the end of the tunnel. We've got him at home and my missus is keeping a close eye on him.'

Walt's voice breaks momentarily, then he continues. 'Mate, thanks so much for helping me. But, tell me, are you okay? You didn't look too good on Saturday when you came back into the centre with that woman.'

'Yeah, I'm okay,' Jack lies, 'she's an old friend who needed a hand. It's all good'. He suddenly needs to end this conversation. 'Mate, I'll talk to you later, okay?'

As Jack walks out of his office, he spots his communications technician sitting at his desk, busy on some chore. This image triggers something in his head. There is something related to communications that Walt has said, something that may be important, but he can't for the life of him pin it down. *It's probably nothing. Anyway, what to do about Jenna?* Jack decides that he doesn't want to talk to her just yet. He has had enough bad news for one day.

He catches a taxi back to the flat. Susie is waiting for him, sipping a cup of coffee. She sees the glum expression on his face and in a concerned tone asks him what the problem is. He tells her, and they both sit in silence as they contemplate the sheer scale of the conspiracy that has been mounted against them.

Finally, Susie turns to him and says contritely: 'Jack, I'm so sorry that you are involved in this. Shit, if I'd have known half of what you just told me, I'd have caught the first train out of town and disappeared'. Fear is etched on her face. 'What are you going to do now, Jack?'

He sighs, and looks at her in frustration. 'I just don't know, Susie, I don't know.'

Neither feels like eating so they go to bed; Susie in the bedroom, Jack on the lounge. Jack tosses and turns, mulling over the problem and cursing the uncomfortable lounge. Finally, his troubled brain allows him to sleep. At around three in the morning he sits bolt upright, and yells out, 'Yes, packet switches, that might work!'.

Clad in her underwear, Susie runs into the lounge room, fearful that Jack has had some sort of seizure. Instead, Jack grabs her and kisses her on the forehead.

'Susie, I may have a way out of this.' Susie wants to know what he is talking about, but he fobs her off. 'Susie, it's best if you don't know anything about what I'm thinking. If it works, I'll tell you then. Please don't ask me any questions, just trust me, okay?' Subdued, Susie nods in agreement.

Barely able to contain his excitement, Jack rushes to the small alcove that he uses for a study and grabs a pen and notepad. Mystified, Susie returns to bed as Jack scribbles frantically on the pages.

Chapter 59

Just after daybreak two days later, Jack waits expectantly for H to appear through customs at Sydney International Airport. He has borrowed the family car from Jenna who was initially reluctant to give it up, but finally succumbed to Jack's pleas. Jack has thought his plan through and now has much of the details covered.

Jack smiles broadly as a tired-looking H emerges into the arrivals hall amongst a large group of travellers. H is startled; he has expected Jack to be down in the dumps—he is anything but. Before H can speak, Jack excitedly blurts out that he has a plan. When H looks blankly at him, Jack laughs.

'Come one, mate, it will wait until we get to my office. I'll give you chapter and verse in words that even a computer illiterate like you could understand.'

If H takes exception to this, he doesn't let on. Jack seems to be up to something, and he seems confident that it might work. That's enough for H.

Jack and H buy coffee and sit down in Jack's office. Jack closes the door and pulls down the venetian blind over the half window, ignoring the puzzled glances from his staff. He starts to talk.

'H, have you heard of SWIFT payments? No? Well, I'll give you an example: let's say you want to transfer a thousand bucks from your bank to Gene's bank in Washington. The bank uses what is called a SWIFT transfer. SWIFT stands for Society for Worldwide Interbank Financial Telecommunications—I know this because I've been dealing with a couple of banks lately including, as you know, the Nugan Hand Bank.'

Jack pauses to take a sip of coffee. 'You with me so far, H? Good. Now, I won't go too much into the technical details, but the transfer involves a process called packet switching. In layman's terms that simply is grouping data into blocks, or packets, for transmission from point to point.' Jack smiles in memory. 'I thought of this the other night when someone accidentally triggered my memory. The beauty of the SWIFT system is that real money doesn't actually get sent, only an order from the sending bank to the receiving bank. This happens a lot, so the banks settle up a few days later with actual money.'

Seeing H look blank again, Jack smiles and continues. 'Stay with me, H, I'm getting to the point. So, let's say it's me we're talking about, and I want to send a very large amount of money, say a couple of million, overseas. I will need to have an account at the transmitting bank, and of course the right amount of money in that account.'

Jack adopts a serious tone. 'Now let's talk about the real world. As you know, I don't have any money to do anything like that. I'm broke. The bastards have stopped my credit, and I can't access any funds.'

H is now completely confused. 'Then how can you transfer money that you don't have, Jack?'

Jack smiles triumphantly. 'H, this is the kicker: I don't transfer my money; I transfer the Nugan Hand Bank's money.' Seeing the light dawning in H's eyes, Jack says gleefully: 'Yes, H, I'm going to steal their money and deposit it in an overseas account. I've done some checking. The Nugan Hand Bank has a financial arrangement with several banks in the Cayman Islands. That country is a tax haven, and the banks there provide account holders with maximum secrecy and security. I'm going to set up an account in one of the banks there that is linked to Nugan Hand—or rather, hopefully one of Gene's contacts will do it for me. And, just to be doubly safe, the money will immediately be transferred out of the Cayman Islands to the Channel Islands—you know—between England and France. That place is a tax haven as well. By the time it reaches the Channel Islands, it will be untraceable. I'll need a similar favour from Gene for that too'.

H is impressed with the audacity of the idea, but he has one question: 'But how are you going to steal this money? Surely you're not contemplating just walking in and holding them up like a bank robber?'

Jack laughs at the absurdity of this. 'What's my business, H? I just installed software and communications infrastructure to allow the workstations the bank uses to talk to the minicomputer that controls all the financial transactions. I'm going to give the computer instructions that will transfer money into an account I will set up using one of their workstations, and then instruct the computer to effect a SWIFT transfer of that money overseas to my new account. The timing is important, as the linked banks settle up at the end of the month, and I don't want anyone at Nugan Hand to cotton on until the physical money has been transferred. So I'll have to pull this off in the next few days before the end of November to minimise my chances of getting caught. And, given the volume of overseas transactions Nugan Hand makes every month, unless they're very clever, they won't know for a few weeks that the transaction is fraudulent.'

H whistles appreciatively. 'How much money are you

contemplating, Jack?'

Jack smiles coldly. 'Well, H, there are a couple of factors to take into account here. The first thing I intend doing is pay the loans back to my bank so that my name isn't dragged through some legal quagmire—but that means whoever put a stop on my credit will know about it fairly quickly, and they'll find some other way to come after me, so it's most probable that I'll never to be able to operate my business in this country again. That points to going elsewhere, under a new name, and that means a major change to my, and hopefully my family's, lifestyle.'

Jack stares at his friend grimly. 'So, in order to compensate for the shit they have put on me, and in order to set us up in a new life, I'm thinking big.'

'How much is big, Jack?'

'I reckon five million bucks should do it.' Jack looks at H for a moment, and they both burst into laughter. After a few moments, they stop laughing and contemplate the enormity of the challenge facing Jack. He finally says: 'Come on H, let's work through the details. I want to present Gene with the nuts and bolts, including what I need him to do for me, when he gets in tomorrow'.

*****

Chapter 60

Gene arrives a day later. With H in attendance, Jack outlines his plan in Gene's hotel suite at the Hilton. Gene is stunned for a moment at the audacity of the plan, then he smiles and says: 'Shit, Jack, you're a fucking genius. I never would have thought of that in a million years. You are some devious son of a gun. It's so out there, I think it just may well work'.

Gene then fixes Jack with a serious gaze. 'Buddy, in my former life I thought I was on the side of the good guys, but after a while, working out who were the good guys became just too hard. So, I'm not going to judge you, Jack. We're talking about drug money here, and my sources tell me that many hundreds of millions of dollars are laundered through that bank every year. The way I see it, they're gunna get what they deserve.' He turns his attention to H. 'And I'd say that H feels the same way. Ain't that right, H?'

'You bet,' H replies seriously, patting Jack reassuringly on the back.

Jack smiles in relief. 'Thanks guys, I really appreciate your support. This is not an easy thing to do. To step outside the law goes against everything I have previously stood for, but I'm not going to stand by and watch those assholes destroy me and my family.' Jack is momentarily overcome by emotion, but recovers quickly. 'Gene, there are a few loose ends to tie up. Can you get your guys to open those accounts as soon as possible?'

'Sure, Jack, what name?'

Jack thinks for a moment, and then smiles. 'How about Mr J Swift for the Cayman Islands account, and Mr J Sloe for the Channel Islands? They have a nice ring to them.'

They all laugh at the pun. Gene will arrange for sufficient fictitious ID to be created to satisfy the fortunately lax security requirements of the international banking system. All his guys will need are copies of these IDs to present them when opening the necessary accounts. The system is wide open to shady transactions.

Gene then turns his attention to the rest of Jack's scheme. 'So, how are you going to get into the bank's system? Won't they have some sort of security, like passwords or something?'

Jack is dismissive. 'Being a new business, computer security hasn't yet caught up with the speed of technological advance, Gene. The computing environment has more holes than a Swiss cheese, but I don't need to know what password they are using, or even if they have one; I have my own. Every program I have devised has what is called a back door, which allows me to get into the system without the client knowing. I use it as a fail-safe mechanism in case I need to sort out some major software glitch. So, all I need is access to a workstation at the bank.'

Gene and H are intrigued by this information, and Gene makes a mental note to ensure Jack secures his own system in the near future. Then he asks Jack a question, 'Surely you can't just waltz in there and start operating a workstation without someone looking over your shoulder, even if you are the architect of the system?'

'A good question, Gene. Well, I'm planning to use a bit of subterfuge, a little like a magician. I'm going to direct my good friend the security manager's attention away from what I'm up to.'

'How, Jack?'

'I'm hoping to use Susie's charms, assuming she'll cooperate. But it won't be the Susie anyone will recognise. She'll be someone else entirely.'

H and Gene are impressed, but Gene has an observation. 'My man, you're going to need a complete set of new documentation, including a new passport, for you and your family, given you'll have to move somewhere else in the world. That is gunna take a week or so to organise.'

Suddenly a thought strikes Gene. 'Have you told Jenna what is going on?'

Jack shakes his head. 'No, she doesn't know about any of this yet, and neither does Susie. She'll need a new ID as well.'

Gene explodes. 'Goddam, Jack, you haven't told your wife about something as big as this? This isn't some bloody game, man, this is life-changing stuff, and there's a good risk that they'll come after you big-time, wherever you are. And the timeline is tight, so you'd better get on with it.'

At this outburst, Jack feels like a fool. He realises he hasn't thought this all the way through. Gene is right: he needs to get Jenna in the loop. He resolves to do it immediately.

Gene regards Jack closely. 'One other thing: Is there anything you need to tell us about you and Susie?'

Jack looks him in the eye and replies: 'Absolutely not, Gene. We're just friends. I'm married to Jenna, and I want to continue that way. All I want for Susie is a means for her to escape to wherever she wants to go'.

*****

Jack's conversation with Jenna at the front door of the house doesn't fare well. She demands to know the full story, but Jack feels he is unable to fully confide in her about his plans for the Nugan Hand Bank because he doesn't want her to feel unnecessarily scared or to try to talk him out of it.

Without full disclosure, Jenna stubbornly refuses to cooperate. She yells at him in anger: 'I'm not taking Natalie anywhere with you just because you say we have to. You come here and tell me some cock-and-bull story about people trying to put you out of business—which somehow puts us in danger—and you won't give me the whole picture, so why should I uproot us and just go off with you to God knows where?' Jenna stares at him in disgust. 'This is probably another one of your ploys to keep me in my place as the dumb little housewife. Well, I'm not having it, and that's that.'

Jack can see that Jenna is close to tears, and as she closes the door in his face, she speaks in a miserable tone of voice: 'Just go, Jack. I need to know what is going on, all of it, so don't come back unless you're prepared to tell me. That's the only deal I can offer'.

Jenna shuts the door and collapses to the ground in tears. Jack's heart goes out to her. He knows he will have to tell her everything, otherwise he will risk losing her. That he will not tolerate, but he doesn't know how she will react if he tells her that he is planning to steal a fortune to fund their new life. He decides to spill the beans if he is successful in transferring the money. If he isn't, it won't matter too much—he will be either dead or in jail.

Resolved more than ever to go through with his plan, Jack knows he will fight with every fibre of his being to keep Jenna and Nat safe. This sudden shift in fortunes has given him a much-needed wake-up call. After this scam is over nothing—not work nor the pursuit of fame and fortune—is ever going to get in the way of his family's happiness and security again.

Jack has more success with Susie. She listens intently as he outlines the plan, including her leaving the country afterwards. She asks a couple of questions and seems satisfied with Jack's answers.

He finally arrives at her part in the scheme.

'What I need you to do, Susie, is to act … well … promiscuous. Do you think you can do that? It's worth two hundred grand, if that's any incentive.'

She smiles wickedly at him. 'What you mean is that I've got to pretend I'm a slut. Well, that will be no problem at all, and the money will be most welcome, even though I intend to live cheaply where I think I'll be travelling to. But I'm going to need some accessories to help pull this off.' She grabs a pen and paper and writes down a list. 'Don't worry, I'll get these. I don't want to embarrass you, dear boy.'

*****

Chapter 61

Three days later Jack, smartly attired and armed with the SWIFT code and account number of the Cayman Island bank account, walks into the Nugan Hand Bank, Susie beside him. Jack could have been wearing nothing at all, no-one would have noticed. All eyes are on Susie. She is wearing a bright red micro minidress with matching shoes and handbag. She is not wearing a bra, and her nipples poke saucily through the thin dress material. On her head is a blonde wig. She looks like sex on a stick.

Whilst everyone is gawking at Susie, Jack quietly asks to see George Horner, the security manager. The pair is escorted to George's office by a prim-looking female secretary who frowns at Susie disapprovingly. Jack extends his hand to shake George's hand, but George is too focused on Susie to even look his way.

During the installation of the bank's new system, Jack couldn't help noticing that George had a roving eye. He constantly seemed to be mentally undressing young women who work at the bank. Jack thinks that George will be an excellent mark and he, with Susie in tow, has just the right bait.

Susie sits down and crosses her long legs, aware that she is exposing a flash of white panties as her dress rides up her thighs. George smiles lecherously at her. Susie, managing to hide her revulsion, smiles back coyly.

Jack speaks to George. 'I don't think you have met my new assistant, Miss Penny Lane.' George, not a fan of the Beatles, has no idea of the origin of this bogus name. 'George, I just need to tweak a couple of things in the system. I found a small glitch in the Beta model the other day, and I want to make sure that everything is okay. I won't be touching the operational parts of the software—I know that's a no-no.'

As far as George is concerned, if Jack would have asked him for the keys to the vault, he would have agreed. He is wondering how to get to know this gorgeous Penny creature a little better. 'Sure,' he mutters, as his eyes sweep over her body again.

Susie/Penny helps him out. 'Mr Horner, I'd just love to see around the bank. I get so excited at the thought of all the money you probably have in your vault. Could you give me a conducted tour? I'd be so grateful.' She bats her eyelids at George, and recrosses her legs. Jack tries not to smile.

George is beside himself with excitement. 'Why, Miss Lane, I'd be only too pleased to do that. We'll just let Jack get on with things, while I take you on the grand tour, including a sneak peak at our vault.'

He stands, making no attempt to cover the bulge in his trousers, and gestures for her to precede him out the door. His hand hovers near her tight little bottom as she passes. As they walk out, George says to Susie: 'You know, I'm also a banker in my own right. Would you like to hear about the size of one of the client transactions I handled the other day?' George's voice fades as the pair moves away from the door.

Jack stifles a laugh, and gets to work. He will need at least ten minutes. He hopes Susie can fend off George for that long.

Jack quickly crosses to George's desk and accesses the workstation. Within thirty seconds he is into the system. He quickly creates an account in the name of Swift, and electronically transfers five million dollars from the bank's general fund into it. Then he sets to work on the SWIFT message. Using the proper proforma, he creates a one-page document containing details about the originating bank, the date and time, the coding details of the receiving bank, the name and number of the new account in Sydney, and the amount of money to be transferred.

The only remaining item to be inserted on the document is George's name and his internal bank code. Jack opens George's desk draw and removes his diary. The code is written on the inside cover, as Jack has suspected. Jack is momentarily contemptuous of George's lax personal security, then smiles: it is to his advantage, so why should he care. He puts the diary back and starts to type.

Just then, George's door opens and a bank employee walks in. He stops in alarm when he sees Jack at the workstation. He eyes Jack suspiciously. 'Who are you? What are you doing at George's desk? Where's George?'

Inwardly quaking, Jack smiles easily and replies calmly: 'Hello to you too. I'm the guy whose team installed the update to your computer system to allow the workstations to talk to the main computer. I'm just testing it. George has gone somewhere temporarily. He'll be back in a few minutes.'

The man is clearly not convinced by Jack's explanation.

'I think you'd better stop right now. I'm going to get the security guard. You stay right here.' With that, he rushes out the door, calling out for the guard.

Jack reckons he has less than a minute to finish what he is doing. He frantically works to complete the SWIFT message, his heart racing inside his chest wall.

Jack is just finishing off when the door opens. Susie and George enter. Susie's clothes are slightly disarrayed, and George is smiling. Jack presses a button on the keyboard, and the SWIFT transaction enters the system.

Loud voices approach George's office. Jack figures it is the suspicious bank employee, obviously accompanied by the security guard. Jack ignores the approaching noise and addresses George—'All done. The system is working just fine …'—as a guard and the nosy bank employee burst through the door. They stop in confusion when they see George standing there.

The man nervously addresses George, but not before getting an eyeful of Susie. 'Uh, this fellow says he is doing something to the computer system with your approval. Is that right?'

George looks daggers at the guy, who visibly wilts under his stern gaze. The security guard stands by, impassive.

'Of course that's right, you idiot. Do you think I'd let just anyone walk in here? Besides, the system is secure. This man is simply testing the communications. Now Roger, I suggest you go back to work and stop sticking your nose in where it isn't wanted. And take the sheriff here with you.'

Although Roger is looking angry and embarrassed, he and the guard make a hurried exit. George looks jubilant; he has put them well and truly in their place. That surely must have impressed Penny. He smiles at her in anticipation. Jack thinks it's time to leave as well, before anything else happens.

'We'd better be off, George. Lots of work to do, and I'm sure you're busy as well.'

Susie turns to George, smiling falsely.

'It was a pleasure, Mr Horner. Maybe we could do it again some day.'

George gallantly kisses her hand and goes to better this by moving his lips towards her face. Susie nimbly evades him and walks quickly out of the door, followed by Jack. She sighs with relief as they exit the bank.

'God, that man, I swear he's got tentacles for arms. He was all over me like a rash. He tried to put his hand inside my knickers in the lift, but I told him that I am having my period. That got his hand out pretty damn quick.'

Jack laughs and gives Susie a hug.

'It sounds like you had the harder job. Mine was pretty bloody easy by comparison—apart from a moment of sheer terror when that nosy bugger came snooping around. Come on, let's go and catch up with Gene and H.'

*****

They walk the few city blocks to the Hilton and take the lift to Gene's floor. H lets them into the suite where he and Gene are waiting. They note that Jack and Susie are smiling, so it must have gone all right. H and Gene admire Susie's outfit. H says approvingly, 'Jeez, Louise, don't you look the goods'.

Susie laughs. 'I'll take that as a compliment, H.'

Gene says: 'So, phase one is successfully completed. But remind me, Jack, how do you know that they won't cotton on to the scam?'

'I've got a fair understanding of how the SWIFT system works from my last two assignments with bank clients. As I told you two before, the sending and receiving banks normally balance their SWIFT transactions at the end of the month. Seeing as we're in the last week of November now, that only gives us a few days grace. Jenna is refusing to budge unless I tell her the full story, and now that we've pulled off the scam, I'm going to talk to her straight away. The deadline with my bank runs out in early December, so we need to be out of here before the bank forecloses on the house. There's no way I can get three hundred grand from overseas back to Australia in that time without giving the game away. Even a short-term loan from you, Gene, is no good for the same reason. That amount of money will raise too many flags, and we don't want that.'

Gene is pensive. 'So there is no reason why they would come after you and your family for a week or so. They are convinced that they have got you right where they want you. But I wouldn't hang about, Jack, once you've got your new identities and your plane tickets.'

He turns his attention to Susie. 'But you, girl, are another matter entirely. It was you they were after in the first place, so why would that change? Susie, you're going to have to be very careful. What are your plans?'

Susie smiles. 'I don't have Jack's problems. I'll be heading to the other side of the planet early next week, thanks to the money you have advanced me, and the new ID and passport. Until then, I'll hide out at Jack's place. No-one but you will know I'm there, and Jack tells me his wife is the only other person who knows where he lives. I've got no intention of being anywhere near Sydney when the shit hits the fan.'

Gene stands and the others follow.

'Okay, I guess that wraps it up. I'll be staying in Sydney for a few more days to bed in with H a new contract that the company has just won. As there should be no reason for us to meet again between then and now, this is it. Y'all have a nice new life with that money. Jack, we will be able to communicate through a special channel I will set up with H, just so I know everything is okay in the future. That applies to you too, Susie. Take care, both of you.' Susie gives Gene and H a hug and Jack shakes their hands.

They take a taxi back to the flat. Jack sits down and forms in his mind the sequence of the story he will tell Jenna. Then he has to tell his staff that the business will be closing down, effective immediately. That will be hard enough, but the Jenna conversation is likely to be a doozy. He decides he needs another day before he confronts her.

Chapter 62

Late in the morning on the last day of November, Nugan Hand's vice-president in charge of Australian operations receives a visitor. Like many of the bank's senior staff the VP, a recent appointee, is an ex-US senior military officer with no previous bank experience. Like them, he has been hired for his connections into the covert world of the CIA and ASIO—the Australian Security Intelligence Organisation.

The visitor is the Sydney branch's internal auditor, a prissy grey-faced man named Bolt. The VP greets him warmly and offers him coffee, even though he has little idea what Mr Bolt's duties entail. After all, apart from his cronies, visitors to his office are fairly rare, and almost never on a Friday.

When they are both settled, the VP asks Mr Bolt politely how he can help him. Mr bolt smiles blandly.

'This is just a courtesy call, really, to introduce myself. Amongst other things, my job is to undertake random audits of the bank's transactions and to report on anything unusual that I think warrants further scrutiny.'

Smiling inwardly, the VP assumes a serious expression. *Unusual transactions? My God, most of them are unusual. Is this guy an idiot? Surely he must know what is going on?* It would appear Mr Bolt does indeed know what is going on.

'The reports I prepare go straight to Mr Nugan, and as I understand it, he uses them to minimise the risk of anyone outside the bank from finding out about such transactions. As you may be aware, the bank has been coming under increasing scrutiny in certain financial circles of late. So, you could say, it is a risk-minimisation process.'

The VP smiles. This is good news. Frank Nugan is one smart cookie.

After exchanging small talk over coffee, Mr Bolt proceeds to the area where the records of bank transactions are kept. He removes his coat and starts the lengthy process of sifting through the hundreds of overseas transactions made during November. He carefully sets aside those that require further attention. The pile grows.

By late afternoon he has completed his task. Amongst the large volume of transactions he intends to discuss with Frank Nugan is one that mystifies him. It involves a five million dollar SWIFT transaction made several days before that seems not to have been cleared at the required level in the bank's hierarchy. All the codes on the inter-bank transfer message are correct, but there is not the usual statement on the message that the funds transfer has been checked by a higher authority. He knows that the check is not necessary to effect the transfer, but the omission of the authority is unusual. Perhaps someone has been a little less diligent than normal?

Mr Bolt decides to consult with Frank Nugan but, when he calls at Frank's office, Frank's secretary informs him that Mr Nugan is away for the day attending to urgent family business. No, he cannot be contacted, but he will return on Monday. Mr Bolt knows that the settlement process for international transfers will be completed by the time Nugan Hand opens on Monday, but there is nothing else he can do. He makes an appointment with Frank for first thing on Monday morning, and leaves for the day. His garden bed awaits, and a little weeding and pruning will be just the thing to take his mind off this puzzle.

*****

At the allotted time Mr Bolt is ushered into Frank Nugan's plush office. Politely declining the offer of tea or coffee, he gets straight to the point. Although Frank Nugan seems at first distracted, Mr Bolt's story quickly gains his attention.

Frank stares at the auditor in disbelief. As if he hasn't got enough on his plate—with the impending court case against the family company—and now this.

'Five million bucks? And the money has been transferred already? Shit! No, I didn't okay the transfer, and there's no-one else here at the moment who has that level of clearance. What the fuck is going on here? Why isn't there a rule that makes that clearance mandatory?'

The auditor smiles apologetically.

'That's exactly what I advised the security manager to do a few weeks ago. Unfortunately, it would appear that it hasn't yet come into force after the recent upgrade to the computer systems.'

Frank is very angry now.

'Upgrade, what upgrade? Why don't I know about that?'

'I'm afraid you'll have to direct that question to the security manager, Mr George Horner.'

Mr Bolt looks impassively at Frank, then adds maliciously, 'By the way, George's name was on the authorisation for the transfer'.

Without another word, Frank charges out the door, screaming at the top of his voice for George Horner. He finds him in his office.

'George, what the fuck are you doing? Why did you authorise the overseas transfer of that five million bucks last week? Are you crazy?

Or are you on the take?'

George's expression resembles a stunned mullet. He stammers: 'Wha … what? Five million dollars? You've got to believe me, I didn't do it. It's impossible. There's no way it could have happened, Mr Nugan, please believe me.'

Frank fully intends to punch George in the mouth, but he is interrupted by a knock on the open door. Roger enters timidly.

'Uh, excuse me, Mr Nugan, I don't want to interrupt but … George, you remember that guy who was fiddling with the computer? Maybe he did something while you were away from your desk with that attractive blonde women.'

Gleefully, Roger stares at George, who looks stricken. *Got you, you bastard*, he thinks.

Frank is now apoplectic with rage.

'You, George, stay right here. You—Roger isn't it?—you go straight to my office and get my secretary to call Terry Bannister. I want him here straight away. Now, go, Roger, fast as you can.'

Roger scurries away, hearing Mr Nugan's shouts of anger as he berates George. He almost feels sorry for the security manager. Almost.

Thirty minutes later, after parking his car illegally outside the bank, Terry runs inside and heads in the direction of the shouting. Frank is so angry that Terry thinks he will have a heart attack. He shouts over Frank's outrage.

'Frank, calm down and shut up, will you? Let me handle this. What has this bloke done?'

Frank takes a few deep breaths and provides a brief account of what has happened. Terry listens in amazement. *You could drive a truck through the holes in the bank's security*, he thinks. Terry addresses the guy cowering in his chair.

'Now listen, pal, who was the guy who was fiddling with the computer? Surely you must know that.'

George gulps out a reply. 'He … his name is Martin. He was contracted to upgrade the bank's system and to install a way of allowing the workstations like this one here to communicate with the main computer. But there's no way that he could know my password. I don't write it down; it's in my head. And I never told him, honest.'

Frank once again explodes in anger.

'Martin? Isn't that the guy we …' Terry hastily shuts him up lest Frank spills the beans.

Terry thinks about this, and points an accusing finger at the security manager.

'Well, it seems that he must have got in some way, unless you helped him.'

George almost falls over himself to deny this. 'I wasn't even here. I was showing his female assistant around the bank. It wasn't me.'

Terry has a flash of insight. 'Describe the woman he was with.'

'Well, she was very attractive. She had blonde hair and a terrific figure.'

Disappointed, Terry doesn't think it fits Susie's description. The right sort of body, but the wrong hair colour. Suddenly he stiffens, and asks George, 'What colour were her eyes?'.

George smiles in memory. 'They were the most extraordinary green. Just like the sea on a sunny day.'

Shit, Terry thinks. *It's Susie. That cunning bitch obviously kept this sucker busy while Jack worked on the computer. But how did he do that?*

Frank provides the clue. He asks in an ominous tone: 'George, where do you keep your SWIFT authorisation code? You must have a written copy somewhere'.

George's face registers confusion at first, and then turns bright red. 'Ah … in my diary, in the drawer here.'

Frank's anger is fully unleashed. He shouts at him in fury, 'George, you fucking idiot!'. He reaches over and strikes George a stinging blow across the face. 'Get the fuck out of here, you moron, you're fired. If I ever see you again, I swear I'll kill you.'

George flees in terror. Frank stares at Terry and says deliberately and slowly: 'Find them. Get the money back. Then kill them both'.

Terry grins savagely. This time they won't get away. He leaves Nugan Hand and goes to find Dozer.

*****

When Jack rides his motorbike to the house on the last Friday of November to tell Jenna the whole story, there is no-one there. Worried, Jack returns to his flat and calls Jenna's parents. Her mother tells him in a frosty tone that Jenna, having completed her university studies for the year, has gone off with Natalie and a girlfriend for a few days to the beach somewhere north of Sydney. No, her mother doesn't know how to contact Jenna, but she should be back late on Sunday evening. Jack feels angry and completely powerless. He can't speak to her, and time is running out. He chastises himself for not having the gumption to take her fully into his confidence earlier. Jack can't help but feel a sense of impending doom as the potential consequences of his recent actions settle on his shoulders.

First thing on Monday morning Jack calls the house and is relieved to find that Jenna is back. Part of him wants to lash out in fury at her for not being available earlier, but wisely he holds his tongue, instead merely stating that he wants to tell her the whole story. Jenna agrees with Jack's suggestion that Nat should not go to school that day, but neither should she be there whilst they have it out. He has someone who can care for Nat for a few hours. Jenna, her mind focusing on the fact that he has elected to come clean, does not think to ask who will be looking after Nat, nor does she object when he asks if he can call into his office for a short period before returning to talk to her.

Jack drives his motorbike around to the house, and leaves it there whilst he picks up Nat and some toys. He drives the car back to the flat and introduces Nat to Susie, who is packed ready to leave for the airport midafternoon to catch her flight. They seem to hit it off right away. He leaves for his office, promising to be back for Nat in a couple of hours. The office thing is not going to be easy, but he realises that it will be a walk in the park compared with the impending chat with Jenna.

*****

Terry and Dozer sit outside Jack's house an hour later. Terry recognises the motorbike. Through the front window he can see a woman in the kitchen. There is no sign of Jack. Terry makes a decision and gets out of the car and heads towards the house, his gun concealed in his jacket. Dozer will jump out of the car and come to help, if necessary. Terry is completely focused. If the wife gets in the way, he will shoot her and take Jack.

Jenna hears a knock at the door. *It must be Jack*, she thinks. *Natalie must have forgotten something.* She opens the door. Instead of Jack, a stranger is standing there, smiling.

'Yes, what do you want? If you're selling anything, I don't want it.'

The man replies, the smile still on his face. 'Sorry to bother you, Mrs Martin, but I'm Terry, an old mate of Jack's. We grew up in Newcastle together and I haven't seen him for years. Is he at home, or if he isn't, can you tell me where I might find him?'

Jenna is cautious. She doesn't know the man; he might be anybody.

'So you grew up together, eh. Then you must have known Jack's parents.'

Terry's smile remains fixed. *Bitch*, he thinks. *She's trying to trip me up.*

'Yes, I knew Henry and Gladys quite well. Me and my family lived just around the corner from their house.'

Chapter 62

Jenna asks cagily, 'Were you in the surf club as well? What was the name of that beach?'

'It's Bar Beach.' Seeing Jenna still hesitant, Terry adds: 'Look, I can see you're worried about talking to me. For all you know, I might be some mad axe murderer, right? What I can tell you is that I haven't seen Jack since he left to join the army. So, if that isn't enough, never mind, I'll trace him another way. Thanks for your time'.

Terry steps back and makes as if to leave. Jenna quickly apologises.

'I'm sorry Terry, but you can't be too careful, you know. No, Jack isn't here. He's gone to his flat, not far from here. I'm afraid we aren't living together at the moment. He has just taken our daughter, Natalie, around there for a visit before popping into his office. Hang on a second, I'll write down the address, I'm sure he'll be pleased to see you but you'd better hurry.'

Jenna hands Terry a piece of paper with Jack's address. Terry thanks her, and mutters as he walks back down the path, 'Yes, he's going to get a real shock'.

Jenna is left at the doorway puzzling over that last remark. After a moment of reflection, she dismisses her slight misgiving. *He's an old mate. I hope he doesn't take too much of Jack's time. Our own talk should come first.* Jenna closes the door and walks inside to the kitchen, her mind on the forthcoming conversation with Jack.

Terry's smile is predatory as he reaches the car. Dozer regards him questioningly.

'Dozer, I think we have got the perfect solution. With a bit of luck, we are going to get Jack Martin and his daughter. That cow Susie will be next. Leverage. Just what the doctor ordered.'

Within minutes they arrive at Jack's flat on the ground floor of a small complex. There is no sign of a car in the car park. *Jack must have already left for work. No matter, his daughter will do nicely.* Terry sends Dozer around the back to cover the exit. He strides up to the front door and kicks savagely at the flimsy lock. After a few solid blows it smashes open. He rushes inside. He grins savagely when he realises that the woman with the kid trying to get out the back window is Susie. There is no sign of Jack.

In a couple of long strides Terry reaches Susie, who tries to dodge him and heads for the kitchen area. He swings a clubbed fist at her head. Blood erupts from her nose as she goes down. The kid is screaming in terror. As Dozer smashes in the window, Terry grabs the kid and covers her mouth. The young girl's eyes roll up in her head as she faints from fright.

Dozer heaves Susie's limp body over his shoulder and effortlessly carries her and the child from the flat. He drops them in the back of the van and proceeds to tie and gag them. Terry scribbles a note, which he leaves on the kitchen bench. They are gone within two minutes.

*****

Feeling depressed, Jack leaves his office. His staff members have taken the bad news surprisingly well, no doubt buoyed by the very generous severance pay Jack has promised. This will leave him with only a thousand dollars or so to make good the family's escape. *At least the flights are paid for*, he thinks, *hopefully a grand will be enough to cover the other expenses.*

He is not looking forward to talking to Jenna.

When he arrives at the house Jenna, who has now recovered her wits, immediately asks who is minding Nat.

Jack, a little taken aback at this question, replies quickly: 'Relax, Jen, she's fine. When I left Nat she was playing with my friend Susie'.

'Susie?' Jenna is suspicious, but suddenly changes tack. 'Speaking of friends, did your mate from Newcastle catch you at the flat?'

Jack is confused. 'No, I haven't seen anyone. Did he give you a name?'

Chapter 62

'He said his name was Terry. Does that ring a bell?'

Jack panics. No, no, it can't be. They can't have cottoned on so quickly. He grabs her by the arms fiercely. 'This Terry, can you describe him?'

Jenna pulls away in pain. 'Jack, you're hurting me, stop it. I don't know, he was just a guy. He said he grew up with you. Don't you know him?'

Jack grabs her again. 'Oh shit, Jen, that's very, very, very bad news. Come on, we have to go. I'll explain on the way. I pray to God we're in time.'

Jack, driving like a maniac, gives her a condensed version of the story on the way. He screeches to a stop outside the flat, rushes to the boot and pulls out a tyre iron. He sprints to the door, followed by Jenna. It is ajar. Jenna screams out, 'Nat, Nat, where are you, baby?' but there is no answer. Jenna collapses to the floor, sobbing.

Brandishing the weapon like a club, Jack quickly but cautiously searches the flat. His heart feels like it is going to burst out of his chest. His left side throbs painfully; he must have damaged the torn muscles in his haste.

In the kitchen he finds a broken window, as well as a smear of blood and a note. He scans it rapidly.

> We've got your kid and the luscious Susie, pretty boy. That was a very nifty bit of work at the bank. You are obviously a lot smarter that I thought you were.
>
> But Jack, it isn't going to do you any good, because I'm smarter. We want the money back—all of it. In return, you get to see your darling little daughter and that slut Susie again. Whether they are unharmed will depend on your cooperation.
>
> You will receive a phone call tonight at your house with further instructions. And don't think of bringing the cops into this. We've got lots of friends in the police force, so we'll know straight away.
>
> So just do as you're told, and everything will work

> out well.
>
> P.S. The blood belongs to Susie, not your daughter, just in case you are wondering.

The note is unsigned, not that this matters to Jack. *Oh, Natalie, what have I done*, Jack thinks miserably. He goes to find Jenna.

Jenna goes into hysterics when she reads the note. In desperation, Jack slaps her lightly on the cheek to try to bring her to her senses. She recoils from him and screams in rage: 'You useless bastard, you've fucked everything up. Our house will be gone in a few days, our darling daughter has been kidnapped by some lunatic, and you can't even manage to knock off some money without being caught. And I suppose you're fucking this Susie woman, as well'. Jenna collapses again, sobbing bitterly.

Jack sits beside her and tries to comfort her.

'Jenna, I promise you that I will fix this, even if it kills me. I will do anything to get Nat back. The money means nothing to me. Nor does Susie. Yes, I had sex with her, but only once. I apologise. But she knows that I love you, Jen, and I always will. Come on, we've got to get through this together. I need you, and your support, Jenna, if I'm going to set things right.'

Jenna stares up at him through her tears. Part of her hates what he has done to them, even though he undoubtedly felt it was justified. She knows deep down that she loves him, and she realises that she doesn't have much choice other than to support him to do whatever it takes to get Natalie back unharmed. As for this Susie women, well Jenna isn't exactly innocent either, is she? Sighing she takes a deep breath and says: 'You really mean that, Jack? You're not just saying it to shut me up?'

'Jenna, I love you. I don't know how to say it any other way.'

She stares at his face, trying to see the lie, but she senses it's the truth. She calms herself and decides to clear the air.

'Jack, as long as we are in confession mode, I had a fling too.

With one of the lecturers at uni. But, don't worry, it was only sex.'

Despite the desperate situation, Jack can't help but laugh.

'Touche, Jen. I deserve that.'

Jenna returns his hug.

'Jack, we have to do something. I don't think we can trust that horrible man, do you?'

'You've hit the nail on the head, Jen. The only thing I can think to do is to call the cavalry. By that I mean Gene and H.'

They stand up and Jack puts in a call to Gene's hotel. By now it is midafternoon; hopefully he will be there.

Gene hears him out in silence. 'Fuck' is the only word he utters. But Gene is used to crisis situations. He speaks decisively to Jack.

'Go back to your house, right now. I'll round up H and we'll be there as soon as we can. We'll come in the back way—no telling who they've got watching you, so it's best not to take chances. You and Jenna hang in there. The most important thing is not to panic. Can you do that for me, Jack?'

Jack can, and the couple drive back to the family home to await H and Gene and the phone call. Ironically, this dreadful affair seems to have brought them a little closer together. Jack thinks it is the sense of shared pain. He is realistic enough to know that there is a long way to go to repair the relationship, and without Natalie there is no chance at all. For the moment, their objective is simple: get Natalie back safe and sound. If Susie is okay too, that's a bonus. Jack is sure Susie would understand.

H and Gene knock gently on the back door. Jack lets them in. They are both dressed in dark clothes and carrying guns. Gene and H hug Jenna briefly. Jack and Jenna look at Gene hopefully as he speaks quietly.

'We can't see any form of surveillance out there. That's good.' He looks compassionately at them. 'Obviously, they got onto the missing money much quicker than you thought possible, Jack. We would be wasting our time and efforts in trying to figure out how. What's done is done. There's no point in beating yourself up about it, pal.'

Jack shudders and suddenly there are tears in his eyes. He wipes his face with the back of his hand.

'Terry and his mates seem to hold all the aces, guys. I don't know what to do, apart from give them what they want.'

They sit on chairs around the kitchen table, thinking hard.

H speaks up. 'You both should know that there's a good chance that this won't end well. I'm sorry to have to say that, but we have to be realistic.' H sees the impact these words have on the couple. 'That said, they don't hold all the cards. Now, listen up. When this Terry guy rings, you're going to need to demand proof of life. Jenna, you have to be strong then; it's the only way you're going to get through this.'

Jenna raises her chin defiantly, and nods agreement. Watching her, Jack feels a warm glow of love and pride.

Gene steps in. 'Now, they're going to want those codes, Jack, and my guess is they will want you—or even you and Jenna—to deliver them personally, not by phone. We have to put ourselves in their shoes. The inescapable fact is that they will want you both out if the way, along with Susie. In their view, anything that happens to Natalie is collateral damage.' Jenna starts to weep again. 'You have to bear up, Jenna; come on girl, if there is a way out of this, we'll find it. We have to talk it through.'

H speaks up: 'If they do want you to deliver the information in person, then that may give us a chance. My ex-SAS guys are on standby at the office. They're real good at sneaking around without anyone seeing them, and Terry has no idea we're involved. That's a card we hold. Now, if Terry and his mates come by car to the meeting point, maybe my guys could get to their car undetected and plant a tracking device on it. Gene, we can use that new LoJack prototype homing device you brought in from the States to trial. Perhaps they may lead us straight to where they're holding Nat and Susie'.

Jack and Jenna stare at each other in sudden hope. The plan sounds good, but Jack sees a flaw.

'Let's say both of us go to deliver the codes—how the hell will we get away? If your guys come in shooting, we'll never find out where they've got Nat and Susie.'

Jack slumps in his chair, head hanging low. He grasps his side again, wincing in pain. Gene asks him what is wrong, and Jack tells him in a few words. Gene thinks that Jack isn't going to be much use in a fight in his condition. *Hang on, isn't Jack a great marksman? Maybe he might have a use after all.*

It's Gene's turn to improvise. 'Hmm. What we would need is some sort of diversion; something that appears to be coincidental, but allows you to get away unscathed. We can't risk you having to run, Jack, not with that hip problem. Now, what might work?'

Again, they mull over possible solutions. In their high state of anxiety, nothing occurs to Jenna or Jack. All they can think about is Natalie.

H suddenly jumps to his feet. 'I've just thought of something that might work.' The others look up expectantly. Jack wants to know what it is, but H cuts him off. 'No, I'm not going to tell either of you, just in case you both have to go to the meeting point. You'll need to be just as surprised as them when it happens.' He walks to the phone. 'I'm going to make a call. You three talk amongst yourselves.'

H talks quietly into the handset. His voice is pitched too low for Jack or Jenna to hear anything of the conversation. Gene takes over.

'Okay, we'll call this plan A; there will be a few more plans to put in place in order to cover the most likely scenarios. If something else happens, we'll just have to improvise—that's what we ex-military folk are good at. H and I will discuss his brainwave in a minute. In the meantime, Jack, let's run through what you're going to say when they make the call.'

Gene and Jack discuss this while Jenna watches silently. Jack doesn't know whether she's absorbing all this, or if she can't get her mind past Nat. Gene makes a point.

'Jack, you're not gunna want to appear too enthusiastic if whoever calls tells you that it's a face-to-face meet. You need to make them think you want the exact opposite. That make sense? And, you'll have to sound real scared. We need them to think they are running the show.'

Jack nods in affirmation. He must not think about Nat or Jenna; he has to focus on the plan. He is so much in the zone, he forgets entirely about Susie.

*****

Susie is strapped securely to a chair, a gag over her mouth. She can move only her head. They have been a little kinder to Natalie; she is tied only by the hands, her legs are free, but she is also gagged. Susie can see that the little girl is petrified with fear. She is shivering with fright at the trauma they have experienced. There is nothing Susie can do except move her eyebrows and shake her head in an attempt to attract Natalie's attention. It isn't working.

Dozer sits and watches her steadily. His gaze is like a cat stalking a mouse. She knows intuitively what he wants to do to her, and this sends a little frisson of disgust through her body. Dozer sees this and his smile is unspeakably evil. He has already had a quick grope, leaving her feeling soiled.

They appear to be in an old warehouse. Susie can smell sea air; they must be near the harbour as the journey in the back of the van wasn't long enough to have reached the ocean—besides, she cannot hear the telltale roar of the surf.

There is a single dim light above them, but the rest of the

warehouse is in darkness. Susie guesses that it must be sometime after nine o'clock as the sun set at least an hour before. Terry is somewhere in the darkness. She can hear him talking on the phone.

Susie is in despair. There seems to be no way out of this predicament. She fears the worst for herself, but hopes that maybe they will spare Natalie.

Terry is talking to Jack, who is pleading for him to release Natalie and Susie. Jack says in a wheedling tone: 'I'm begging you, Terry, please let them go. I'll do whatever you want. I've got the codes you need to transfer the money back. I'll even come into the bank and you can watch me do it—or I can just give them to you over the phone and you can do it yourself. For the love of God, Terry, please don't harm them. At least let me speak to my daughter. Please.'

Terry smiles malevolently. Jack is just where he wants him. Excellent.

'She's not available to come to the phone right now, but she's okay. You'll just have to trust me on that. Tell you what, Jack, how about you bring those codes to me, and that pretty wife of yours can tag along as well. It's about time we had a little reunion. Maybe I can tell you both all about the good times I had in that stinking jail in Holsworthy. Ah, the good old days. Don't you wish you were back in 'Nam, getting shot at? No, I suppose not.'

Jack jumps in quickly. 'Terry, why can't I just give you the codes over the phone? That would be quicker. You can have your people check them and the money would be back in the bank in no time. Then you can let Nat and Susie go. You know we'll never talk to anyone about this. Please, Terry.'

'Shut your trap, you snivelling prick. You'll do what I say, or you won't like the consequences. Now, write down this address.'

Terry dictates a number and street in Pyrmont, an inner-Sydney harbour suburb with many derelict buildings—remnants from its heavy industry days. He continues: 'Now Jack, you and your missus had better be there in forty-five minutes, or I swear you'll regret it. Remember, I'll have my men scattered around, so don't try any tricks. If you want to see your daughter alive again, do exactly as I say'.

Terry terminates the call. He is sure Jack is too terrified to try anything, but he will take no chances. He calls to Dozer: 'Doze, get the van. I'll get the boys rounded up. We're off to meet Mr Jack Martin and his wife, and it ain't a social visit'.

*****

Chapter 63

H opens a map of Sydney. He traces his finger to the address Jack has written down. 'It's the old Ultimo powerhouse. It closed down about twenty years ago. It used to supply power to half of Sydney. Jeez, the bastard has picked a good spot. The good news is, it'll be dark. That will give my guys a good chance of attaching the tracking device to his vehicle.'

Gene breaks in. 'We'd better get going. H, call the guys quick smart and tell them where to meet us. We'll use those Magnavox squad radios for short range communications. There are a couple in the trunk of the car. They work just fine over a few hundred metres, and the FM band they use will make it difficult for anyone to pick up the transmissions. Not that I think that's likely—I reckon we have the advantage in technology. My take on these guys is that they're run-of-the-mill thugs who fight with weapons or their fists, not gadgets—but just in case, tell the guys to turn the volume right down, H. You take Jenna in your car, Jack. We'll be right behind you until we get close to the rendezvous. We've got your back, but don't take any unnecessary chances.'

Jack and Jenna drive across the Harbour Bridge, through the

CBD and turn right through Haymarket, finally reaching Harris Street. The old power station is only a few hundred metres away. Gene's car has left them in Haymarket. Jack feels Jenna's hand on his arm as he drives cautiously along. There are only a few street lights working, most have been smashed by vandals. Jenna's hand is drumming nervously on his skin. He is just as edgy as she.

The derelict facade of the old building looms up ahead and he slows the car to a crawl. Suddenly, a heavy-set man wearing a balaclava appears in front of him, armed with a shotgun. He points the weapon menacingly at Jack, and motions for him to stop the car. The man waves the shotgun in an obvious order for them to get out. Jack and Jenna do as commanded, and raise their hands in the air.

Another man, similarly garbed, appears from their left, a pistol in his hand. The man with the shotgun scans up and down the street, but all is quiet. He says something to the other guy, who immediately disappears back into the shadows. *He must be the lookout*, Jack thinks. His earlier nerves have gone; his combat experience kicks in. Jenna grabs him in fright. He murmurs words of encouragement to her as the heavy-set man motions for them to walk into a nearby alley.

They stumble their way forward for twenty metres. The only light comes from a crescent moon above. Without warning, a torch flicks on, pinning them in its glare. It moves towards them.

Terry shines the torch into their faces. He grunts in satisfaction. They are here, and alone. It's time to tango.

'Hey, Jack, and Mrs Jack, good of you to come,' Terry calls out. 'Let's get straight down to business, shall we? Jack, where are the codes?'

Jack motions to his pocket and says quietly, 'In here, Terry'.

'Okay, take them out very slowly. My mate Dozer here has his shotgun trained on you. We don't want any accidents, do we?'

Jack does as he is told.

'Now, Jack, throw them over here, and don't move, or you and the missus will be on the receiving end of both barrels of Dozer's twelve-gauge. That would make a real mess of you two.'

Terry bends and picks up the envelope and checks inside. They appear to be codes, but Terry is not that interested; what he wants is standing in front of him. Before Jack dies, if these are fakes, he will give Terry the real codes. He puts the envelope in his pocket.

Jack seems to have read his mind. 'They're the real thing, Terry. Now, we've met our end of the deal, are you going to do the same?'

Terry smiles chillingly. 'All in good time, Jack. But there's a slight change of plan, pretty boy. You and wifey here are gunna come along with us. When we find out about the codes, then we'll let you all go.'

Jack has had enough of this as adrenalin courses through his body. He replies in a scoffing tone: 'Why do I think that's a load of bullshit, Terry? You've got no intention of living up to your end of the deal. That's because you're a fucking liar and a rapist, and God knows what else. Yeah, Susie told me what you did to her'.

Terry loses his cool. He rushes at Jack and, before Jack can move, Terry strikes him viciously across the face with his gun.

'Don't you fucking well lecture me, you asshole. I failed to kill you in Vung Tau, but this time I will make sure you die. And slowly, you prick.'

Terry attempts to regain his composure, his breathing harsh in his mouth.

'Get up, cunt. You and your missus have got an appointment with Dr Dozer—except he doesn't like using anaesthetic when he operates.' Terry laughs maniacally.

Jack's face is streaming with blood. He spits out a tooth as he climbs to his feet. His blood is up; he will kill Terry with his bare hands if he gets the chance. So finally he knows it *was* Terry who shot him in Vung Tau. Jack wants Terry dead, and if necessary will die trying to make that happen, as long as he can get Jenna and Natalie out of this mess.

Terry and Dozer march the couple to the end of the alley where the van is parked. Jack is desperate; *where is the help that H has organised?* If they get in the van, they will have no hope.

Just as they reach the van, bright flashing lights appear at the end of the street, moving rapidly towards them. Then they hear the distinctive wail and yelp sirens of several fire trucks. Terry and Dozer stand, open mouthed, as the fire trucks scream to a halt in front of them. One has a ladder mounted on top of the chassis. The other looks to be a pumper.

Terry and Dozer hurriedly hide their weapons as the door of the leading truck opens and out jumps a figure dressed in a black jacket and pants over thick safety boots. Although the man is wearing a helmet, Jack immediately recognises H's face. H yells to the group standing in front of him: 'Where's the fire? Have you seen any smoke?'

Jack grabs Jenna and motions for her to keep quiet. Terry is confused and suspicious as a dozen firemen climb out of the trucks and surround them. Some are carrying fire axes. Unseen, a figure dressed in black, his face camouflaged, slides under the van and attaches a small tracking device to the bottom of the chassis. He is finished in ten seconds.

Terry responds angrily: 'Fire? What fire?'.

H takes a step forward and replies. 'We got an emergency call to say that there was a fire in the old Ultimo power station. You sure you haven't seen a fire?'

H turns his attention to Jack and glares accusingly at him.

'Say, mate, what's that blood on your face all about? Have you got anything to do with any fire? You look downright suspicious to me.' H turns to the nearest firemen. 'Guys, grab him and this woman who is clinging on to him, and stick them in the truck while I go check for smoke.'

Before Terry and Dozer can react, Jack and Jenna are quickly escorted to the rear truck. H heaves a mental sigh of relief. Now to get rid of Terry.

H addresses Terry aggressively. 'Would you like to come with me, sir? Perhaps you can explain what you and your friends are doing here in the dark. Fire is a serious issue, and anyone involved in deliberately lighting fires can get jail time.'

Seeing the couple disappear into the second fire truck, and conscious that there are upwards of twelve firefighters standing between him and Jack, Terry decides to make a tactical retreat. He is suspicious of the timing of the arrival of the fire brigade, but he reasons that as long as he has the kid, Jack will not do anything that might cause her grief. Anyway, he can get Jack back anytime; all he has to do is call him. He might not want to come now that he knows what Terry has planned for him, but it's not as if he has a choice. His thoughts turn to Susie. *Perhaps it's time to let Dozer have some fun with the bitch.*

Backing away, Terry declines H's offer. H pretends to be offended. Terry motions to Dozer and they jump into the van and drive off. As they do, he is thinking hard: *this may well have been a set up—although if it is, it's pretty plausible. Best to take no chances.* Just in case, he needs to ensure that no-one is following them.

Terry steers the van back into Harris Street and speaks to the other thug who is guarding the front of the abandoned building. He instructs the guy to follow the van, doing a sweep to check that they don't have a tail, while Terry goes on a detour through the narrow streets of Haymarket. Terry will meet the other car in thirty minutes at the top end of Kent Street, under the approaches to the Harbour Bridge.

As he watches them leave, H hopes that the LoJack beeper is working. It's up to Gene now.

*****

One of H's ex-SAS guys is driving Gene's car as they tail the van, staying well back. Gene is watching a small red dot on a receiving device about the size of a cigarette packet. If the dot moves upwards, the van is going straight ahead. If it moves to the right, that's where their quarry is headed. He is impressed; this gadget is so simple to use, and it has a range of several kilometres, even in built-up areas. They can stay safely out of the way of any counter surveillance.

He calls H on the squad radio. 'H, you got Jack and Jenna?'

H answers immediately. 'Affirmative, Gene. And our other two guys. That tracker thing working okay? Where are you?'

'We're doing a tour of this Haymarket suburb. Terry is obviously suspicious—not that it is going to do him any good. He appears to be heading generally north, despite all his antics to get rid of us. So, head north slowly and I'll keep you updated.'

*****

Once Terry and Dozer have departed, H runs back to the fire trucks and opens the door where Jack and Jenna are sitting. He hugs them both. Jack has cleaned most of the blood off his face, but there is a large welt on his cheek. Jenna is balled up in the corner, weeping softly. H can see that she is just about at the end of her tether. *Hang in there, girl*, he prays silently to her, *we may just well be into the end game*.

H thanks one of the firies for their help.

'Charlie, we owe you big-time. Thanks heaps for helping out at such short notice. The beers are on me as soon as we finish this business off.' Catching a glimpse of himself in the truck mirror, H says in satisfaction, 'You know, I reckon I look pretty good in this uniform'.

Charlie grins. 'Mate, I think you should stick to your day job. From what I hear, you'd be much better at it than fooling around with fires. You'd probably shit yourself if you got anywhere near one.'

Chapter 63

A car driven by a firefighter pulls up nearby, and the guy jumps out and climbs into one of the fire trucks. Waving in acknowledgement, H sheds his firefighter's gear and escorts Jack and Jenna to the car. Jack thanks him profusely for saving him and Jenna from what was certainly a death trap. H drives the vehicle back towards the city centre, awaiting Gene's radio message. As H drives, he and Jack start to argue about Jack's role in the possible rescue mission. Jack wants to lead the charge; his anger at Terry is so great it clouds his reason. H is placatory but firm.

'Steady on, Jack. Your face is a mess, and that hip of yours isn't going to stand up under any hand-to-hand fighting.'

Jenna suddenly speaks up. Her face is red and puffy from crying, but both Jack and H notice her jaw is set in determination.

'H, I know why Gene has a stake in all this. But you, why are you getting yourself involved? It can't be just because Jack is a mate.'

H stares ahead at the road as they wait for his reply. Then he gazes out of the window, his face softening in sorrow.

'I never told you about my younger brother Sam. He was a brilliant law student with a big future, then he got himself involved with the wrong crowd. He starting using heroin, and he died of an overdose when we were in Vietnam in 1967.' H glares back at them angrily. 'I've got no use for scumbags that peddle dope, and these guys seem to be at the top of the list of those who deserve everything they get.'

Jenna pats his arm in sympathy as Jack looks blankly at his mate. Jenna says softly to Jack: 'You listen to H. He's making sense; you're not'.

The radio suddenly squawks into life.

'H, it's Gene. We're on Kent Street heading north. The van seems to have stopped about five hundred metres ahead of us. Benny here tells me that they are close to Hickson Road. At the end of that road are some old wooden warehouses. They are built on a couple of finger wharves that jut out into the water near the Harbour Bridge. It's a pretty quiet area, so it may be the place where they've stashed Natalie and Susie.'

H grunts in acknowledgement. 'That makes sense. Those warehouses are not too far away from the Cross.' He adds a warning. 'Be careful, Gene.'

'Yeah. We're gunna cut across to the other end of Hickson Road and come in from the north-eastern side. That's where we'll meet up. If my gadget tells me the van has stopped near those wharves, we'll know that's the spot.'

'Righto, Gene, let me know if there is any change of plan. We're about five hundred metres behind you.'

H fixes Jack in a hard stare.

'Jenna's right, Jack. In my view, your job is to do what you are real good at.' H sees a glimmer of understanding form in Jack's eyes. He continues: 'Mate, in the boot of this car is a long gun, and I want you to be the sniper, just in case one or more of those bastards who've got your daughter needs to be taken out quickly. The rifle is an M40A1, the latest variant, with an infrared Redfield scope so you can see in the dark. It's a good rifle, with a range of around nine hundred metres, which will be more than enough, even in darkness. It's been zeroed by my guys, so with your skill you shouldn't have too much of a problem hitting anything you aim at'.

Although Jack's heart tells him to protest, his head agrees with H. He knows the M40 well; it was a sniper rifle used by the US Marines in Vietnam with devastating effect. He has fired one a couple of times on the range in Nui Dat, and he knows it is a very capable weapon. Jack nods his head in agreement.

H gives Jack a pep talk. 'You know, there's a simple but big difference between us and the people we're gunna go up against tonight, and it ain't just goodies versus baddies. They mostly *want* to kill for the sheer perverse pleasure it gives them. Us, well, we were trained by the army to *have* to kill if necessary to achieve the mission. Remember, we've got a distinct edge; our training, our equipment, and our *will* are much better weapons than they'll ever have. Terry and his mates are gunna be in for a shock.'

*****

Gene is watching the red blip as it starts again after stopping for a short period at the end of Kent Street. He and Benny are now in position at the most northerly point of Hickson Road, facing south. The blip moves steadily right towards the water, then heads north-east towards them. Benny jumps out of the car and runs silently, ghostlike, down the road, scanning ahead for the van.

Benny sees headlights coming up the road and immediately drops prone on the ground and wriggles quickly into hiding. The beams of the headlights move sideways as the van makes a left turn and drives through an open gate onto the closest of what appears to be four wharves. The car pauses at the gate and a guard, armed with a pistol, appears. Then the car moves forward onto the wharf.

As Benny watches a second car, with its lights turned off, comes up the road about one hundred metres behind the first car and stops near the gate. A figure gets out and joins the guard. After a few moments the guard remains whilst the other person disappears onto the wharf. The gates close silently.

Benny whispers into his transceiver a succinct version of what he has observed. Gene acknowledges this intelligence and instructs Benny to stay put and keep watch. H also hears Benny's whispered summary as their car glides to a stop just behind Gene's. Gene checks his watch. It is just after midnight. The area seems deserted.

Gene and Willie, the driver—also ex-SAS—alight from their car and meet H, Jenna and Jack. Gene's gaze is directed upwards towards the bridge supports as he searches the skyline for a vantage point. They are too low to see anything from their current position.

They need higher ground. Gene makes out in the shadows a short hill leading to what appears to be a park nestled under one of the main stone supports of the famous coathanger arch. Gene instructs H and Willie to bring the gear, including the rifle, and motions for Jenna and Jack to follow as he quickly climbs the low hill.

Within thirty seconds they all reach the park, Jack limping awkwardly with his bung hip, Jenna helping him. There is a bundle of clothes and blankets on the ground, and Gene realises that it must be some homeless bum seeking shelter under the bridge. They silently move past the sleeping figure.

The park is about ten metres above the waterline and in inky darkness. Gene turns back to look across at the wharf area. Right in front of him, and running parallel to the road, is a two-storey wooden building with a curious triple-peaked roof. He realises he can't see the wharf that Benny is surveilling. They must move further south.

Gene steps noiselessly off, followed by the others, all of them keeping to the pitch-black conditions under the bridge. After about one hundred and fifty metres Gene pauses and examines the immediate surrounds. They are crouched on a narrow path that has a low wall running beside it. He peers cautiously over the wall. The second wharf is now in clear view. It juts out like a finger into what Benny has called Walsh Bay. It has a similarly shaped wooden building of the same size erected on it, covering most of the wharf. Like the first building, it is showing signs of deterioration.

The elevation is good enough to view the wharf in its entirety. He estimates it to be about one hundred and sixty metres long. On the side of the warehouse that Gene can see, he notices that the outside wall is indented under the roof line at the road end for about half the length of the warehouse, with the wall at the seaward end immediately under the roofline. *Hmm*, he thinks, *that indentation provides good cover, but for half of the warehouse length we will be exposed.*

Chapter 63

Looking to his left on the other side of the road a few metres below him, Gene notices that there is a row of terraced houses stretching as far left as he can see. Next to them, just below and immediately to the left of their position, is a set of concrete steps leading down to Hickson Road.

Gene's gaze turns back to the wharf. Although it's only a quarter moon, the night sky is clear of clouds and the dim moonlight reflects off the van. It is parked at the seaward end of a narrow strip of cleared area that extends along the wharf from the gate. The distance from their observation post to the van is a touch over three hundred metres—*not really much of a challenge for Jack and the long gun*, he thinks, *even in this light.*

He takes a small pair of binoculars from a pack he has around his waist and scans the wharf where the van is parked. He sees a boat tied to the wharf near the van. There is a man standing at the stern, smoking a cigarette, with what appears to be a shotgun resting under one arm.

Suddenly Gene sees movement at a warehouse door near the van. Terry steps out of a pool of light and stands next to a smaller man, who seems to be guarding the door. Gene can see that they're both armed with pistols. He pivots his binoculars towards the gate. The guard is still there, peering out at the road. *That's four*, he counts to himself. The bulky form of Dozer is not visible. So there are at least five of them, with possibly more inside. At least two shotguns, and at least three pistols. Gene hands the binoculars to H for him to assess the situation whilst he starts to plot out the rescue operation. Jack is busy familiarising himself with the rifle.

*****

Chapter 64

Inside the warehouse, Terry cautiously orders another of his henchmen to check for any sign of intruders. They have around two tonnes of marihuana stored inside, with a street value of about one million dollars. Terry is taking no chances. He mentally checks off the safeguards in place: a guard at the entrance to the wharf; one outside the door; one on the boat; one inside; plus Dozer and him. *Good*, he thinks. *Plenty of firepower in case someone comes calling. And an escape route via the boat.*

Terry turns his attention to his captives. He can see Susie watching him, fear in her eyes. The little girl seems lost in a world of terror. Dozer is gazing at Susie, his eyes full of lust. Terry smiles, and says loudly enough for Susie to hear: 'Soon, Dozer, soon. Once we've got everything locked down, you can get down and dirty with little old Susie. I'm sure she's going to love you attentions'. He laughs as he sees Susie renewing her efforts to free herself.

*****

Gene has finished his deliberations and motions for the group to gather around. Gene also gets Benny on the walkie-talkie.

Chapter 64

'Right, here's the plan,' Gene whispers to ensure the sound of his voice doesn't carry in the still night air. 'Willie, I want you to ghost your way down those steps over there and, when you get to the bottom, pull a drunk act to distract the guard at the gate to the wharf. When he comes out to move you along, take him out. But don't kill him. We don't want any unnecessary bloodshed. Willie, you take over the guard's position so that the opposition will think everything is okay at the gate. That's stage one—any questions?'

There are none. Gene continues: 'Okay, now to stage two. Benny, then I want you to get into the warehouse any way you can. I'm betting that they have a store of drugs inside, as well as Natalie and Susie.' Pausing, Gene pulls out a metal can from the pack. 'Benny, use this smoke canister to create a diversion inside the warehouse. Hopefully, they'll think any drugs that are inside have somehow caught alight and come running to check. Be careful, keep your head down, but take anyone out you can. Disable, but not kill. We need to reduce the odds as much as possible because there's probably a hell of a lot of firepower in that shed.'

Gene turns to H. 'Whilst Benny is doing his thing, you and I will go up the wharf very fast and, when we see smoke or hear noise from inside, we will take out the guy on the door, and then go into the warehouse through the door that Terry used a few moments ago. We'll need to keep an eye on the guy in the boat. Jack, your job is to cover him with the rifle. H, once we're inside, you look for Natalie and Susie while I cover you. Willie will act as backup at the gate.' They all whisper in agreement; the plan seems sound.

Gene turns to Jack. 'Jack, you're gunna have to do what you've been trained to do. You need to be ready to shoot the shit out of anyone who comes through those doors that isn't us, or if there is any prospect of the guy in the boat getting the drop on us. The thing is, once you fire that long gun, everyone is gunna know we're here, so use it only if you have to.' Gene turns his attention to Jenna. 'Jenna, you're gunna be Jack's spotter. Jack will explain what that is. I'll leave the binoculars with you. Jack, I trust you to be able to differentiate between us and them when things start to get hot. And, I've no doubt they will.'

Jack silently processes this. He hopes that he is able to shoot if somehow Nat is anywhere near the bad guys. He looks at Jenna. She stares back and nods resolutely.

'Okay,' Gene whispers, 'let's do it.'

*****

Inside the warehouse the thug checking the drug stash returns to report that all is secure. Terry turns to Dozer to give him the go ahead. Smiling, Dozer moves towards Susie purposefully. Terry's plan for her is simple: once Dozer is finished, they will kill her, then Susie's body and Natalie will be taken to the boat and Susie's body weighed down and dumped in the middle of the harbour. Terry and Dozer will take the little girl to another secure location and, after that, they will give Frank the bank codes. If they are correct, Terry will give some thought to releasing the girl—but only after he has his hands on Jack.

Seeing Dozer coming at her, Susie struggles franticly. Her wrists and hands are bleeding from her attempts to dislodge, or at least loosen, the bindings. She manages to loosen the gag and pushes it up with her tongue.

In a voice raspy with terror, fatigue and thirst, Susie gasps out: 'For God's sake, don't let Natalie witness this. Please, I beg you, either take her somewhere else or make sure she can't hear and see. Please, please, if you do this, I swear I won't struggle. Please, Terry, show some mercy.'

Dozer pauses, and when Terry nods agreement, he grabs a roll of duct tape and begins to wrap it sideways around Natalie's head, covering her eyes and ears, but leaving her nose free. Nat begins to hyperventilate in fear, and Susie tries to calm her down. It takes a few minutes, but Natalie begins to breathe more easily. Her head is almost entirely swathed in duct tape. She certainly can't see, and Susie hopes that she is unable to hear.

Dozer has had enough, and reaches Susie in two strides. He leans forward and grips her blouse, tearing it effortlessly from her torso. She is not wearing a bra. He cruelly grabs her breasts and squeezes hard, and then tugs hard at her nipples. Susie gasps in pain. This makes Dozer all the more excited.

He bends again and fumbles at her waist, attempting to undo her slacks. Frustrated at not being able to undo the fastening, he simply pulls the waistband apart and tugs her trousers down, where they snag on the tape binding her ankles. With one hand he snaps the tape and pulls her slacks off. She is now clad only in a pair of brief powder-blue panties.

Ignoring her struggles, Dozer gazes lecherously at Susie's body for a moment before he grasps the front of her panties and rips them from her body. She is naked. He quickly snaps the final bindings on her wrists and pulls her to him.

Susie can feel the outline of an enormous erection bulging out of the front of Dozer's pants as he grinds his body into hers. Pinning her hands behind her with one hand, he fumbles for the belt on his trousers and releases it. He lets his pants fall to his ankles and he slowly bends her backward until she is lying on the bare concrete. Susie braces herself for his assault.

Suddenly, there is a shout from the thug in the warehouse. 'Shit, Terry, I smell smoke. What the fuck …'

Terry, who has been watching Dozer and Susie with a malevolent grin, spins around and stares back down the warehouse. Sure enough, grey smoke is billowing out of the darkness.

Terry acts quickly, shouting at the thug: 'Get down there and find out what the fuck is going on. I thought you told me that everything was okay, you idiot. Dozer, get up off her … leave her … but tie her up. I smell a rat here'.

Hastily Dozer pulls up his trousers and wraps duct tape around Susie's wrists and legs. She is shivering with fear and relief, her nudity forgotten in her temporary reprieve.

*****

The guard at the gate is bored. There is no-one around, but he dare not leave his post otherwise the boss will give him to Dozer to play with. He shudders. Anything but that.

Suddenly he hears the faint sound of singing. He peers out, but can't see anyone. Then, from the direction of the Hickson Steps staggers a guy who is obviously as pissed as a fart. His clothing is in disarray, and he is clutching a half-empty bottle of something as he weaves his way across the road towards the gate. The guard watches him in amusement. *What a tosser.*

The drunk pauses at the gate and then unzips his fly and starts to pee on the gate. The guard is offended and calls out to the drunk angrily: 'Hey you, fuck off. Go piss somewhere else. This is private property. Go on, get out of here'.

The drunk peers around, startled and finally looks up and spies the guard. In a tipsy voice, he says: 'I gotta take a pish, man. I'll only be a fuckin' minute. Hold your fuckin' horses, asshole'.

The guard is incensed at the drunk's tone. 'Who are you callin' an asshole? Go on, fuck off before I come out there and kick your ass.'

Hearing this, the drunk tries to adopt a pugilistic stance, but only succeeds in stumbling against the gate. 'Come on fuckface, I'll give you a whuppin'.'

The guard has had enough. He leaves his vantage point and opens the gate just enough to slip through, expecting the drunk to be either already trying to run away or trying to keep upright. Instead, he sees an arm arc with blinding speed towards him holding something dark, which strikes him on the side of the head, and then everything goes black.

Willie eases the unconscious guard to the ground inside the gate and gives a click on his walkie-talkie to signify that the coast is clear. Within thirty seconds Benny, Gene and H are inside the gate, crouching in the shadows.

'Well done, Willie,' Gene praises him. 'Put on the guard's shirt and stand by the gate. Benny, off you go. Try this side wall as you'll be out of view of the guy near the boat. One click, you're in—two clicks, you can't find a way in. Then, if you're in, one click when you let off the smoke grenade.'

Gene fervently hopes it won't be two clicks. Plan B involves direct confrontation, and this is high risk.

Benny silently moves through the shadows, searching for a way in as he disappears from view. A minute passes, and Gene becomes increasingly worried. Then a single click is heard on the walkie-talkie. *Good fella*, Gene thinks approvingly. H and Gene wait for the next click.

Benny has found a way into the warehouse via an open window high up on the side of the building. Noiselessly, he enters. In the dim illumination from the lights further down the warehouse, he spots a large cache of plastic bags. He smiles. Time for some fun. He moves to the stash of drugs and takes out the canister, then pops the pin. Immediately, smoke silently billows out and starts to spread through the warehouse. Benny melts into the shadows and, whilst waiting for a reaction from inside the warehouse, gives a single click.

Hearing this, H and Gene crawl silently but quickly through the darkness until they reach the end of the indentation. Suddenly, shouts ring out from inside the warehouse. Someone has noticed the smoke. Lying on the ground, Gene sneaks a quick peek around the indentation up the wharf. The dumb ass outside the door is staring into the warehouse wondering what is going on. The guy in the boat is doing the same. No one is looking in their direction.

Gene gives H the okay signal and they race the several hundred metres up the wharf to where the guard is still distracted by the noise inside. At the last second the guard sees them and tries to bring his weapon to bear, but H is too quick. He is on the guard, chopping his pistol savagely across his head. The guard drops like a rock and lies motionless in the doorway.

Gene is focused on the guy in the boat and swings his revolver towards him, but the guy doesn't seem to have any taste for action and raises his hands, dropping the shotgun. This threat neutralised, Gene's attention swings back to the warehouse door, which is partially open. Seeing Gene's head turn away, the guy on the boat jumps to the rope holding the boat to the dock, casts it off and dives into the wheelhouse. Almost immediately the boat's motor fires up and the boat moves smartly out into the harbour. Gene isn't interested in what is happening to the boat, he is focused on the warehouse.

*****

Inside the warehouse, the thug moves cautiously through the smoke searching for the source, pistol in one hand, the other hand attempting to wave the smoke away. He is angry; everything was okay no more than five minutes ago. He walks slowly, the gun waving from side to side. *What the fuck is going on?*

He finds out when Benny's sap strikes him on the side of the head, poleaxing him. Before Benny can catch him he drops to the ground with a thud. Benny's action in bending over to try to grab him saves his life.

Dozer is following along about twenty-five metres behind and hears the thud of a body hitting the ground. He instinctively fires one barrel of his Mossberg shotgun at waist height into the smoke in the direction of the noise. He doesn't care who he hits. Dozer is really pissed off about missing out on enjoying Susie's body, and he is in a killing mood.

The twelve-gauge buckshot pellets emerge from the shotgun barrel at just under four hundred metres per second. Initially tightly clustered, they spread out about sixty centimetres whilst travelling the distance to Benny. In his bent position, most fly over his torso, but a few strike his left side. Even though the velocity of the pellets has dropped considerably due to the short range of the weapon, it is enough hit to put him down in shock, but not enough to kill or even seriously wound him. Although in a lot of pain, Benny silently slithers into hiding, moving an agonising centimetre at a time. Once there, he waits patiently for rescue.

Dozer doesn't attempt to find out if his single shot has hit anyone. Hearing Terry urgently calling his name, he charges back to the lighted area of the warehouse. Terry has grabbed Natalie and is holding her in front of him as a shield. Dozer quickly crosses to Susie and roughly pulls her to her feet, and pulls her in tight to his body. Both Terry and Dozer have their weapons pointed at the warehouse door, the likely attack point.

Terry is unsurprised when a head cautiously pokes through the doorway at ground level. He lets off a shot but the figure at the door is too quick and the bullet misses by a considerable margin.

Outside, Gene swears under his breath. 'Fuck, they're onto us and Terry and the one called Dozer are using the girls as shields. Dozer has Susie, and Terry has Natalie. Quick, H, get behind the van. We'll have to play this a step at a time.'

Both scuttle silently to the other side of the van and peer cautiously around at the doorway. Shortly after, Susie appears, Dozer crouching behind her, his shotgun at the ready. Dozer scans the area quickly before his gaze settles on the van. He smiles horribly and says something softly to another set of figures mostly behind the door. Thinking quickly, Gene keys the walkie-talkie to send, hoping that Jack and Willie will pick up any voices.

Terry's voice rings out: 'You can see we've got the kid and the bitch. If you want them to live, back the fuck away. We're gunna get on that boat out there, and you're not gunna stop us. Get the message, you fucks?'

For the benefit of Jack and Willie, Gene repeats the message in the guise of considering it. Then he says: 'Okay, Terry, just chill, man. We're not going to stop you, but we are not going to expose ourselves in the open on this wharf so that you can gun us down. We'll stay behind the van, but we won't stop you'.

'Listen, you Yank asshole—yes, I recognise your accent—we're in control here. Throw those guns out where we can see them. You can hide behind the van all you like, but you're not getting the chance to play the hero, so do as I say, and toss those guns, now.' Terry's voice is harsh and strained and Gene has little doubt that he and Dozer will shoot the females if they don't accede to his demands.

Gene says in a voice loud enough for the walkie-talkie to pick up: 'Okay, H, let's do it. Throw your pistol away, but not towards them'. Both H and Gene do this, tossing their guns into the semidarkness at the far end of the wharf.

Terry is still suspicious. 'Say, Yank, where's your little mate, Jack? He around somewhere?'

'No, Terry,' Gene replies, doing his best to sound convincing, 'he's in hospital being treated for that pistol whipping you gave him earlier. He's out of the equation'. Gene hopes that Jack can hear. To his relief, he hears a single click.

Up on the hill above the wharf, Jenna gasps in disbelief as Terry and Dozer slowly ease their way out of the warehouse door, holding their daughter and Susie in front of them. She turns to Jack and asks beseechingly: 'What do we do now? They're got our darling girl. Jack, please, they can't take her again. You have to do something'.

Jack is shocked, but recovers quickly. He has set the rifle up to his satisfaction. Using a spare pack placed on the wall, Jack has fashioned a firm base on which to rest the barrel. Bending slightly, he has Terry in his sights, his image magnified and enhanced by the backlighting and phosphorous-based contrasting capabilities of the Redfield 3-9 scope, which provides very good resolution of the target. He ignores Susie; if he can save her he will, but Nat has priority.

The problem is that Terry is cunningly using Natalie's body to shield his body from head to knee. Although he is an excellent marksman, Jack cannot be confident of hitting Terry and not harming Nat. Jack gives a frustrated sigh. He attempts to quieten Jenna, who is becoming increasingly hysterical as Terry and Dozer edge closer to the boat, which has returned to the wharf.

'Jenna, please, quieten down, you aren't helping. Please, I need to concentrate, and you need to be watching for me. And, for God's sake, keep your voice down. They don't know we're here, and that's the only advantage we have. We can't let them know that, otherwise Natalie may be in even greater danger.'

This last plea seems to have an effect, and Jenna's voice quietens. 'Just do something, Jack, please.'

Jack watches as Terry and Dozer step onto the bow of the boat, still holding the hostages tightly. Gene and H are powerless to intervene, and Willie is too far away to help. Jack knows it is down to him, and him alone.

He risks a quick glance up away from the rifle to survey the area. The angle of view he has over the water out from the wharf is limited by the southern end of the closer finger wharf building. Jack estimates that he has no more than a thirty-degree arc in which he can fire, otherwise the boat will go out of sight either behind the building Terry has recently vacated or the one to its right. He has an idea. It is risky to Gene and H, but it may be their only chance.

Jack keys the walkie-talkie. 'Gene, listen carefully. You must keep them moving out in front of the wharf, otherwise I won't be able to get a shot. Got that?'

Gene responds. 'You realise what you're asking, Jack?'

'Yep,' Jack replies, 'it means you and H have to put yourselves in the firing line to give me a chance at taking them out'. Jack lets out a long breath. 'I can't think of any other option, Gene.'

Gene's response is immediate. 'Okay, my man, as long as H is agreeable, we'll do it.'

H obviously is. Suddenly Gene and H break cover and race towards their weapons at the end of the wharf. This attracts immediate attention from the boat, which by now is fifty metres out into the harbour. It stops, and Dozer and Terry let fire a volley of shots, the deeper blast of the Mossberg shotgun almost drowning out the thinner and flatter crack of Terry's pistol. Gene and H throw themselves to the ground, but H is hit. Gene scrambles to cover his body.

Jack's shooting eye is back at the scope and he has the sights on Terry. Infuriatingly, he still holds Natalie up in front of him. Jack makes a snap decision to take out one of Terry's legs. The range is about five hundred metres, almost at the edge of the night scope's capabilities in the dim light. He takes several deep breaths and lets them out slowly. *Do the Minute of Angle calculation*, he thinks. *Once fired, the 7.62 millimetre NATO standard round will drop vertically some 2.9 centimetres every hundred metres, therefore, the expected drop is about fifteen centimetres over five hundred metres. So, if I want to hit Terry around knee height, I will have to aim for about mid-thigh, or approximately where the bottom of Natalie's foot is.*

Jack knows he has no choice, and only a few seconds to take the shot. He doesn't see Dozer laughing or Terry gesticulating to Dozer to shoot again. All Jack sees is the target. The crosshairs rest on Terry's thigh at the level of Natalie's shoe, and slowly he squeezes the trigger. The round leaves the rifle muzzle at a velocity of almost eight hundred metres a second and in less time than it takes Terry to open his mouth, the shell strikes his lower thigh just above the knee cap, shredding tissue, muscles, ligaments and anything else in its way. Terry gives out an agonised grunt, drops his pistol and falls to the deck, letting go of Natalie at the same time. There is blood everywhere, but Natalie is unharmed.

Although astonished at what has happened to Terry, without hesitation, Dozer swings his shotgun up to Susie's head and pulls one trigger. The impact is catastrophic and she falls lifeless to the deck, half her head missing. With a snarl, Dozer swings around and starts to bring the shotgun to bear on Natalie's body.

But Jack has already chambered another round and, aided by Jenna's guidance, swings the sights left and lines up on Dozer's throat. Again he squeezes the trigger, and the bullet strikes Dozer in the centre of the chest, creating a massive exit wound and instantly stopping his heart. Dozer is dead before he hits the deck.

Jenna's frantic whisper alerts Jack to another danger to Natalie. Terry is slowly crawling to retrieve his pistol.

Jack gives him no chance. Jack's third shot strikes Terry in the chest and lifts him clean off the deck and backwards into the water. Natalie sits sprawling on the deck, head wrapped in tape, but she is safe. Thank goodness she can't see Susie's or Dozers' bodies.

Jack lifts his head to see what is going on. He hears Gene's voice through the walkie-talkie calling out to the boat driver to bring the boat back to the wharf, or suffer the same fate as the other two. The guy needs no persuasion. He quickly pilots the craft back to the wharf and throws a line to Gene, who scrambles onboard and scoops up Natalie into his arms. As Gene steps back onto the wharf with Natalie, Jenna hugs Jack in relief and begins to cry quietly. Jack has a tear in his eye, too, and is not ashamed to seek comfort in Jenna's arms. Distractedly, he notices Gene jump back onboard to retrieve Susie's body. He gently rests her lifeless body on the wharf.

Jack can see H moving slowly and then notices Willie running into the warehouse, calling out on his walkie-talkie for Benny. Following Benny's directions, Willie locates him and uses a fireman's lift to bring him out of the warehouse. The smoke has nearly dissipated inside the shed. Gene, ever professional, instructs Willy to retrieve the LoJack beeper from under the van.

By this time, with multiple gunshots being fired, the neighbourhood has woken up. Dogs are barking, and Jack can see several lights now on in the row of terraced houses to his left. They need to get out of there, fast, because someone has undoubtedly already called the cops.

Jack gathers Jenna, the rifle and the packs and, stopping only long enough to retrieve the three shell cases—no sense in leaving evidence for the police—limps down to where the vehicles are parked. He relays to Gene his intention for him and Jenna to drive the cars down to the warehouse gate, collect them and then get the hell out of there.

Throwing the gear into one of the vehicles, Jack jumps into the front seat and accelerates down Hickson Road closely followed by Jenna in the other car, lights switched off to reduce the chances of someone identifying the number plates. They come to a halt at the gate, where Willie has Benny over his shoulder, Gene is helping H who is clutching his side, and their beautiful Natalie is holding Gene's other hand, the duct tape now mostly removed from her face. Although obviously frightened out of her wits, she is able to follow directions.

Jenna leaps out of the car she has driven and gathers Natalie in her arms, crying out her name and sobbing. Jack wants to go to her desperately, but right now his priority is to bundle them into the vehicles and get away. In the distance they can hear sirens.

Jack helps Gene and Willie ease H and Benny into the back of the cars and the able-bodied ones jump in. Gene, in the car driven by Jack, says: 'Sorry, man, but we had to leave Susie there. We just couldn't bring her'.

Jack peers at Gene in the rear mirror and gives him a curt nod. He knows Gene would have brought her along if possible. He will grieve for her later.

Jack and Jenna do a quick U-turn and speed back north under the Harbour Bridge. Behind them, Jack can see the lights of several police cars as they pull up at the entrance to the warehouse, then they are gone from view as he rounds the corner. Gene is busy trying to stem the flow of blood from the wounds suffered by H and Willie is undoubtedly doing the same for Benny in the other car. In the car behind, Jack can see that Jenna is trying to comfort Natalie as she drives. His heart goes out to the little girl.

Gene suggests that they head for his company's office. They can hide the cars in the private underground car park and find someone medically qualified to discretely assess and treat the injuries to H and Benny. H is aware enough to gasp out that he knows a doctor who owes him big-time from a previous job.

The cars cross the Harbour Bridge, heading for North Sydney. Jack can see the lights of police cars near the finger wharf, but they again fade as he moves north.

At the office, Jack is finally able to hug Natalie, delighted when he receives a small squeeze in response. Jack and Jenna exchange a meaningful glance. They need a chance to talk to Natalie somewhere quiet and safe. The doctor will be useful for checking her over as well. And they need to have a heart-to-heart discussion themselves. Their lives have undergone a radical upheaval, and there will be more to follow.

*****

Chapter 65

Soon after dawn following the rescue of Natalie, the friendly doctor extracts a handful of shotgun pellets from H's torso, and does the same for Benny. The doctor applies sterile dressings to both men and gives them a course of strong antibiotics to help prevent infection. He leaves without asking any questions, happy to help H out and to repay the favour.

A few hours after the incident, the press gets hold of the news of the firefight on the wharf and, armed with little in the way of fact but plenty of speculation, runs the story of a gang-fight over a large cache of drugs that have left two dead—one found floating in the harbour, the other a woman apparently killed on the wharf—as well as two thugs who were knocked senseless and are now helping police with their enquiries.

The police let slip that the female has been identified as Susan Adams and, from the state of her body, she had been subjected to some form of physical abuse before her death. The press has found out about her connection to the drug clinic in Kings Cross and the conjecture is that she has suffered a similar fate to Juanita Neilson.

The guy found in the harbour is identified as Anton Kocher,

aka Dozer, an employee of Mr Bernie Houghton who runs several nightclubs in Kings Cross. Mr Houghton denies any connection to the affair, and claims Mr Kocher must have been involved in something sinister that is not linked to the nightclubs. Neither the police nor the press make any mention of Terry Bannister, nor any link to the Nugan Hand Bank.

Gene, Jack and H are left to do their own speculating about Terry. Jack is convinced he is dead—surely he couldn't have survived the last shot—but H and Gene aren't so sure. No other body has been recovered from the harbour, so it is possible he has somehow survived. In any event, he is off the radar and, if not dead, then undoubtedly severely wounded. But he had the bank codes on him, so something must be done to minimise the risk of the money being traced and possibly retrieved.

H and Benny stay in the company office suite for a few days in a small self-contained apartment, fed by Gene and Willie who also change their dressings when directed over the phone by the doctor. By then, both declare they are well enough to leave the office and finish their recuperation elsewhere. Willie, always the professional, will go back to the mercenary business.

Jack acts quickly and Gene arranges, through his contact in England, to set up a new account in the Principality of Andorra, a tiny country on the border between France and Spain, and then transfer the entire five million dollars into this account from the Channel Islands. This only takes two days and goes off without a hitch.

Jack is also very happy with the outcome of a very long discussion with Jenna. Holed up in an apartment in Sydney's northern beaches with Nat, they sorted through a great deal of emotional issues and resolved most of them. Most importantly, Jenna wants to continue the relationship and agrees that they have to disappear if they are to survive. Jack pledges that, never again, will he let anything or anyone come between him and his family. The trauma they have gone through convinces Jenna to believe him. She will give the new life a go and reserve judgement on Jack. She realises she has no other choice.

Jack deals with Susie's death as a separate issue, but Jenna is quite understanding about his feelings towards her. He is extremely sorry that he cannot attend her funeral, but they will be long gone before this can happen. Jack is sad that there will be no-one from her family to farewell her. He will send a bouquet of lilies with an unsigned card. That is all he can do.

Jenna mails a brief note to her parents, advising them that the family are taking an unscheduled and prolonged holiday overseas. As they have no set itinerary, she will send postcards when she can. She tells them not to worry, knowing full well that this is a futile gesture. Her parents are no fools; they will know something is up, but she must protect them as best as she can.

*****

A week after the firefight at the wharf, five people sit in the bar of the International Departures Lounge at Sydney Airport. Jenna is nursing Nat on her knee with Jack sitting next to them holding Nat's hand. Nat has lost that fearful look, but she is still finding it difficult to sleep at night, so both of them have been spending a lot of time with her. Jack and Jenna agree that, if some sort of therapy is required to help her recover from the trauma, then Nat will have it. H sits opposite the family unit, his torso bandaged under his shirt.

Jack notices that their flight to London via Singapore is boarding and quietly announces to Jenna and Nat that it is time to go. The trio emotionally embrace Gene and H—they have all gone through a lot in the past few weeks, and this may be the last time they will see these two for quite some time. They say their goodbyes, and the family with the new identities walks confidently into the entrance to Customs and Immigration. Their new life is about to commence.

Chapter 66

Sydney 1992

Jack Curtiss walks up the path to his daughter's apartment in Randwick. *It is well located*, he thinks, *under a kilometre from the beach and not far from the bars and restaurants*. She lives on the top floor of three, and her balcony faces north-east towards the coast and has a limited view of the ocean. *It will be worth quite a deal of money in the forthcoming years*, he predicts. Money well spent when he purchased it a year ago, soon after Nat first expressed a determination to return to Australia. He presses the buzzer for her apartment and she quickly answers.

'It's me,' he says and she releases the front door lock to allow him into the apartment complex.

She meets him at the door and they kiss and hug. Natalie is now in her late teens and has blossomed into a beautiful young woman. She looks nothing like she did when she was younger, which is a distinct advantage for her security.

Jack and Jenna are very proud of Nat. Academically gifted, she is studying for a degree in science, aiming to major in biology, at the University of New South Wales. She has gained entry as an international student, funded entirely by her parents. Her parents had tried to talk her out of moving back to Australia to study, but Natalie would have none of it. She chose the university because of its high international ranking, and she proved to be as obstinate as both of them put together. She believes they finally relented when she threatened to just walk out on them and make her own way to her place of birth. That is not quite the case, but it matters not to Natalie.

She knows there is risk but, with the nightmares of events a decade ago having faded, Nat is adamant that nothing will happen to her. Jack is equally determined to make sure it doesn't.

After she graduates Natalie wants to undertake research in the fields of biotechnology and genetic engineering. She loves university life and is very happy to be in Sydney—even if it is incognito. She has told Jenna recently during a phone conversation that she is seeing a young man named Will, who is also studying at the same university. Jack is pleased that there is no sign of Will tonight.

Natalie has prepared a simple but delicious dinner of chicken and vegetables. Jack has brought a cold bottle of Eden Valley riesling and they enjoy the crisp flavour of the wine as they eat their meal. Nat asks after her mother and her brother, Ben, and is pleased to hear that Jenna is doing very well thank you, even though she misses her baby like crazy. Jack adds that he does too, and Natalie hugs him. As for Ben—well, he is in his mid-teens and is inclined to be a little lax in his study routine. Maybe that is because he is very popular with the girls back home. Her father expresses his frustration at his son's attitude. Natalie smiles fondly at the worried tone in Jack's voice.

They discuss Nat's studies in detail and she is pleased that her dad is very interested in the minutia of her courses. Jack casually asks after Will, but Nat can see right through this and tells him that he is just a friend. He smiles and mentally ticks off that one. Jenna has given him a list of questions to ask but he only has a few more to get through. Jack knows Jenna will give him the third degree about Nat when he returns home.

Chapter 66

Dinner finished and the pots and pans washed up, Jack realises with regret that it is time to leave. He would dearly love to stay but he has stuck religiously to his rule of minimising his time in Australia. He has booked a room at a hotel near the airport as his flight to London leaves the next day and there is still a lot to do before he boards the plane.

Jack and Natalie hug and kiss for the final time and he quickly makes his way back down to the hire car, blinking back tears. *Why didn't she choose to live and study in Europe?* he asks himself for the hundredth time. *Everything would be so much easier and safer.* He consoles himself with the knowledge that he, Jenna and Ben will see her on Nat's next trip to Europe in six months' time. As for him, the next few hours will determine whether he will be there when she comes home.

A man sits in a car across the street, watching Jack as he exits the building. When Jack starts his car and pulls away, the man carefully does a U-turn and follows.

Terry Bannister has been waiting patiently for a very long time. He will not let Jack get away again. It is time to finish this once and for all.

*****

Epilogue

In the early hours of a Sunday morning in late January 1980, two police officers come across a Mercedes sedan parked on the side of a road just south of Lithgow, a small town west of Sydney. Curious as to what the car is doing in a relatively remote area, the cops cautiously approach and shine a torch inside. Slumped sideways in the driver's seat is a man, apparently dead. A rifle rests with its butt on the floor of the passenger's side of the car and its barrel near the man's head. The dead man's left hand is on the barrel, and his right hand on the trigger. There is a large amount of blood and gore around the body. The car is unlocked.

Whilst one of the policemen calls in the incident to the Lithgow police station, the other, a sergeant, carefully searches for clues, conscious of the need not to contaminate what could be a murder scene. The copper gingerly extracts a briefcase out of the car and, opening the driver's door, is able to ease the man's wallet from his back pocket. With a handkerchief covering his hand, he opens it. The name on the driver's license is Frank Nugan. This name means nothing to the policeman, but Frank's death is to cause consternation not just in Australia, but in many parts of the world.

The car and its surroundings are treated as a potential crime scene, but the sergeant, well-experienced in this sort of thing, has already come to the conclusion that it is a suicide. There are no signs of anyone else having been in the car and the large amount of blood is undisturbed. There are, however, several curious items found in the briefcase. One is a long list of notable Australian business, sports and political identities and alongside each is written a five- or six-figure sum of money. The sergeant concludes that this man must be someone very important indeed.

The other item that sparks a lot of interest, particularly with the press once they get the details, is a business card. The name on the card is William E Colby, and on the back of the card are several dates and locations in Hong Kong and Singapore. As those in the know are well aware, William E Colby is a former Director of the CIA, now retired and working as a consultant. Mr Colby is placed in these cities at the dates named on the card. Mr Colby subsequently denies knowing Frank Nugan.

The news of Frank Nugan's death spreads like wildfire. Michael Hand is in Sydney at the time, and Bernie Houghton in Switzerland. Bernie immediately orders the bank's Saudi Arabian staff to leave the country, fearful that they may be arrested for suspected fraudulent activities. The wheels are starting to fall off the Nugan Hand Bank.

Back in Sydney, Bernie and Michael Hand start removing files from Frank Nugan's office. Curiously, even though the police are aware of this and of the high profile of the case, they do nothing to stop them. Soon after, Michael Hand warns the directors of the bank, at a hastily called meeting, to keep their mouths shut and do as they are told—otherwise they and their wives might meet with a fatal accident.

Quietly, Michael Hand begins paying out money to selected clients. Others are not so politely stonewalled. All wait for the coroner's inquest, which is held several months later.

To the relief of many influential Australians—not to mention the many American stakeholders in the bank—the inquest concludes that Frank's death is suicide, possibly brought on by his impending court case and possible guilty finding concerning the suspect affairs of the family-owned fruit business in Griffith.

However, of more interest to the press—not to mention the many shareholders—is the revelation at the inquest by Michael Hand that the bank is insolvent, with over fifty million dollars in debts.

In attendance at the inquest is a former facilitator for the bank, Fred Krahe. When he hears the finding of suicide, Fred's face briefly lights up in a mirthless smile. *You silly buggers*, he thinks, *why didn't anyone stop to think why Frank Nugan would be parked on a lonely road out in the sticks if he wasn't meeting someone? Why would he drive to some godforsaken place like Lithgow to top himself?*

He also knows that the police, convinced it was a suicide, haven't made a lot of effort to prove otherwise. *Someone has put the fix in*, he thinks, *not that I'm complaining*. He wanders out of the inquest to find a quiet bar to have a drink. *It's a pity Frank acted so stupidly*, he reflects, *too much money, too much booze, and too many girls. He should have paid more attention to business.*

In June 1980 Michael Hand and Bernie Houghton flee Australia using false identity papers. They travel to America via Fiji. One later report has Michael Hand living somewhere in South America. Accompanying them on their escape from Australia is an unidentified man who walks with a distinct limp. Coincidently, prior to this, Terry Bannister's assets have been discretely liquidated and the funds transferred overseas to an undisclosed location.

That month H and Gene each receive a postcard from Portugal. There is no writing on either of the cards, but they get the message.

Bowing to public pressure, the Australian and New South Wales governments set up a joint task force on drug trafficking. The activities of the Nugan Hand Bank are a focal point. The task force report names a number of Americans with links to the CIA, as well as identifying a host of Australians who have previous convictions for drug offenses.

In a related royal commission inquiry into the affairs of the Nugan Hand Bank, the royal commissioner hands down a report in 1985 that 'Nugan Hand Ltd was at all times insolvent … and flouted the provisions of the legislation as it then stood in that large volumes of currency were moved in and out of Australia'. This comes as no surprise to many in the know.

The dead Frank Nugent and the missing Michael Hand are conveniently blamed by the royal commission for the illegal bank activities. The host of Americans with CIA links named in the commission's enquiry, including Bernie Houghton, are found to be blameless.

Confident of avoiding prosecution, Bernie returns to Australia in 1981 and resumes his occupation as a bar owner. He dies in Sydney in 2000 and a plinth is erected in his honour in a Sydney park about seven kilometres from Kings Cross. Partially in recognition of his charitable donations over the years of about one and a half million dollars, it also pays tribute to his contribution to the Kings Cross community.

Bob Askin, former Premier of New South Wales, dies of heart failure in 1981, leaving his widow a substantial windfall of cash and assets.

In 1981 Bob Trimbole, about to be arrested and charged over his role in the Donald Mackay disappearance, flees to America, then France, and then to Ireland. He avoids extradition efforts by the Australian Government and subsequently moves to Spain, where he dies in 1987. His body is returned to Australia and his funeral is held in Sydney. During the service an all-in brawl breaks out between mourners and journalists—something that Bob no doubt would have enjoyed.

A well-known hit man was charged with the murder of Donald Mackay. Despite protesting his innocence and claiming that it was Fred Krahe who did the job, he was not believed and was sentenced to jail for life.

Perce Galea dies of coronary heart disease in Sydney in 1977. He is still betting major sums of money on the horses right up until his death.

Into the 1980s and beyond, some of the dominant underworld figures of the 1960s and 1970s are replaced by younger, more aggressive players who continue to deal in the usual activities: prostitution, drugs, money laundering, bribery, bashings and murder. Names like Arthur 'Neddy' Smith, Stan 'The Man' Smith (no relation), Murray Stewart Riley and Abe Saffron are frequently linked to organised crime.

*****

Where there is an opportunity to make an easy dollar, certain people will always step up to the plate. Greed has a way of overcoming morals. Such is life.

THE END

Author's Note

'*The Stalking Horse*' is a novel of fiction based on facts. Many of the events described in this book such as the battle scenes in the Vietnam War and the rise and fall of the Nugan Hand Bank actually happened. I have taken these historical events and interweaved my story through them. Any mistakes I made are mine alone.

When I first started writing this novel I had a vague intention of attempting to put down on paper the excitement of associated with being involved in the surf lifesaving movement in Australia in the late 1960s. This movement, which I joined at the age of 15, played a significant role in shaping my life. The mateship and camaraderie were, and still are, fantastic and I would commend it to any young person. The motto 'vigilance and service' is entirely apt for such a wonderful public spirited organisation.

The lifesaving equipment and techniques were much less high tech in the period in which the novel is set. There was a much greater emphasis on swimming prowess for rescuing people in the surf although the belt and reel often created dangerous situations if the water conditions were tricky. Nevertheless many people owed their lives to a strong belt swimmer and a good crew on the line and reel.

Being a member of a surfboat crew also provided its share of thrills and spills, particularly in a big surf. The adrenalin rush of successfully getting the boat out beyond the line of breakers and then back into shore on a wave was hard to beat. The four rowers and the sweep hand had to work as a team and as a young man it gave me a sense of belonging and achievement. Even so, the surf always found a way to teach you a lesson about who was really in control.

As I progressed into formulating the story it began to morph into something I had not originally intended, although the Vietnam War part was always part of the plan. I was one of the 'birthday ballot' generation of 20 year old Australian males who were unwillingly involved on a gamble on whether their birthdate would come up in the National Service lottery. I was lucky, but many others weren't. So I felt compelled to have the protagonists Jack Martin and Terry Bannister clash against a backdrop of a divisive and ultimately unsuccessful war (unless you were a Communist). I have to confess the closest I got to that war was as a young Navy officer under training on board the troop transport *HMAS Sydney*, the 'Vung Tau Ferry' as it offloaded supplies in Vung Tau harbour late in 1972. It happened to be the 25th and last voyage that the ship was to make to Vietnam before Gough Whitlam took Australia out of the conflict.

Early on in my writing the theme of drugs came to the fore in the plotting of this novel as I envisaged Terry's character becoming darker and darker, in contrast to the straight laced Jack. Then in my research I came across the drug exporting trade out of the Asian Golden Triangle during, and after, the Vietnam War which in turn led me to the scandal of the Nugan Hand Bank. It seemed to present the perfect opportunity for Terry to get involved with the likes of Frank Nugan, Bernie Houghton and Michael Hand (who has allegedly resurfaced in the USA) and to turn the story in a new and more sinister direction. The historical account of the rise and fall of the Nugan Hand Bank makes for fascinating reading and as ever shows that fact can be stranger than fiction. Having Terry tag along on the coattails of Nugan Hand was a temptation too powerful to resist.

I hope you enjoyed this book. I enjoyed writing it.

David Knight
December 2015

ABOUT THE AUTHOR

DAVID KNIGHT

Born in Newcastle, Australia, David joined the Royal Australian Navy in his early twenties. A trip to Vietnam followed in late 1972 onboard the troop transport HMAS Sydney. For the next 24 years he enjoyed Navy life, one of the highlights being a UK exchange posting, which included shadowing an unsuspecting Soviet nuclear submarine in the North Atlantic in 1984, during the height of the Cold War. David left the Navy in 1996 and entered the world of consulting.

In 2009 David returned to Newcastle to enjoy the more laidback lifestyle. Soon after, David decided to write a fiction book that shared some of his earlier experiences, including the agony of the National Service ballot, Vietnam, and the thrills and spills of surf lifesaving. David's research into Vietnam War drug smuggling led to links to organised crime, shady private bank activities, and the CIA. The Stalking Horse is the result.

David is married, with four children and two grandchildren. When he is not writing, David enjoys cooking, loves a glass of red wine and allows the very active family dog to take him for a daily walk.

David is working on the sequel to The Stalking Horse.

CONNECT WITH ME ONLINE

http://www.horizonpg.net/#!author-roger-monk/c1l4y

http://www.horizonpg.net

*****

MORE OUTSTANDING TITLES

FROM

The shocking truth about

WOMEN
IN ISLAM

And the rights of women in Islamic law.

F. P. HANNA

THE·ANOINTED·ONE

HERB HAMLET

THE BANK INSPECTOR

ROGER MONK

THE BANK INSPETOR

by Roger Monk

Fiction - Bank Roberry - Crime/Thriller

ISBN: 978-1-922238-37-5 (ppk.)

One Monday morning, a bank branch is robbed.

No one hurt or threatened.

Not a hold-up.

Not a tunnel into the vault.

A three minutes' robbery and the robber drives away. Not followed. Not caught.

A perfect, flawless crime.

Detective Sergeant Brian Shaw hardly knows where to start, especially as he is distracted by an attempted murder in a nearby street.

A story of greed, treachery and a heart-breaking family feud.

***"The Bank Inspector"* by Roger Monk (Horizon Publishing Group), RRP AU$24.95, available from any good bookstore and from Horizon Publishing Group's URL: https://www.horizonpg.net/**
OR by emailing:

orders@horizonpg.net

IDENTITY, OBSESSION AND FRIENDSHIPS POISONED BY ENVY

A BLIND FATE

NADA OWENS

A BLIND FATE

by Nada Owens

Fiction

ISBN: 978-1-922238-32-0 (pbk.)

Bridget Gallaway is an ordinary seventeen-year old teenager who is thrown into extraordinary circumstances. She is in her final year of high school and is studying hard to earn a place in a top university, to study law. She lives with her family, including her grandmother, who suffers from dementia. She is trying to live a normal life but is shackled by her childhood best friend, Jordon.

After a number of insidious incidents in her personal life and a series of bizarre events at school, Bridget turns her back on her family and friends and attempts to reconstruct her life in a new environment, but things only get worse.

It is a suspense that delves into identity, obsession, and the impossibility of friendships when they have been poisoned by envy.

Will she succeed and forget the past!

"A Blind Fate" **by Nada Owens (Horizon Publishing Group), RRP AU$24.95, available in 2016 from any good bookstore and from Horizon Publishing Group's URL: https://www.horizonpg.net/ - OR - by emailing:**

orders@horizonpg.net

FROM GALLIPOLI TO COOPERS CREEK

a heartwarming story about the legacy of war and the healing power of love

CATE DAVIS

COLOURS of the Wind

Barry H. Young

COLOURS OF THE WIND

by

Barry H. Young

Fiction - Western

13 Short Stories

ISBN:9781922238290 (pbk.)

"An Epic story of exploration, passion, hatred, treachery, violence, war, despair, passionate intrigue, the culling of a nation, disaster and triumph and survival of those that were to master the Wild West."

THE SINGKEH

by
Terence Campbell

Fiction based on a true story

ISBN:9781922238269 (pbk.)

3 volumes
Vol. 1: NewComer"
Vol. 2: Planter"
Vol. 3: Sunset of an Era"

A fiction based on a true story

The story is set in Indonesia in the immediate post Independence period, and relates the adventures of a young British planter, Andy Anderson, on a rubber estate in the East Indies island of Sumatra. It is a tale of tempest and famine, riots and rancour, corruption, jealousy, intrigue and murder, and friendship, joy, love and passion. It also heralds the sunset of an era.

Chapter 1 is a prologue describing the outward voyage from Southampton to Belawan and introducing some of the characters who will reappear later in the story. The true adventure begins when Anderson sets foot on Sumatran soil.

"The Singkeh" by Terence Campbell (Horizon Publishing Group), RRP PER VOLUME A$24.95, THE SET OF THREE VOLUMES: 59.95, available from any good bookshops and from Horizon Publishing Group's URL: https://www.horizonpg.net/
OR by emailing:
orders@horizonpg.net

"A CITY GIRL STEPS OUT FROM HER COMFORT ZONE FOR A CHALLENGING LIFE IN THE OUTBACK"

Life as it is

REBECCA BURGE

Life as it is

by
Rebecca Burge

Non-fiction - Biography

ISBN:9781922238603 (pbk.)

"*Life as it is*", is what it is-My Life! My name is Rebecca Burge and I haven't always lived on a cattle property in far North Queensland. I was born and bred in Adelaide, South Australia. Growing up in the small country town of Gawler and then spending all my secondary years in Adelaide. The story only touches on my early years and is predominantly about my years on Lamonds Lagoon Station, North Queensland.

I married a "cattle man" and moved from the comforts of city life to the isolation of the bush. It is about all the little stories along the way and some of the different experiences I have had to deal with.

Lamonds Lagoon is four to five hours from the major towns of Charters Towers, Townsville and Cairns. I educated my five boys through Distance Education to the end of year 7. The boys all have their different personalities and this is characterised in this story.

In summary, I moved out of my comfort zone into an unknown "world" away from family, friends and shops. I have experienced so much in these years and it has not always been easy but what stands out beyond all doubt is how important family is, and while we are all healthy and happy, then we are the lucky ones!

"Life as it is" by Rebecca Burge ***(Horizon Publishing Group), RRP A$29.95, available from any good bookshops and from Horizon Publishing Group's URL: https://www.horizonpg.net/ OR by emailing:***

orders@horizonpg.net

A Place of

Light

[illegible] Warcon

Young-Adult fiction

ISBN: 978-1-922238-46-7

John was a forestry worker responsible for looking after protected forests. His job was to make sure people weren't cutting trees down or stealing precious plants and endangering the forest's ecosystems.

But today he was on holiday getting a much deserved rest, and he knew no better place to rest than in the forest which he loved so much. Lisa also loved nature, and they both wanted their baby daughter to love nature as much as they did.

On the drive to their campsite a couple days before, the little family had stopped at a local shop to look at some antiques. There were some beautiful pendant necklaces said to protect whoever wore them. In the spirit of fun, John bought one each for his wife and baby. Although the chain was much too long for one so small, John had immediately fastened one of the pendants around the baby's neck. Instead of wearing hers, Lisa had fastened her necklace to the wrist strap attached to her camera.

They lived only a short drive from this forest, but they wanted to explore parts of it at their leisure—something John couldn't do with his family when he was working. Today they were going to hike to the top of the mountain near their camp. They readied their supplies and put the baby into a backpack on John's back. They put out the fire from the night before and headed off on their hike, leaving some of their gear at the campsite. They knew no one else would be in the forest at this time of year and their campsite would be safe.

***"A Place of Light"* by Monica Warcon (Horizon Publishing Group), RRP AU$19.95, available in 2016 from any good bookstore and from Horizon Publishing Group's URL: https://www.horizonpg.net/ - OR - by emailing: orders@horizonpg.net**

Anaimon

THE STARFALL

TIMOTHY DANCARROW

Anaimon

THE STARFALL

by Timothy Nancarrow

Science-Fiction

ISBN: 978-1-922238-44-3 (pbk.)

The reign of the Gods of Anaimon is sundered abruptly, when Propagatoris, ruler of Anaimon's divine pantheon, casts himself into the twin suns of the world, obliterating him from existence and triggering a cataclysm that tears apart the Gods' star-lit ethereal home. Their divine forms broken and ruined during the sudden, violent descent, the Gods fall and smash into the great cities of Cpharan and Cphesus, killing thousands, almost destroying with them their most beloved priestess, Burning Flower.

Amidst the desolation and chaos, the Gods utter a final pulse of communication, telling Burning Flower with their dying breath that Anaimon is but one world, and that other cycles of Anaimon exist beyond even the Gods' reckoning. If Burning Flower can find the three sigils that lead the way through these worlds to 'Horizon', she may be able to restore Anaimon and the Gods, and undo the great calamity that has occurred.

Burning Flower is not alone in her search for the sigils, as a bestial enemy breaks free of their borders and begin to march across Anaimon; ravenous nightmares and misshapen hordes come to destroy all that Burning Flower and the Orders have fought for. Amidst such turmoil, the human enemies of the Order find new resolve; the nomadic, scattered tribes of the Iera who have been persecuted for their animistic beliefs and customs; the Aletheians, apostate criminals, smugglers, and exiles who value free will and their 'ultimate truth' above all else; and the Syndicals, rebellious heretics who have devolved into a broken people concerned only with survival in the bleak, barren emptiness of the world.

These factions and forces surge and swell even as the Orders slowly fray and tear themselves apart in the wake of the Gods' death. Pursued relentlessly by friend and foe across their slowly dying world, Burning Flower and those survivors willing to restore Anaimon must journey across the lands in search of the sigils, to find their way to 'Horizon', and the enigmatic power that lay beyond.

"Anaimon: THE STARFALL" by Timothy Nancarrow ***(Horizon Publishing Group), RRP AU$30.00, available from any good bookstore and from Horizon Publishing Group URL: https://www.horizonpg.net/ OR by emailing: orders@horizonpg.net***

Heretics

Ryaed Owens

HERETICS

by
Ryaed Owens

Fiction - Historical

ISBN:9781922238078 (pbk.)

Heretics is a novel of forbidden love, set against the backdrop of the Hundred Years' War and the Inquisition. It follows the point of view of Marcus, an English orphan boy and atheist who fights the French as a bowman. Wounded in battle, he flees to the town of Auch where he disguises himself as a Frenchman. In a tavern, he meets Claire, the daughter of a former priest, who is to be married to the knight Robert, and who has snuck out of her house dressed in her father's clothes to escape her plight.

When Claire's father and sister fall under the suspicion of the inquisition, Claire's marriage is hastened to keep the good family name. Marcus and Claire form a deeper bond, and find themselves embroiled in a net of vengeance, witchcraft, and on the run from the inquisition intent on spilling their blood.

Heretics is a novel that takes you back in time to medieval France and gives you an adventure story typical of this era.

"Heretics" by Ryaed Owens (Horizon Publishing Group), RRP A$24.95, available from any good bookshops and from Horizon Publishing Group's URL: https://www.horizonpg.net/ OR by emailing:

orders@horizonpg.net

A searing erotic romance set in the magnificent Australian outback

Pink Diamonds

Jodi Delaney

PINK DIAMONDS

by

Jodi Delaney

Fiction - Erotic

ISBN: 9781922238023(pbk.)

Alex is repetitively haunted by the tragic death of her husband. Leaving the security of her home, changing her life's path, she travels the Outback where she hopes to find inner peace.

Along the way visiting an old friend, Rex, and with an unsuccessful fling, Alex believes she'll never find love again, until she meets Eric. They both find themselves fighting their own demons as they work towards a trusting relationship. Her travels and her love for Eric are soul searching allowing hidden emotions to evolve.

The colourful characters Alex meets all leave their thumb print on her heart, although not always positive, she prays the love of one man will hopefully bring her back to the person she once was.

"Pink Diamonds" by Jodi Delaney (Horizon Publishing Group), RRP A$26.95, available from any good bookshops and from Horizon Publishing Group's URL: https://www.horizonpg.net/
OR by emailing:

orders@horizonpg.net

THE CAMROS BIRD

INSPIRED BY TRUE EVENTS

DIANA GREENTREE

Bestseller on Refugees, Love & the trauma of detention centres

THE CAMROS BIRD

by
Diana Greentree

Fiction based on true events

ISBN: 9781921369452 (pbk.)

The Camros Bird is a remarkable, heart-wrenching and thought provoking story about one man's desire for freedom. It draws the reader into the highly emotional journey that Amir makes fleeing Iran and seeking a home in Australia. Olivia becomes an integral part of Amir's story and her search for love, family and happiness is just as remarkable.

It is an astonishing tale of freedom and love that is certain to impact on the readers who will be shocked to learn just how poorly refugees are treated in Australia and how the Australian government has implemented a detention process that deliberately abuses and psychologically damages people seeking asylum.

Gaining freedom in this country can be extremely costly on an emotional level.

This the story of persecution, escape, detention, freedom, trauma and certainly … love.

"The Camros Bird" by Diana Greentree (Horizon Publishing Group), RRP A$32.95, available from any good bookshops and from Horizon Publishing Group's URL: https://www.horizonpg.net/
OR by emailing:

orders@horizonpg.net

power is a drug and drugs are power...

The

RED CHILLI

MICHAEL BATCHELOR

by Michael Batchelor

Fiction - Druggs/Crimes

ISBN: 978-1-922238-41-2 (pbk)

Bowden: A small town in rural Queensland – divided by two powerhouse drug lords. Known only as The Red Chilli and Carmen, these two charming drug pushers have their markings imprinted all throughout the small community where cocaine is their currency.

Here we introduce our hero. A young high school student named Jack whose curiosity gets the better of him as he becomes entangled with The Red Chilli and Carmen's twisted agenda. So what will become of Jack as he struggles to climb up from the underground drug scene of Bowden? Will he find his solace and his escape? Or will cocaine and the seduction of a town of druggies bring him into the shackles of a corrupt town where the lawmen are lawless, and The Red Chilli reigns King.

***"The Red Chilli"* by Michael Batchelor (Horizon Publishing Group), RRP AU$24.95, available from any good bookstore and from Horizon Publishing Group's URL: https://www.horizonpg.net/**
OR by emailing:

orders@horizonpg.net

"A memoir on the family of the man who committed affray in front of Prince Charles in January 1994."

Forty Bibles and Forty Dictionaries

Letters from THE FRONT

Carte Postale — Postcard

DOROTHY GILDING

LETTERS FROM THE FRONT

by Dorothy Gilding

Non-fiction - World War One - Gallipoli - Australian History

ISBN: 9781921369544 (pbk.)

"There were dead men everywhere, and a good number of our cavalry. We passed Fritz artillery with dead horses attached to their limbers. I come across a wounded Fritz. He was just a young boy and our tanks had run over him. A crew of five had a gun mounted in a shell-hole and the tank had flattened it into the ground, killing the rest. He had both his legs broken and had a very pitiful look. I gave him a drink of water and poked a stick in the ground with a white rag around it so our stretcher bearers would pick him up."

Letters From The Front is an authentic account of World War One through the eyes of an ordinary soldier, the story of one man. It seeks to add to our national consciousness of the immeasurable value and sacrifice of all those who have served our country, and our damaged heroes who survived, without in any way glorifying war.

Jim McConnell takes us with him to Gallipoli, Villers-Bretonneux and the Somme Canal to gain another glimpse of the events that symbolise courage, comradeship and sacrifice, and that cost Australia a generation.

As a first-person narrative, it strives to preserve the authenticity of the time and place in which these events occurred; to simply tell the story without twenty-first century judgements, embellishments or condemnations. Much of the story comes directly from this important primary source of actual diary notes. This is a valuable contribution to our World War One literature because so little was passed on in the generations that followed.

It also teaches us how to live well in an imperfect world. Jim McConnell saw people as people, and treated them accordingly, willing to fight and quick to forgive. He then made the most of the life he was left with in postwar Australia.

"Letters from The Front" by Dorothy Gilding (Horizon Publishing Group), RRP A$49.95, available from any good bookshops and from Horizon Publishing Group's URL: https://www.horizonpg.net/
OR by emailing: orders@horizonpg.net

Horizon Publishing Group™

Publishing for Generations to Come

2016

Printed in Australia
AUOC01n0659040416
274937AU00002B/2/P

9 781922 238535